WIDOWS OF THE
SUN-MOON

What Reviewers Say About Barbara Ann Wright's Work

The Pyradisté Adventures

"…a healthy dose of a very creative, yet believable, world into which the reader will step to find enjoyment and heart-thumping action. It's a fiendishly delightful tale."—*Lambda Literary*

"Barbara Ann Wright is a master when it comes to crafting a solid and entertaining fantasy novel. …The world of lesbian literature has a small handful of high-quality fantasy authors, and Barbara Ann Wright is well on her way to joining the likes of Jane Fletcher, Cate Culpepper, and Andi Marquette. …Lovers of the fantasy and futuristic genre will likely adore this novel, and adventurous romance fans should find plenty to sink their teeth into."—*The Rainbow Reader*

"*The Pyramid Waltz* has had me smiling for three days. …I also haven't actually read…a world that is entirely unfazed by homosexuality or female power before. I think I love it. I'm just delighted this book exists. …If you enjoyed *The Pyramid Waltz*, *For Want of a Fiend* is the perfect next step…you'd be embarking on a joyous, funny, sweet and madcap ride around very dark things lovingly told, with characters who will stay with you for months after."—*The Lesbrary*

"This book will keep you turning the page to find out the answers. …Fans of the fantasy genre will really enjoy this installment of the story. We can't wait for the next book."—*Curve Magazine*

Thrall: Beyond Gold and Glory

"…incidents and betrayals run rampant in this world, and Wright's style successfully kept me on my toes, navigating the shifting alliances… [Thrall] is a story of finding one's path where you would least expect it. It is full of bloodthirsty battles and witty repartee…which gave it a nice balanced focus. …This was the first Barbara Ann Wright novel I've read, and I doubt it will be the last. Her dialogue was concise and natural, and she built a fantastical world that I easily imagined from one scene to the next. Lovers of Vikings, monsters and magic won't be disappointed by this one."—*Curve Magazine*

"The characters were likable, the issues complex, and the battles were exciting. I really enjoyed this book and I highly recommend it." —*All Our Worlds*

Paladins of the Storm Lord

"An intricate…novel one that can be appreciated at many levels, adventurous sci fi or one that is politically motivated with a very astute look at present day human behavior. …There are many levels to this extraordinary and well written book…overall a fascinating and intriguing book."—*Inked Rainbow Reads*

Visit us at www.boldstrokesbooks.com

By the Author

Thrall: Beyond Gold and Glory

Coils

The Pyradisté Adventures:

The Pyramid Waltz

For Want of a Fiend

A Kingdom Lost

The Fiend Queen

The Godfall Novels:

Paladins of the Storm Lord

Widows of the Sun-Moon

WIDOWS OF THE SUN-MOON

by
Barbara Ann Wright

2017

WIDOWS OF THE SUN-MOON

ISBN 13: 978-1-62639-777-4

This Trade Paperback Original Is Published By
Bold Strokes Books, Inc.
P.O. Box 249
Valley Falls, NY 12185

First Edition: January 2017

Credits
Editor: Cindy Cresap
Production Design: Susan Ramundo
Cover Design By Sheri (graphicartist2020@hotmail.com)

Acknowledgments

Like all my books, this one wouldn't be possible without Mom and Ross. Another big thank you to Angela, Deb, Erin, Matt, and Natsu for reading and making my work better. We're the best writing group ever, AND we have the word "beaver" in our name. Thanks also to Pattie for reading. You're the bestest.

A special thank you to everyone who's ever said they liked my work. You have no idea how important it is to hear that. Without you, I couldn't keep writing.

Dedication

For Erin Kennemer and David Slayton,
two of the best friends I've ever had.

Prologue

Jack grinned as he slid into his chair and laid his napkin across his lap. "Sorry to keep you waiting, Copilot Dué. Has your copilotship ordered wine, or would you like me to summon a lackey to do it for you?"

Patricia saw right past the grin to the resentful undertone. She sighed and closed her eyes, listening to the murmurs of the other couples scattered through the restaurant. In the foyer, someone played a soft melody on a piano, and glasses clinked from the bar. "Is that your idea of a congratulatory speech, or are you trying to get me to break up with you right after my promotion and right before the most important mission of my life?"

He picked the menu up and studied it. "I thought marrying me in a year was the most important mission in your life."

"Are you a deep space colony? Or maybe you're the ship with the revolutionary engine that I get to pilot to said deep space colony."

He gave her a leer. "Pilot me anywhere you like, baby."

She sputtered a laugh. "Shut up. I'm trying to be mad at you for being late and resenting me."

He sighed, put the menu down, and lined up his silverware next to his plate. "Oh, don't listen to me. I'm just a jealous worrier."

"You should be jealous. The *Atlas* is a very nice ship. It would put any mere human being to shame."

The grin was back. "So, are we breaking up so you can have an affair with your ship?"

She took his hand, staring into his blue eyes so she could remember them all the way out in the deep blackness of space. "There's no way I'm leaving you here without an engagement ring on your finger." She trusted him completely, but she knew petty jealousy warmed his heart.

"I love you, Ms. Copilot."

"I love you, too, Mr. Copilot."

He smiled wider. "We'll have to remember that for the invitations."

When he winked, she wanted to climb over the table and kiss him until the staff asked them to leave. She opened her mouth to suggest they skip dinner and go straight home, but the sounds of the restaurant faded, and her voice wouldn't climb above a whisper.

That wasn't right. In her memory, she'd said, "Let's get out of here," and he'd said something like, "And go on our own deep mission?" and she'd laughed until she nearly choked.

No! She didn't have to settle for "something like." She could remember everything clearly, every head tilt, every vocal nuance. Everything. All she had to do was focus.

In the restaurant, she tried again. "Let's…"

Jack was still watching her intently, but footsteps caught her attention. At the next table, a server set a covered dish between a smiling couple. He raised it with a flourish, revealing a long knife and a meat fork.

"No," Patricia whispered. "That's not right. They had the mousse."

Jack was still frozen in time, waiting for the right words.

The couple at the next table kissed each other before the woman took the knife and pressed the tip to her cheek, drawing it upward to her eye. Blood oozed from the wound to curve around her smiling lips as she cut down at an angle and then across, carving a perfect triangle in her cheek. Her partner took the fork, speared the triangle of flesh, and brought it slowly to his lips, eyes closing in bliss.

Patricia clapped a hand over her mouth and tried to breathe down bile. "That didn't happen!"

With blood pumping down her face, the woman at the next table took the fork and plucked an eye from her partner's head. The optic nerve trailed behind it as she brought it to her teeth.

Patricia leapt up. "It didn't happen this way!"

The restaurant blinked, and the gore disappeared, replaced by a happy couple sharing chocolate mousse, ignoring her and Jack in their bliss. Jack was still waiting, still frozen, and Patricia sat again, smoothing her hair. She could fix this. She could still have this memory, could exist in it.

"Go back to the wink," she said to herself.

The memory unwound to the spot where she wanted to have him right then, when she'd never loved him more, but this time, after he winked, his eye vanished and became wheeling stars, infinite space, everything.

"No." Panic crept up her neck. "Why won't you leave me alone?"

As the sounds of the restaurant faded again, she leapt from her chair and ran. The foyer had become a pilot's chair and console, and Patricia slid in and buckled the harness. Her console flared to life, and she primed the engines before starting them.

"Jack, hold on!" she yelled, but he wasn't really there. None of them were. There were no screams echoing from the restaurant as it pulled into open space, no crashes and clatters as the tables slid and fell. "If I go far enough, I can go back to where I was."

Lies. The restaurant ship stopped as if gripped by an invisible hand, but everything in it was gone. All she had now was her flight suit and the mangled bridge of the *Atlas*. But if this was the crash, then she looked up right about...

"No!" But there was no stopping this memory. The bulkhead above her collapsed, and a shard of shrapnel rammed into her right eye and let Naos inside.

The agony of the wound was nothing compared to the woman who brought with her the whole of existence. Or maybe she *was* the whole of existence or simply a more powerful Patricia Dué, the woman Patricia had always feared to become.

She rose from the rubble but saw no Dr. Lazlo to greet her. Maybe he'd been consumed along with her mind. She didn't speak, feared to breathe. Maybe the vision would stop here, and she could go back to reliving her past, far from a place where she was a visitor in her own body, where she didn't understand her own actions.

The ship began to creak, slowly at first but growing into a shrieking metal tear. Huge fingers punched through the roof of the bridge and tore it away. Patricia screamed at them and lashed out with her powers, but her own hand caught fire, and she cried out anew. The ship began to shake as it tore apart, and a babble of sounds poured inside, every noise in the entire universe and with them the goddess who claimed to need Patricia's help just to bring a little sanity to the chaos.

Patricia fell to her knees and put her hands over her head. She tried to resist, tried to retreat, but before this power she was nothing. When her one eye opened, she looked through it as through a window, fought impotently for control before she gave up and sighed.

"Don't cry, baby," Naos said to her inside their shared mind. "Let's have some fun!"

❖

The Deliquois people wept for their absent goddess. Ap led them in prayers, begging the mighty Contessa to speak in their minds once again, but she stayed silent. What had they done to fall out of favor? The goddess could be fickle, but she'd never stayed silent this long, with moon after moon passing and no word. They'd lit many bonfires on the shore, danced until their feet bled and their voices died, but she failed to whisper her thoughts to them. Ap had even sent several villagers into the sea to die and search for her in the afterlife she'd promised them, but she hadn't said she'd received their gifts.

This night, they simply cried out and raised their arms to the heavens where she lived. Some smeared their faces with soot and ripped at their garments, tearing shells and feathers loose from the soft, woven grass of their kilts. Ap knew their grief could turn to grumbling soon enough. They might think it was the shaman who'd failed them, that only his sacrifice could bring the Contessa back.

"Please, Goddess," he whispered. "Return to us. Save my life." He'd always been her favorite. She'd taught him secret ways to bend others to his will, her will. She'd shown him how to meditate, to be one with his surroundings, as well as secret ways to kill his enemies, fast and silent ways.

When he opened his eyes, her hazy form hovered above the fire. Ap gasped, not daring to blink. She had never appeared before him, had always spoken in his mind and the minds of her followers, but if this wasn't a sign of favor, what was?

When the crowd fell silent, he knew everyone could see her above the flames. Her unbound hair curled around her naked curves as if possessed of its own life, and her sad smile filled Ap's heart with both joy and sorrow.

"My beloved people," she said, her voice faint, and her lips not moving in time with her words. "I come to say good-bye."

They cried out as one, but Ap waved them to silence. "Dear Contessa, why?"

"The Storm Lord has murdered me, and I must hasten to the place where dead gods dwell. Avenge me, or lose me forever!"

As the outcry came again, she vanished. Ap stared at the place she'd been while some of the others leapt to their feet. Some ran wildly, tearing at their hair. Others fled into the reed huts lining the shores, letting the flaps fall shut behind them. Some clasped their arms around their kin and wept while still others remained on the ground, staring with Ap.

He took a deep, shuddering breath and tried to contemplate a future without the goddess who'd led them for generations, when their ancestors had first come to this planet. She comforted them, protected them. She was the sun and sky and stars. When she was happy, the weather was calm and mild. When she was angry, her storms rocked the coast until they appeased her. She knew all, saw all. She could be fickle. They often didn't know she was angry until they were already pounded by rain and wind, but she always forgave them. And she held the honored ancestors in the palms of her hands. Without her, what were they?

Ap staggered to his hut and let the flap close behind him. Murdered? By another god called the Storm Lord. She'd mentioned him before, sometimes as lover, sometimes as enemy. He must have tricked her somehow, must have followed her to her home beyond the clouds and used some ruse to disarm her. How could they avenge her?

With numb hands, Ap fumbled for the small bag hidden in a hole under his mat. There had to be more to the Contessa's message. If she couldn't come to them, Ap would go to meet her. He took a small wooden bowl and upended the bag, spilling out a rustle of crumbling leaves.

When he left his tent with the bowl, those that saw him followed. "The shaman's going to dream!" someone called, and then people were spilling out of the darkness to watch.

Ap knelt by the bonfire, knocked a coal out of the flames and tipped it into the bowl, setting the leaves alight. He inhaled the stinging smoke, and the burn in his lungs spread through his body to lodge in his mind and tug his soul free. He flew above his body into the clouds, searching for the goddess under the full moon.

"Has this worked before?" she asked in his mind, though her voice sounded different than he remembered. "You just get high, and...oh, well, never mind. What can I do for you? Were my instructions not clear?"

"Goddess, please, tell me what happened to you? Where can we find the Storm Lord?"

"Right. Directions. Okay, wait a second. I'll think up something properly godlike."

He waited for a few moments, poised in the air.

The Contessa cleared her throat. "Woe! Hear the tale of my death, O Shaman, and glean from it what you may."

Ap saw the beautiful Contessa hounded by a fierce god clothed in metal, the Storm Lord. She laughed as she ran, and the Storm Lord grew angry when he couldn't catch her. He begged her to slow and love him, to bear his children, but she refused. Foolish god! He should've plied her with gifts and flattery, but he had only anger to offer. When her back was turned, he struck her down with a bolt of lightning.

Ap cried out as she collapsed. He tried to go to her, but her image dissolved like smoke, reforming in front of him again too far away to touch. Her dead eyes would haunt his dreams.

"He's taken human form," she whispered in Ap's mind. "But you can get him if you're quick enough. Probably. Maybe. Who knows?" She showed him where the Storm Lord was hiding; they'd have to cross the water, but they'd done it before when they'd traded with those on the mainland. "I'll wait for you in this cold place, alone until he's dead. Avenge me!"

Ap wept and thought he heard another voice beyond hers, a tiny, unfamiliar voice calling for help, but it fell silent after a noise like snapping fingers. Ap waited, floating. "Contessa?"

"What are you waiting for? Get going!"

Ap awoke with a start. The Deliquois jumped where they huddled around him. He clasped the hands of those nearest, used their help to stand, and rubbed at his burning throat. "We are hunters no more! We do not gather roots or reeds. We do not carve or weave or cook. We are god killers, every one of us, and we will avenge our goddess, or she will be lost forever."

They wept anew, but before dawn had broken, they gathered what they'd need and unwrapped the canoes from woven reed covers. One by one, they came to Ap, and he cut their hair as he did when they'd displeased the goddess. No one would be beautiful or happy until she'd been rescued from the void.

CHAPTER ONE

Natalya could acutely recall being insane. Though she'd never been a healer, she'd known a few yafanai telepaths and micropsychokinetics who dealt with mental illnesses ranging from the mild to the extraordinary. Sometimes their neural pathways could be changed or the mix of hormones regulated, but some were beyond yafanai abilities: those who heard voices that compelled them to act contrary to their nature or those who suffered such a break from reality that they never found their way back. Some were so dangerous their minds had to be wiped by telepaths, and they were left to drift like shadows through life.

Eight months ago, she knew she would've qualified for the mind wipe. After Simon Lazlo had augmented her, she'd heard voices, oh yes, every voice on the planet, maybe the universe, and she wasn't even a telepath. They came charging in via her micro-psychokinetic abilities, and she couldn't just hear the words; she could feel the words being formed by the brains around her. She'd felt heartbeats and organs and a cacophonous mix of so much feeling that she wanted to silence them forever. On top of that were the sensations her macro-psychokinetic powers delivered: the feeling of large objects and the spaces they occupied, of the gravitational pull of the planet itself. The whole universe seemed to breathe around her, and she'd just wanted it to stop.

At first, she'd thought she could handle it. She'd thought her new abilities would let her prove herself to the Storm Lord, and he would reward her for her strength and faith. But the feelings had just kept building, pushing her outside her own head; only she couldn't drift like those insane shadows she'd seen in Gale. She was inexorably connected to herself, and it *hurt*. The pain kept building until she needed to tear and kill, needed to get her hands around Simon Lazlo's neck for doing this to her!

And then, like a balm, the goddess had come. Naos, titanic force, had hushed the power inside Natalya, muting it to tolerable levels while still letting her access it. Naos had seen the potential in her where the Storm Lord had seen only madness, so Natalya had changed gods as quickly as changing a shirt.

Naos had a touch of madness all her own. She knew how power screamed inside one's mind, and because she knew, she could grant sanity. They had made a good team for a month or so, exploring each other's pain, plotting against Simon Lazlo, until Natalya had awoken in the middle of the night standing over a ditch. The long grass of the plains had whipped around her legs, all of it bathed in silver from the full moon. It wouldn't have been a bad fall, but she might have hurt herself. She stumbled back from the drop and tripped, falling over one of the rocks that dotted the plains like wandering animals.

"Was I sleepwalking?" she mumbled. "I've never…"

"It wouldn't have hurt," Naos said, as if that distinction made all the difference.

They'd gone back to fun: wandering, spying on various groups of plains dwellers. Naos told her tales of Earth, the planet that had birthed humanity, and the true story of how a group of colonists had gotten thrown off course and wound up here on Calamity two hundred and fifty years ago. She told of the accident that had made some of them very powerful, how those with superior micro-psychokinesis could keep someone alive forever. The Storm Lord had taken credit for all of it before.

"So you have to be cautious if you're going after Simon Lazlo," Naos said. "His micro powers are as great as mine."

Natalya snorted. "He can't be a match for you and me together."

"Speaking of together…"

Natalya's belly went cold and she remembered the fall she'd almost taken. Naos explained that she'd wanted to borrow her body for a bit, but Natalya had thought it sounded as if the goddess wanted to wear her like a suit.

"It's fine if you don't want to," Naos said. "You can always go back to being alone. And mad, let's not forget that!"

And then what could Natalya do but agree?

Slowly, Naos started taking little trips in Natalya's body, and Natalya had to watch behind her own eyes as Naos operated her like a puppet, steering her through the grass, tripping over rocks, and plunging her headfirst into more ditches. Naos could never get her arms up in time, and Natalya had to heal her own cuts and bruises, the occasional broken ankle.

"I don't know what you're always complaining about," Naos said one day. "You can fix anything." As if that made everything forgivable.

Natalya sighed and stared into the green sea of the plains. She never knew exactly when Naos was listening. Sometimes the goddess was absent for days, though her lingering power kept madness at bay.

"Just keep that in mind," Naos said, an angry tinge to her voice as she read Natalya's thoughts.

Natalya sighed again, missing the times when Naos had pretended to be beside her rather than inside her head, but she couldn't keep Naos out if she tried. Not that she wanted to, she added hastily.

"Good girl."

"You know that makes my teeth ache," Natalya said aloud. "Can you please wait until I speak before you reply?"

"Oh, do excuse me. It's so easy to tell speech from thoughts while in orbit, you know."

It was a good point, but still...

"Enough moaning. Time for practice."

Before Natalya could groan again, her body jerked upright and stumbled around for a few moments before Naos got her back on track.

"I'm putting a scheme in motion," Naos said, her words coming in stutters from Natalya's own mouth. "And I need a vessel." After a few jerky steps and another fall, Naos retreated with a frustrated sigh. "Your flesh doesn't suit me."

"It doesn't fit you!" Natalya cried as she sat up, rubbing her hip. "I'm already in it!" As soon as she heard the words, she regretted them, not wanting to give the goddess any ideas.

"Relax," Naos said, "you're right. And you're all grown. Your muscles have their own memories. I need someone younger."

Natalya stayed quiet as Naos's presence withdrew. She didn't know quite what Naos meant, but anything that would keep the goddess out of her body was worth a try.

"I sense someone close, a fight."

Natalya felt around with her own powers and detected a group of people, adrenaline pumping, maybe a mile away. Some heartbeats fell silent as she watched. "A battle."

"Let's have a look. There's one that feels perfect!"

Natalya ran with Naos hastening her along. With her augmented powers, she didn't get tired anymore, though she still liked to sleep from time to time. She clambered onto a rock and spotted a camp just beyond.

Many of the plains dwellers were nomadic, moving camps and homes wherever the hunting was best. They usually followed the rivers that wound through the plains or went from this lake to that stream, keeping water close by. Sometimes they fought, but from what Natalya had seen, most traded; sometimes people left one group for another, often if they fancied themselves in love. Whether or not they returned if disappointed, she didn't know.

But this was no simple dispute. Adults scattered through the camp, cutting down the elderly and adolescents, all but the children. These they lifted into the air and sought to comfort as if they hadn't just murdered everyone else.

One of the attackers spotted Natalya and started toward her; she expected to see glee or anticipation in his expression, but he seemed pale, his mouth turned down in determination as if he took no pleasure in what he did, but it had to be done.

Her power flowed over his mind and turned it elsewhere as she erased herself from his vision. He shook his head and sought other prey. "Looks like they're after the children."

"Including ours," Naos said.

"Ours?"

"Follow them."

Natalya hopped down as the raiders withdrew, bearing the children with them. She stepped over bodies and threaded through the camp. The attackers hadn't bothered to take food or water. They hadn't even taken the few pieces of metal she saw here and there, the rarest substance on Calamity. She also didn't see many young, healthy looking adults among the dead. Those were probably out hunting, and they would return to find the rest of their people slaughtered and their children gone.

She hurried in the footsteps of the raiders until they stopped to light a campfire at dusk. Ten adults sat around a circle of children and tried to comfort them with words or gestures, and the kids seemed too small to care what form comfort took as long as the violence had stopped.

"Good," Naos said. "They're young enough to work with."

Natalya looked to the children. Most seemed under five. "Too young, surely?"

Naos only laughed. "She'll make a lovely vessel. Her mind is so bright. Her mother named her Kora."

One of the children lifted her head, searching for the source of the voice, but it would only echo inside her head.

"Bring her," Naos said.

Natalya lifted the girl with macro powers and pulled her over. The adults leapt to their feet, crying out as Kora flew into Natalya's arms. She stared with wide brown eyes, her little mouth open, and her four-year-old mind racing to understand. "Sleep." Natalya's power flooded the girls' mind, switching it off. The raiders rushed closer, screaming, some of them weeping.

"No!" one cried. "We need the children. We need them! Get your own."

"You're one to talk." Natalya tore the woman limb from limb with her powers. Naos melted one and flung several high into the air to land with wet thumps, unmoving. Natalya removed the heads of a few more while Naos attacked the brains of others, leaving them as mindless hulks, spittle flecking their mouths, soon to die. Before the sun had even fully set, there was nothing but a field of corpses and the whimpering children who'd seen too much death in one day.

"What about the rest of them?" Natalya asked.

Naos's power skated over them. "We've got what we want in dear little Kora."

Natalya frowned. One of the babies was crying in the grass. Several of the others tried to crawl away from her. "They'll starve if we leave them."

"Do whatever pleases you."

With a sigh, Natalya laid her power over them. They quieted, hypnotized but not asleep, but their trauma would probably remain. She'd never been good at healing, not like Horace. She missed him and not for the first time. He'd know what to do in a situation like this.

"Get up and follow me," she said.

The children obeyed, and Natalya lifted the infants with her power. As she walked, the children tottered behind her, and the infants drifted as if carried by the wind. She felt Naos watching her, felt a bit of amusement, all that Naos would let her see. Natalya didn't care. Let the goddess be amused. Abandoning the helpless to starve to death was a line she wasn't willing to cross, that was all. She headed toward the largest gathering of people she could sense, the children following her through the long grass.

As night got deeper, they began to stumble, and Natalya made camp, lighting a fire far away from the people she'd killed. She coaxed the children into true sleep, though she imagined it would still be filled with nightmares. Naos sighed and mumbled impatient noises until Natalya turned her attention to Kora, who lay closest to the campfire, her chest rising and falling steadily.

"Now what?" Natalya asked.

"Let's comb through her memories. See what she's got so far."

Before Natalya could remind Naos that she wasn't a telepath, Naos towed her along into Kora's head. Natalya tried to protest, but Naos was inescapable. And this was worse than just seeing. She *was* the girl, going as far back as memory could take her, which luckily wasn't far. Kora knew three faces well: Maman and Fatan, her mother and father, and Shufu, her older brother. Naos sped through her memories without rhyme or reason, settling on a fall here or a laugh there. Kora knew her people were the Miri; they wore the finger bones of the beloved dead around their necks. Her mother wore Grandmaman's; her father bore his grandmaman's and his fatan's. Someone had told her she would have a necklace of her own one day, but she didn't understand what that meant. She didn't yet know death.

As the memories caught up to that morning, Naos slowed over them, lingering on Kora's terror as the strangers attacked. She'd heard shouts from her elders. The raiders were of the Svenal, Shufu had said, and the word blazed in Kora's mind.

"Hatred," Naos said. "Anger like she's never known before."

And fear that caught Natalya as surely as it had Kora. Fatan had been gone for the day, hunting, and Kora had begged him to come save her. Maman had fought the Svenal with a long bone knife. Even Shufu had fired arrows until Kora lost sight of them, until the screams and smells of frightened people surrounded her, and she'd fallen and gone to sleep.

When she'd awoken, she'd been wrapped in a blanket, and though terror still lurked in the back of her brain, she'd thought it a bad dream. Then she'd seen that the blanket was the end of old Lilian's skirt, and she'd laughed to think they were sleeping outside until she'd noticed Lilian's blood-spattered face. She'd screamed for Fatan and Maman, but a strange man had carried her away. She recalled the long walk and flying through the air. That feeling had thrilled rather than frightened her, and then Natalya was looking up at her own face.

"Stop!"

With a laugh, Naos pulled them from Kora's mind. "You didn't enjoy reliving childhood?"

Natalya shivered and breathed hard. "Mine was never like that."

"You should appreciate it more, then. Watch."

They went inside Kora's body this time, and Natalya watched with horrified fascination as Naos commanded Kora to grow.

Kora's eyes snapped open, her mouth opening in what would surely be a shriek, but there was too much pain for that. Natalya sensed white-hot agony crippling her, cramps flooding her limbs as her legs stretched by inches. She whimpered and mewled. Natalya scrabbled for Kora's pain centers and tried to dull them, to put the girl back to sleep, but there was too much torment for that.

"I'm sorry, lovey, but you're too short!" Naos said.

Kora gagged and dry-heaved as her body continued to grow. Tears poured down her cheeks. Natalya wiped them away and tried to do what she could with her power, but she paled next to Naos and could only watch as the transformation took place. She helped Kora struggle out of her dress as her body elongated, limbs growing, hips spreading, and breasts developing as if the girl was being baked into a woman. Her face grew along with her hair until the young woman she would have eventually become lay before the fire, twisted up in anguish.

"Maman," she said softly, "Fatan." She grabbed her throat; her voice had to sound so different in her ears.

"Take a look," Naos said. "I think you'll be pleased."

Kora looked at herself, a four-year-old in a body that looked about sixteen. She shook, eyes as wide as a skull's. "It's not me! It's not right!" She slapped at herself, shrieking.

Natalya grabbed her wrists. "Calm down! Goddess, do something!"

Kora managed one more scream before Naos's power rolled over her, and she slept.

Natalya sat back, breathing hard. "Oh, shit." She couldn't have seen what she'd just seen. It had to be a trick, a joke, a mistake.

"Calm down yourself," Naos said. "I just have to age her mind a little."

"Wha...what?"

"Stay out here if you want, if you can't appreciate power."

Natalya felt Naos withdraw. Kora twitched in her sleep as Naos became part of her dreams. Natalya rubbed her hands together, wondering what she should do. She took the child-sized leather dress, laid it over Kora as best she could, and waited.

When Kora sat up with a gasp, Natalya nearly leapt to her feet. "I knew everything," Kora said, and Natalya knew that look in her eyes. She'd seen the universe.

"What did you do?" Natalya asked softly, but Kora didn't look at her. That didn't matter. She wasn't talking to Kora anyway.

"She told me what I needed to know," Kora said. "How to exist in this body, to exist with her." She smoothed her long, tangled brown hair over her shoulders. "I lived all those years with her. I grew up with her, with you." Her aged eyes pinned Natalya to the spot. "We used to go on picnics."

"Did we?" A hollow pit opened in Natalya's stomach. Maybe it would have been kinder to let her starve. "Was I your mother?"

"You worshipped my mother. Everyone did."

In Natalya's mind, Naos cackled before she said, "We're not far from the clan you sensed earlier, but they'll move at first light. We should go now."

"In the dark?" Natalya said.

At the same time, both Naos and Kora said, "I don't need light to see."

Natalya shepherded the hypnotized children to their feet and bade them walk again. If left on her own, Kora directed them around ditches and holes. When the power and presence of Naos filled her, she danced naked over the grass, luxuriating in the moonlight, a beautiful puppet.

"What will we tell them?" Natalya said as she helped the children down a steep rise. "These people we're going to meet? Won't they wonder about the naked girl, her handmaiden, and her retinue of small children?" When neither Kora nor Naos answered, she sighed. "I guess they'll think whatever you want them to think."

"Exactly!" Naos called with Kora's mouth. "You'll tell them I'm your daughter, and we rescued these children after we were attacked by the Svenal."

"And if they want the name of our clan?"

"Make something up! Do I have to do everything?"

"I can't just—"

Kora spun, and her eyes glowed electric blue in the dark. "You'll do as I say, or I might start to wonder what to do with you now that I have my perfect vessel."

Natalya shut her mouth until they were nearing the next camp. Though it was late, a few fires still burned in the dark. Natalya staggered forward, trying to put on a show while Kora leaned on her arm as if wounded, Naos chuckling through her mouth the entire time.

"Help!" Natalya called. "We've been attacked!"

CHAPTER TWO

The drums kept time with Cordelia's heartbeat. A loose circle of humans and drushka cheered her on as she faced her opponent, a man maybe two or three years her junior. His skin was duskier than hers, like many of the plains dwellers who spent so much of their life outside, but he still wasn't as brown as a drushka. Cordelia suspected they'd all be darker before their time on the plains was done, if the Storm Lord ever lifted their exile.

As she and her opponent circled each other, she tried to put the past out of her mind. Beside her, Nettle sized up her own opponent, an older woman who'd grinned when Nettle offered to be a quarter of the night's entertainment. Even after the eight months they'd known each other, some of the Uri still looked at the lean drushka and saw people who'd break easily.

The older woman leaned back as if she would step away but instead spun and aimed a kick at Nettle's head. Nettle bent, her torso kinking like a snake's. She caught the leg and shoved, sending the woman off balance. The older woman stumbled but recovered. She eyed Nettle with new appreciation, and Nettle darted forward and slashed with the poisonous claw on her middle finger.

The older woman scrambled back, but Cordelia saw the ruse for what it was. A drushka wouldn't risk paralyzing a human. Most humans could survive the poison, but there was always a risk. As Nettle darted again, launching a punch, Cordelia's foe finally attacked.

A clumsy rush. Cordelia almost pitied him as she grabbed his arm and planted her feet. After a wink at his startled face, she fell backward, letting his weight slow her. As she connected with the ground, she pulled her feet up and planted them in his chest, still holding his arm. She rocked his body onto her feet and threw him up and over to slam back first into the ground.

Still keeping hold of his arm, she twisted and rolled to her knees. While he tried to catch his breath, she kicked to the side, thumping his ribs and driving a harsh wheeze from his mouth. She flipped him onto his belly and folded his arm up behind his back until he squealed.

Beside her, Nettle had a foot in her opponent's back and an arm in each hand. "Enah!" the woman said, the plains word for stop.

Cordelia's foe couldn't seem to say anything, so she took the call of uncle to count for both of them. She and Nettle released their opponents at the same time, and the circle of watchers pounded their feet or clapped. The drums banged out a fast rhythm as the Uri chafa, Wuran, pronounced Cordelia and Nettle the victors.

After a slap on the back, he led them to sit. "I like it when you fight," he said. "I always leave a richer man."

Nettle sucked her sharp teeth, the sign of drushkan confusion. The firelight glinted off her dark brown skin, picking out the darker whorls and patterns that ran across her flesh like lines in tree bark. "I do not fully understand this wagering. You do so against your own people?"

"With you two? How could I not?"

He waved for them to make themselves comfortable on a pile of leather cushions. Cordelia took a handkerchief from her pocket and wiped her sweaty face. Wuran took off his large brimmed leather hat and fanned himself. He'd already taken off the long, sleeveless leather coat many plains dwellers wore, revealing a blousy white shirt and leather trousers. He grinned when he caught her studying him, showing the gaps in his teeth and adding many more wrinkles to his lined face. "Soon, no one will want to fight you," he said.

Cordelia chuckled. They'd been on the plains nearly a month before they'd met Wuran and his clan. Her uncle Paul had been communicating and exchanging emissaries with the plains dwellers for some time, and she'd been thrilled to find that some of her renegades spoke the language of the plains, and some Uri spoke Galean. Luckily, the languages were similar enough that everyone soon picked up a bit, though Cordelia had to admit she was particularly bad at it. The words didn't want to stick in her head, so even now, eight months after coming to the plains, she mostly spoke to Wuran; his Galean was perfect.

Another drushka threaded through the crowd to sit at their side and speak with Nettle. Reach, the former drushkan ambassador to Gale, had taken to new languages far easier than Cordelia. She supposed that was one reason Reach had been chosen as ambassador and probably one of the reasons Paul found her so fascinating, enough to pursue her as a lover. Even Cordelia had found her attractive, once upon a time.

And now that she'd found Nettle, Cordelia would have given plenty for the chance to take back all the shit she'd given her uncle about having a drushkan lover. But she'd given him shit about everything else, so why not that, too? If he'd lived, that's probably what he'd have said.

She sighed and tried to think of something else, an exercise that came easier the more time that passed. She'd missed him keenly when they'd first arrived in their new home among the long grass and tumbled boulders of the plains. He would have been able to coax the drushka out of their tree much sooner. Even now Pool hesitated to bring her tree close to any other humans. She left it to Cordelia and a few others to journey to the plains dwellers' Meeting Rock, a spear of stone that stabbed into the sky, the largest object around save for Pool's tree. Wuran and his people had seen the tree from a distance and asked about it, but Cordelia had let Reach answer, letting the drushka keep their secrets however they wanted.

She took a leather cup as it was handed around and gulped down some scuppi, a plains dweller brew that a person had to fight through drinking in order to get drunk. Liam had said it tasted like fire, and as she winced, she thought he wasn't far wrong.

"Careful, my friend," Wuran said. "It snuck up on you last time."

Cordelia chuckled. "Scuppi doesn't sneak. It strides right up and knocks you over the head."

He slapped his knee and smiled. "Truth! Are you frowning in anticipation of that?"

She shrugged. "I feel as if…something should be happening. Or maybe that something will happen soon. I don't know." There was a prophet among her renegades. Maybe she should just ask, but the prophet claimed that seeing the future changed nothing, and it did no one any good to see it coming.

"I know what you mean," Wuran said. "Like the air before a storm."

"Or maybe that's bullshit." She already felt a little dizzy. Adrenaline, even when fading, plus scuppi equaled…a bad equation. "If we're already anxious, we might make things happen."

He shrugged and looked to the night's next fight. "I've heard rumors from the other clans."

When he didn't say more, she prodded his knee. "And?"

"The Svenal, a clan to the southeast. Sickness walks among them, and some of their neighbors claim they have attacked, but I haven't heard from anyone who's actually fought them."

"They won't be hard to beat if they're sick," she said. He shrugged again, but maybe their illness only affected their brains, not their bodies. "Are you going to send someone to check?"

He shrugged yet again, and after a moment, Cordelia wandered away from the fire, staring up at the stars that stretched from one horizon to the other. She put the Svenal and any rumors out of her mind and focused on what was around her, searching for the peace she'd felt when she'd decided to leave Gale.

Geavers, large pack animals for the Uri, milled around the outskirts of the camp. Bigger than the beetle-like hoshpis of Gale, the geavers stood nearly twelve feet tall and twenty feet long. Their rough, scaly hides provided the plains dwellers with all the leather they'd ever need, but the creatures didn't seem to resent their fate as transportation and then clothing. They trundled through the landscape on four stumpy legs, with long necks and flat heads bearing scraggly manes that shaded their huge, dull eyes. Cordelia stepped around them carefully. They could kill her by accident with a badly placed foot, and Cordelia had no intention of dying such a shitty death.

She found a boulder and climbed it. The Uri gatherings were a welcome break from digging latrines or wells, settling petty disputes or explaining to Liam once again why they couldn't go attacking the Storm Lord. The Uri liked a good fight, and Cordelia had never been so glad to meet someone who enjoyed it as she did. Liam, her frequent partner in extracurricular fighting, didn't join in anymore. The only fight he still craved was the only one he couldn't have.

Cordelia breathed deeply of the night air and wasn't surprised at the hint of greenery coming closer. She never heard Nettle walking, but the woodsy scent gave her away.

"Do you wish to be alone?" Nettle's voice asked from the near darkness.

"Only if I'm alone with you."

Nettle chuckled and climbed up on the rock. It was a corny line but true. Spending time with other people and spending time with the woman she'd fallen for were two different things. She'd never meant to fall in love, hadn't wanted to, but it had sneaked up on her. She'd been afraid of a sharp, sudden change, but as time passed and she never wanted to be without Nettle, she knew she'd eased into love rather than fallen.

"Are you thinking on the past again?" Nettle asked.

"I'm trying not to, but you know how it goes."

"Drushkan lives are long. We must look at now or forward, not behind." She shivered. "But I admit, I do not know if I will ever get used to the feeling of so much space. It makes the swamp large in my memory."

Cordelia chuckled. The plains were as different from the former drushkan home as it was possible to be. Though the swamp was large, its trees enormous, the ropy branches that crisscrossed it and the murky water threading through it made it seem suffocating when compared to the endless rolling hills of the plains. "Just how old are you, anyway?"

"Did I not just say we do not count the past?"

"Roughly, then. Approximately," she added when Nettle sucked her teeth.

"Perhaps seventy summers. Perhaps more."

Cordelia grunted as if she'd been punched. "Seventy!"

"I knew it would upset you."

"I'm almost thirty. I thought you had to be the same, but... You look so young!"

"Your people may take that as a compliment, but it means nothing to a drushka. To some, it might even mean you think them inexperienced. You know the age of the queen?"

"Yes." Pool was over two hundred, but she looked the same as the rest of the drushka, with their skin whorled like tree bark. And now it hit her that she didn't know how long Nettle would live, how long any of them lived, and she didn't want to ask. She fumbled for Nettle's hand and gripped it. Nettle rolled her middle finger into her own palm, tucking away her poisonous claw.

The long line of Nettle's body bent close, molding itself to Cordelia. She nibbled up Cordelia's neck with her sharp teeth and whispered, "Do not fear, Sa. I will be by your side for many years to come."

Cordelia sighed at the touches and the sentiment and the drushkan name. It seemed at times as if Nettle could read her mind or at least share her feelings as drushka could among one another. Cordelia had once done the same, right before the exile, when the Storm Lord had hit her with his lightning just as the healer Simon Lazlo had saved her. Her spirit had been propelled from her body, and she had sensed the drushka as they sensed one another. Even now, with Nettle so close, Cordelia could feel the love between them; her own feelings and Nettle's feelings returned, along with a vague awareness of the drushka who'd come to Wuran's encampment.

Before she could sink too far into the feeling and freak herself out, she sat up. "How old is Shiv? Sixty? Sixty-five?"

Nettle sighed, and Cordelia sensed her irritation, though she told herself it was from months of getting to know each other well.

"Perhaps…fourteen summers?"

With a groan, Cordelia put her head in her hands. "And now I have to tell Liam he's a pervert."

Nettle grabbed her before she could slide from the rock. "He and the queen's daughter are enjoying themselves. Leave them!"

"You're the one who didn't want them together in the first place."

"I thought two fools together would birth a thousand mistakes, but they have matured, and she is not a child. She has not been a child for some years."

"So you mature faster and live longer than we do! Fantastic. We can't know if we're coming or going."

"That makes no sense, Sa. Stay. Liam has the same number of summers as you, ahya?"

"Yes."

"But his mind is younger than yours, especially when we first met, ahya? As Shiv's mind is younger than most drushka you have met."

Cordelia sighed and relaxed into Nettle's embrace, seeing where this was going. "I suppose they are a good fit together, brain-wise."

"At last." She wrapped her long arms around Cordelia and nuzzled her neck again.

Cordelia fought the images of screwing teenagers or the elderly and tried to relax, but she knew it wasn't going to be easy.

Bathed in the first rays of dawn coming through his windows in the Yafanai Temple, Dillon grunted his way through a second set of pushups. He'd gotten soft on the space station. Everyone had, but with Lazlo's boosts of immortality, no one had noticed. Now, after eight months without Lazlo, Dillon had to keep on top of his fucking exercises.

Luckily, his muscles still remembered his old workout routine. Well, mostly. He'd floundered at first, unable to remember where the pushups went in relation to the sit-ups. Did he jog before or after? He'd been hesitant to join the paladins' routine, scared he would fuck up worse than the new recruits, but now he ran with them regularly, getting a kick out of the way they picked up their feet when God ran by.

And with Captain Jen Brown around, he didn't have to worry about handing any new recruits their asses if they fell. She was more than happy to yell for him, so much easier to get along with than old Captain Carmichael. It had been a mistake to let anyone on this rock know he was human, but she was too dead to tell anyone now. And with luck, no one would even suspect he wasn't immortal.

With a final grunt, he finished the pushups and stood, draping a towel around his shoulders as he breathed. He opened the window wider and looked at the courtyard below.

A tree blocked most of his view, but that was by design. He wanted to look upon the yafanai, his favorite children, unobserved. So many round bellies among them made him smile. He tried to have a kind word for all the women who were bearing his children. The visibly pregnant ones were easy, but he sometimes forgot those who weren't showing. Even then, if they were disappointed, all he had to do was turn on the charm, and they forgave him. Perks of being God again. A nursery full of superpowered offspring was a good idea all on its own. Odds were, one of them would be as good as Lazlo, and then immortality would be in the bag again.

"Wow, how many have you screwed?" a voice behind him asked.

Dillon turned, knowing that voice but not believing it, not until he saw Lazlo standing there, arms behind his back, neck craned to look out the window.

"Looks like most of them if that's all your handiwork," Lazlo said.

"Laz, what…" But what and why and how didn't fucking matter. Lazlo was back! Dillon reached out even as he knew he shouldn't, even before Lazlo popped like an overinflated balloon, covering Dillon with red tendrils of gore.

"What the fuck!" Dillon scrubbed at his clothes but felt nothing. The fluid rolled away from his hands and coalesced into a willowy female form.

With a snarl of disgust, Dillon turned away. "You really are an asshole, Naos." He cursed himself for falling for her amateur hour bullshit. Ever since she'd fucked with him when he'd thrown the renegades out of Gale, she came back every now and again for shit like this, and if he called her Dué instead of Naos, she only did it more.

"How can you say such things to your fairy godmother?" she asked, her voice echoing around his head. Her mouth didn't move with her words as she stepped to his side, but her vacant right socket glimmered with starlight.

"Fuck you." He crossed his arms and knew he should ignore her, wait for her to get bored, but she pissed him off so *much*.

"Are those *all* your unborn children?" she asked.

"Just fuck off."

"Trying to make a new Simon Lazlo from scratch?"

"I said fuck off!" The sound echoed across the courtyard, and even with the tree, most of the yafanai stared at him. When any caught him looking, they tried hesitant smiles.

Naos jerked a thumb in their direction. "Ooh, that's not good. That's a smile to foster rebellion, a my-god-is-crazy smile."

"You're one to talk." He closed the shutters. "Get out of my room."

"Or you'll what?"

He crossed to his bed and pulled his sidearm out from under the pillow. He'd brought a rack to the temple so he could charge it and the set of armor he'd claimed for his own. It made him feel better to have it around, just like now, when he was holding a gun even though he was having an argument with someone in his goddamned mind.

Naos grinned and slinked closer, her subtle curves draped in a long black evening gown streaked with nebulae. "I've heard all the ladies like your big gun." Her face and form flowed into Lazlo's again. "It's a shame you won't share it with the boys."

With shaking hands, he put the gun down, not wanting to fire random holes in the wall. "What do you get out of this shit, hmm? Does fucking with me get you off? Or are you mad you drove all the others away, and now you don't have anyone to play with?"

"I visit because I care."

He snorted and turned away, but the back of his neck tingled, and he knew that if he turned, she'd be right behind him.

"They're coming for you, you know," she said. "I put them on the path."

He told himself not to fucking listen, but he couldn't help thinking of the graffiti he'd seen, of Paul Ross's last words, of the looks he'd seen in the streets. When the renegades had left, they'd taken more than just a few nonbelievers. They'd taken the faith of some of those who'd remained.

Unless she meant someone else entirely. "Who?" He knew in his gut he'd hear from the renegades directly again. Former Lieutenants Cordelia Ross and Liam Carmichael were their leaders, and he'd killed her uncle and his mom, mayor and paladin captain. If he was them, he'd sure as shit be plotting revenge.

And then there were former lieutenants Christian and Marlowe, the Sun-Moon. He'd banished their followers from his city, killing a few just to make sure the point got across. That might have gotten back to the lieutenants themselves, and they wouldn't be happy about it. Could be another revenge plot in the works.

A feeling of emptiness behind him told him she'd left. He sighed, but as he cleaned up, he felt lighter than when he'd started his workout, his annoyance with Naos gone. If someone was coming for him, he needed to prepare, especially since he didn't know much about the drushka and their walking tree. He'd talk with Captain Brown. She'd been in the swamp, had fought the trees face to…bark. His spies kept an eye on the renegades from afar. Maybe he needed to get a little closer.

The lieutenants he could easily make a plan for. That would be a numbers game, follower against follower. A big enough storm might render their powers all but useless, except for the telepathy. For that he'd need an expert.

Down the hall, he took a quick peek in on Caroline, only weeks away from bearing his first child. She was asleep in the hammock chair she'd sworn was more comfortable than her bed. His most powerful telepath, she'd be able to better understand just what the lieutenants could do. He didn't want to wake her to ask. He slipped out and walked to the set of rooms near the Yafanai Temple gates, those he'd adopted as his study. Captain Brown waited for him as if summoned by his need. The thought made him smile, but she didn't return the look, all business, another reason to admire her.

"Captain," he said as he entered. "To what do I owe the pleasure?"

She bowed. "Storm Lord. A drushka came to the city."

He froze, his belly warming in anticipation. "One of the renegades?"

"She says she's a representative of the Shi, the leader of the old drushka. We've got her in the keep if you want to take a look."

He did indeed. Here he was wanting someone who could tell him about the walking trees, and a drushka showed up on his doorstep. He almost thanked Naos and then wondered if he was getting religious in his old age. The thought made him chuckle out loud, and when Brown glanced at him, he waved her concern away. "Lead the way."

Dillon didn't shake hands or speak to the populace as he walked from the temple to the Paladin Keep. He didn't like to glad-hand anymore, not after the boggin attack. Even after every story he'd made up about how the boggins had killed Mayor Ross and Captain Carmichael, with the departure of some popular people among the renegades, some of the townspeople still didn't believe. Popular graffiti included, "Paul Ross Lives" and "Where is Our Real God?" He'd like to meet the author of both of those so he could address them personally.

It was a shame that Gale wasn't as happy as it used to be. There'd been plenty of time to rebuild, but he still saw empty lots where burned-out buildings had been cleared. Some people clearly didn't want to move on. He'd made many a speech about how they all had to come together, but with the loss of so many, it seemed the living found that harder than necessary. After too many suspicious looks, he usually stayed in the temple or the keep, leaving the daily stuff to Brown and whomever she chose to take care of the city side of things. They hadn't elected a new mayor, though Dillon supposed Brown fit the bill well enough. Maybe he should've installed someone, though, so the populace would have someone else to blame.

Still, his paladins gathered to greet him. He nodded at those ringing the large open floor beyond the keep's bailey, but when a few turned in surprise, he realized they weren't waiting for him but staring at a drushka loitering in the hall.

No one had seen a drushka since the renegades left. He supposed any one of them would cause quite a stir, but this one was worth a second look. Her hands sported poisonous claws on her middle fingers, the only way to spot a female. She tapped both claws against her leather-clad thighs as she slowly turned. Dillon followed her long legs down to the floor before he took his time looking up again. She was tall, like all drushka, nearly his height, and she had long, lean limbs. Her hair glimmered silver, braided in three plaits that reached her waist before looping back up to her head. All the drushka he'd seen before kept their hair cropped short. He'd thought it was a fighting thing, but maybe it meant they were from different tribes.

This drushka's skin was nearly the same silvery color as her hair, like gray tree bark, and she had the lines and whorls that all drushka had, dark patterns like tattoos. As she turned full circle, eyeing everyone in the room, her yellow eyes finally found Dillon, and she inclined her head with a slight wrinkle of her narrow nose.

She took a step toward him, and the susurrus of the paladins' shuffling feet echoed through the hall. Dillon raised a hand to calm them. If she made a threatening move, he could blast her across the room faster than anyone could draw a gun. He smiled, and she did the same, cupping her chin as she looked him over. She tapped her claw against her cheek, and he didn't know if she was offering danger or threatening it.

"Looking for me?" he asked.

"If you are the Storm Lord." Her voice was husky and her accent thick. It sent a shiver through him. "I am called Enka."

"Let's go upstairs to the captain's office." He sauntered past her, letting her take all the looks she wanted. Brown followed on his heels, between him and the drushka, and Lieutenant Lea brought up the rear. Dillon went into the captain's office and took the seat behind the desk while Brown stood at his side, and Lea guarded the door. The drushka draped herself across the one other chair with lithe fluidity.

"Well," Dillon said, "what can Gale do for the drushka?"

"We have learned that trading with humans can be useful." She flashed those sharp teeth. "A hard lesson, learned during the last battle."

"That was the old regime. Tell me why you and I should be friends."

She spread her hands. "Why not? Friends share weapons, information…" She gave him another slow glance. "Many things."

An old ploy, but one he could still appreciate. "Captain Brown, would you excuse us?"

She glanced at him with doubt written on her furrowed brow, but when he nodded toward the door, she left. Dillon stood, and Enka followed suit. When he came around the desk, she met him, molding her lean body to his and kissing his chin with thin lips.

"I see you've negotiated before," he said.

"I sensed your liking of me. I enjoy the sight of you, too."

"Good to know."

"We will trade, ahya?" Her tongue flicked out and teased his earlobe as she caressed his chest. "Weapons?"

Dillon smiled and grabbed her wrists. She tried to jerk away, and he pumped the tiniest amount of electricity into her, making her gasp. She stiffened and stilled, staring at him with wide eyes.

"As if I'd ever be stupid enough to trade weapons for a piece of alien ass, never mind how much I 'enjoy the sight of it.'"

She tensed, and he hit her with another jolt, enough to make her teeth click together. She gasped but stilled again, and when he let her go, she sagged into the chair.

He stepped behind the desk and sat again. "Nice ploy, though, one I've used myself a time or two, but it's not going to work here. Now, if you and your people want to stay in the swamp, be my guest. You'll get no trouble from me. But if you come into my house, you play by my rules."

Enka licked her lips and sat up slowly. He noticed her hands shaking, but she smoothed them across her legs. "What do you want in return for weapons?"

"We could spare some slings. No guns, no metal. As for what I want…" He tilted his head back and forth. "Hoshpis, for a start. Maybe the services of some of those walking trees."

She narrowed her eyes. "You do not know of what you speak."

He shrugged. If she didn't want to talk about the trees, he'd just have to find someone who would. "I'm guessing you want weapons to go after your renegades? Better work fast, before they dig in. Hell, I know where they are. Maybe we can have some kind of joint mission, but not before we have trust."

She stared before lifting her chin. "I will consult with my leader."

He nodded toward the door. "Feel free to come back and stick your tongue in my ear anytime."

She looked back over her shoulder, and he expected to see offense, but she grinned. "I shall."

He chuckled and turned his attention to Brown's desk, seeing what she had going on, but someone said, "A piece of alien ass. I like that."

He sighed as he recognized Lessan's voice. Over two hundred years since she'd died, but he hadn't forgotten what she sounded like, a side effect of Lazlo's immortality treatments. And of course, Naos wouldn't let him forget. He turned, and Lessan was leaning against the wall, hands in the pockets of her blue flight suit.

"I know that's you, Naos," he said, "Why do you bother?"

She kept her eyes pinned on him, and Dillon waited for her to explode or melt.

"Trading with the drushka was quite lucrative," a man's voice said.

Dillon turned and saw the former mayor, Paul Ross, leaning against the wall opposite Lessan. Blood covered his torso where Dillon had stabbed him after electrocuting him, and he scratched idly around the wound.

"Lucrative but still dangerous," the ghost of Captain Carmichael said as she walked through the wall beside Paul, a bloody mark across her forehead.

"Oh, this is a new one," Dillon said. "We almost have enough for a parade!"

"You always did like flirting with danger," Marie Martin, the former Contessa, said as she appeared beside Lessan, arms crossed in front of her blackened torso.

Dillon nodded. "I was wondering when you'd get to her."

Lazlo materialized in front of the desk, hands outstretched. "All your kills! I thought you might like the company."

Dillon sighed and hoped she'd get whatever the hell this was over with soon. "But Lazlo's not dead." A chill crept up his spine. "Is he?"

Lazlo blew him a kiss. "Miss me, big boy?"

"Just tell me."

"All these dead people not good enough for you?"

"Oh, fuck off if you can't be useful!"

"Storm Lord?" Brown poked her head in, Lea looking over her shoulder. "Drushka's gone, Storm Lord. Can we help with anything else?"

He marched around the desk and past her. "I don't think anyone can." The laughter of the ghosts echoed behind him. He hurried past the paladins and out into the street, but halfway back to the temple, he stopped. Someone had scrawled, "God Is Dead," on a half-finished shop, the words a dull black like charcoal. It hadn't been there earlier.

He whirled around, and several people avoided his gaze or hurried back from it. "Who the fuck did this?"

Heads shook, and people backed away. One man even dropped what he was carrying and held up his hands as if Dillon might throttle him right there in the street.

"Someone clean that shit up." He strode away. Fucking people didn't know how lucky they were.

❖

Enka paused inside the tree line and let the rhythms of the swamp embrace her. She wished she had a safe pond handy to wash away the city stink, but she supposed that would have to wait, like many things. With a long sigh, she jogged into the trees until the ground gave way to liquid, and then she climbed high among the ropy branches of the proper swamp where each tree's long limbs entwined with the others.

"Hunt leader?" Thesta, her second, called to her. "Are you well?"

Enka waved the younger drushka to her side. "Frustrated."

"The Storm Lord did not succumb to the scent?"

"He seemed as if he might, then bent in another direction." She rubbed her aching arms, her chest. "His power is great."

"A shawness is within call," Thesta said.

"I am not badly hurt." She stalked into the branches, and her band fell in behind her. They hurried deeper into the swamp until they found the seventh queen, Daishi, waiting for them. Enka climbed among the queen's branches, and the great tree moved even deeper into drushkan territory.

Enka found the queen's perch, where drushka and tree joined, the seventh queen nearly encased in the wood. Enka sat and opened her mind, letting the seventh queen serve as a link to the Shi, the ninth queen, leader of all drushka.

Well, all real drushka. The renegades only followed one queen, she who had torn the drushka asunder two centuries ago, she who must now be returned to the fold at any cost.

"Your will, Queen," Enka said.

She felt the mind of the Shi envelop her, taking over the seventh queen's mind as if it was her own. "The Storm Lord did not take you for bait."

"Ahwa. We will have to find another way."

"He seeks hoshpis. That could be the seed of his undoing."

Enka sucked her teeth. "How?"

"We will weaken the humans, and then no one will stand between us and the Anushi queen. With her human allies decimated, she will have nowhere to run but back to her home."

Enka squirmed, anxious to see it done.

"Patience," the Shi said. "We acted too hastily before. We did not know of all the human weapons. Now we will be as saleska, waiting, biding our time, and when we strike, the humans will be dead before they know they have been attacked."

Enka thought quickly. "Poison?"

"Not all at once." The Shi paused, and Enka felt her amusement. "Gather hoshpis for the humans and feed them spyralotus leaves. It will not kill the animals, nor the humans who eat the meat. But it will linger in their bodies, and then we will give them veira pollen, perhaps in their water."

"The two will combine inside the body to make poison," Enka said. "And the humans will be weakened."

"Too weakened to stand against us."

CHAPTER THREE

Simon awoke with a twinge in his back. Even after eight months, he still had a brief flash of confusion. Spending two hundred years with the ability to heal himself and everyone around him had made him forget pain. In the few days following when he'd burned out his power, small pains had even made him smile, such a strong reminder that he was alive. Now they were simply annoying. He wondered if Horace felt the same way.

But he'd stolen Horace's power. His intentions had been good: to make sure the crew of the *Atlas* could never make a healer their slave again, but he doubted Horace saw it that way. If he woke up with an ache, he probably cursed Simon's name to hell and back.

Even as Simon thought about it, the twinge faded slowly. He and Samira had slept on the ground a lot in the months since they'd left Gale, but the twinges had followed him east, into Sun-Moon territory and all the way to Celeste, the capital city of former Lieutenants Christian and Marlowe. He'd finally had to conclude that he just had a bad back, but he knew that being almost three hundred years old should probably come with an ache or two.

Snug in her own bed, Samira muttered in her sleep and turned over. Simon heard footsteps going downstairs outside their door. It sounded like the man with the limp who'd checked into the wayhouse just before them. Simon sat up, pulled on the loose fitting trousers he'd bought just outside of Celeste, and slipped on the long robe that sported slits from the ankles to the waist. He hated the way it slapped his legs as he walked, but wherever they went, he and Samira endeavored to fit in, so in this country, he wore the embroidered sun of the men, and she the moon of the women, making them seem like a bonded pair.

In the common room of the wayhouse, Simon grabbed two mugs of hot, spiced tea and two delicate, flaky pastries and brought them up. As more guests came downstairs, he flattened against the wall to let them pass, not wanting to risk a fall. During the past few months, he was glad he'd never let his healing powers make him reckless. Even though he could have fixed any injury, he'd stayed careful, and that care now served him well. He never blundered into danger like Dillon had, depending on old Laz to fix everything.

Samira sat up as he came back in, smiling at him and then smiling wider at the breakfast. "Are you sure you're not a telepath?" she asked, a question she often put to him, but she knew he was good at reading people, just like she was.

"Think we'll see the ocean today?" she asked as they ate. It'd been nearly dark when they'd gotten to Celeste the previous evening, and they'd been in a hurry to find shelter for the night rather than explore.

"If you like. We'll have plenty of time for—" A tingling feeling slid over his scalp, making him twitch. Even though he no longer had power, he could still sense it when someone was trying to use telepathy on him.

Samira sat up straight. "I felt that, too. The Sun-Moon?"

"Maybe." But of course, he had no way of checking, and Samira wasn't a telepath. He sighed. He'd considered the fact that he might run into them, of course. Celeste and the surrounding countryside was their domain, but he'd hoped to bump into them rather than have them seek out his mind.

Of course, if it was them, why weren't they saying anything? He might not have power, but that wouldn't stop them. They could speak in anyone's mind.

"Should we try to find them?" Samira asked.

Irritation thrummed through him. "If they want to find us, let them."

She grinned, and he answered it with a smile of his own. She liked the rebellious nature he'd discovered after leaving Dillon; she even fostered it. He'd been doing what someone else wanted for over two hundred years. He liked hanging out with someone who appreciated going against the grain.

They dressed and went out together. Celeste sported buildings made of white and rose colored clay. Flowers and plants flourished in the sea air, and the people of Celeste kept them in pots and window boxes, and more than one storefront or home was covered in climbing ivy. He and Samira started down to the left, heading for the market rumored to be near the city center. According to the owner of the wayhouse, the city was laid out in concentric circles, with many small spokes connecting them, very different from the grid of Gale.

And that wasn't the only difference. Sun-Moon worshipers were raised as pairs, partners, and they spent their whole lives together. Simon had cringed when he thought that pretending to be partners would mean he and Samira would have to pretend to be lovers, but it wasn't the case. One half of a pair could be married to one half of another pair and so on until great groups of people lived in the same house with spouses and partners and children until it was hard to tell who was bonded to whom, though the Sun-Moon worshipers always seemed to know.

And their language hadn't drifted much from what was spoken aboard the *Atlas*—just like the language of Gale or that of the plains dwellers—and Simon found this one as easy to pick up. Samira still tripped over unfamiliar words like those of local food or animals, but she'd quickly learned the words for Sun-Moon, and both of them were careful never to impugn those names.

The crowd parted ahead, pairs scurrying out of the way, eyes downcast. Simon and Samira mirrored them, though he sneaked a peek, guessing at what he'd see. A lone man strode past; large, exaggerated teardrop tattoos stained his cheeks. The black marks were red around the edges, newly done, as was the black circle that surrounded the embroidered sun on his back. In one of the outlying towns, Simon had asked what it meant, and in hushed tones, the partners had named such people widows, those whose partners had died. And to spend too much time in their presence was to tempt unseen forces into killing one's own partner.

Simon felt pity for the man, but he kept his eyes downcast like everyone else. It wouldn't do to draw too much attention. He wouldn't need to be a rebel if no one gave him a reason, after all. Still, after the widow passed, Simon glanced after him. Partners often shared the same interests, often had the same careers, but even if they didn't, a widow had to devote what remained of his or her life to preventing whatever had killed their partner. If it was illness, the widow had to become a medic. If an accident, he must work to protect others from the same fate. If it was murder, he must hunt down other such murderers, even after avenging his partner's death. Indeed, groups of widows often hunted together. If a partner died from old age, the widow had to care for and comfort the elderly as best he could.

When the widow passed, life in the street resumed. Samira nudged Simon's arm. "Maybe we should get one of those when we leave." She nodded ahead to where two men were hustling a band of animals up the street.

Simon stared at them and shuddered. As large as an ostrich, the ossors were giant insects, just like the hoshpis of Gale. They stood on two legs covered in spines and had a pair of vestigial wings that a rider could tuck his feet under. Two huge, bulbous, multifaceted eyes stuck out from the top of their head, just below long antennae, but what drew the eye was the pair of mandibles that clicked together constantly.

Simon could feel the blood draining from his cheeks the longer he stared. In one of the villages, he'd been persuaded to ride one, but when those wings had closed over his feet, encasing them in the bug's warm... meat, he'd nearly gagged. "No thanks."

These ossors had yokes around their necks, and they pulled a cart of injured people. He thought at first they were going to a hospital, then he noticed the bonds.

"Prisoners?" Samira asked.

"Plains dwellers." He craned his neck. He'd heard of some fighting between the plains dwellers and the Sun-Moon worshipers. He'd hoped it was isolated, as the two cultures had developed a trading system after years of conflict, but if captives were being taken to Celeste, the fighting must have spread.

"Dr. Lazlo!"

Simon was glad he was turned away from the voice. It gave him a moment to get his face under control. "Lisa," he said as he turned, recognizing her high-pitched voice.

She flung her arms around him as if they were old friends, and she wasn't one of the worst breachies on the *Atlas* for gossip and cliques and other petty, school-like bullshit that drove him nuts. She stood with Aaron, another breachie, who gave Simon an embarrassed wave as if he acutely recalled every petty torment he'd levied Simon's way. And all that because Simon was quiet and unassuming; it never seemed to matter that he also kept them all immortal.

Lisa beamed and held him at arm's length, not even deigning to glance at Samira. "It's so nice to see you! I thought I felt your mind earlier. We don't get to talk to many equals."

If Dillon had been there, he would have howled with laughter, probably after giving Lisa a leer. The powers of the bridge crew dwarfed those of the breachies. In fact, Simon had met many yafanai, like Samira, who could rival them. Marie Martin, the strongest breachie, was killed by Dillon shortly after they arrived, so maybe Lisa meant she had no one around with a power as equally weak as her own.

Of course, everyone was more powerful than him now. "Um, were you looking for me?" he asked.

"Just taking a quick telepathic scan, seeing if there's anyone interesting." She sniffed. "The Sun-Moon don't care as long as we don't try to influence anyone."

He fought the urge to roll his eyes. Those among the bridge crew had always called one another by their real names, but the breachies loved the names they picked out for themselves. If Lisa and Aaron had a god name, he'd never bothered to find out what it was. As far as he knew, they didn't even have worshipers, or maybe they borrowed some from Christian and Marlowe.

He felt another tingle as she scanned him again, and he automatically reached for his shields to keep her out, but all he got was a headache. Still, she narrowed her eyes as if she detected something, and he hoped it was his spike of anger.

"We should be going," he said, turning.

She laughed. "Wait, Dr. Lazlo, I'm sorry. I was just curious."

He didn't feel her reach for him, but Samira said, "Keep your hands to yourself."

When Simon turned, Lisa looked at Samira at last, her eyebrows raising. "What did you say?"

Aaron looked embarrassed. "Come on," he said. "Let's go."

Lisa shook him off. "Who in the world do you think you are?"

Samira glanced at Simon, and he knew she would follow his lead, but he must have looked even angrier than he felt. "Simon's not going to be your emotional punching bag anymore."

She'd said something similar to him once, that she wouldn't be a sponge for other people's feelings. He knew the idea ticked her off. Lisa narrowed her eyes, and then staggered back a step as Samira used her power, making Simon's head tingle all over.

Lisa's eyes widened. "How dare you!"

"Stay out of our heads."

Simon opened his mouth to ask them to break it up so they could all get away from one another. So much power was flying around, and his head was starting to ache. But Lisa launched into an angry tirade, and

Samira met her word for word, and Aaron was stepping up behind Lisa as if he'd changed his mind about getting into a fight. He was a bit of a telepath and a bit of a micro, nothing like Simon used to be, but together, they'd be more than a match for Samira.

And all Simon could do was glare at them, more handicapped even than when he'd had power but had been unwilling to use it. And he could feel their power gathering. He had to stop them. "Samira."

But even if they ran, Lisa and Aaron could follow them, find them, attack them from a distance. He snarled and focused again on the way their power gathered, pushing at something inside himself in a way he hadn't had to do in a long time until he could actually *feel* their power.

It was enough to make him gasp and lose the feeling. All those back twinges that had been fading faster and faster each morning. He'd thought it had just been the transition from camping to sleeping in a bed, but...

Lisa left off arguing and stared at him, Aaron staring with her. Their mouths dropped open, and he knew they had to feel something. When Lisa's face broke out in a delighted smile, he knew what she was thinking, what all of them would be thinking when word spread. If his power had returned, if his brain had mended itself, that meant they could all be immortal again. They just had to catch him and keep him as if he was some leprechaun out of an old story.

"Samira," he said, a harsh whisper.

She couldn't know what was going on, but she had to see his panic, and it made her brow darken. When her gaze darted to Lisa and Aaron, they flew across the street and smashed into a fruit cart. She didn't hesitate but grabbed Simon's arm and ran, threading through crowds.

"Are you all right?" she asked when they were several streets away. "What did they do to you?"

He shook his head. He couldn't tell her out loud. "We have to get out of here."

And go where? Back to Gale and Dillon? Beg the Storm Lord to protect him? He snarled at the thought, but he needed to do something. He reached deep inside for his power and felt a soggy, weak response. As he was, any breachie could catch him. He'd run first and think about where later.

Horace. The idea almost stopped him dead. If Simon's powers were coming back, Horace's might be as well. And Dillon at least knew about Horace's augmentation, knew that he could grant immortality as well. Simon had to warn him.

"We need some supplies," Samira said. "Or we won't make it far."

The crowd parted ahead of them as it had earlier, and Simon thought it might be another widow, but people were falling to their knees, and as they did, Simon caught a glimpse of a familiar face, two faces, that were never far from one another.

He grabbed Samira's arm. "Down!"

"What?"

"Don't think of me. Don't think of anything!"

She closed her mouth and kept her face down. The crowd had fallen silent, and Simon cast one glance down the lane to see the lieutenants, Christian and Marlowe, walking arm in arm among their prostrated followers. Quadruple damn! He tried to think random thoughts, little songs and grocery lists. The lieutenants turned down a side street, and Simon thanked his lucky stars, guessing there were just too many minds around for them to focus on anyone. He hoped like hell Lisa and Aaron hadn't reached out to them.

"That was the Sun-Moon!" Samira said.

"I hope they didn't sense us."

"Maybe they can teach those other two to mind their manners."

"They'll be so much worse, believe me."

They headed away from the lieutenants and found the outdoor market. Like the Galeans, the people of Celeste used metal coins as currency, and Simon haggled while Samira kept lookout. He'd just bought salt when a tingle passed over his scalp. He gripped Samira's arm and tried to find his random songs again. The tingle passed, and he hoped it was only Lisa looking for him. She wouldn't forgive them anytime soon.

"Someone's scanning for us," he said. "We need to hurry."

"We have enough for a day or so. We can pick up the rest in that little town by…"

She trailed away, and he almost didn't want to look, but he knew that if they ran, they'd find their brains so scrambled they couldn't move, or perhaps Marlowe would slam them into the ground with her macro-psychokinetic powers, or Christian would burn them to death with pyrokinesis.

"Dr. Lazlo," they said as he turned. "So good to see you again."

Everyone else had fallen to the ground. Simon managed a sickly smile. He started to greet them by their human names, but a warning prickle along his scalp stopped him. "Lords?" he tried.

With a laugh, they nodded. "That will do. Lisa told us you were here. We felt you in the crowd."

"Oh?"

"Those songs, Dr. Lazlo. No one here knows them."

He cursed himself, and they smiled wider. "Well," he said, "I suppose I just proved it's possible to be smart and stupid at the same time."

"All those years with Colonel Tracey must have taught you that," they said in his mind, and he fought another wince.

"Come," they said aloud. "Be our guest at the palace. You won't have to see Lisa or Aaron again. We promise."

He glanced at Samira, and she shrugged. The invitation hadn't been a question, after all.

Samira sat on a divan, hands folded in front of her. Since she'd entered the Yafanai Temple as a teenager, she'd been learning how to school her thoughts, curb her emotions, and control her temper. All those exercises were supposed to help her control her power, but only the third lesson really benefitted her. She suspected the other two were to help telepaths who were trying not to be distracted by the powerful thoughts of others.

Faced with the Sun-Moon inside their palace, she didn't know if any lessons would help. Simon had told her they could read minds from space. Even the most determined mental exercises wouldn't keep them out. All she could hope for was to remain slightly unnoticed.

The Sun-Moon glanced at her and winked.

The room was opulent, with tall ceilings and windows. Rugs covered the cool stone floor, and she and Simon sat on one heavily padded divan while the Sun-Moon occupied another. The number of stairs they'd climbed to get here indicated a second or third story, and before she'd sat down, Samira had glimpsed the blue expanse of the sea through the windows. Two servants opened the large doors at one end of the room, stirring long curtains. The servants set a tea service on a low table before scurrying out again, passing a lone side door on their way.

Samira didn't reach for the drinks, letting the Sun-Moon hand them around. She held hers tightly in case it might prove useful. Simon put his in front of him and adjusted his robe for the twentieth time. He hadn't stopped fidgeting since they'd been discovered. Occasionally, his hand wandered toward his temple as if looking for something, but he simply toyed with his dark blond hair before lowering his hand to his lap and starting the whole process over.

She'd pictured the Sun-Moon as looking exactly alike, but they differed in almost every way: him with straight blond hair and her with dark curls and him paler than her. He had blue eyes, and hers were hazel, and as she stared, all four eyes fixed on her.

"We've never gotten to study a yafanai this closely," they said together, their voices matching perfectly.

Samira nodded, but at the sudden speech, Simon started. Samira tried not to sigh. He was the one who'd spent centuries with these people. He'd told her they did everything in unison.

"Not always," the Sun said.

"But most of the time," the Moon added. Without looking at each other, they joined hands, and she supposed having such a deep telepathic connection meant they always knew where the other was.

One of the mugs rose into the air and settled in the Sun's hands before steam billowed anew from the liquid inside. Her macro-psychokinesis and his pyrokinesis, working in harmony. Samira smiled to show she admired them. They could all be friends.

"Indeed," they said with a smile.

"Will you stop that?" Simon shouted. When everyone looked, he glowered. "Oh yes, you're powerful, but you didn't bring us here to wow us, so will you stop dicking around and tell us what you want?"

Samira swallowed a chuckle that she knew would sound more than a little nervous. Simon didn't lose his temper often, but when he did, he didn't do it by halves.

If the Sun-Moon had a response to that thought, they kept it inside. "There's no reason we can't be civilized," they said. "We were hardly ever at odds aboard the *Atlas*, if you'll recall."

"A lot has changed," Simon said. "Don't try to finesse or cajole, or whatever it is you're doing. If this was a friendly cup of tea, it would have been an invite instead of an order, so…" He waved for them to get on with it.

"Samira," they said, "would you excuse us a moment?"

She looked at Simon, and with an exasperated sigh, he shrugged and nodded. If she didn't go, she supposed they'd throw her out, and she didn't want to try to match her macro powers against theirs. It wasn't until the doors had closed behind her that she realized no one had mentioned her name, and she hadn't even felt the prickle along her scalp that said they were looking. Maybe she was rusty. Before that morning, she hadn't felt the touch of a telepath in a long time, but more likely, they were just that good.

She stood in a long hallway lined with windows similar to those in the room beyond. She pressed her ear to the doors but heard nothing. But there'd been a smaller door, much closer to where they were seated. Keeping it out of her thoughts, she focused on the look of the hall again as she traced the walls around, looking for the smaller door. She turned the corner and stopped in surprise.

A woman with short dark hair knelt in front of it, head turned down. Her clothing was torn and dirty, bloody in spots, and when she lifted her head, Samira saw blood crusting under her nose. She seemed a bit younger than Samira, nineteen or twenty. Staring into her dark eyes, Samira recalled her from the cart earlier that afternoon, one of the captives being taken through the city, but this one had apparently escaped. She pulled a small bone knife that looked dull, something used for spreading butter or cheese. With a grim look, she shifted as if she might spring for Samira's throat.

"I'm a bit harder to cut than butter," Samira said softly.

The woman looked to her knife and then at Samira. "I know your voice. You were inside with the spirits."

Samira stepped closer, her power ready just in case. "Don't worry. I'm not going to turn you in." She nodded toward the room. "We're not allies." Though she supposed if the Sun-Moon turned their attention this way just a little, they'd know everything. They probably knew already. "What's your name?"

She swallowed. "Mamet of the Engali."

A plains dweller name. "I'm Samira. Where are you from?"

"The Engali," Mamet said again.

"I don't know them, I'm sorry. The north?"

Mamet's eyes widened. "So, you're beautiful but not smart?"

Samira put her hands on her hips. "When all you have is that pitiful knife, insulting someone isn't smart either."

Mamet stood up. "You have no weapon at all."

"None that you can see."

Mamet gave her an up and down glance before nodding at the door. "Then you're a spirit like they are?"

"They're people, and so am I."

She frowned. "They're the spirits of the sun and moon!"

"No, they're the Sun-Moon. There's a difference." And she didn't have time to explain right then.

Mamet tucked the small knife in her cloth belt. "Not stupid. You're a beautiful lunatic."

Samira sighed a laugh. She'd never been called beautiful twice in one day. "Look, my friend is in there, and if you don't mind, I'd like to hear what they're saying."

Mamet waved her close. "Come on, lunatic." She smelled as coppery and dirty as Samira thought, but there was nothing for it. She knelt and pressed her ear to the door.

Simon tried to keep his temper in check, but the lieutenants kept dragging their feet through the conversation. And they kept calling him Dr. Lazlo, a name and title he hadn't even thought about in months before that morning. He knew they were reading his mind, too; the pact they'd made to leave each other alone on the *Atlas* clearly hadn't followed them to Calamity's surface.

"Did you start the fight between your worshipers and the plains dwellers?" he asked, interrupting them.

They shrugged. "We must secure our borders."

"It seemed as if they were all doing just fine until you got here."

"They stole from us."

He nodded. "In the past. They're trading now. Given time, they'd probably merge."

"If they want to submit to our rule, to live as we instruct—"

Simon rubbed the bridge of his nose. "Funny, I thought I'd left the megalomaniac behind in Gale."

"And how is the Storm Lord?"

He sighed. "You tell me. You're the one who can speak with him from here. Is that why you brought me? You think I can give you some insight into Dillon?"

"Your powers have returned."

His mind became a black pit, letting out nothing, not even the suggestion of thought.

The Sun laughed while the Moon shook her head. "Keeping your surface thoughts blank won't help you."

As he wondered when he'd let it slip, they smiled. Oh, he'd let nothing slip, and they hadn't gone deep diving in his mind. He'd just confirmed their suspicions with his surface thoughts. "Sneaky bastards." He clapped his hands slowly.

"What about the other one?" they asked. "The other micro whose powers you burned?"

"His aren't coming back. Ever."

"But if yours—"

"Ever."

"Ah."

"So, you're going to lock me up to be your immortality dispenser?"

"There is comfort here."

"And discomfort, too, I suppose?"

They shrugged, but their smiles said it all. "You won't ever have to see Lisa and Aaron if you don't want to."

"So immortality just for you two, then? What happened to all the others?"

"They're here and there. Most went wandering."

Seemed a fine idea to him. He made as if to stand, but an invisible force held him still. His anger flared, tapping into his power, and with a desperate push, he broke their grip. Funny how quickly it all came back to him. With a lash of his mind, he shut off Marlowe's powers, and both of them recoiled, their synchronicity briefly shattered.

"Samira!" Simon shouted. He shut off Christian's abilities, too, but his own power flagged, and they hit him with a telepathic attack. He reeled, staggering. "Samira!"

Someone was pounding on the doors, probably the servants. Swaying to his feet, Christian grabbed for him, but Simon tapped his power again and gave Christian's lungs a squeeze. Christian grabbed his chest and tottered, falling over the low table. Marlowe picked up the tray, sending the tea things crashing to the floor. She raised it over her head.

The side door burst in, and Samira strode inside, another woman just behind her. Samira looked at the lieutenants, and they flew across the room under her power. The large doors opened, and a pair of servants took one look at the scene and called for the guards.

The lieutenants stood, faces red with anger. Pain stabbed through Simon's head, and he moaned. Without a word, Samira threw both lieutenants into the wall again. Their heads slammed into the stone, and Simon focused all his power on their minds, putting them out completely.

"We have to get out of here," Samira said. Her companion had shut the main doors and moved a piece of furniture against them, but cries were coming from the hallway.

"Where?" Simon moved to the window, but the ground was at least thirty feet below.

The new woman looked down at his side. "We wouldn't survive such a jump."

Samira ripped down one of the long curtains. "I don't have the control to lower you down, but I could hold this against the wall with my power, and you could climb." She dangled it down the wall, and it stuck as if glued in place. "Hurry."

The new woman scurried down but was left with a ten-foot drop to the street. She let go of the curtain and rolled when she landed. Simon expected her to run, but she glanced around and waved for them to follow.

Simon licked his lips. "I don't know if I can."

Samira grunted, lines of stress creasing her face. "You can heal yourself if you have to. I heard about your powers."

He gaped but did as she asked. Halfway to the ground, he heard the doors inside the room give. The curtain dropped without warning, and he fell, bruising himself on the ground, but it didn't feel as if anything was broken. He looked up. "Samira!"

She leaned out, looked over her shoulder once, and jumped. Simon sensed it as she tried to slow herself with her power, but she'd never had that kind of careful control. Few macros did. She fell fast, her dark hair fluttering behind her.

When she hit the stones, Simon cried out as he felt something snap within her. Broken ribs and cracked vertebrae, a fractured pelvis. He took back all the times he'd wished to be normal and laid his power over her, clutching her hands at the same time. Her pain-wracked expression relaxed as his powers flowed through her, but he could hear the sounds of guards calling for help. He wasn't fast enough.

"We have to go," the new woman said.

"Just a little more," he whispered.

"Pick her up and come!"

"Almost done. Almost. Hold on, Samira, please."

She gasped, and life seemed to rush into her eyes where it had been ebbing before. "I can walk." She struggled to her feet. "Finish me as we go."

She still wheezed, and he put everything into one last push. Red spots bloomed in front of his eyes, and he heard a roar in his ears. He clasped the new woman's shoulder as Samira was healed, and his sight returned. The three of them hurried into the city as cries of alarm spread through the palace behind them.

❖

Fajir stepped over the ruined furniture and fought to keep from frowning in front of her gods. The partnered servants looked away quickly, fearing to look too closely at her tattoos, a stupid superstition, though one she'd held when Halaan was alive. When she'd first been promoted to seren, the leader of a Celestian patrol, she'd seen respect in the eyes of her troops and fear in the faces of recruits, but it wasn't until after she'd lost Halaan that she knew what real dread looked like in the faces of others.

But her gods did not show fear. They stood among the wreckage of their sitting room and stared at the window through which their quarry had escaped.

"Shall I kill them for touching you, Lords?" she asked, though they had no doubt already plucked the thought from her head, as was their right.

"Their escape had to be believable," they said together. "Dr. Lazlo's power hasn't recovered as much as he thinks, but we had to make it seem so, or he wouldn't have had the confidence to escape."

Fajir bowed. "Your will in all things."

"Was their little Engali helper your idea?" the Lords asked.

Fajir smiled. "I thought a native guide might be helpful, Lords, so I let one escape." And she'd picked her most hated clan on purpose, but no doubt the Lords already knew that, too. An Engali had killed Halaan, so she must forever hunt them, but she would also do as her gods bid, two purposes merged into one.

The Lords gave her a kindly smile and cast a knowing look at the bone sword on her hip, as if confirming that it would soon drink Engali blood. "Give them enough time to get out of the city and then track them. If we're right, Dr. Lazlo will head straight for this other healer to warn him. Take them both alive and bring them here."

Fajir bowed again and left. As she crossed the threshold of the palace, her company fell in behind her, all of them raising their hoods to block out the sun. It was a warm day, but that didn't matter. Warm days, cold ones, rainy or dry, she marked all of them the same. Eight months, seven days since Halaan had been taken from her. Tomorrow would be eight months, eight days, and time would go on that way until it ended, until she ended. All those in her company counted days the same way.

Nico, her second, fell in beside her. Shorter than her, he was still stocky and strong, fast with a sword. For him, it had been three years, four months, ten days. They all knew one another's counts. As they mounted their ossors and turned out of the city, entire crowds averted their eyes.

Eight months and seven days ago, it had been a warm day, too. She and Halaan had been patrolling a ranch near Celeste's northern border. The keening of ossors drew them close to a paddock, and they laughed as they bet on what predator would be harrying the animals this time. Halaan had strode fearlessly into the pack, shouting to make the ossors scramble out of the way. She'd watched the play of light on his hair, the sweat along his bare, muscled arms and wondered if they had enough time before they were due to report to be alone together.

When he fell, she called out, asking if he'd tripped. He didn't answer, and she'd hurried over, but even when she'd seen the spear sticking out of his chest, she hadn't believed. She'd thought his staring eyes must be some trick, the blood dripping from his mouth a shadow. Then she'd screamed as she'd fallen by his side, as she'd torn the spear loose and cast it away. He'd sucked in air then as if the shock revived him, but he could only grip at the hole in his chest and try to breathe, a wet, sucking sound that would rattle in her ears every night to come.

She'd rolled him flat and put her hands to the wound, thinking she could stop the blood by sheer will. He'd given her a confused look, frowning and working his bloody teeth. He'd mouthed something like, "Am I dead?" but before she could tell him he lived, his eyes rolled back, and his arms fell limp to his sides.

She'd screamed his name and shaken his dead weight. When she paused to breathe, she heard a gasp, turned, and saw him. He'd pulled his scarf down below his mouth and looked at her in horror. "I...thought he was a grelcat."

The long-limbed predators of the north. That was probably what Halaan had thought was scaring the ossors, too, but it had been an Engali raider. Fajir memorized his every feature and lunged for him. He'd leapt atop an ossor and fled. Fajir had run in his track until it was nothing but a dust cloud, and even then, she'd run until she collapsed.

The Engali had sent an envoy later, claiming Halaan's death had been an accident. They'd sent her *skins* and *food* to pay for his death, the death of her partner, her one love.

In the saddle of her ossor now, she kept her rage close, letting it seep into every pore. Only the arrival of her gods had kept her from hunting all the Engali down. She'd thought their arrival a sign that she should do as tradition demanded and keep the Engali out of Sun-Moon territory, but now the Lords had chosen her for this mission, to follow their prey, and she had made sure it was an Engali who led them. Perhaps on their journey, they would take her to the Engali territory, maybe to find the one that killed Halaan, maybe just to kill as many as she could.

CHAPTER FOUR

After they'd ridden all night through Calamity's grassy plains, Simon begged a halt; his thighs couldn't take anymore. From the moment Mamet had suggested they steal ossors to make their escape from Celeste, he'd known it was a bad idea. Problem was, sticking around to feel the wrath of the lieutenants was a far worse idea, so he had to clamber aboard one of the large insects and secure his legs under its wings, fighting down the urge to vomit as their pulsating warmth encased him.

Mamet bounded out of her saddle and held the reins for Samira. She'd barely taken her eyes off Samira long enough to introduce herself to Simon, let alone guide them toward her people. He tried not to roll his eyes at the obvious smitten-ness.

"Where are we?" Samira asked as she stretched.

"We went north," Mamet said. "Close to where my people camp this time of year."

"Did the Sun-Moon capture you way out here?"

Mamet shook her head, and in the growing light, Simon spotted a flush on her cheeks. "We were sent to another village to trade."

"They attacked you just for being there?" Simon asked.

Mamet ducked her head farther. "They had huge herd of ossors, and we thought..."

Samira gave her a wry smile. "That they wouldn't miss a few? Let me guess, everyone in your trading-turned-raiding party is as young as you?"

"I'm nineteen!"

"Ah," Simon said, "the age of wisdom."

Samira turned her head to hide a laugh while Mamet glared at Simon.

"They caught us," Mamet said slowly, "with their mind powers." She gave Samira a nervous yet admiring glance. "But your powers are so much better! If we hadn't been in such a hurry, we would've killed them, I'm sure, and then we could've rescued my people from the dungeon and...avenged the dead."

"Oh." Samira laid a hand on her shoulder. "I didn't know some had died. I'm sorry."

She gave Samira a glowing smile, and Simon fought the urge to sigh. With Samira's natural tendency toward kindness, Mamet would be nursing a hell of a crush in no time. "Samira, a word, please. Sorry," he said to Mamet, "it's, um, a mind power thing."

Mamet nodded slowly and let them walk out of earshot.

"I don't think we should get attached to Mamet or her people," Simon said.

"I wasn't planning on it." Samira narrowed her eyes. "Or are you saying you want to leave her behind now?"

"No, if we go to her people, we can get our bearings. Maybe they can give us directions. I just..." He nodded over her shoulder. "She's already staring at you."

Samira shrugged, but the look on her face said she knew very well what was going on.

"So, you're going to let her...woo you?" he asked.

"You sound like my grandmother."

"I'm older than your grandmother, young lady."

She gave him a flat look. "What would you suggest? Tell her to leave me alone? Insult her so harshly she bursts into tears and vows never to love again?"

"Don't be ridiculous. I'm just not..." He didn't know how to finish, didn't want to admit that he wasn't ready for another person to join his life, to join Samira's life. As Dillon would have said, they had a good thing going.

"I know how to care for my own heart, Simon, and I know what to do with someone else's." She poked him in the arm. "Including those stubborn friends who don't tell me their powers are returning."

He sighed and slumped, feeling tired all of a sudden. He reached for his powers and let their sluggish flow fill him, cleansing her fatigue as well.

She stretched again. "I can't say I'm sorry for that. How long have you known?"

"I wouldn't let myself suspect, or I never would have suggested we go to Celeste. I didn't put two and two together until yesterday."

She nodded. "And then it was too late."

"It was foolish. I'm sorry."

"Too late for regrets." She gave him a one-armed hug. "Use your powers to help my paramour, and let's get going."

Simon did as she said, and Mamet stared at Samira with wide eyes again. "Truly," she said, "you are more powerful than the sun and moon combined. And you're twice as lovely."

Samira chuckled. "Thank you, but that wasn't me."

She looked to Simon. "Both of you?"

"We don't use our abilities to capture people and make them do our bidding, though," Simon said.

Mamet nodded. "My clan will be anxious to meet you."

Not too anxious, Simon hoped, though he had no doubt that if it came to an escape, he and Samira could get away from a group of people who had no abilities to speak of, especially since they'd already succeeded in getting away from two of the most powerful people on Calamity. How much trouble could a group of nomads get them into?

The next morning, they reached a camp made up of hide tents, ossor pens, and a few of the large geavers. Simon and Samira waited while Mamet entered the camp first, and as she did, a man and woman drew her into a frantic embrace. Parents probably. It made Simon sigh to see it. He didn't often think of his family, but even at their happiest or saddest, they'd never thrown their arms around one another.

Mamet led the couple closer. "Maman, Fatan, these are Samira and Simon. They helped me escape."

The couple put their hands over their hearts and bowed. Mamet had a mix of their features and shared both dark hair and eyes. And they were probably the reason she couldn't hide her emotions. They hugged everyone as they led the way into the camp, and Simon fought down the urge to shrug them off and run for it.

"You'll be welcome here until the sun no longer rises," Mamet's mother said.

"And what of the others?" her father asked. "Are they alive?"

"Some," Mamet said softly. "The others are still prisoners. We had to run when Simon and Samira attacked the Sun-Moon gods."

People were already gathering, and at these words, murmurs started in earnest.

"You have to meet Chafa Yuve," Mamet said. "He'll want to hear the story."

They were led to a tent, a respite from the sun and crowd. Simon used his power to try to calm himself, but the feelings of everyone around him beat at his shields.

Samira sat between him and the door as if shielding him with her body. "Say the word," she whispered, "and we're out of here."

He nodded and squeezed her hand. When Mamet's parents served tea, Simon sipped the bitter liquid and tried not to grimace, using his power to numb his tongue. How quickly he fell back into old patterns. He'd thought his nerves had gotten better since he'd left Gale. He'd been in crowded villages and among strangers, and at first his anxiety troubled him, but as he and Samira traveled farther east, it seemed to fade.

Maybe the anxiety came with the power. He'd always been anxious, so he'd never thought the two related until now. He'd been pressured to excel when young, pushed into a degree in biology when all he wanted was botany, and he'd nearly driven himself crazy trying to study both at once, but he'd managed it. Going to a far-flung colony in space had drawn him as the perfect escape, but then he'd spent over two centuries on the *Atlas*, and seeing to the needs of Dillon and other egomaniacs hadn't helped him.

He tried to shake the memories off. His anxiety was back because it was a stressful time; that was all. He'd nearly been kidnapped. Again. He had to warn Horace of danger, and that wasn't going to be a pleasant conversation, *and* he was wandering closer to Dillon's territory. Anyone would have been nervous.

Samira was chatting to Mamet's parents while Mamet stared worshipfully. When Samira glanced at her tea, Mamet's mother nudged the father and then nodded at Mamet and Samira with a knowing smile. The father raised his hands slightly and shook his head, but he wore a little smile, too. Wonderful. Mamet's parents thought she'd made a match. The last thing Simon needed was the smitten plains dweller following Samira and him around like a lost puppy.

A young woman poked her head into the tent flap. "The chafa is coming," she said before ducking out.

Mamet and her parents stood. "Chafa Yuve has been looking for all of you," Mamet's mother said. "We'll greet him with the others." She waved at Simon and Samira to stay put. "A proper introduction is always made indoors." With another smile, Mamet and her family left.

Samira picked up her teacup. "Sounds important."

"How can you drink that stuff?"

"It's an acquired taste."

"I bet people would say the same if they had to drink their own urine." He drummed his fingers on his knees. "Did you see the look between Mom and Dad?"

"Yep."

"Thoughts?"

She shrugged. "She's cute enough." He gave her a dark look, and she chuckled. "I told you. The best you can do about a crush is wait. We'll be gone soon."

"And if she's so struck that she follows us?"

"You think her parents will follow, too, and guilt me into marrying her? Or do you think she'll carry me off in the night like in those old raiding tales?"

He snorted. "Only if she wants to find herself knocked across the plains."

"Exactly. Think about when you were nineteen. The more people told you not to do something, the more you wanted it, right?"

Wrong. He remembered caving to anyone with a will stronger than his, which seemed to be everyone at the time. "Maybe you *should* break her heart, tell her she's not good enough for you."

She gave him a long look.

He smiled. "But you'd never do that to anyone, even to save them."

"If anyone ever needs me to hurt them like that in order to save them, we're in too much trouble already."

He began a retort, but Mamet's parents stepped back in. "Chafa Yuve of the Engali," Mamet's father said. He held the tent flap open, and a short man entered. With such an impressive title, Simon expected tall and forbidding, but Yuve walked with a bowlegged shuffle that spoke of many years atop an ossor. A quick scan placed him near sixty, but Simon could have read that in his face, as brown and lined as a well-weathered boot. He had a permanent squint, and the hair poking out from beneath his broad brimmed leather hat was as white as his beard. His dark eyes glittered with intelligence as he studied everyone.

"These are Simon and Samira," Mamet's mother said, gesturing to them in turn.

He put a hand to his chest. "Thank you for aiding one of my clan."

"Mamet aided us, too," Simon said. If they weren't being touted as the only heroes, maybe Yuve would sooner see them go. The last thing he wanted was to be pulled further into a conflict between the plains dwellers and the Sun-Moon worshipers.

Mamet beamed, and Yuve nodded to her. "A pity you couldn't save everyone."

"They're alive," Mamet said. "Waiting."

Yuve sat, and the rest of them followed. Mamet passed around more of the cursed tea. Simon pretended to sip his, waiting for the first chance to get away. Yuve rubbed his own back, but Simon resisted the urge to ease his hurts, not knowing how he might react.

"We've lived in peace with the Sun-Moon people for many years," Yuve said, "but when their gods came, a sort of bloodthirst began among them. But I've learned they might not have been the aggressors. The Svenal, who live far to the south, have been attacking Sun-Moon villages." He shrugged. "Who knows who struck first?"

"Raiding again instead of trading?" Samira asked.

He swirled the tea in his cup. "Rumor says they steal children."

Everyone glanced at one another, frowning.

"When we searched for you," Yuve said, "we met survivors from such an attack. Any adults who weren't hunting were killed, the children taken."

"Why?" Mamet's mother asked.

Yuve shrugged and shook his head.

Simon thought back to everything the Sun-Moon had said, but they hadn't mentioned any preemptive attack or stolen children. They'd spoken as if eradicating non-believers was their plan in the first place. But why would anyone take children? No one that he'd met practiced slavery or the like. Maybe they were trying to wipe out the other denizens of Calamity but drew the line at killing children? A genocide wasn't complete until all your enemy's genes were dead.

"Whatever their reasons, the Sun-Moon won't stop," he said, feeling he should at least warn these people about what might be coming. "And once they've taken care of everyone close, they might reach out this far."

"But you bested them once," Mamet said.

"We were lucky," Samira added before Simon could say he wasn't anyone's bodyguard.

"Perhaps if the Svenal are quieted," Mamet said, "the Sun-Moon won't be so anxious to attack everyone else. There can be peace!"

"Not until you find out why the Svenal want kids," Simon muttered.

"And how will you find out, friend Simon?" Yuve asked.

He was staring, and so were Mamet's parents. Simon nearly cursed. "I didn't…" He trailed away, trying to think of a way out, but it seemed the perfect excuse to leave quickly, before the Engali expected him to solve all their problems, and if he stumbled on the reason for the Svenal's abductions, he could always send word back. "I won't know until I ask!"

They glanced at one another again, and Samira patted Simon's knee. "Maybe they'll tell us if they think we can help them," she said. "If word spreads about how we got away from the Sun-Moon, we might be able to convince the Svenal that we're on their side."

Yuve leaned back, scratching his beard. "My new friends seem very helpful."

"We're not being altruistic," Simon said quickly. "We're travelers, Samira and I, and we can't go where we want as long as the fighting continues. And if we solve this problem, maybe even the Sun-Moon will see we're more valuable free than in captivity."

Yuve nodded as if that made sense.

"I'll go too," Mamet said in the sudden silence. When everyone looked to her, she held her chin up. "When we find something out, I'll ride back to tell everyone."

"I don't think—" Simon began just as Samira started to say, "It might not be safe."

Yuve held up a hand. "Then it's settled." He stood, and everyone followed suit. "We'll ready mounts and supplies for the morning." He paused before stepping outside. "If the Sun-Moon are looking for you, it's better for us if you're not here anyway." He grinned. "Don't worry. We'll claim we never met you."

When he left, Simon resisted the urge to curse again. Mamet was still there, beaming at them, and now Simon had to find a way to get rid of her before he got to Horace. Their lives were complicated enough already.

❖

The night before their journey began, Samira watched with amusement as Simon tried every tactic to rid them of Mamet. Several times he mentioned that the Svenal might be more receptive to outsiders without another plains dweller present. Whether he believed that or not, Samira didn't know. One by one, he tried many different arguments, showing every emotion from fearful to frosty, but Mamet brushed it all off with a sea of unrelenting optimism.

She also never seemed to tire of casting amorous glances Samira's way. Samira still believed most crushes would go away on their own, but when her second day of ignoring Mamet's bursts of poetry and random compliments were met with the same affection, she started to rethink. She didn't want to hurt Mamet—she still didn't see the need—so she tried to think of some way to help Mamet instead, to maybe transfer the affection to someone else, but when they camped that first night, and Samira stared up at a sky bright with stars, she started to wonder why she was trying so hard.

Was it fear? As much as Simon liked to go on about Mamet's age, she wasn't that much younger than Samira, though they'd led far different lives. Among her people, Mamet had been an adult for a long time. She would have been newer to adulthood in Gale, though at nineteen, Samira had nearly been a full-fledged yafanai, as deep in her training as any soldier or journeyman.

She glanced at Mamet where she reclined on the other side of the fire. Mamet looked away quickly, but when Samira stared, Mamet turned back and smiled. She was cute with her soulful brown eyes and her dark hair just long enough to get caught in her lashes. Samira liked the traits they shared: optimism, faith in others. But something about her, some innocence, kept Samira at bay. Mamet acted as if she'd never been hurt, at least not emotionally, and Samira didn't want to be the first one to hurt her, and lovers had to do so occasionally. It just happened.

She thought maybe she should wait some more, but when they were mounting their ossors the next day and Mamet was still giving Samira longing glances, Samira pulled Mamet aside, signaling to Simon that she wanted to have a word alone. He sighed, a look of relief, and she knew he thought she'd tell Mamet to go home.

"You know what we're doing is dangerous," Samira said. "Even though we're trying to figure out why the Svenal are doing what they're doing, this could get...messy."

Her chin went up. "I'm not afraid."

"No," Samira said, ducking her head to hide a little smile. "I know you're not, but with our powers..." She took a deep breath. "Simon and I can make sure no one gets hurt unless it's necessary."

Mamet frowned. "Are you worried for me or them? I won't attack unless I have to, I promise."

"And I'll hold you to that if you still insist on coming with us."

"I won't let you down. You'll see!"

Samira narrowed her eyes and knew what was putting her off. Mamet was so eager, and she seemed to think that if she behaved the right way, she'd be rewarded. "Even if you impress me, even if you save my life or Simon's, I don't owe you anything romantically. You know that, right?"

Mamet's mouth dropped open, and she seemed genuinely horrified. "Of course! If you would ever...if we could ever..." She went pink and took a deep breath. "I...admire you, Samira. So much." Her eyes filled with hero worship. "If we could ever be anything together, even close friends, it would mean nothing if one of us felt...obligated." She looked away and shivered, her mouth turned down in distaste.

Samira smiled, and her estimation went up a few notches.

Another day of riding passed, followed by a night of camping as they angled southwest, and Samira told Simon she didn't think they should drive Mamet off just yet. Simon sighed. "I guess we really are going to the Svenal then. I was hoping to veer off and look for Horace."

She nodded. "But while we're out here, we may as well see."

"With our little helper along, it seems like the only way." He gave her a look, but she shook her head.

"I can't just make her leave, Simon."

"Can't or don't want to?"

She put her hands on her hips and stared.

He hung his head. "I know I'm being a pain. I'm sorry. I didn't want to get pulled into this plains dweller thing. I just wanted to warn Horace."

"And we will. But I know you're intrigued by this Svenal thing. Let's take a look, find out what we can, and we'll be on our way again."

He nodded, and Samira bet he was at least a little happy for a delay. Then he had more time to think of what he'd finally say to Horace when they met again.

They approached the Svenal camp in the afternoon, a loose collection of leather tents, much closer together than those of the Engali, and the site looked unkempt, broken baskets and torn clothing strewn through the grass. Tent flaps waved untied in the breeze. One tent, larger than the others, dominated the center, and the only murmur of voices came from there.

Someone wandered out of the central tent and caught sight of them. He wore no shirt, and his ribs showed through his skin. Before they could call out, he darted back into the tent, and others poured out, weapons ready. They snarled, their eyes haunted.

Mamet drew her bone sword, but Samira grabbed her arm. "Wait, let Simon try first."

Simon slid off his ossor. Samira felt a prickle along her scalp as his power engulfed everyone, radiating calm. Her tense muscles relaxed, and she fought to keep her eyes from going half lidded. The Svenal staggered to a stop, staring in wonder before looking to one another. They walked forward again but seemed more curious than angry. Their clothing was dirty and their hair disheveled as if they had too much to do to worry about their appearance. No one appeared to have eaten well recently, and Samira didn't need to come closer to know how badly they smelled, like a group of sick people.

"We're not going to hurt you," Simon said in the plains language. "We're healers. We've come to help."

Now the light in their eyes changed from wonder to hunger. They stumbled forward again, and Samira readied her power just in case, but Simon's abilities had recovered more than she'd thought. Another wave came off him, and the Svenal slowed, stumbling. Samira was glad she was sitting down.

"A healer?" the lead man said. His blue eyes were bloodshot above his blond beard. He licked his lips, twitched as if barely in control of himself. "I am Chafa Onin, and if you are truly healers, please, please help us."

CHAPTER FIVE

Natalya stared while Kora sat cross-legged under the smoke hole in the small tent. What was left of the girl, the real girl, only came out when Naos didn't have hold of her, and that was rare indeed. Natalya cocked her head. She thought she'd be happy now that Naos wasn't trying to possess her anymore, but Kora's transformation still unnerved her, and against her better judgement she felt sorry for the person Kora might have been. But what was happening now *might* have been better than whatever her kidnappers had planned. And she seemed to have gotten over her grief for the loss of her people, her family. Now she had new memories of growing up with Naos and Natalya, and Natalya wondered if she remembered her old life at all.

Kora sighed as if reading Natalya's mind, and Natalya supposed she might be, that or Naos was. When one of them was paying attention to her surroundings, there was a clear difference between girl and goddess, so when Kora opened her eyes and smiled slowly and cruelly, Natalya had no doubt who was looking out.

"Talking with one of your old friends?" Natalya asked, knowing Naos often explored Calamity with her roving telepathy.

"Just keeping an eye on them."

"Are you going to let the girl out today?"

Naos gave her a cold look. "She's perfectly happy, you know. She likes it when we're together, unlike some people." When Natalya looked away, Naos sighed. "If you won't either fight with me or fall to your knees and worship me, I'm going to get bored with you."

Natalya swallowed hard. "I think you should give her some time to herself."

"Oh for fuck's sake, fine. I don't want to talk to you anyway." Kora's eyelids fluttered, and she fell back as Naos's presence withdrew.

Natalya grabbed her shoulders and hauled her upright again. "You all right?"

"Every time she leaves, it's so cold."

"Here, put a blanket around your shoulders."

"We were in the park watching the space elevator haul people up to the ships." Her brow wrinkled, her gaze far away. "I said I wanted to be a pilot, and my father smiled, but my brother laughed at me."

"Those are her memories, not yours. We don't have anything like that here." She frowned. "So, she stashes you in her own mind when she uses your body?" It had to feel like being trapped in the suffocating swamp.

"If those are her memories, what happened to mine?"

Natalya shrugged. "We found you on the plains. That's all I know."

Kora stared into the middle distance again. "My mother had a necklace made of bones."

"Hmm." That sounded like something Naos would say, but Natalya couldn't be sure. "Maybe you should sleep. Or are you hungry?" She could never tell what people needed. Maybe she should have never left Gale, should have gone happily mad instead. Maybe Horace would have found a way to fix her as he'd promised. Maybe he was back in Gale right now with a way to solve all her problems. If she ever saw him again, she probably owed him an apology for the way they'd left things, but he'd understand. He always did.

"I feel as if I've been asleep for years." Kora stood and wrapped the blanket tighter around the leather shirt and trousers the plains dwellers had given her. She slipped on soft shoes and stepped outside.

Natalya looked out behind her. A group of young people were practicing fighting some ways off, hitting one another with long bone staves that clattered in the stillness of the plains. As strangers, she and Kora had been given a tent far from the others, but when the youngsters saw Kora and Natalya watching, they moved a little closer, sneaking glances.

Natalya was tempted to tell them to go away. She'd claimed Kora as her daughter since that made things easier and said she'd rescued the children after the rest of the Miri had been slaughtered. Natalya supposed the children might still have relatives elsewhere, but she didn't mention that, and with Naos's help, the children thought of themselves as orphans, too.

"They're using bones," Kora said. "Bones instead of wood."

As if the child had ever seen a wooden staff. Trees were too scarce on the plains. She had to be drawing on Naos's memories again. "Do you remember the geavers? Large animals, long necks? Your people use them as pack animals. You make weapons from their bones, clothing from their hide, and use their dung for fires."

"I wonder if they'll let me try."

Natalya climbed out of the tent. "I'm not sure that's a good idea."

Kora flashed a smile of such confidence, it had to be a bit Naos.

Natalya let her power linger over Kora as she walked to join the youngsters. They clustered around her, curious, and when she asked to try the fighting, Natalya read every reaction from pride to anger and curiosity to nervousness. Young people were always balls of hormones.

From the way some of them nudged one another, Natalya thought they were laughing at the clumsy way Kora held the bone staff. Some felt pity while others seemed as if they would take enjoyment in thrashing someone new.

Natalya moved closer. Kora still had pieces of Naos inside her even if she wasn't being possessed. With all the work Naos had done on her, the two were linked, probably permanently, and as such Kora could use Naos's power. When Kora looked to her, Natalya nodded toward one boy who seemed particularly anxious to knock the new girl down.

Kora nodded and asked the boy to practice. With a smile more like a leer, he agreed. "Be with me?" Kora asked in Natalya's mind.

Before Natalya could respond, Kora pulled her along as Naos would, though with a far gentler hand, a link that could be broken if Natalya fought, but she went along, curious. She shut her own eyes and looked out from Kora's. The boy took a ready, practiced stance, and Kora let her prophetic powers play out.

Natalya gasped. Naos had never shown her this. She saw the field from above. The boy swung at Kora's shoulder, and Kora read in his mind that he thought it'd be an easy hit.

Kora's focus snapped to the present, and she avoided the boy's strike. His anger spiked, and Natalya laughed. Kora kept traveling milliseconds into the future and then snapping back to the present, reading the boy's mind and moving to avoid him. When she foresaw a move that would leave him vulnerable, she whapped him hard with the staff, getting in three hits before he could back away.

Kora released Natalya to her own body, and she clapped.

The boy glared. "You said you didn't know how!"

"I'm a fast learner," Kora said.

"That's a load of geaver shit. You cheated!"

"Watch your mouth," Natalya said.

They glanced at her, Kora with a smile. "I love that you want to protect me," Kora thought.

Natalya smiled back, though she didn't know why.

"It wasn't cheating," Kora said. "The goddess told me what you were going to do. For the faithful, the goddess has many gifts."

"You're not talking about the One-Eye?" one of the youngsters asked. "That's a story for oldsters."

Kora held the staff out and let go. The long length of bone hovered in the air until she grasped it again. "When the goddess chooses you, she's realer than anything."

They gawked, and one of the girls stepped forward. "My mother said one of the old women used to worship the One-Eye."

Kora's opponent shook his head. "She died a long time ago." He had one foot back but leaned forward at the same time as if torn between standing his ground and running away. "Why haven't we heard from anyone else if this goddess is so real?"

"Because the time wasn't right before," Kora said. "And if you're speaking of Clauda, she is with the goddess still, only in a different form."

The youngsters looked to one another. "How did you know her name?" one asked.

Kora waved a hand. "The goddess knows all."

Natalya resisted the urge to scoff. When a person could read minds, it was easy to know everything. People hid things in their minds that they weren't even aware of. And who was this old woman Naos had contacted before? Had she tried this whole scheme in the past?

"She wants you to join her and gain power as I did," Kora said.

"Why does she want us?" one asked.

"Because you're worthy."

They seemed to like the sound of that, particularly the bully. Kora held up her staff. "Who's ready to learn?"

All through the day, the members of the Nevan clan clustered around Kora, watching her fight or listening to stories of Naos's glory. Natalya watched from the edge of the crowd, wondering what Naos was up to now. She had no doubt this was part of some plan. The Nevan seemed to grow more enamored of Kora as the day grew on, and maybe that was mind-tampering, maybe not.

Only one person seemed to regret the decision to let her stay. Chafa Lanet, leader of the clan, watched Kora with a frown that occasionally deepened into a look of such disgust, it made Natalya nervous. If he snuck up on Kora when she wasn't paying attention, he might be able to wound or kill her. She wasn't safe up in space, unlike the goddess. When Lanet spat out the blade of grass he'd been chewing and took a step in Kora's direction, Natalya moved to intercept him. He turned a suspicious look on her, and she tucked a loose strand of hair behind her ear with a nonchalance born of confidence in her own abilities.

"Something wrong?" she asked.

He gestured at where Kora stood surrounded by admirers. "Soon she'll have everyone changing their name from the Nevan to the One-Eyes. We don't want any of your tricks."

"It's power, not trickery."

He jabbed a finger at her. "Control your daughter, or I'll see you both ridden down."

"Challenge her if you like, or challenge me. See where it gets you."

He sneered. "If a little blood will get you gone, so be it."

Natalya gathered her power, but Kora said, "Wait," in her mind.

"Chafa Lanet," Kora called aloud. "Is there something you'd like to say to me?"

He marched toward her, drawing his knife. "I'll prove your powers a trick, and then your false goddess—"

Kora's power flexed, and Lanet's head popped free of his neck, leaving an oozing stump. The body toppled, though the head stayed aloft for several seconds. People screamed or shouted, their eyes wide. Lanet's head dropped as Kora released it.

"Like a champagne cork," Kora said as she marched over.

"A what?" Natalya asked, not believing her own eyes. She knew what Naos could do, but she didn't expect Kora to...

Unless. She glanced up, but it was still Kora's face, not Naos's. Power flowed from Kora again, and the panic of the Nevan faded as she comforted them.

"He's dead," Kora said wonderingly. "I never thought it would be so easy." She nudged Lanet's body with her foot. "And dead is forever, right?" With another swallow, Natalya nodded. Kora cocked her head. "Why do you look so sad? Is everyone sad?" Kora turned to the plains dwellers. Slowly, they all bowed their heads, and when Kora looked back, her face was all Naos. "I guess the rest want to keep their heads."

"Did you do that?" Natalya whispered. "Did you make her do that?"

Naos frowned. "Some people do things because they like me, you know." She jerked a thumb over her shoulder. "And now I have a lot more. If it makes you feel better, Kora wanted to be friends with the chafa, but she didn't like that he threatened you and me." She sighed dramatically. "I guess what they say is true, jealousy makes a person lose their head." She brayed a laugh.

Natalya looked to the bowing plains dwellers. "So now you're gathering worshipers? Or are you building an army?"

Naos gave her a dazzling smile. "You never know what you might need. I'd forgotten how intoxicating worshipers could be, and I can't help thinking what it would be like to be the only one that has them."

That night, Natalya sat alone in the tent, looking out the open door, waiting for Kora. When she came in, bright and bubbly, Natalya turned away. She kept seeing the headless chafa, and she couldn't make that image match with this effervescent child.

"What's wrong?" Kora asked.

"Nothing."

"That's a fib, and fibbing's not right."

Natalya sighed. "And who taught you that?"

"Everyone knows that." She flopped down in front of Natalya, squeezing against the side of the tent so she could see Natalya's face. "You don't like what happened to the chafa. He shouldn't have said he'd hurt you."

"I could have stopped him, Kora. You don't need to take care of me."

Her head cocked. "But you think you need to take care of me, and I'm more powerful than you are."

True, and that still didn't make everything that had happened to her right or justified. "You shouldn't have to worry about even thinking about killing people. You should only be worried about toys or other kids pulling your hair. Parents that won't give you sweets, that sort of thing."

She frowned at the tent floor. "I don't like that killing is forever. I can't feel the chafa's mind anymore. It's as if there's a hole."

Natalya grabbed her hands, feeling as if she had to say something, try something. "Don't kill anyone again! Make her do it if it's got to be done."

"Make her?"

Like making a mountain do anything. "Ask her, then! She...she enjoys it!" Maybe not the best advice, but it would help keep a few stains off Kora's soul.

"Would that make you happy?"

That hurt her, though she couldn't quite say why. "Yes."

The bright smile came back. "Okay! If the goddess wants holes, she'll make them."

And if she put it like that, maybe Naos would be amused enough to not resent it. Natalya could only hope. And a promise not to slaughter people wasn't much, but it felt like a step in the right direction.

CHAPTER SIX

The sun was warm on Cordelia's shoulders as she rolled rocks into what would be the newest of Pool's little ponds. The giant Anushi tree had dug out various swimming and watering holes—the drushka dried out without large amounts of water—and the tree could have moved these rocks, too, but Cordelia liked the activity. Good for the muscles and good for the heart. She sometimes feared she'd get soft sitting out in the plains with little to do. Wuran's fighting parties were too few and far between.

Sitting under the shade of a lean-to, Liam didn't seem to have the same concerns. He watched her work with a little smile on his face as if he knew she was doing it partly because she couldn't stand sitting still.

"You could help," she said.

"Why rob you of your fun?" He stretched and leaned back, resting his head on a bedroll. Pool created little cubbies in her bark for her people to sleep in, and many humans stayed with them, but others preferred some time on the ground. "If you said we're finally going to pay back the Storm Lord, I'd be up before anyone else."

She sighed. His stumping for revenge had been louder ever since Pool's scouts had spotted a Galean spy watching them from afar the day before. But the Storm Lord still had weapons and forces, powered armor, and a fight with him would have meant a fight with other Galeans, something she'd never done. And she didn't want to drag the drushka into it, either. She didn't know how many of them would volunteer, but Nettle and Reach would certainly go, and they were too important to her. "I'm not having this argument with you again unless you pick up a shovel."

He rolled out from under the shade and marched toward her, grabbing a wooden shovel and levering rocks at her side. "Let's dance."

She coughed a laugh. "I didn't think you'd do it. I'm unprepared."

"Why'd we stop so close to Gale if you didn't want to march on him one day? And if he's watching us, he's planning something."

"You do realize the Storm Lord isn't sitting there alone. You'd have to fight the believers to get to him. Brown. Lea."

He shook his head. "After we tell them—"

"We told them already, Liam. If they didn't believe us before, they're not going to change their minds now. They'll figure him out in time."

"So, you're saying they need rescuing?"

"At the end of a truncheon? Or did you forget that those are the only weapons we have?"

He pointed at her. "Ah ha! We also have slings. And the drushka have weapons."

"So now we've got the drushka attacking Gale. Even if people don't side with the Storm Lord, they'll side with their own kind against a bunch of aliens."

He threw down his shovel and walked in a wide circle, putting his arms up, palms resting on top of his head. "He is planning something! How can you sit still knowing that?"

"You're not sitting still. You're helping me." She kicked the shovel in his direction.

With a grumble, he picked it up.

"If he is planning something, he'll have to come out here. Then we can punch it out, and civilians won't get hurt."

"Brown and Lea will still be with him."

"If we take him out, they might fall in line."

"And the rest of the true believers?"

She shrugged. "I guess we'll figure it out when it happens."

"When we're old and gray, maybe."

"Speaking of," she said loudly, "did you know that Nettle is seventy and Shiv is fourteen?"

She expected him to gawk, but he only stared before nodding. "So?"

It was her turn to drop the shovel. "You knew?"

"That they mature faster and live longer? You didn't?"

"Are you in the habit of fucking teenagers or the elderly?"

"Teenagers? Not since I was one. The elderly?" He looked to the sky as if remembering. "Well…"

She kicked a small rock at him, and he dodged, laughing.

"They're aliens, Delia. What did you expect?"

"Not…" She didn't know what to say.

"Let's put it this way: does knowing stop you from daydreaming about your lover's thighs, a characteristic you've spoken often about?"

She sighed and thought about Nettle, all long and lean and muscular. "No."

"Why just daydream?" a voice behind them said.

Cordelia turned slowly. Nettle sat on the edge of the pond, no telling how long she'd been there. Liam certainly hadn't given her away.

"Hello," Cordelia said and heard the way her voice changed, the soft, deep quality reserved for Nettle.

"That's my cue," Liam said. "I'll leave the shovel over here, not like you're going to care."

Cordelia ignored him and went to lean her head against Nettle's knees. "I'm sorry it's still bugging me."

"My thighs? Or are you speaking of my age again, Sa?"

"All my worries disappear when you're with me, if that makes it any better."

Nettle reached down, helping her clamber out of the pond. When Cordelia sat on the edge, Nettle swung on top of her, knees resting on either side of Cordelia's legs. She took Cordelia's hands and placed them on her outer thighs, giving them a squeeze. "You make my mind easier, too." She bent forward, and Cordelia thought their lips would meet, but Nettle leaned around her face and tongued her earlobe.

Cordelia gasped and let her hands wander higher, but the tip of a brown root broke the ground nearby, and she sighed, knowing what that meant. Pool had something to say.

The root coiled around Nettle's wrist, and her gaze went elsewhere as they spoke mind to mind. Cordelia waited for Nettle to tell her what Pool said, but a shockwave traveled up her legs from where she and Nettle still touched.

She felt Pool's amusement but also a slight current of reprimand as Pool conjured the image of Wuran. He was coming to meet with them any moment, coming to trade leather for the wood that Pool shed as easily as cast-off hair. Pain slid through Cordelia's temples, and she felt the shock of Pool and Nettle before Pool's root withdrew.

Cordelia would have slumped back, but Nettle caught her shoulders. "Sa?"

"I'm…all right."

Nettle stood with sibilant grace and pulled Cordelia up. "You heard the queen?"

"Heard, saw, something like that." She rubbed her aching temples. "Sometimes I get these…visions or feelings, as if I can see a light when I look at Pool's tree or Shiv's, but nothing like that has ever happened before."

Nettle looked to the root. "The queen is coming."

"I know." Cordelia could feel her moving closer.

"She will know what to do." She smiled a little. "If you can speak as drushka can, perhaps it is a boon."

"Hurts like hell." She rubbed her head again.

More roots broke the ground, bringing Pool. They could move her underground for quite a distance, as long as her roots could reach. There hadn't been that much solid earth in the swamps for her to stretch, but on the plains, she'd popped up quite a few places when her human associates weren't expecting her.

"Sa." Pool bent and peered into Cordelia's face, her green eyes wide. She was taller than Cordelia or any of the drushka, and she'd once told Cordelia that any drushka who could live as long as a queen would continue to grow. Her green hair, the color of queens, curled over her shoulders, longer than any of her tribe. "You do not look any different, but the feel of you…" She sucked her teeth. "I have noticed the change."

"How do I stop it?"

She cocked her head. "Why should you wish to?"

Because it was alien and different! But she couldn't say that. It was just like the age thing. Or was it? As a child, she'd passed all the aptitude tests that would have let her become a yafanai. She'd chosen to be a paladin instead. Maybe this was like that, and being electrocuted and healed had awoken some yafanai part of her brain. It didn't mean she had to be a yafanai or a drushka or anyone but herself.

"I don't know," she said.

Pool chuckled softly. "Never doubt that you are human, Sa. Only one of your kind would be so bothered by something which could benefit you greatly. Perhaps something new yet familiar will be a comfort." She held out her hands, and one of her roots laid a wooden sword across her palms.

Cordelia took a step forward. It was an almost perfect replica of the paladin blade she'd once wielded, except for the color, a deep brown that was almost black, and the twining ivy motif on the hilt and grip. "It's beautiful."

Nettle took her arm, giving it a squeeze while Pool wrinkled her nose. "I knew you would appreciate it. It will keep itself sharp."

Cordelia tore her gaze off the weapon. "Are you saying…"

"Call to it. We shall see how far your connection to us has grown."

Cordelia licked her lips. Pool hadn't just made her an ordinary blade. She'd created a living weapon, the kind she made for her own people, which kept itself sharp and would obey the mind of the user, but that mind had to be able to connect to the queen.

Her hand shook as she took the blade. A weapon no one could take from her? It was still weird, but it was weird and *good*.

She focused on the feelings she'd been denying, the connection she'd felt. The whisper of the wind faded to a dull hum, and she saw the sword as a shard of light in her grasp. She didn't know what to say or how to call it. She would have felt like a fool speaking aloud, so she pictured what she'd seen drushkan weapons do: sprout little wooden tendrils that held them to the wielders' hands.

Little limbs snaked from the sword's grip and twined around her fist. She sucked in a breath, losing control and turning the sword back into a sword, but the tendrils stayed put.

"You will have to practice," Pool said. "It will come easier."

"You're seriously giving this to me? I don't know what to say."

Pool chuckled. "As long as you can see the good in it at last." To Cordelia's surprise, she leaned forward and touched her lips to Cordelia's forehead as she would one of her drushka. Cordelia resisted the urge to lean away, wishing they could have hugged like humans instead.

Horace waited for Wuran with Cordelia and the others on a slight rise near Pool's great tree. She still seemed hesitant to bring the tree close to any other humans, and Horace didn't blame her. Trust shouldn't always come easy.

As whenever he thought about trust, his thoughts wandered to Simon Lazlo, though they didn't go there as often as they did eight months ago. When Simon had first burned out Horace's psychokinesis, it was all he could think about. He still had his telepathy, but he'd spent long hours searching inside himself for something that wasn't there anymore. When Simon had first augmented his power, Horace had thought it a curse. He'd had a hard time keeping everyone out, more trouble than he'd ever had before, but Simon had apologized over and over and then he'd helped Horace control it. It had seemed like a gift again, especially as he realized just how many people he could help, how many he could heal. He'd brought people back from the brink of death. Without that ability, what was he?

Now, with telepathy, he'd helped his new drushkan and human family by aiding the occasional insomniac or person plagued with doubt or drowning in their own troubles, but when someone had cut herself badly, he'd searched hard inside himself before it even occurred to him to look for a bandage. One of the drushkan healers, a shawness, had taken over, wrapping the wound and crooning a healing song. Horace had found a quiet place to cry.

Now he tried to look forward, missing his gift less and less, or so he told himself. He liked meeting with Wuran and the Uri. They distracted him from fantasizing about what would happen if Simon walked over that hill, across that valley. Would there be hugging or murder? With the help of the drushka, Horace had dived back into his first aid knowledge, but he didn't know if it would be enough to ever forgive Simon or not.

Cordelia wandered over to him, and he smiled. He'd liked her ever since their journey into the swamp. She was muscular and tall, intimidating, but the slight lines at the corners of her brown eyes spoke of frequent smiles, and as she gave one to him now, he was reminded how good of a friend she could be.

She tucked a strand of brown hair behind her ear. It was longer than when he'd known her in Gale, and he wondered if she'd grown it out a little since she wasn't a soldier anymore, or if it was a symptom of something else, some kind of metaphorical letting down of her hair as well as a literal one. Or maybe she just didn't have the time to think about it with all her new people to manage.

"Wuran is nearly two hours late," she said.

"And you hate waiting."

"More than anything," she said with a sigh. "Some of the drushka went looking."

"Why didn't you go?"

"I'm not as fast."

He chuckled and patted her on the back. "I'm sure it won't be long now."

She gave him a sardonic smile. "I'm glad you can be mellow."

He shrugged. In his darker moments, she'd brought him some of the plains dweller scuppi, and there had been a few drunk, long nights with her or Liam or both. He liked getting drunk with her alone, though. Even though Liam had Shiv, he also had a tendency to flirt, and when Horace was drunk, he did more than flirt. His friends in the temple had once declared drunken Horace to be the king of bad decisions. Cordelia had to sit between him and Liam a few times. Horace dreaded to think what Shiv would do, though he wasn't sure how the drushka felt about monogamy. Some seemed to have multiple lovers at once. Best to avoid a reason to have that conversation, though. And he didn't want to play around. He was a one man at a time man.

The drushkan scouts hurried over the next rise, Nettle at their head. Horace squinted, thinking them awfully bunched up until he noticed they carried Wuran between them. Cordelia streaked toward them, and Horace shook his head before jolting into a run. Reach hurried, too, calling for Nettle to put Wuran down.

"What the hell happened?" Cordelia asked.

"Attacked." Wuran's face was a mask of blood, one eye swollen shut. "The Svenal."

Horace felt along his head while Reach searched the rest of his body for injuries. A deep cut curved along his forehead into his hair. Horace reached into his medical bag, a drushkan gift. All shawnessi carried one, they said. He pulled out a roll of soft bandages and wound them around Wuran's forehead.

Cordelia fired off questions, but Wuran could only mumble answers, his non-swollen eyelid fluttering.

"Sa," Reach said, "go easy."

"We need to know!"

Frustrated, Horace pulled at the place where his micro powers used to be. They needed Wuran to tell them what had happened but also if he was hurt anywhere else. Reach was doing her best, but if his back or organs were injured, and it didn't show…

Wuran took a deep breath, and his swollen eye opened slightly as his other opened wide.

"Wuran?" Cordelia asked.

"The Svenal!"

She knelt and took his hand. "What happened to the rest of your people?"

He shook his head, and tears leaked from his eyes, leaving tracks through the blood. "Some went hunting. Others were taken, killed. They wanted the children!"

"Where? How long ago?"

He gripped her hand and tried to sit up. "Help us."

"I will." She stood. "Come on, Horace. Leave him with Reach. His people will need your help."

Horace left Wuran in Reach's hands. Nettle called for reinforcements, and when they came from over the hill, Liam leading them, they all followed the drushkan scouts into the plains. But running had never been Horace's strong suit. The drushka and the ex-soldiers were pulling away, and he cursed. Cordelia was right. Wuran's people would need his help, and he couldn't do that if he was leaning on his knees and wheezing.

When he pulled a burst of speed out of nowhere, he thought he'd gotten a second wind, but Wuran's clearing head came back to him. Maybe he'd given Wuran a telepathic nudge, but he didn't think so. He'd reached for his micro powers both times, and something had answered.

He pulled at his power again. Soggy and weak but *there*, and the realization almost made him stumble. His powers were returning. What could that mean? Were Simon's powers returning, too? Simon had been healing people for so long, he'd no doubt forgotten about the body's miraculous ability to heal itself.

But Simon had burned out their powers for a good reason. Everyone would come running to him for immortality now. And some wouldn't be asking. He looked to those around him, those he trusted. In the end, Simon hadn't trusted anyone, maybe with good reason. Horace let his power die back down and kept his mouth shut.

Cordelia had to admit, it felt good to run into battle again, even while worried about Wuran's people. She pictured the men, women, and children she'd befriended, and her battle rage bubbled to the surface. But this would still be human against human. She told herself to wound if she could, to only kill as a last resort, just as her paladin training had taught her when it came to dealing with other humans.

"How far?" she called.

"Just there," Nettle said, pointing over a rock-strewn hill.

It was late afternoon, and she hoped they could get this settled before dark fell. When she spotted movement among the rocks, she called, "There!" Before she could speed toward it, an invisible force sent her flying.

The drushka and humans scattered. Cordelia rubbed her chest, but nothing had hit her. "Yafanai!" she shouted, hoping to give everyone a heads-up. Maybe it wasn't the Svenal. Maybe the Storm Lord had attacked the Uri for some reason.

Liam slid to a stop at her side. "What the fuck?"

An arrow plonked into the ground nearby. She dove behind a boulder with Horace while Liam took cover by another rock. "Arrows!" Liam shouted.

Everyone went for cover, Nettle ducking at Liam's side. Liam cocked his hand to the left and held up two fingers. She nodded. He'd spotted two people and would go for them. After a word in Nettle's ear, the two of them took off.

"Find that yafanai," she said to Horace. He nodded and closed his eyes. She drew her wooden sword and covered him.

"A macro," he said. "Not a yafanai. Untrained, hardly more than a boy." He slapped the ground. "This would be so much easier if my micro powers were better."

"Better?"

He took a deep breath and started to open his eyes.

She waved at him to concentrate. "Where is he?"

"He's lashing out. I don't think he has much control. There are more people, there and there." He pointed over his shoulders. "He is terrified, Delia."

She pressed her lips together hard. She didn't want to hurt a kid, but if it was him or her people… "Can you attack him power to power?"

"Maybe. He's…" His eyes flew open. "No, he's a telepath, too!" He grabbed her arm, and she felt a tingle pass over her scalp, probably as he tried to raise his shields over them both, but when he sagged like a ragdoll, she knew he hadn't been quick enough.

"Shit." She lowered him to the ground, checked his pulse, and peeked over the rock. The telepath had knocked him out, but if she could get the telepath, he might wake up. She ran around the boulder and took cover on the other side of an occupied one. When a woman with a shortbow stood to take a shot, Cordelia grabbed her and dragged her over. She squealed until Cordelia elbowed her hard in the face, silencing her. Cordelia rolled the woman out of her long vest and put it on, hoping to blend in enough to take more of them out.

She got close to a man before he blinked at her and pulled a long bone knife. She charged, but a sling bullet bounced off his head. From behind him, Liam gave Cordelia a salute. She grinned as she crouched, but his eyes widened, and he flew toward her as if on invisible wings. Cordelia braced herself to catch him, but they slammed together and fell.

Her head connected with a rock, and everything went fuzzy. Her heart pounded in her ears as the world spun in and out of focus. She pushed Liam off, but he was shaking his head, woozy. Someone tiptoed into her periphery, his eyes wide. He seemed barely more than a boy. She tried to get up, to leap at him, but her legs betrayed her, and she slipped into darkness.

CHAPTER SEVEN

S imon sat on a cushion and let his powers drift over the Svenal woman in front of him. The problem was in the uterus, easy to spot, but that was just a symptom. He focused harder, but the ultimate cause for her illness eluded him. He resisted the urge to let go of his trance and tear his hands through his hair. He'd been with the Svenal nearly a week, but it wasn't enough. He needed more of his power back, and he needed more time, something the Svenal didn't seem to understand.

Samira entered the tent behind him and cleared her throat with a deliberate edge.

Simon opened his eyes and sighed. "Thank you, Sheila. That's all for now."

She put a hand on her belly. She was in her first trimester, but if he couldn't figure out what had gone wrong with the Svenal, her pregnancy wouldn't progress past that. "It's all right now?" she asked.

He didn't know if she meant the baby or the pregnancy. Desperate as they were, the Svenal seemed to distance themselves from what might happen to them by referring to all babies as it.

"No," he said, unable to lie to her earnest face. "But I won't give up. Just give me a little time to think."

She gave him a fearful smile. "I'll come back."

After she left, Mamet followed Samira inside and stationed herself by the flap to stop anyone else coming in. Simon looked to Samira, taking in her worried frown. "They've captured more, haven't they? Damn it!"

She nodded. "Another group of children."

"That they might infect! Why don't they listen to me? I need time!"

"They're desperate," Samira said. "This whole circle of life thing, birth and death, it's very important to them." She lifted her hands, dropped them. "I mean, it's important to everyone, but to them, they… worship pregnancy." She bit her lip. "That's not the right word, but—"

"I know what you mean," he said. If any group of people were unable to carry a pregnancy to term, he imagined they'd be frantic, but the Svenal had responded by attacking their neighbors and stealing any children they found, and it seemed they wouldn't be happy until they had them all. All his pleas to stop and retreat from the rest of the plains dwellers and the Sun-Moon worshipers until he could help them fell on deaf ears. Even if Onin agreed, he doubted that would stop the rest of them.

"The new captives aren't all children," Mamet said.

He massaged his temples. "Pregnant women?"

Samira knelt. "Two adults. One of the guards told me one is a woman with a wooden sword, and the other has powers like Pakesh."

He held his breath. They weren't close enough to Gale for that to be a yafanai. It had to be someone among the renegades, and by the looks Samira was giving him, she had to suspect it was Horace, just as he did.

"Heads up," Mamet said.

Onin pushed into the tent. His bloodshot eyes passed over all of them before settling on Simon. "You heard?"

"About those you could infect? Yes."

He shut his eyes. "The rest of my clan wouldn't hear me. You've been here a week. We've seen nothing new."

Simon tried to keep his temper in check. He let his power flow over himself and gave Onin a jot to calm him down.

Onin sighed. "You must find a way to protect the new children."

"If you returned them, I wouldn't have to."

Onin gave him a dark look but instead of responding, left the tent, the flap falling shut behind him.

Simon paced in a tight circle, Samira and Mamet watching him closely. The Svenal seemed to have no confidence in his abilities while at the same time having all the confidence in the world. Maybe they were comfortable believing in the dream of his powers, a fiction they could create around him rather than any actual ability he might have.

And now they'd caught a yafanai or someone yafanai-like, and if it was Horace, Simon had to help him escape.

"Should we flee?" Mamet said. "Take the new children with us?" When they both looked to her, she went a little pink. "I'm not afraid. It's just…well, I believe in you, but they might not." She shrugged. "They don't know of your power, Samira. We could take them by surprise."

They'd only managed to keep some secrets because Simon could shield them from Pakesh. Somehow, Onin had gotten his hands on some of the yafanai-maker drug and had fed it to one of his kinsman without the necessary training, making the sloppiest yafanai Simon had ever seen. Early yafanai had tried the same thing in Gale, and Simon remembered they'd had many of the same problems Pakesh had; those that hadn't died outright. He used his abilities often without warning, reading random thoughts, throwing things around. If he'd been trained, if his brain had undergone the necessary nudges, he could be a genuine threat.

Simon sidled close to the tent flap and peeked out. Onin stood not too far away with one of the tribesman who watched Simon's every move. He couldn't quite hear what they were saying, but he felt Onin's excitement, and as he turned, he caught the words, "Pakesh says he's a healer, too."

Simon's heart thumped loudly. Well, that cemented it. "It's Horace," he said to Samira.

She grabbed his arm. "We have to rescue him." More than altruism shone in her eyes. A hopeless romantic by nature, she wanted everyone to have a happily ever after.

"We have to be smart."

"Who's Horace?" Mamet asked.

"Simon's true love," Samira said before he could stop her. "They had a falling out, but now…"

"Ah," Mamet said, a knowing look in her eye that claimed knowledge beyond her years. "You must rescue him, Simon. It'd go a long way toward pledging your heart."

Simon rolled his eyes. He wanted to see Horace again but from a distance first. He needed time to think of what to say, time to drink in the sight of Horace again, time to line up every apology, and time to see if Horace had another lover. He needed to know if it would be better if he left Horace alone.

But he couldn't do that now. Horace had to have his micro powers back if Pakesh had sensed them. And since the Svenal already knew, Horace would probably try to help them, to maybe bargain for freedom for himself and whoever this woman with the wooden sword was.

Simon rubbed his jaw as he remembered one woman Horace had left Gale with, Cordelia Ross, who had a punch like an iron bar. "Oh, I hope it's not her," he muttered. But no matter who it was and what was happening, one thing was clear: they couldn't let another healer rot here. "Let's make a plan and wait for dark."

It was only a few hours before darkness fell. Simon left the tent with Samira and Mamet, their guard wandering in their footsteps as they approached one of the cooking fires. They angled close to Pakesh's tent, and Simon sensed him inside. He preferred to be alone most of the time. Though the Svenal used him, they weren't exactly friendly toward him. With a little nudge of power, Simon caught Pakesh off guard and put him to sleep. He hadn't managed to cure the Svenal, but his powers grew stronger every day.

Not many Svenal were out; they didn't often hang around each other. Even though the illness had spread to all of them, they seemed to think themselves safer if they stayed separate, though some of those who'd lost children consoled themselves with their captives, something else that gave Simon the shivers.

Samira took a bowl of soup to their guard, and he eyed it warily, but he had to know it wasn't poisoned. They didn't even have anything to poison someone with, but as soon as the guard was distracted, Simon short-circuited him and sent him off to dreamland, too. Samira caught him, and she and Mamet hid him in the dark.

They headed toward the central tent where the captives were usually kept. The inside had been subdivided into what Simon thought of as prison cells, though there were no doors, just leather flaps that created a maze to everyone but the Svenal.

The guards at the entrance waved them past. Any new captives had to be seen by the healer, after all, though the looks they gave him reinforced Samira's earlier thoughts that the Svenal were running out of patience. He turned down one hall, putting out a tendril of power, looking for an answering call. They passed a group of children, but Horace wasn't among them. Simon kept going, but Onin turned the corner, bringing them up short.

"Where are you going?" he asked.

"I'm…here to see the captives."

Onin pointed behind them to where the children sat.

"Um, well." Simon went through a myriad of horrible excuses. "Oh, screw it." He hit Onin with his power and made him collapse. A woman rounded the corner behind them and called out.

"Well, that's done it," Samira said. They broke into a run, and as people came to see what was going on, Samira threw them with her power, sending them careening through leather walls until the tent began to sag overhead.

Simon kept searching as Mamet drew her bone sword, and cries began all around them. Finally, he felt an answering signal and headed for a familiar mind pattern in as straight a line as he could. He broke into a large space to find Horace and Cordelia Ross tied to stakes in the ground. She had a wooden sword that clung to her leg with wooden tendrils, and both were bound hand and foot.

Horace's eyes went wide. "I knew that was you! Your powers are back."

"I've come to rescue you!" He hoped it didn't sound as ridiculous to everyone else as it did to him.

"So get rescuing," Cordelia said.

"Right." He darted for Horace and paused at his leather bonds. "Mamet, lend me your—"

"Look out!" Cordelia shouted.

Simon twisted to the side as one of the Svenal rushed him. Horace's power blew past, squeezing the air from the man's lungs and knocking him unconscious. Simon could only stare for a moment, wondering who had taught him that, but circumstance had probably done it.

"Simon, his knife!" Horace said.

"Right." He sliced through Horace's bonds just as Mamet cut Cordelia's. Samira was holding the door, and when Simon pulled Horace to his feet, Horace grinned before his expression twisted into something more complicated, as if he didn't know what to do or say.

"I wanted to say—" Simon started.

"Save it." Cordelia lifted her own sword then staggered, her eyes going unfocused. Horace reached for her, but she shook him off. "Our ride's here. They must've been tracking us."

A tree root erupted from the ground, and Mamet jumped back with a strangled cry. It arced to Cordelia, and she bit her lip but grabbed it and closed her eyes. Simon felt her nerves jump as something passed between her and the root before she opened her eyes again. "Everybody, brace yourselves."

"What about the Uri children?" Horace asked.

The tent was still sagging. The Svenal were crying out, hurrying toward them. "The Svenal aren't hurting them!" Samira said. "They can wait."

More roots erupted around them, and Simon yelped as one curled around his waist. He shut his mouth as the root pulled him under the soil, and then he was flying through the dirt, the roots undulating around him, digging a hole so they could pass him along, but it was hard to focus on such thoughts, so much easier to scream inside his own mind and listen to the panic of Samira and Mamet and the comforting voice of Horace assuring him that everything was going to be okay.

Cordelia breathed deep as she surfaced. As the others breached, the young plains dweller drew her sword and spun in a rough circle as if fighting off invisible attackers while she coughed and hacked, cursing.

Cordelia got under her swing and plucked the sword from her grasp with a simple twist. "Calm down, kiddo."

The girl rubbed the dirt from her face and coughed some more. "What was… Give me my sword!"

Cordelia nodded over her shoulder where the Anushi tree loomed against the night sky, small fires alight among her branches. One of those lights rushed toward them, and the tree set Pool on the ground, a candle in her grip.

"Pool, queen of the drushka, this is…" She gestured to the plains dweller.

"M…Mamet." She took a breath. "Mamet of the Engali…Madam Tree."

Pool chuckled. "Sa, are you all right?"

"We're all fine." She tossed the sword back, and Mamet fumbled with it but didn't cut her own hand off. After another marvel-filled look, she moved to stand with Simon Lazlo and the friend he'd called Samira.

Drushka hopped down from the tree, and Nettle's long arms slipped around Cordelia, pulling her close.

"I knew you'd find me," Cordelia said.

"The queen did, not I, though I searched. She is far faster."

"I guess talking like a drushka can be useful after all."

Nettle wrinkled her nose and kissed Cordelia's neck. "We must move."

"Come on," Cordelia said as she stepped back. "Everybody into the tree. The Svenal will be after us."

The newcomers balked at first, but their faces relaxed into smiles once they were aboard, and the tree began to move, its long roots propelling it along, digging into the soil as more roots undulated along the ground. Cordelia caressed the sword at her hip. The Svenal had tried to take it from her numerous times, but it wouldn't let go. Even when she'd been unconscious, it had clung to her.

Pool leaned close to Cordelia's ear. "Is that not shawness Simon? The one shawness Horace sometimes speaks of?"

"It is."

"Did Horace not wish to kill him?"

"A few times. I think we've all been there."

When Pool sucked her teeth, Cordelia added, "With humans, saying a thing and doing it are different. We like to tell ourselves we'd be happy or angry if something happened, but we won't know until it does."

"So Horace has forgiven him?"

"Maybe, maybe not. After the shine of seeing him again wears off, I guess we'll have to see." She sighed. "And it seems they've both got their powers back." And that might lead the Storm Lord right into their laps, but at least they'd have powerful people to face him with.

Liam slid down from a higher branch, Shiv beside him. He pulled Cordelia close until she pushed him away with a laugh.

"When I woke up," he said, "And you weren't there..." His face creased in pain, and she knew he was thinking of all the people they'd lost.

She punched his shoulder lightly. "You knew I was kicking ass somewhere else."

He sighed a laugh and hugged her again. Shiv gave her another hug before she moved to Horace and held him close, too. She peered at the newcomers and said, "Are you not shawness Simon, who stole Horace's powers from him and made him cry?" Everyone went silent and watched them. Shiv snarled, her hands curling and uncurling, clawed fingers flexing. "Humans cry when they are very sad, and I do not like to see my friends sad."

"I'm sorry," Simon said. "Really."

"Shiv," Horace started.

She waved at him to be quiet. Her little tree wasn't with her, but it was probably near. "Horace is my friend."

"I'm glad he has such protective friends," Simon said hurriedly. Samira and Mamet made a block behind him.

"Shiv, please," Horace said.

She bristled, but Pool called, "Come away, daughter. Let the humans settle themselves."

Shiv pointed a long finger in Simon's face. "You must make all your apologies, shawness. You must say it so that he believes it." She spread her hands. "Then and only then may you bite each other's ears." Simon gawked at her, but Shiv only leaned close to Horace. "Call upon me, shawness, if you tire of his words, or if they do not please you."

He gave her a kiss on the temple, and she moved to join Cordelia, who kept down the urge to laugh. When the tree stopped for the night, Horace and Simon wandered away by themselves. Samira and Mamet sat alone, too, but by the way curious drushka and humans clustered around them, they wouldn't be alone for long.

Liam leaned close to Cordelia and nodded after Horace and Simon. "Think that's going to get naughty?"

She laughed. "Who knows? Horace could punch him."

Shiv frowned. "Do you think he will call if he cannot punch hard enough?"

Liam hugged her close. "I think you'll be the first one he calls for."

"Shawness Horace is of our tribe," Shiv said, still with the fierce look. "He should cry no longer."

Cordelia thought maybe one more cry was in order, as long as it was the good kind. Horace wasn't one to be cruel or hold a grudge, but there would have to be words between those two, maybe some punching, maybe something naughty, but something that would put an end to the past or at least a beginning to the future.

The stars stretched like a beautiful sparkling canopy overhead, making Simon forget about his troubles, forget about everything but the man beside him. He was happy and nervous and so excited he was almost giddy. He'd pressed down all memory of Horace and the moments they'd shared, their kiss on the roof, their parting caresses in Gale, but now those memories came flooding back. But he also kept remembering Horace's face after Simon had burned out their powers: the hurt, the betrayal.

"I'm sorry," Simon said. "Horace, I'm so sorry. I thought it was the right thing to do. I thought it would keep you safe."

He could barely make out Horace's features, but he didn't need his eyes. With his power, he never did. Horace was also a tangle of emotions, but through the hurt and anger, Simon detected a hint of joy. He tried to turn his power away, to not pry.

"You hurt me, Simon. Not just physically. If you'd given your reasons, I might have agreed—"

"There wasn't time!"

"So, if you could go back, knowing you'd have to face me again one day and you couldn't just run away, would you hurt me again?"

Simon paused, wanting to think, to search for some other way. "I'd have to."

Horace turned away, and Simon curled his hands into fists as he fought not to use his power and see what Horace was feeling. Instead, he sat on a low rock, one of many that glowed white under the starlight.

"If you'll excuse the terrible pun," he said, "living with Dillon was like living with a live wire. Exciting, yes, and as long as there's just a little bit of current, it feels wonderful, invigorating. You don't see the danger. It took me a while on the *Atlas* to realize just how dangerous he is, how little he'll give and how much he'll take. And even after I knew, I couldn't let go because there was nowhere *to* go. It wasn't until I was here that I could finally leave." He felt tears gathering but willed them away. He'd shed enough tears over Dillon to fill a well.

"It doesn't matter who you are," Simon said, "or how good you are at reading people, or how powerful you are. He can trick anyone and bleed them dry."

"You don't think I'm smart enough to have figured that out?" Horace said. "When I found out he was a murderer, I left. I would never have worked for him, never would have given him anything."

"You say that," Simon said, feeling his anger grow, "but you don't know!" He surged to his feet and paced. "It doesn't matter how smart you are because you're not cruel, Horace! No one is as cruel as he is. And if all his pretty words, all his crumbs of friendship weren't enough to sway you, he would find another way! He'd go through your friends, your family. He would twist and warp until he made you think he was all you had!"

And then he was lost in memory again, Dillon being both carrot and stick. He'd never had to threaten Simon, never held friends or family hostage, but he didn't have to. Simon couldn't get away from him, and in the end, he'd let Simon go, but only because the power was gone.

For years, Dillon had called them friends when he didn't even know the meaning of the word.

Someone touched his shoulder, and he whirled around, visions of Dillon still in his head, but it was only Horace, and Simon couldn't help feeling the concern that washed over him.

"Simon, it's all right. You're free. He's gone. It's all right."

Simon breathed deep, and tears filled his eyes again. "I pictured you under his thumb, under all their thumbs, and I had to do something, Horace. I won't do anything like it ever again," he said, and the tears were coming now, twisting his words into sobs. "But I had to then."

Horace pulled him into a hug. "Oh, for goodness' sake, Simon, don't cry! Shit. I knew you'd do something that'd make it easy to forgive you."

Simon kept sobbing but let out a bark of a laugh. "Glad I could help."

Horace held him at arm's length. "I've thought so hard about this, imagined how this would go a million times. In the space of a few days, you went from someone I'd never met to the most important person in my life, who kept my sanity together, and when I found out you were as attracted to me as I was to you, I...saw a future."

He was crying now, too, and Simon couldn't stand it. He pulled them back together, and they wept like a couple of children. How Dillon would laugh.

"I'm sorry," Simon said. "I'm so, so sorry. I never meant to hurt you. I mean, I knew it would hurt, but I didn't want it to."

"I know, and I think I understand, but it still makes me so angry!"

"You can hit me!" Simon said as he stepped back, drunk on emotion. "If it will make you feel better."

"I'm not going to hit you. Don't be ridiculous."

"I can hurt myself with my power if that—"

Horace stepped forward and grabbed his chin. "If you even try to do something so idiotic…" His eyes were bright, and so close, they were easier to see though the night made them colorless. Still, Simon saw when Horace's gaze traveled to his lips, and he let his own mind wander to their kiss. When desire flooded him, he didn't try to hide it, nor did he try to avoid looking into Horace and seeing that desire returned.

Their kiss was hurried and brutal, teeth knocking together, hands rubbing over tear-stained cheeks. They pawed at each other like animals, tearing away clothing as their power entwined; sensations passed back and forth so that they reveled in the effects of their own touches as well as those they received. Simon couldn't tell where one of them ended and the other began. He just knew he couldn't get enough, and Horace felt the same as they rolled across the grass, grabbing and kissing and thrusting until the world faded to nothing, and everyone and everything else was a far distant memory.

The roar in Simon's ears finally faded, and he realized he was on his back, staring up at the starry sky and breathing hard while Horace lay in his arms, the cool night air gusting over their sweat-streaked bodies. Simon held his breath and waited for all the negative things to return, but for the moment, they stayed at bay.

Horace lifted his head. "Are you all right?"

"Perfect." And he hadn't thought of Dillon, not even once. He kissed Horace again, but this was tender, thankful. "Are you cold?"

"You know I'm not, and you're not either. This is the kind of power sharing that I like, by the way."

"We should have grabbed a blanket."

"Were you thinking we'd wind up having fantastic sex together? Was that your plan?"

"I wasn't thinking with my brain."

Horace's jaw dropped. "Simon Lazlo! That's a very naughty thing to say."

Simon stammered. "I meant heart! I was thinking with my heart!"

With a laugh, Horace kissed him again. "Do you want to go back for that blanket, or shall we stay here? What does your *heart* tell you?" His hands went wandering, but they didn't stop at Simon's chest.

Simon gasped and decided to show his answer instead of speak it.

CHAPTER EIGHT

Whenever Caroline said she needed a walk, Dillon tried to go with her. As pregnant as she was, he didn't want her walking the streets alone, never mind that she could always call for help with her power. He liked to think that if something went wrong, he'd be there to help before anyone else.

She liked to walk near the warehouse district. The sight of the hoshpis always made her laugh. He did his best to ignore everyone but her, but she didn't talk much. She liked to enjoy the silence, so he tried to enjoy it with her as they strolled, never going far from certain shops with "clean places to pee" as Caroline said, but any house would probably do. Who would deny the odd outhouse or chamber pot to the woman carrying God's baby?

Probably some. He hadn't seen any graffiti that day, but he couldn't help scanning every alley and wall. The people in the warehouse district didn't seem to have time for that sort of nonsense, though. They were always hard at work with the animals or shifting goods from one area of the city to another. Even the shop owners were pure business. He was starting to relax when Caroline's voice vibrated through his head. "Look out!"

He turned in the direction of her pointing finger, shook off her other hand, and flexed his power. Stabbed by a burst of lightning, the man she'd pointed at flew backward and bounced off a wall. A knife dropped from his hand to the street, and all around, people screamed and scattered.

Dillon drew his sidearm, jogged over, and kicked the knife farther away, though the would-be assassin was too busy twitching to try again.

The strike hadn't been enough to kill him. Dillon had been practicing. Caroline approached, rubbing her belly as if soothing it.

"Do you sense anyone else?" he asked.

She shook her head.

He frowned and looked to the fleeing people, but none seemed exactly murderous. Sun-Moon assassins would come in pairs, but he supposed this could be a gift from the renegades or one of the graffiti artists putting on his big boy pants. "Pump him."

She grimaced and rubbed her belly faster but nodded all the same. Dillon waited while her eyes moved back and forth as if reading or searching, and after a few heartbeats, she blinked. "Done."

Instead of wasting a bullet, Dillon touched the man with one foot and sent another strike into him, stopping his heart. He waved over one pedestrian who didn't seem too terrified to move. "Call the paladins to clear this body away." With another look at his face, the pedestrian fled. Even if he didn't obey, someone would.

Dillon took Caroline's arm and led her back toward the temple. "What have you got?"

"There was a lot of pain," she said softly.

He put an arm around her shoulders, trying to hide his irritation, even if he did wish she hadn't had to do it. "I'm sorry, but I need to know."

"He was going to kill you. He knew other people who want to kill you, too. They want revenge for their god. Is it Simon Lazlo? Is he the god they're talking about?"

He couldn't help a flinch. "He isn't dead. And he isn't a god." But he knew which god he had killed. How the fuck had Marie Martin's followers gotten wind of him? She hadn't been a weak telepath, though not as strong as the Sun-Moon. Maybe she'd been able to call out to her people before he'd killed her? Naos's words about people coming after him echoed in his brain. Oh, that fucking asshole! Was she sending random followers after him now by playing Contessa?

He sighed. "Maybe he was crazy."

"I've read the minds of those with mental illnesses," she said, not adding if this was the same or different.

He rubbed her shoulders. "You know I wouldn't ask you to do anything you're not capable of."

She gave him a bright smile, and he didn't have to be a telepath to know how much she loved him. After he dropped her off at the temple, he went to his office, not wanting to walk the streets again now that people were literally out to kill him. Strange as it was, having an enemy with the intestinal fortitude to just come at him made him giddy. He'd often tended toward paranoia; he tried to control it, but many people on Calamity were *actually* out to get him.

And maybe this pathetic attempt on his life meant those people were working together. Caroline wouldn't necessarily have detected that. Since people didn't think about names and faces in neat, orderly rows, minds were often hard to read; he remembered Christian and Marlowe saying that same thing once. Maybe he should have kept the assassin alive a little longer, but he didn't want anyone else talking to the man, and they couldn't risk an escape. It didn't matter. If the bastards were going to come after him with knives, they were going to fail, over and over. Even without his power, he had a gun, for fuck's sake. It would be nice to smoke them out, though, before they tried again.

He pulled a piece of paper over and dipped a pen in his inkwell, trying to remember the last time he'd written a note. He ordered people to carry his messages from one place to another, but he needed to brainstorm now and didn't have a handy computer.

"People who want to kill me," he wrote. After a moment, he underlined it, the ridiculousness making him chuckle, even as a pleasant feeling scythed through him, leaving him warm and tingly.

Despite the part about killing a god, he listed the renegades at the top. If there was a conspiracy, they were part of it. They'd be recognized in Gale, if not by him, then by someone, and word would get around. He'd thought gossip on the *Atlas* was bad, but at least it was contained. Events didn't just get passed around in Gale; with so many ears and mouths, they got distorted, too, but a kernel of truth remained. So, the renegades would need someone to do their dirty work.

He listed Marie fucking Martin's followers next. "Deliquois," he said aloud. He didn't know how far that was from Gale. He remembered it as an island chain to the south and wished he could see it from above again so he could send a lovely hurricane their way.

"Naos," he said loudly, "care to do me a favor?"

No one answered, and he sighed. He should have known she'd never be helpful. He listed Christian and Marlowe under Marie's name. Any Sun-Moon pairs would also stand out in Gale, but he supposed they could shuck their symbols in order to disguise themselves. Unless…

Maybe the assassin hadn't been thinking about Marie but about the lieutenants. If something had happened to them, their people might blame him. Some of the breachies might have carried word about their final meeting with Dillon to Celeste and might have claimed he did something to them, and then if they'd died, maybe even been murdered by the breachies, the Sun-Moon worshipers would definitely set that at his feet.

He wrote "Breachies" last, but Caroline had said god and not gods, so either just Christian or Marlowe had died, or his original thought about Marie was the right one.

Unless something *had* happened to Lazlo. Even without powers, Laz had knowledge that people might find godlike, especially where plants were concerned. He started to write Lazlo's name under the breachies, then scratched it out hurriedly. Angry as Lazlo might be, he wouldn't send assassins or encourage anyone to go that direction. No, any worshipers Lazlo gained would be pacifists sitting around communing in a field or growing a garden together.

He turned back to the top of the list. He had people watching the renegades, but he could spare a few more. They'd been quiet for a long time, trading with the plains dwellers and staying put, but they were too close for comfort. He'd send a few more telepathic spies and find out what they were up to, see who visited them. He'd also put someone to watch for any plains dwelling clans wandering close to Gale, see if any of them could be Marie Martin's people.

As for the assassins already in Gale, he wouldn't be able to find them until they acted. Even if he wanted to set his telepaths loose on the city, reading minds willy nilly, they could never read everyone, not deep enough to predict their movements. And random thought reading was still against the law. He didn't want to give the graffiti artists more ammunition.

Luckily, Dillon didn't have long to wait. Brown rushed into his office not two days later, dragging one of the telepaths with her. Dillon jumped from his seat and helped the winded man into an empty chair.

"A gathering, Storm Lord," the wheezing man said. "Plains dwellers and renegades, but more of them than usual."

"Coming here?"

"To the large rock they've met at before."

Dillon smiled and rubbed his hands together. They could be getting ready to mount an attack. Perfect. "Captain Brown, let's put together a welcome wagon." He gestured for the spy to go with Brown. "Tell her everything you know."

Now they were cooking. Maybe the renegades thought he wasn't watching, that they'd catch him unawares. Or maybe this was the prelude to an attack, and they were still gathering their forces. Well, he wasn't going to sit and wait for the fucking soup pot. He'd remind them why staying so close and sticking their necks out in his direction was such a bad idea.

❖

Fajir had been following the winding trail of her prey for over a week. She'd kept her distance as they stopped at the Engali camp. They hadn't stayed long, not even long enough for Fajir to snatch up a captive and question him, which seemed a shame, but Nico suggested caution, and Fajir had never known him to be wrong about such things.

As the nights wore on, though, she'd wished for at least one captive, someone she could torture in Halaan's name. She began to wish she'd stayed near the Engali and sent Nico, excellent tracker that he was, on the trail of the prey, but she didn't dare disobey the Lords.

Now her band lay along the side of a hill and watched the Svenal scurry about their camp like insects. She could almost smell their agitation on the wind. People raced from tent to tent, and she hadn't seen her quarry for two days. They had to have escaped and sent their captors into a panic.

Fajir signaled one of the others to watch and slid farther down the hill, Nico at her side. They'd have to wait. They couldn't search the surrounding area for tracks while the Svenal were so stirred up, so they'd wait for the clan to move, and then pick up the scent again. She pulled a small jar from her pack, untied the tiny knots that held it closed, and then breathed deeply of the oil inside. The acrid scent brought back Halaan and lazy afternoons. He'd always taken meticulous care of his bone sword, rubbing it with oil so it never turned brittle.

She drew her blade, then dipped her fingers in the oil and rubbed them along the sword's pitted surface, just as Halaan had done so many times. She could almost feel his hand over hers, his whisper in her ear.

Nico settled at her side and wiped his short dark hair away from his face. Shorter than her but stocky and strong, he made a good second, would have been a good friend if she'd allowed herself time for such things. His small, rounded face had been the first one she'd seen after she'd awoken from chasing Halaan's killer. He'd found her on the plains after she'd passed out. He'd said her dark hair stood out like a stain upon the grass, as she would be a stain upon the hearts of the Engali.

Comforting words. She'd let them guide her as he guided her. One night, as he'd held her while she wept, he'd told her he was a dual child, born as a male soul in a female body. The Lords had spoken to him even as a young child, reassuring him that he would be the male in his partnership. He'd had a true partner, like hers, but his love had died in a storm, lost and alone. He'd kept a house in the middle of nowhere, helping lost travelers, and that was how he'd found Fajir. He'd claimed no one was as lost as her and said he knew her anguished look as he knew his own heart.

Nico had stayed with her when they wrapped Halaan for burial. He'd held her hand while other widows tattooed her, her real tears mingling with the ink of her fake ones. He'd whispered his memories in her ear, and it had calmed her to know she had company in her loss. On the day of Halaan's funeral, he'd wrapped his strong arms around her waist, and she'd wondered how he'd known she planned to throw herself onto the pyre and join Halaan in the other world, but of course he'd known. Someone had once kept him from doing the same.

"He needs your revenge," he'd whispered.

And one day, he would have it. As she cleaned her sword, Fajir smiled at Nico. He leaned back, surprised. "Seren?" A hesitant smile started on his own lips. "Is there something…"

"I just wanted to thank you."

He ducked his head. "You needn't."

"You don't even know what I'm thanking you for."

Though he shrugged, she thought she saw a twinkle in his dark blue eyes. "You never need to thank me."

Above them, the scout waved, and Fajir capped her jar and crawled up to join him.

"Someone came into camp and went into a tent with their leader," the scout said.

"One of our prey?"

"No, Seren. Two strangers, one of them very odd."

She frowned but nodded. "Get ready. If they move, we follow. Circle out for now, far. I want to know if anyone else is coming."

"Your will, Seren."

They spread out, and when they returned, the two who'd entered the camp still hadn't left, but they found other tracks, as if there were more watchers who'd recently fled. Fajir didn't want to follow old tracks. She had to stay with those who'd last seen the prey. "Maybe we can catch one," she said, "And wring the truth from him."

Nico cleared his throat. "They are not Engali, Seren."

"Then they may live or not." She shrugged. "I don't care either way."

CHAPTER NINE

On her way to the Meeting Rock, Cordelia couldn't help but think of how tenuous peace seemed. Her time with the plains dwellers had always felt a little hazy, as if she was waiting for something to happen, not unlike her time with the paladins before the Storm Lord's arrival. But back then the waiting had made her feel anxious, as if she was missing out on something, and only her street fights with Liam made her feel calm again. Now part of her had enjoyed the peace with Wuran and her friends and family, and she was sorry to think it had ended.

After her escape from the Svenal, she'd had an uncomfortable talk with Wuran, who was anxious to know if his children were safe and his allies were going to help him take revenge. He wanted to know why Cordelia hadn't rescued the children when she escaped. She'd told him that Pool hadn't been able to tell one plains dweller from another. She'd only taken Cordelia and those closest to her at the time. That seemed to mollify him for a bit, but when he kept demanding they seek out the Svenal camp, no matter that it was still dark, she had to calm him until Simon and Horace stumbled back to camp just before dawn.

Simon had explained that the Svenal were sick, unable to have their own children, and Wuran raged that he didn't care what was wrong with them. Simon claimed he had an idea how to make everyone happy: he and Horace would heal the Svenal, they'd give the children back, and no one had to fight.

Wuran had said that wasn't good enough. He'd stalked out of camp when day had fully dawned, saying he would call on his other allies. Cordelia felt as if she should prevent bloodshed if she could, yet again, a side she'd never seen herself on. People usually called on her when they *wanted* it.

Liam had come to her after she stared at Wuran's retreating figure and said, "I remember when fighting was what you lived for."

She kept herself from sighing. "We used to think killing was the only way to keep others alive. Now that we've got a chance for another way, shouldn't we take it?"

After another long look, he'd shrugged. "Yeah, my heart's not in this fight, either. I want to save all my energy for you-know-who. I can talk to the Svenal if you want, bring them to the Meeting Rock, and we can try Simon's plan."

It was her turn to stare at him, but he didn't have a conniving bone in him. He'd always been honest about what he wanted, and he had no reason to piss the Svenal off or prolong this fight. And after all the shit his mother had always given him, he was hard to ruffle. Maybe he would make a good peacekeeper. "Take Reach. They need to see a drushka up close, to see what they're up against if they decide to fight instead of talk."

So they'd gone with an escort, and the Svenal had listened. Liam had said they'd been angry, but still desperate. If they couldn't be healed, they'd rather die than waste away with the generation they had. But after they'd spoken, there was still no more sign of Wuran.

Pool's tree stayed far back now, as it always did in these meetings. Cordelia walked with Simon, Horace, Samira, Mamet, Liam, Nettle, Reach, and several ex-paladins and drushkan warriors. Ahead of them at the Meeting Rock, the Svenal had brought their whole clan. Their tents were arrayed around the base of the jutting tor, but Cordelia wasn't worried. Pool was close, and Cordelia could feel her watching through her roots, her drushka. If the Svenal decided to fight, they'd soon find themselves overwhelmed.

A group of Svenal came out to meet them with their chafa, Onin, but there was another among their group that Simon identified as Pakesh, the half-yafanai who'd knocked Cordelia out. Onin sat cross-legged in the long grass rather than waiting for a tent. Maybe he wanted everything out in the open where everyone could see. She appreciated the same thing. He glared at Simon, at everyone, but it seemed he didn't want to be the first to speak.

The rest of them sat down, too. "I know you're angry," Simon said at last. "Lots of people are. Chafa, it wasn't my intention to deceive you. I said I'd help, and I've come back to keep that promise. I only left because you abducted my friends."

Onin took a deep breath and put his hands on his knees. "You injured some of my people."

"But didn't kill any," Cordelia said. "And we don't want to start now."

"The Svenal are strong!"

Cordelia didn't need the hand Simon laid on her arm to keep her from retorting. She knew bluster when she saw it.

"There's no need for violence," Simon said. "I've...learned a few things since I saw you last. Please, let me see Sheila, and I'll show you."

Cordelia didn't even glance at Horace. If Simon didn't want to reveal they were going to work together, she wasn't going to tell anyone. Most likely, they already knew Horace had powers. Pakesh probably felt them; by the way he was staring at them, Cordelia guessed he was trying to figure out who could do what, but Horace and Simon combined might be blocking him.

"You get one for free," Cordelia said. "Then you release the kids you've stolen, and our healer will do the rest."

When Simon glanced at her, she raised an eyebrow, and he nodded.

Onin sent someone back to the tents, and he led a young woman forward. She was pale and drawn and looked as if she'd lost weight when she should be gaining it.

Simon shut his eyes, but Horace kept his open, and Cordelia felt a tingle pass over her scalp as they worked. "The fetus can't fully attach, that's the problem," Simon mumbled.

Horace said nothing but frowned a little, and Cordelia knew he was probably speaking telepathically.

"Right, yes," Simon said. "It's in the blood. She can't sustain the child, and..."

Cordelia didn't need that sentence finished. A species that couldn't procreate would eventually die out. Question was, was it a natural disease or something that had been done to them?

They sat in silence for a long time, both Simon and Horace frowning. Beads of sweat shone on both their faces, and Cordelia began to wonder if they could do anything, fix anything. Their power might have healed somewhat, but what if it never fully recovered? What if Simon *had* crippled their ability?

Onin stared at them, too, as well as the young pregnant girl. Cordelia eased her legs out to the side, the better to stand quickly if anyone lunged. Onin would go for Simon and Horace first, she thought, as soon as he suspected they couldn't do what they'd promised. Cordelia had only seen a look that desperate once before, on a woman frantic to avenge her wife's murder. When the paladins had taken the murderer into custody instead, the woman had leaped at the paladins as if she needed to get her hands on someone's throat.

Onin fidgeted, and Cordelia tensed. His gaze shifted to hers, and he licked his lips. She let her hand fall close to her hip and the wooden blade.

When Simon cried, "There it is!" everyone started and then stared. He took Sheila's hand. "Yes, yes I see it now!"

She gasped and gripped her belly. Onin tensed, but she said, "The pain is gone, Chafa."

He sprang to his feet, and Cordelia did the same, but there were tears in his eyes.

Simon breathed deep. "Done. She's cured."

She leapt to her feet, too, and threw her arms around Onin's neck. "She's moving! The baby is moving!"

"He, actually," Horace said softly. When Cordelia turned to him, he winked. Onin and Sheila didn't seem to notice. They were too busy laughing and hugging and chattering like mad.

Cordelia kept her face calm as Onin called for the rest of his tribe to come and be healed, but she said, "Not yet."

He blinked as if she'd just offered him a lifeline and then snatched it away before realization spread across his face. "Release the children," he called.

"We'll give them a quick scan," Simon said. "Make sure they're not infected."

Cordelia nodded. "Let's see if we can find Wuran and head him off with the good news."

Cordelia took the children in hand, leading them off across the plains. Simon trusted that she'd set things right. She seemed like one of those people who was always putting things right in one way or another. He let his hand dangle at his side, his fingers finding Horace's before he told them to. That was silly, romantic stuff, the kind that would have had him rolling his eyes before, but when Horace turned a smile his way instead of a sneer, Simon's contempt for himself blew out the window. Maybe that was love.

Okay, too much. He coughed a little chuckle, and when Horace raised an eyebrow, Simon thought loudly, "I'll tell you later."

That was another thing. He never thought he'd be used to speaking mind to mind with someone, but ever since their powers had let them entwine so completely, it seemed natural. Simon couldn't read Horace's mind, but Horace could project his own thoughts as words, and the tingle constantly passing over Simon's scalp told him that Horace was listening for surface thoughts, "loud" thoughts. The only time they'd shut it off was during Pakesh's clumsy attempts to scan them. The boy was a battering ram of power, but so unfocused, he was easy to brush away if they were expecting it.

Simon needed Horace as close as possible as they healed the Svenal. Simon was better at using his stronger powers, but he hadn't had much to cure on the *Atlas*. Horace was used to wounds and illnesses. Even before augmentation, he'd been seeing to the sick. And with Simon's greater knowledge of biology, they knew what to look for. Scanning the women and trying to get ahead of the disease had been so frustrating; Horace made him see there was no getting ahead of it. It was everywhere, integrated. The invader had become part of the whole, just like Horace had said. The thing to do was to scan the uninfected and look for the differences. It was only then they'd been able to spot an insidious pathogen, but they didn't know if it was a naturally occurring disease that humans had stumbled upon on this planet, or if it was something that'd been engineered. There weren't many people who could do such a thing; there were no germ labs on Calamity. The only people with the power to make a disease were Dué, Simon, or now Horace, and Simon was pretty sure he and Horace hadn't done it.

Onin approached them again, leading many of his clan, all of them shifting and fidgeting. Simon had focused his efforts on the pregnant women last time, but the disease was part of all of them. They'd all have to be scanned.

"Are you the second patient, Chafa?" Simon asked. "We'll check everyone, but now that we know what we're looking for, it should go faster."

Onin nodded and rubbed his hands together. "I have a request."

Simon almost said, "Besides healing your entire tribe," but Horace gave him a warning squeeze.

"My mind bender," Onin said, looking at Pakesh. "What's wrong with him? Sometimes, he seems crazy."

Horace cleared his throat, but Simon said, "He ate some powder you stole from Gale, and now you want him fixed?"

"Simon," Horace said, "easy."

Onin stared, but he must have seen the folly of holding things back. "We knew some of your people had power, and…"

Simon nodded. He was surprised no one else had tried it. "Someday, I want to hear the story of how you got your hands on it, but for now, what do you want me to do?"

"Can you heal him?"

Horace rubbed his forehead. "He *ate* it?"

Onin nodded.

"How much?"

Onin held his hands apart, but it was difficult to tell whether he meant the container the drug came in or the amount itself. It looked to be several ounces. He couldn't have eaten all of it at one time, or he'd be dead.

Horace nodded as if he'd heard that thought. "Cleansing him would take too much time, might even kill him depending on how the drug has changed him." He sighed and added mentally, "It might be easier to change his brain like we would a trained yafanai. At least then he'd be able to control himself."

"No matter what we do," Simon said aloud, "we aren't staying after we heal the disease. If you want us to help Pakesh, he'll have to come with us."

Onin rubbed his chin. "Begin the healing, please."

Time dropped away as Simon entwined his senses with Horace's. He tried to block the memories of when they'd joined for more intimate reasons and keep himself focused, but they kept bubbling to the surface.

Horace's amusement was a bright bloom. "Keep your mind on the mission."

With precise attacks, they overpowered the illness, going cell by cell, changing it into something each person could dump from their system. They sat on a rock together, Simon letting his eyes slip shut and knowing Horace kept his open. The drushka were watching, as well as Samira and Mamet. The joy of the Svenal twined around them, and as silly as it sounded, it felt like a great big blanket of happiness spreading to the horizon.

Almost. On the edges of Simon's thoughts was a black cloud, and he didn't know who or what it could be. He felt determination and anger and had time for the thought that some people were never happy before booms and screams shattered his attention. He opened his eyes to see pieces of Meeting Rock break from the top and rain down on the Svenal camp.

He stood slowly with those around him, staring in wide-eyed horror before the booms came again, and more rock came crashing down.

"What?" Horace said. "What is—"

"Get down!" Simon cried. "Everyone down. Take cover, take cover!" He dragged Horace with him and hoped everyone was doing the same.

"So many wounded," Horace said. "What's happening?"

"Rail guns," He'd never seen them, but he knew what they were, just like he knew what that black spot was. The guns sounded again, and Horace clapped his hands over his head. Someone else screamed, and Simon cried, "I told everyone to stay down!" But they couldn't stay that way forever, and Simon felt powers reaching for him, Dillon's telepaths, who'd be telling the soldiers where to aim.

His bile rose, and he clung to Horace. "It's Dillon. Can you feel his telepaths? Tell them I'm coming."

Samira grabbed his ankle. "You can't!"

"He won't kill me. Please, do it, Horace."

He felt Horace use his powers, and the gunfire stopped. Shakily, Simon stood as those around him called to him to stay down. He looked into the distance, where the soldiers were mere specks, but they wouldn't need to be close with all their tech.

"I'm coming with you," several people said at once.

He turned to see Horace, Samira, and Mamet standing as well as several of the drushka. "No, Horace, please, tend the wounded. And I don't think he'll do well seeing drushka. Samira…"

She shook her head. "I'm coming with you. He knows who I am."

Well, he might remember her body, but not her name, not exactly. He couldn't remember what he'd never bothered to learn.

"Simon—" Horace started.

"Please," Simon said as he stepped close, planting a quick kiss on Horace's lips. "I don't want him near you."

Horace gripped his hand. "I'll be watching. If he does anything, I'll come running."

Simon smiled softly, not willing to admit his terror. "I'm more powerful than he is." And it was true, even if his powers hadn't fully recovered. He'd always been the more powerful one. He just hadn't wanted to admit it. As he walked over the hill, he kept telling himself that over and over and over again.

He headed toward the soldiers at a steady gait, gesturing for Samira and Mamet to stay behind him. Dillon waited until the three of them had crested a hill, probably until he could see they weren't surrounded by a plains dweller escort. He stood, obscured by armor, but Simon knew it was him. He expected anger or surprise, not the big smile that took over Dillon's face or the shaky step forward, the grin faltering as Dillon said, "Tell me you're not her."

Simon stuttered to a halt. "Um, I'm not her. I'm me."

The grin came rushing back, tugging Simon's own lips into a smile. "Simon."

Simon brayed a laugh and fought the urge to clap a hand over his mouth. He always picked the worst times to guffaw. "I see you remember, but let's stick to Laz, shall we?" It was familiar and comfortable, and it let him remember how they'd left things.

Dillon turned to his paladins and waved at them to stay put. He jerked his head to the side, signaling a little way from the others. Simon gave a look to Samira that he hoped conveyed, "Please don't let me get dragged back into this shit."

She gave him a nod and a reassuring smile, crossing her arms and radiating the idea that she wasn't going anywhere, no matter what.

"So," Dillon said once they were out of earshot.

"Let me stop you right there."

Dillon quirked an eyebrow. "With so?"

"I know what you're thinking. You found out a lot of people are gathering on your doorstep, you thought it had something to do with you, so you attacked first. You probably didn't even intend to ask questions later."

Dillon shrugged, still with that same old smugness, and Simon felt any good feelings he remembered dissolving. "If it's not about me, what's it about?"

Simon resisted the urge to snarl and lay all the blame Dillon deserved at his feet. After all, the idea was to get Dillon the hell out of there as quickly as possible. "It's an internal dispute between the plains dwellers. There's a disease…" Too late, he realized he should have lied, should have been thinking of a lie all the time. Any talk of curing diseases would point back to his powers. He told himself to keep still, to not react. Hoping the pause didn't show, he started talking again. "Some of the renegades know about my background in biology. They asked for my advice."

Dillon's gaze flicked toward Meeting Rock, and Simon could feel his excitement building. Damn, damn, damn. He knew Dillon, but Dillon knew him, too, knew what a pause could mean, knew that Simon couldn't set up a lab in the middle of the plains, so all his knowledge would be worthless without power.

"Were you able to help them?" Dillon asked.

Simon's temper spiked. "Want to make sure there's more of them to kill?"

Dillon had the decency to look sheepish. "I thought they were massing to attack."

"You didn't think to maybe, I don't know, ask! You had to have been spying on them, why not just keep doing that! Then maybe you would have asked the important questions like, would they bring their kids to war!"

"Hey, I haven't had it easy, you know! There's some kind of assassin group trying to kill me in Gale right now. I can't be too careful."

Simon took a deep breath. "Before you make this any worse, please just get the hell out of here."

"Are you going to stay? Going to keep *helping* them with their disease?"

"Yes, so keep your bullets to yourself."

He looked at the ground and kicked at it like a child. "Do you think...do you think you could visit, or I could visit, or..." Sincerity flowed from him in waves.

And even though they'd known each other for hundreds of years, it seemed Dillon could still surprise him. "Maybe. I don't know. Probably. If you behave."

So far, so good, Dillon thought. It didn't seem to be Naos standing in front of him. By all the nagging, he knew it was definitely Laz, and by the little bit he'd said, the brief frozen look on his face, he was holding something back, and Dillon knew it had to be the return of his powers. Why else would the plains dwellers want him?

"Caroline," Dillon thought as loudly as he could. "Am I right?"

"If I scan him, he'll know," she said in Dillon's mind, "but I can feel his shields from here."

And he wouldn't have those without powers. Dillon wanted to do a little dance but was afraid Lazlo would see through his glee. He *was* happy to see Laz. When they'd first clapped eyes on each other, there'd been a significant tug in his chest. He'd even nudged a little rainstorm closer without meaning to. It rumbled in the distance, its energy traveling up and down his spine.

"It's good to have you back, Laz."

A smile started on Lazlo's face before it faded. "I am not back. I'm just…"

Dillon tuned him out as he prattled on about what he was doing. He *was* back; he just didn't know it yet, and this time, he was going to stay. "When I say," Dillon thought to Caroline, "you and the rest of the telepaths give him a burst, knock him out."

"He's very strong—"

"He'll be off guard." He couldn't keep the glee off his face and put his hands on Lazlo's shoulders, letting all his affection shine through.

This time, it seemed Lazlo couldn't help a smile. "What?"

Dillon punched him in the face, lightning quick, as he said, "Now!" Even his scalp tingled as Caroline and the yafanai attacked with all their might. Lazlo dropped like a stone. While his friends gawked, Dillon sent two short bursts of power their way, knocking them flat but not stopping their hearts.

The whole thing had taken under a second. Brown's gun hadn't even cleared its holster.

"What the hell?" she asked. "Storm Lord?"

"Cover our retreat, Captain," Dillon said as he lifted Lazlo and hung him over one shoulder.

"Retreat, sir?" She jerked her chin toward where the renegades had gathered.

"We've got more than we bargained for. It's enough for today." And if his newly forming plans for Lazlo didn't go well, Laz would take it better if his friends were still alive. Dillon laid him in a cart beside Caroline, and the armored paladins began towing it back to Gale.

"It's going to take a lot to keep him asleep," Caroline said. "His powers keep trying to heal him even without him using them."

"Not for long," Dillon said. "Not after you're done with him."

CHAPTER TEN

Cordelia thought she'd have to take the kids all the way to Pool, but she spotted Wuran in the distance just as Pool sent a message to the drushka that he was coming. Cordelia shivered as the hazy pictures formed in her mind, as if she was trying to play a vid on the wrong device or at the wrong speed.

The children cried out and broke into a run when they saw Wuran. He sprinted forward, his leather hat flying from his head. Two little girls headed for him like a shot, and he caught them up and kissed them, all of them laughing and crying and speaking over one another. It was a happy scene, the kind Cordelia knew would stay with her in dark times.

The children spread around Wuran, asking questions about their parents; others raced to the adults scattered around him. Cordelia tried not to focus on those who'd never see their parents again. That had been her once, though she'd still had Uncle Paul. She couldn't help wondering if the orphans would forget their anger or if it would stay with them as it had with her.

Wuran stepped toward her, wiping his eyes. "I can't believe it."

"Sorry it took so long."

He threw his arms around her, and she laughed, slapping him on the back. He pushed her to arm's length and clasped her shoulders. "Thank you."

"Just remember this when we're quibbling over prices."

He only laughed and hugged the little girls again. Cordelia turned to leave, and he called, "The Svenal?"

With a sigh, she stopped. "Can you let us handle them?"

"What of the dead?"

Yes, there were always the dead, more and more of them. Before she had to answer, a boom echoed from Meeting Rock, and the breeze carried the sounds of screams across the rolling plains.

"Run!" she shouted.

Wuran grabbed every child within reach and sprinted back the way he'd come, those around him doing the same. Cordelia ran toward the screams, sliding to a halt as she came within sight of the Svenal encampment. Pieces of the rock had rained down among them, but most people looked to be up and moving. Cordelia ran for Horace.

"What happened?"

He bent over a bloody man and didn't answer.

Onin ran over, carrying a wounded person to lay at Horace's feet. "They say it was your old god. His wrath."

Cordelia curled her hands into fists. "He's not a god, just a man with some fancy tricks." Liam had been right. The Storm Lord had come for them, but she hadn't been there to greet him. "He's gone?"

Onin waved into the distance. "Your strange friends have gone to see. Do you think he knows of the One-Eye, the old god?"

Cordelia shuddered, though she didn't know why. "Who?"

"My father once spoke of strangers who wandered the plains claiming they spoke to a goddess." He stared at the carnage instead of her; no matter what she said, he wouldn't hear. "They say she knows all, sees all."

The sounds of crying, wounded people slipped out of her mind, pushed by the memory of the power that had shown her the universe when she'd floated above Calamity and through the whole of existence, pulled by an infinite hand.

A tingle passed over her scalp, and a voice inside her mind whispered, "I remember you."

She gasped and came back to the present. Onin still wasn't looking at her, but Horace glanced up. "These are healed enough to survive. I'm going to look for Simon."

She grabbed his arm as he started to the west. "Hold on."

"The drushka followed him." He pulled against her, as deaf as Onin.

"So we wait for them. We can't go blundering around."

When Nettle finally jogged back to meet them, Horace pulled away so hard, Cordelia had to either let him go or rip his sleeve off, maybe his arm.

"The Storm Lord has retreated," Nettle said, "carrying shawness Simon with him."

Horace ran. Cordelia cursed and followed, Nettle with her, and Reach broke off from the crowd to join them.

"Is he hurt?" Reach called.

Cordelia didn't bother to answer. She could tackle Horace, but she didn't want to hurt him. And if the Storm Lord was gone, Horace couldn't get himself into too much trouble, and he would tire long before he got close to Gale.

"We did not see what became of Samira and young Mamet," Nettle said. "I did not wish to be too close."

Horace stumbled and cried, "Samira!" as he angled off to the side.

Cordelia followed to where Samira and Mamet lay in the grass, hidden. Horace put his hands on both of them, but by the charred, ozone scent, Cordelia guessed they'd earned the Storm Lord's personal attention.

Nettle lifted her face to the wind, nose up.

"What is it?" Cordelia looked toward Gale, trying to see if the Storm Lord had left any surprises behind.

"Oily," Nettle said, frowning, "and acrid."

"A gun?"

Nettle sucked her teeth. "I do not—"

"Simon!" Samira cried as she bolted upright. "Where..." She glanced at all of them before whipping her head around, looking wildly. "Where is he?"

Reach knelt at her side. "You must calm yourself."

"The Storm Lord hit him!" Samira struggled to her feet as Mamet did the same. "He hit him, and then..." She rubbed her chest.

"He's gone. Taken." Tears hovered in Horace's eyes before he took a deep breath that seemed to banish them.

"By the Storm Lord?" Reach asked.

Samira started toward Gale without another word.

"Stop!" Cordelia said, resisting the urge to ask if going off half-cocked was part of yafanai training. "What can you do?"

She whirled, frowning and sneering, and Cordelia could almost sense her gathering her power.

"He defeated you easily," Nettle said. "How will you help shawness Simon if you are dead?"

She opened her mouth but couldn't seem to think of anything to say. Finally, she nodded. "So, we'll sneak in, Mamet and me."

"My...my sword and heart are yours," Mamet said.

Cordelia fought the urge to yell at all of them and the woman she'd been a short time ago, who would've been thinking the same thing. "With all his tech and the yafanai? We need a plan."

"The plan is to rescue Simon. I'm sure the rest—"

An arrow thudded to the ground in their midst. Cordelia whipped her sword out as a woman with large, teardrop tattoos stood from the grass. Several stood with her, all dressed in the robes of the Sun-Moon. Several had bows, and she sported a long bone sword.

"Everyone will stop," she said, her accent heavy.

"Ah," Nettle said softly, "the ones I smelled before."

Horace froze as he stared at the strangers' tattooed faces. The day just kept getting weirder.

"The healer and the Engali vermin are coming with us," the lead stranger said.

Samira responded in a different language, similar to the plains dweller tongue, but by the way she sneered and the way the lead stranger frowned, it seemed an insult. He would've preferred to talk, but an insult would have to do. He needed this over so they could get back to rescuing Simon. He didn't care what these people's problem was, though calling Mamet a vermin wasn't a good start.

Samira took a step as Cordelia called out a warning. One of the tattooed people fired an arrow, and Samira shoved him with her power. Cordelia cried, "Down!" as more bowmen took aim, and Horace dived into the long grass.

The battlefield went quiet, and Horace sent his senses out, trying to find out who was where, but it was hard to sort one body from another unless he already knew them well, like the other healers from Gale, maybe Natalya.

And Simon.

Horace clenched down on worry. He located one of the drushka, either Nettle or Reach, and tried to crawl silently. He reached out with telepathy, hoping surface thoughts might direct him, but he pulled back when he sensed massive power. One of the tattooed people might be a yafanai, but this felt as if it came from farther away, watching the tattooed people, maybe communicating with them.

One of the drushka was on the move, and Horace sensed a spike of fear. A deeper probe told him one of the humans had been paralyzed, drushkan poison coursing through her veins. He crawled closer, hearing nothing but wind sighing through the grass. A push of psychokinetic power caught his attention, and one of the tattooed people flew upward, crying out before landing with a thud.

"Samira?" Horace sent.

"Stay hidden!" she thought back, and he got flashes from her mind as she let him in: looking for attackers in the grass and feeling around with her power but not daring to use it wildly lest she hit someone she cared about.

With "cared about," he got a flash of Mamet's face and a little trill of worry and embarrassment. She cared about Mamet and didn't want to? "Be careful," he thought. "Someone is using telepathy, massive power."

"The Sun-Moon. These are widows, worshipers of theirs."

His senses picked up movement. "Someone's coming toward you. Human. Can't tell who."

"I've got them."

He sensed it as she tried to unleash her macro powers again, but telepathy poured from her attacker like a hammer, and her mind voice cried out as loudly as her real one before both fell silent, smothered by a telepathic attack.

Horace put a hand over his own mouth and pulled away. The Sun-Moon, more of Calamity's gods. Why couldn't they just leave people alone?

Something tickled his micro powers, and he sent out again hesitantly, sensing a new wound in Samira's abdomen. She'd bleed to death if he didn't see to it. He gritted his teeth and repressed the need to call the widows cowards for attacking someone who couldn't hurt them anymore, but if he gave away his position…

He'd killed a boggin once with his powers; how was this any different?

Because they were people! Incapacitate them? How, with his power still so soggy and weak?

"Cordelia?" he thought loudly, trying to zero in on her. "Samira's hurt!"

No one responded, but he felt weak signals nearby. "I'm going to help her," he thought.

He crawled toward Samira, his senses wide open, but her attacker had fled. He tried to mend her wound across the distance, but he needed to get his hands on her. He inched forward again, listening.

He parted the grass and saw her outstretched hand. He reached forward when his senses prickled again. He turned, trying to bring his powers to bear as he saw a tattooed face, but a telepathic burst battered his mind, and as his vision dimmed and voices exploded in his head, he realized that such a power could hide from him whenever it wanted.

❖

Cordelia frowned hard as tingles passed this way and that over her scalp. Someone was using telepathy nearby, but damned if she could hear any of it. Maybe being so close to the drushka had robbed her of her ability to hear human telepaths? Or maybe someone was talking and didn't want her to hear.

She heard a grunt, though. Ever since Samira had stopped throwing people around, the battlefield was like a tomb. "Fuck it," she whispered.

Sword drawn, she peeked over the top of the grass and saw the tattooed leader lifting an unconscious Horace and dragging him away.

"No you don't!" She leapt to her feet.

The tattooed woman held her sword under Horace's chin. "Do not move!"

"Or you'll what?" Cordelia said as she stopped. "You want him. You won't hurt him." Cordelia heard the twang of a bowstring and dropped again, but she couldn't afford to get distracted. She jumped up as Mamet rushed the tattooed woman from the side, but another of the tattooed crew leapt on Mamet's back, bashing her in the head with a sword pommel.

"The healer we may care about," the leader said, "but the vermin can die here."

Two people lifted Mamet, using her as a shield for the leader, and when Cordelia tried to see a way around them, one of them nicked Mamet's cheek, showing they were serious. Cordelia halted, and they gathered their wounded and watched each other's backs as they crested a hill. A line of whipping grass followed them, and Cordelia knew Nettle was on the move.

Reach stood from where she hid. "I smell Samira's blood."

Cordelia followed her to where Samira lay in the grass again. Reach rolled her over and loosened her clothing, looking for the wound. "Somewhat healed," she said when she found it. "Shawness Horace's last gift to us."

Cordelia left her to her healing songs and followed in Nettle's footsteps, but Nettle jogged back to meet her before she got far.

"They rode those insects," Nettle said. "The ossors Wuran told us about. Too fast for me to follow."

"Shit!" Cordelia yelled. "We lost two healers in under an hour!"

"We must regroup," Nettle said. "If the Svenal decide to attack again..."

She nodded. There were still enough Svenal to do some damage if they decided all this was Cordelia's fault. She felt Nettle call to Pool, and they carried Samira in her direction.

"I'm going to get Liam," Cordelia said. "And the rest of the humans. We need to find out what the Svenal are going to do now."

Nettle laid a hand on her arm. "I will go with you."

They both looked to Reach, who waved them on. "Ahya, you will always be a creature of action, Sa. Go, but be safe."

Cordelia ran back to where the wounded were gathering, but so far, there didn't appear to be any dead. Cordelia went to where Liam and Onin stood in conversation. Liam turned to her and told Onin to stay a moment, but he trailed in Liam's wake.

Cordelia didn't have time to worry about diplomacy. "You're going to be pissed," she said in Galean, "and you've got the right to tell me that you told me so, but the Storm Lord kidnapped Simon Lazlo, and then this group of tattooed people carried off Horace, and if we're going to do anything about one of them, we have to do it quickly."

He didn't yell but did turn several shades of red. "You know what I want."

"To attack the Storm Lord."

"Yes, but that's not what you should do."

She stopped in mid-argue, stunned. "What?"

"Go after Horace. They're a smaller group with no guns. You should get on their track yesterday."

"You...don't want me to go after the Storm Lord?"

He grinned, and it was a tiny bit horrible. "No, I'll go after him when the time is right. You get Horace. Right now, I have to explain things to Onin."

"The diplomat. I like it."

"Yeah, yeah." He turned to Onin and said in the plains dweller language, "We need a mount. Our healer's been stolen, and we're going after him, for your sake and ours."

He stared and then nodded, his expression unreadable. He waved one of his people over and spoke with them quickly.

Cordelia shuddered as she felt the drushka speaking again. Pool was coming closer, and Cordelia sensed her anger over someone abducting a shawness. Cordelia shrugged and twitched, trying to cut off the contact, but it was flying between so many of them.

Nettle laid a hand on her arm. "Sa, are you well?"

"No." And now she felt Nettle standing there, more than with the usual senses. She could almost sense the workings of Nettle's body, her connection to root and soil, to Pool, to all drushka.

She felt surprise from all of them, but instead of letting go, Nettle's grasp tightened, and Cordelia's skin felt too small, just as it had when she'd toured the universe. She was trying to contain too much, sense too much. She tried to push the feeling away, shrug it off, and the tight feeling slipped a little, but her sense of the drushka only grew. She shivered, closed her eyes, and fumbled inside herself for another way to ease the tightening feeling, as if trying to wriggle free from too tight clothing. Something gave. She opened her eyes in time to see her body collapse in Nettle's arms while she floated above it.

Nettle sent a panicked call to Pool, and Cordelia heard it as if she was some sort of relay, but it didn't bother her now. Nettle glowed, but her light was nothing compared to Pool's, whom Cordelia could see and sense coming closer.

"Sa?" Pool thought, the words clear as glass.

"Right here."

She felt the drushka jerk as they heard the words, felt them searching for her through Pool.

"What has happened?" Pool asked.

Cordelia floated a little higher, amazed by how much fear she *didn't* feel. Like flying in a dream, it was effortless, her spirit secured to her body by a long silver cord. When Nettle held her close and passed a hand over her forehead, the sensation hummed down the string. Nettle's light reached for the silver string, and she felt an outpouring of love and fear.

"Sa," Nettle said, "my heart's friend, come home."

Cordelia followed her silver string, a little afraid she wouldn't know how to get back inside, but it was like sliding into warm water. She didn't even have to try. With a gasp, her eyes opened, and she stared into Nettle's fear-filled gaze. "It's all right. I'm fine."

Liam was shouting that they needed a shawness, a healer, anything, but Cordelia stood without effort. "It's fine!" she called. She tried to explain and couldn't, settling for, "Um, I think I left my body but could still talk with the drushka."

He stared. "You're not a yafanai."

She shrugged. "Remember my tour of the universe?"

"Side effects?"

"Possibly."

He rubbed his chin, but as Onin approached with a team of people leading a geaver, they didn't have time to discuss it.

Liam eyed the animal and frowned. "Aren't they a little slow?"

Onin shook his head. "As fast as you need."

She thought about taking a larger force, but the enemy was too far ahead for a simple attack. They needed to be able to get to wherever the tattooed people were taking Horace and then sneak him out, and a smaller force would serve them better.

She gave Liam a wave. "Take care."

His mouth worked as if there were so many things he wanted to say, but he settled for, "You too." With a crooked grin, he added, "Fuck off."

She chuckled. It was the way they'd said good-bye when they were paladins. She'd nearly forgotten it.

The handler tapped the geaver and called a word. It knelt, and Cordelia and Nettle climbed atop its back into a box-like saddle. They sat on a leather pad and hung on to poles sticking up from the pad's corners. The geaver took a few ponderous steps, just long enough for Cordelia to think she could walk faster, then it broke into a lope, a stomach-churning, ground-eating stride that had the wind whipping around them. She and Nettle grabbed each other at the same time and had to laugh at the fear on both their faces before they settled for hanging on to the straps with one hand and each other with the other.

She felt for Pool, hoping someone told her the plan. That feeling of tightness surrounded her again, but she didn't try to push away from it this time, not wanting to leave her body unless she wanted to.

"We will find you, Sa," Pool said in her mind. "Always."

CHAPTER ELEVEN

They just kept coming. Word of the amazing godchild had spread like fire across the plains, and more clans arrived every day to see the wonders she could do. Natalya could only cross her arms and watch as Kora spoke to them, sometimes with Naos inside her, sometimes alone. She felt the ground shifting under their feet. She'd gone from thinking every other day that she'd made a mistake going with Naos, whether she risked madness or not, to knowing she'd made a mistake but not knowing what to do about it.

She could leave now, could grab some provisions and walk away, but Naos would follow in her mind. Naos could take away her stabilizing powers and let the madness sink back in until Natalya tore herself apart. Well, at least if she was dead, she wouldn't have to see the hoshpi-eyed worshipers anymore, wouldn't have to watch Kora's continued transformation into a puppet.

Kora bounded up and grasped her arms. "They love me! And they love you, but most of all, they love the goddess! Some of them have heard of her before, but not since they were little."

Natalya kept her arms crossed as Kora tugged at her. "They told you this?"

"I read their minds!"

Natalya frowned. She'd thought some of Gale's laws restricting the yafanai were silly, but she'd been raised among them, and prying into heads at random seemed wrong. Since she wasn't a telepath, she liked to keep her thoughts her own.

Kora's face fell. "What's wrong?"

"Maybe you should stay out of their minds."

"Why?"

"Because it's rude!"

Kora spoke those words again to herself, her face scrunched up as if trying to comprehend. By the Storm Lord, Natalya forgot how young she'd been when they'd gotten her. Finally, Kora shook her head. "When the goddess is with me, it's like…I'm a bottomless well. But when she's gone, part of her remains, giving me power, and it's the power they worship. Naos told me. So, how can touching them with what they worship be rude?" Her head tilted, but she wasn't looking at Natalya, and it seemed as if she was asking herself.

"Am I me?" Kora asked, turning her gaze to Natalya. "I have my thoughts, and she has power, but since I've got some, is there any part of me that's just me? Would they want me if I had power, but I was just me?"

Natalya sighed. "Best advice I can give you is that if you're alone in your head right now, you should enjoy it."

Kora's smile came out like the sun. "All right." She turned and regarded her gathering of followers again, the plains dweller camp that was growing bigger by the day. "We'll have to figure out something to do with all of them."

Nearby, a group was trying to put up a large tent, but one of the poles kept collapsing. Someone was yelling that they should have replaced the pole long before, and they all fell into what sounded like a long held argument. Kora crossed to them with eager steps and lifted the tent walls with her power.

They stumbled back, gasping and chattering, and she soaked in their praise like the child she was. Natalya leaned against a rock and crossed her arms again. Would Naos keep changing her? Would her thoughts continue to grow to match her body? When would the questions of a child become the demands of an adult? Maybe if Naos continued to groom her, they never would. After all, if she became troublesome, Natalya had no doubt Naos would simply hollow her out and leave her the puppet Natalya feared she would become.

And that was why she couldn't leave, the real reason. She had to see what happened to Kora. She liked to tell herself it was simple curiosity, that she'd grown used to Kora. They slept in the same tent. Everyone treated them as if they were mother and daughter. They ate together, bathed together, spoke first thing in the morning and last in the evening.

Natalya mocked herself, asking if she cared for the girl and sneering at the thought. Well, what if she did? But she'd only ever cared for people when they were useful, and she only worshiped the powerful. What she felt for Kora... Perhaps it was something in between?

The tent stood, and Kora ran back over. "So, if we're an army, we should attack someone, right? But I wouldn't kill them!" she said hurriedly. "We could just prove we're better."

Natalya sighed again. She'd forgotten that children could be bloodthirsty. Like with the chafa, it seemed easy because Kora didn't understand death. "Who would you attack?"

"Whomever we want," Naos said in Natalya's mind.

Kora beamed. "Welcome back, goddess!"

Natalya froze, wondering how long Naos had been lurking in their minds, listening.

"Now you see me, now you don't!" Naos said, and Natalya felt her amusement. "We do have to figure out what to do with all these people, and there are so many others on this ball of rock that could use a good kicking. Now that Dillon Tracey has Simon Lazlo, I don't want him getting complacent."

"Simon Lazlo?" Natalya asked. Hatred still burned in her, though it had cooled somewhat. Still, the root of this predicament led directly to him.

"That's right," Naos cooed, and her sense of vengeance slithered into Natalya, making tingles run from her heels to her hair. "If we play our cards right... Let's head east."

"Is that where he is?"

"No, but that's where he'll be if this all lines up correctly. Let's go poke the Sun-Moon, and see what runs out."

Natalya frowned. "And that will bring Simon Lazlo?"

"Enough talking. Kora, tell everyone we're marching tomorrow."

With a happy clap, Kora ran off to do the goddess's bidding.

But Natalya had too many questions. "If Simon Lazlo isn't there, what's the point of—"

"You're not for pointing!" Naos yelled, making Natalya cringe. "What are you, an Irish Setter?"

Natalya couldn't help a spike of anger. "Pawns are more effective if they know the plan they're supposed to be carrying out!"

"Oh no!" Naos thought, her tones like a mocking child. "She doesn't *wike* me anymore?" She laughed, too delighted by her own plans, it seemed, to mind Natalya's anger. "You're lucky I'm in a honey mood and not a vinegar one."

Raw power filled Natalya, spreading through her core and setting delicious fires through her body. She dropped to her knees and cried out in ecstasy. Why had she ever doubted anything Naos told her? This was a deity, the stuff of legends. Every qualm she had was nothing compared to this! "Oh, goddess! I'm sorry I doubted you!"

Naos roared with laughter. "All better now? Good, now get your shit together."

The power carried her through the day and well into the night, making it hard for her to sleep, even with the comforting warmth of Kora beside her. It helped the next day as they packed and began the ponderous task of moving east, such a large company going slowly, especially with children and the elderly. Problems arose and gnawed on the happy feelings still burning in Natalya's belly. As the power faded, the annoyances kept piling on until she ground her back teeth, hoping that Naos would give her another jolt. She began to consider leaving again, wondering if she was ever going to get out of this fucking loop.

Halfway through the day, Kora called a halt from where she rode a geaver at the head of the column. Natalya stopped fussing with an overturned cart and stomped to the front to find Kora staring into the wilderness.

"What is it?" Natalya said, pushing sweaty hair off her forehead.

"I've been here before."

Natalya glanced around, but it looked like any other part of the plains, rolling hills of grass interrupted by ditches and the jutting fingers of rock.

"The animals have been busy," Kora said. "The bodies aren't whole anymore." She turned flat eyes in Natalya's direction, her expression that of a person who didn't know how to process what she was feeling.

Natalya gasped as Kora's power drew her in. She sent her micro senses careening through the grass, finding bones scattered almost to the wind, the bones of her people. "This is where Maman and Shufu died," Kora said softly. "They're memories, like the spaceships and picnics and eating with Jack."

"Your mother and brother are *your* memories," Natalya said. "Those others are hers."

"Fatan might still be alive. Do you think I'd know him?"

"He wouldn't know you, sweetheart."

"I suppose." Kora touched her chest. "I should wear Maman's bones." Her power arced, lifting the bones from the nests of small creatures and calling them from the soil. As they hovered in the air, everyone watching gasped, and as the bones hurtled toward Kora, the plains dwellers cried out.

Kora's power turned inward, and Natalya felt it as she searched for some clue inside herself that would lead her to the right bones. When she had two skeletons before her, she knelt, lifting the finger bones of one and stringing them on a leather cord she pulled from a pocket.

She beamed at Natalya. "Now all my mothers can go and fight."

Natalya tried to return the smile, but she could only grimace. She couldn't feel Naos anywhere, not inside the girl and not echoing throughout her own mind. She remembered a time when Naos's absence brought hints of madness back, but it seemed like ages ago now, as if her mind had been recovering on its own. If she concentrated, she could nearly keep it in check. The key to not surrendering to the urge to tear the world apart was to use her power with tighter focus. Sanity was a scale, and the right amount of power needed to be poured into each pan.

"We'll camp here," Kora said.

Natalya walked away and didn't see Kora again until after night fell, when Kora crept into their tent and folded in beside her. Natalya fought the urge to sigh, though she found she didn't mind the need for contact as much as she used to. Now it was only the trust that made her shiver. Naos would forever take advantage of Kora, but at least with so powerful a guardian, no one else would.

"Leading an army is hard," Kora said.

Natalya chuckled. "Do we have to be an army?"

"Oh yes. The Sun-Moon killed my family, so there has to be revenge. That's what the goddess says."

Natalya sat up and fumbled around until she found a lamp. Once she lit it, she stared at Kora's wide, innocent eyes. "No, other plains dwellers killed your family. Don't you remember?"

"Like my army?"

Natalya scrubbed her hands through her hair. What the fuck was she doing here? "Yes, like the…army. Who they were or what they wanted, I don't know. Naos and I killed them."

Kora frowned, her mouth working as if reading an invisible page. "But why would the goddess lie?"

"Who says I lied?" Naos said to both of them, but before Natalya could shush her, Kora asked, "Who killed my family?"

"The Sun-Moon."

"See?" Kora said triumphantly. "Natalya was confused."

Silence hung in the air for a moment. "She was, was she?"

Natalya said nothing but kept her power quiet, out of the way, though she felt her shields strengthening as muscles might tighten before an attack. "I suppose it doesn't matter."

"Of course not," Naos said. "Different, the same, what are they really? I'm me and you, and you're me, too. Ha! That sounds like a children's song. The important thing to remember is that we're family, and now the plains dwellers are family, but the Sun-Moon are not, so they're the enemy. That's the way it works."

Kora nodded. "Someone has to pay."

Like she'd wanted Simon Lazlo to pay, the man who'd gotten her into this entire mess, and she still wanted to give him a smack for messing about with what he couldn't have understood, but that had faded, too. And now here they were, with someone having to pay for something, some need for revenge Naos had that was going unfulfilled, or maybe it was just the need she'd mentioned before about being the only god on Calamity.

She felt the goddess watching, but her power was too subtle to detect unless she wanted it known. Kora was staring at her patiently, hopefully, and Natalya gave her a smile. "Why don't we go to sleep?"

Once the light was out, they lay down again, but Natalya still felt Naos's spectral stare. She wondered if Kora felt it and was comforted by it.

"I've met people like you before," Naos said just as Natalya began to drift, making her jump. "You can't ever be happy."

Ringing started in her ears, but she fed power into it, trying to turn the tide, but this wasn't the madness inside her; it was the one without.

"I suppose it's my fault," Naos said. "I gave you a few inches. Why shouldn't you make a grab for the mile?"

"She's not a mile," Natalya thought. "She's a human being."

"Yes, my human being. Or do you miss the old days?"

Natalya's body jerked, but it wasn't a surprise this time. It was that same old sensation of someone trying on her skin.

"Do you miss me that much? Or are you jealous?"

The ringing built to a rushing noise, drowning out thought, turning over reason.

"This is how gods deal with disobedience," Naos said above the noise, her voice still calm, almost sensual. "We aren't friends, you and me. I'm as far beyond you as the stars in the sky."

Natalya's teeth dug into her tongue, and she felt her eyes roll back, her body shaking as raw power ripped through her. She couldn't form words. Thoughts blew away like dirt in a high wind.

"And wherever you go, I can find you."

Images flashed before her eyes, places and views she'd seen before every time she'd peeked beyond the curtain of Naos's mind: stars and planets and peoples.

As quickly as the attack had come on, it fled, leaving Natalya in the tent again, Kora sleeping peacefully beside her. Her muscles were still jumping, and tears streamed down her cheeks, though she hadn't cried in years. She wiped them away and tried not to give in to despair, but for the moment, she couldn't see a way out, not for her and definitely not for Kora.

What the fuck was she doing here?

CHAPTER TWELVE

L azlo heard wind chimes. He opened his eyes and tried to place the ceiling above him or the source of the breeze blowing across his skin. Curtains swayed in an open window, the sound of the chimes coming from beyond. His curtains. His room. Gale.

Something important slipped through his memory like an eel. Gale. Still in Gale. But why wouldn't he be? He wet his lips and looked for water. Pain arced through his temples as he sat up. He smoothed it away, but his powers felt soggy, his brain like a wet mattress. "What the hell?" He pressed the heel of a hand to his forehead.

Someone rapped softly on the door. "Come in?" Lazlo's voice was a croak. Had he gotten drunk the night before?

Dillon slid past the door, a hesitant smile in place. "Welcome back, Laz! How do you feel?" Hope radiated off him like a powerful smell.

"Did something happen?"

Dillon knelt by the bed. "Nothing a little time couldn't cure. We've been monitoring your progress, and the healers felt you wake up at last." He squeezed Lazlo's shoulder, affection rolling off him in waves.

That didn't sit right, either. "What the hell happened, Dillon?"

"What do you remember?"

He cast his mind back. "The boggins attacked, and we… A building collapsed on us?" The memory was hazy, fading in and out. He tried to read Dillon, searching for clues, but his abilities wouldn't work.

"That was nearly nine months ago, Laz. Your brain took a hit."

"Nine months!"

"You've been recovering—"

"My powers should have healed me long before now!"

"Brain damage, I'm afraid." The smile came out again. "But now you're back!"

"Was anyone killed?"

When Dillon frowned, Lazlo felt his real sorrow. "Quite a few people, I'm afraid. Samira among them."

The name felt as if it should have been ringing bells, like something on the tip of his tongue. "I'm sorry...I don't remember..."

Dillon clapped his shoulder again. "That's all right. The healers said there was bound to be some residual damage. You hallucinated quite a bit. Talked in your sleep."

Lazlo felt around with his power again and knew something was wrong with it. "My power is...less."

"It'll get better, especially now that you're awake again, now that you're yourself."

"I haven't regenerated you in a while."

Dillon grinned crookedly, something that had always made Lazlo's heart lurch in the past, but now there was barely a flutter. "You need to heal yourself first."

"I'm fine." He sent his power over Dillon, regenerating cells and tissue. Dillon gave that same appreciative shudder that always made Lazlo feel needed, but it affected him about as much as the smile now. He loved Dillon. Had loved? He felt intense loyalty all of a sudden, but that felt so wrong. He stood up, and Dillon took a step back, but if Lazlo had been lashing out with his powers while he slept, he supposed caution was necessary.

"I...want to take a walk."

"I'm not sure that's wise, Laz. You just woke up."

"I'll be fine. I feel fine." He spotted a pitcher of water and poured himself a cup. His hands shook as he drank. "I just need a few minutes by myself."

"I'll get out of your hair, and you can rest here."

"No!" He laughed to try to take some of the volume away, but he knew it sounded nervous. "Nine months is too much time spent here already."

"At least let me call someone to go with you."

He moved to the door, but Lazlo shook his head. "I'll be fine." Before Dillon could summon anyone, Lazlo pushed past him and fled down the hall. He fought the urge to hug his elbows. Every noise made him jump, every face made him wince. His anxiety hadn't been this bad in...

When? It had always been bad but was worse after he'd come to Gale. The boggin attack had made it worse. The thought made him want to cry, and he told himself to get it together. As he passed into the bright sunshine outside the temple, he paused, letting it warm his face. It had unnerved him when he'd first come to Calamity, but now...

Again, when? He'd been asleep for months. When had he gotten used to sunshine? Maybe they'd let him lay in it while he'd been asleep. He dived into the crowds, striding down streets. People took no notice of him. Signs of the boggin attack still littered the city; buildings were under construction, but any debris or bodies had been carted away. A few storefronts had a half-assembled quality as if the owners had run out of money or energy. Spaces loomed between houses, their former occupants torn down, and nothing new had replaced them. Smaller, shanty buildings stood in some as if awaiting something better.

All of it caused his anxiety to spike as he remembered the fight, the boggins, the progs, the terror. He shouldn't be there, should have stayed in the temple.

Shouldn't be in Gale at all.

But where else would he be? He'd been here since the beginning, been with Dillon since the beginning. They were in this together, would always be together. He didn't have any other friends. Pain careened through his skull as faces flashed past his mind's eye too quickly for him to focus on. He leaned against a railing and soothed the pain away, gasping, trying to hold on to memories that wouldn't stay still.

After a few moments of steady breathing, the pain eased, but the confusion wouldn't go away. How badly had he damaged his brain? How much had he lost? Now that his power was functioning again, he should only get better, not worse, so maybe...

As he used his power, he sensed a yafanai at work nearby, a telepath. He focused and sensed an intrusion in his own mind, something that wasn't supposed to happen in Gale. Lazlo pushed off the railing and looked back the way he'd come, spotting a man staring in his direction. As he watched, the man turned and glanced up and down the street as if trying to find his way, but obviousness radiated off him.

Lazlo frowned. A spy for Dillon? As he continued to stare, the man hurried into an alley. Lazlo started in his direction and felt a tendril of telepathy come his way again. "Got you." His own power followed the signal back, making the man easier to target. Lazlo clamped off the telepath's power and then sent a micro-psychokinetic shockwave.

When he turned into the alley, Lazlo searched the shadows and spotted the telepath lying in the gloom, paralyzed. Lazlo knelt at his side and hauled him into a sitting position. "Who are you?"

The telepath breathed hard, and Lazlo sensed the spasms in his muscles, his brain sending out random signals as it tried to right itself, but he could still speak. He clenched his jaw as if refusing.

Lazlo scrubbed a hand through his hair, angry but unsure how far he should go. "Dillon...the Storm Lord sent you? Why? Or are you some kind of rebel?" The people had reason to rebel, he remembered that, because Dillon had...

With a growl, Lazlo stood and paced up and down the alley. "What am I not remembering?" Swiftly, he knelt in front of the telepath's face again. "Did you do this? Did someone else? Tell me who you are!"

"Stephan," the telepath said. "I would never betray the Storm Lord."

"Good, fine. Stephan, if you're not a rebel, then he sent you to spy on me. You wouldn't do that on your own, would you? There are laws, aren't there? And the only one who can flaunt them is God." He nodded, trying to make things fall into place.

"He cares for you!" Stephan blurted. "You should feel blessed. He wanted to ensure your safety."

"And what could happen to me here?" Lazlo asked. "In his almighty city, what could happen that he couldn't save me from?" He barked a laugh, heard the bitterness, and again wondered why there was so much of it. Dillon's schemes had never bothered him this much before. He flexed his power to make sure he still could. "What could happen that I couldn't save myself from?"

Stephan stared as if he was a lunatic. "He told me you were injured. I was supposed to make sure you didn't relapse."

"Then why not send a micro?" He'd met a few; he remembered that. "Keffy or Leila or Horace?"

Again that pain, that tinny sound he couldn't dismiss. He had to lean against a wall and breathe. Memory fought for release like a moth trapped under glass. Maybe Dillon was right. Maybe he was only moments away from falling into a coma again.

"Go back to the temple," Lazlo said quietly. "I'll sense it if you follow me." He left the alley and wondered if he should follow his own orders, if he should rest. He couldn't do it, not yet, even if it meant risking a relapse, he couldn't be inside those walls with Dillon again.

❖

After Lazlo left the temple, Dillon didn't know what to feel. In some ways, it was the same old Laz, a little grumpy, a little quick to see the gloomy side of things. But there were little differences. That rage that had so surprised Dillon when Lazlo first left was still there, simmering. It was beyond any snit Lazlo had ever shown; it was the same anger Dillon had sensed when Lazlo had said that he'd attack with his power if Dillon didn't let him go.

Dillon couldn't have that. Once he'd set Stephan on Lazlo's trail, he went to Caroline's room, now next to Lazlo's, the better to keep an eye on him. She was sitting in her hammock chair, eyes closed, massaging her belly, and Dillon didn't know if she was resting after the work she'd done on Lazlo or if she was working on him from a distance.

"Can you do anything about his anger?" Dillon asked.

"His mind is strong," she said, not opening her eyes. "And his brain is constantly trying to fix itself. We have to work together to keep adjusting his memory. We can't match him, Storm Lord. I'm sorry." She sounded more than a little grumpy, too, but she'd earned it.

Still, he needed her to work a little harder. He massaged her shoulders, starting gently and feeling his way around the muscles until they gave under his fingers, and she stretched like a cat. He grinned where she couldn't see.

"I'm sorry for all this stress," he said softly. "I know it can't be easy to cope with, especially with the baby."

She sighed. "He squirms when I'm tense. His mind can't be quiet."

Dillon hid a shudder. She'd explained that she could commune with their unborn child; he didn't have fully formed thoughts but could exchange rudimentary feelings. She said the touch of her mind soothed him, but it gave Dillon the creeps.

"Soon now, you won't have to worry, and with Lazlo around, delivery will be a breeze."

She chuckled softly. "I have thought about that, believe me, after my sister."

A difficult delivery, if he remembered her story. He kissed the top of her head, and she reached to caress his hands. She loved him, and he did care about her and about the child. And unlike Lazlo, she wouldn't suddenly stop loving him and start treating him like shit.

"He'll fall in line," she said.

"Of course! You're the best." And she wouldn't read his doubt. She wouldn't dare; none of them would. "Is he...do you know if he's still in love with me?"

She went quiet, and he didn't know if she was hesitating or if she didn't know. "If he is, it's hidden under a cloud of anger. He knows something is wrong, Storm Lord. We'll have to convince him with words as well as this."

And that wouldn't be easy. Lazlo knew when Dillon was playing him. They knew each other too well. He sighed and continued rubbing, and they talked of mundane things until she tensed and grabbed her temples.

"What's wrong?"

"It's Stephan. Lazlo spotted him and sent him packing."

"Fuck! What does he know?"

She stared at nothing. "All I'm getting are hazy details at this distance, but there's no panic, so I don't think he knows more than he did when Stephan started following him."

Dillon strode for the door, but Caroline said, "I'm coming with you."

He didn't ask if that was wise; she'd know her limits better than anyone. He helped her up then forced himself to slow so she wouldn't fall behind. "It might be faster..."

She didn't give him a glare or a dark look. He was still her god, after all, but her chin lifted. As the strongest telepath, she was used to getting what she wanted. "You might need to knock him out again, and if I'm there, you won't have to hit him as hard."

Dillon supposed that was true. It wouldn't do to get Lazlo back just to bash his brains in.

Based on what Stephan had told them, Lazlo was somewhere near the warehouse district. Dillon hurried as fast as Caroline could go. The stink of hoshpis was worse than ever. The new drushkan envoy had made good on her promises to deliver more of the animals. She'd even given them food for the things, something he didn't know if the old drushka had bothered to do.

Caroline kept her telepathic probes to a minimum, and they searched for Lazlo the old-fashioned way, but the streets were crowded. A group of drovers herded several hoshpis out of their pen, and the beetle-like creatures bumbled about, bumping into one another and squealing, some of them humming a bass rumble.

Caroline grasped Dillon's arm. "Something's wrong."

"Lazlo?"

Before she could answer, one of the hoshpis keened, a harsh scream that made everyone grab their ears. The drover pushed toward the animal, but it kicked loose from the pack, breaking into a gallop as if someone had stabbed it in the ass.

Dillon launched a bolt at it as it thundered toward them, and it crashed into a small shanty, bouncing into a half-built warehouse, still alive and kicking. Dillon pushed Caroline behind him, out of the creature's path. The hoshpi clipped Dillon's shoulder and spun him around while Caroline fled into an alley beside the damaged shanty.

Dillon stumbled after her. "What the fuck happened?"

The shanty's supports cracked, the sound of buckling wood echoing up the street. It leaned forward, then slid sideways in a rush, slamming into Caroline and sending her to the ground. Its remaining stilts buckled, and the damaged wood fell on top of her, piercing her legs with bloody efficiency.

She screamed like a banshee, waking Dillon to action. He rushed to help, and the shanty groaned sideways, threatening to crush her. Dillon braced his feet on other side of her and put his back to the wall, trying to hold it aloft, his arms outstretched to catch as much as possible.

It sagged, and Caroline screamed again. Her telepathic power lashed out in waves, and Dillon grunted along with her. "Hold on," he whispered, both to himself and the shanty. He couldn't get enough air to call for help. Where the fuck had everyone gone?

A shadow moved across him as someone loomed in the alley mouth. Dillon began to wheeze for help when he saw the knife shuddering in the man's grip. Another assassin. Fan-fucking-tastic. He licked ragged, thirsty looking lips, glanced up the street, and then stepped forward, knife pointed at Dillon.

One bolt would finish him, but Caroline pressed against Dillon's legs, her nails digging into his calves. If he used his power, he'd catch her and the baby. What then? Let go? Blood already pooled where the shanty dug into her. It might sever her legs if it hadn't already. If he moved, the weight would finish her.

"Come on," he whispered as the assassin took another step. "Come on, you fuck." Fat raindrops pattered on his head, slithering down his neck. Had he called the storm, or was this some kind of poetic nonsense?

He told himself to keep holding, even if he was stabbed. Help couldn't be far. After this, maybe he'd wear armor all the time. He'd even left in too much of a hurry to grab his gun.

Someone else stepped into the alley and took in the tableau with wide eyes. She called out, and people seemed to appear from nowhere. It'd only been seconds since the hoshpi, but it felt like eternity. Now the people seemed motivated.

The assassin spun, but he wasn't fast enough. The people were on him in an instant. Young and old, they beat him with brooms or whatever they had to hand, the wet pounding sounds carrying between snarls of thunder. Those who couldn't get in the fight ran to Dillon and braced the shanty. At least some people in this town still cared about him.

Once they had it steadied, Dillon knelt next to Caroline. "Brace yourself, baby."

She wailed something, but he couldn't make it out.

"I know, I know. Just a few seconds more."

Those bracing the shanty counted to three and then lifted. The broken boards came free from Caroline's flesh with a wet, sucking sound. She screamed again, but it had a desperate, dying sound.

Dillon grabbed her under the arms and pulled her free, setting her next to the bloody lump of the assassin's body. He couldn't look at her mangled legs. She coughed as if trying to draw breath to scream.

"Call Lazlo," he said in her ear. "If you have any strength left, call for Lazlo. He'll fix you."

Her eyes squeezed shut, and he felt the call go out. No directed probes this time. Everyone would hear it. He gripped her hand, feeling her fingers weakening, wondering if it would be enough, if Lazlo would come, if the baby would be all right, if…

Someone gasped and pointed at Caroline's legs. Dillon watched, rapt, as the blood slowed, and the flesh began to knit together. Lazlo slipped through the crowd and knelt, grumbling as he worked, his hands passing over her legs. Her eyes had closed, face slack in sleep, her breathing deep and even.

"Laz," Dillon whispered, "the baby? My son?"

"Fine." He looked up at last. "What am I doing here?"

Caroline was still out, and Dillon didn't know if he meant here in the street or here in Gale or if he'd forgotten what he'd just done. "Helping, Laz. That's what you do."

Lazlo stared at him for a few painful seconds, but when Caroline's eyes opened, he gasped, one hand moving toward his forehead. "What was I saying?"

Dillon didn't answer, only helped Caroline to her feet after she assured him she was fully healed.

"I couldn't have taken this long to heal myself," Lazlo said, breathing hard. "I couldn't."

Before Dillon could say anything, Lazlo stomped away. The way things were going, they might have to keep him in a permanent state of confusion. At least he could still do what he did best, but Dillon was reminded of how much he missed the old Lazlo, the snits, the second-guessing. He didn't just want a healer, though he supposed he might have to settle for one.

❖

Samira's eyes flew open to darkness. "Simon," she whispered. The burn of lightning whipped through her memory along with a tattooed face and the drone of hundreds of insects in her brain. She sat up, and pain gripped her lower back. With a gasp, she grabbed at the rough bandages that swaddled her torso and eased back down.

"Have you learned your lesson?" a sibilant voice asked from the dark.

Samira squinted but saw nothing. "Are you drushka?"

"Ahya, it is Reach. I am tending your wound."

She tried to remember. "The Storm Lord took Simon, and then... that woman...her eyes." She shivered as she recalled her mind being overwhelmed by the widow. Only it hadn't been her, not exactly.

A rough touch grazed her bare shoulder, and she realized she was naked under a thick blanket. She sat up more slowly, and the rough hands helped her upright.

"The enemy hunt leader stabbed you," Reach said. "You were somewhat healed by shawness Horace, or you would not have survived to be tended by me."

Samira pulled the blanket up to her chin. She felt underneath her and found the rough texture of wood. "Where is Horace? Where am I?"

"You are underground among the roots of the tree. We thought it best to keep you in as much quiet as we could. You have been sleeping for a day."

"And Horace? Simon? Mamet?"

Light bloomed as Reach struck a match. As she lit a candle, the dancing shadows made the whorls on her face seem like a widow's tattoos, and Samira had to look away. She lay in a bowl-shaped cavern that was covered in the roots of the enormous drushkan tree.

Reach sat behind her and fussed over the bandages. "Taken, all of them, but we work to get them back." She muttered something as her long fingers probed Samira's side. "I will need to change the moss soon. You will tell me if you feel too warm or cold, ahya?"

"Yes." It came out a whisper. Taken. Her dear friend, his new love, and a young woman she'd grown fond of in so short a time, all gone in a moment. "The widow took Horace?"

"And Mamet."

Ice bloomed in her stomach. They'd called Mamet a vermin. And if they'd come all this way to kidnap Horace, they weren't going to give him back easily. "I have to help them." She braced against the pain and tried to stand, but Reach pressed on her shoulders, keeping her down. Samira took a deep breath. "I can make you let go."

"Ahya, then you would have to escape the queen's embrace to reach the surface, where many drushka wait, and all it takes is one scratch." She pressed the tip of a claw down hard enough to illustrate her point.

Samira fought down a wave of anger. A well-thought-out argument; that was what she needed, enough to make Reach see sense. As she tried to think, all her careful words abandoned her, and she fought down a sob.

Reach sat on the branch in front of her and began to sing. The tension melted from Samira's muscles. "Sa and Ashki hunt leader follow Horace and Mamet. Pool works with the plains dwellers and Liam to rescue shawness Simon. When you feel well enough, we will join them."

"They're still just *talking* about it?"

"Your mother should have named you Usta, the most stubborn of vines."

"What is the Storm Lord doing to Simon while we talk?"

Reach smoothed Samira's hair from her face. "And usta grows like fire, but some of the taller trees of the swamp would not be able to stand without its support."

Samira barked a laugh. "Who could I support right now?"

Reach spread her hands as if to say anything was possible. "Now, we will see if you can walk, Usta. If you can, we venture aboveground."

She put her hands on Samira's shoulders and leaned close. "Look in my eyes, Usta, and tell me you will not try to run from my care."

Samira sighed and pictured herself hobbling away only to collapse far from Gale. "I promise."

Reach stood. "I will find your clothes."

After she made a few stumbling circuits of the cavern, Samira refused to admit she was tired. Reach stayed by her elbow as she practiced walking, and she gritted her teeth whenever she felt a stab of pain. She wanted to see what was happening above, both to know what the drushka planned to do for Simon and also so she could see the sky and feel the wind. She didn't like the idea of spending more time trapped in the dark.

Finally, Reach agreed to go aboveground but ordered Samira to sit at Pool's base while she found out the latest news. The sun was high, and drushkan and human children played in the long grass while the adults went about various chores. Samira spotted a familiar face: Lydia, the ex-prophet of Gale. She seemed happier than when they'd fled, at least a little. Samira remembered that her lover had died in the boggin attack. When their eyes met, Samira smiled, and Lydia crossed over to sit beside her.

"How are you feeling?" Lydia asked.

"Better," Samira said, wondering if everyone knew she'd been injured. "You?"

Lydia nodded and watched the children play.

Samira hesitated then blurted, "Can you tell me what will happen to my friend Simon?"

Lydia's shoulders sagged. "It won't help."

"Why?"

"You won't be able to change anything. If I tell you your friend dies or you never see him again, will that stop you trying to rescue him?"

Samira shook her head hard enough to pull at her back.

"Knowing doesn't change anything."

Samira sighed. She knew that; she'd learned that, but she couldn't accept it.

Lydia gave her a wan smile. "I like the drushka. When someone told them I could see the future, they didn't see the point." She crossed her legs, leaning back and smiling. "I like minding the children. I've been watching Reach's son while she tends you."

"Which one is he?" When Lydia pointed at a human child, Samira frowned. "Reach's son is human?"

"Adopted when his parents were killed in Gale. Careful," she said, winking. "The drushka adopt us stragglers quickly."

"Don't worry about me. I won't be around long enough."

Lydia shrugged. Samira stared and wondered if she could have warned them about the attack or abductions. They could have prepared, but looking into the future made someone react, and that reaction changed what would have happened into whatever the prophet saw. Samira had never gone to see Lydia for that very reason. If the news they gave you was good, you could happily look forward to it. If it was bad, there was nothing you could do to change it. Your negative reaction might even cause the bad thing you were so worried about. Better to hope, she supposed.

Reach approached and helped her stand. "Pool wishes to see you, Usta, and you will have the news you crave."

"Usta?" Lydia asked with a chuckle. "I think you've been adopted already."

CHAPTER THIRTEEN

When the geaver stopped for the first night on the way to Celeste, Cordelia was tempted to thank the Storm Lord. She needed some time on flat ground just to quiet her roiling stomach.

"Fortunately for us, shawness Horace's abductors will have to stop as well," Nettle said as she looked to the east.

The trail hadn't been hard to follow, even as fast as the kidnappers had been moving. Nettle said she could have followed it blindfolded. Cordelia said she could see many uses for a blindfold until Nettle nipped her earlobe and told her to keep her mind on the mission.

They rode hard the second day and had to stop to camp again. The handler seemed content to sleep at the side of his animal, leaving the campfire to Nettle and Cordelia. She lay on a blanket, staring at the stars stretching across the night sky. She'd hoped the kidnappers would have gone to ground before then, but they seemed determined to ride all the way to Celeste. She wondered how Horace was, if he'd awakened yet, or if they were keeping him asleep. She hoped they weren't bashing his head in over and over. After a point, even he wouldn't be able to heal himself.

A tingle grew in her scalp as she realized there might be a way to find out. She glanced at Nettle, who seemed as absorbed in looking at the sky as she'd been. "I'm going to try something."

Nettle turned, and the firelight danced in her lichen-colored eyes.

"When I left my body before—"

Nettle sat up. "Sa, no."

"I know how to get back! I want to see if I can spot Horace."

Nettle's lips tightened, and Cordelia knew the idea frightened her. Cordelia had never heard such panic in her voice as when she'd thought

Cordelia had collapsed from some unseen danger. She'd once said she feared an accidental poisoning between them. She had to have thought that was what had happened.

"It's okay," Cordelia said, squeezing her hand. "I'll just be gone a minute. You were the one who said communicating like drushka could be a boon."

"Communicating, Sa. I said nothing about this leaving of the body."

"Scouting is quite useful, too."

Nettle looked away, but Cordelia knew she was weakening. "I do not like it."

"Only for a few minutes."

"One minute, as you said."

"That doesn't give me a lot of time."

Nettle gave her a long look.

"As short a time as I can manage, I promise."

Nettle didn't like being helpless, either, but she spread her hands at last.

Cordelia gave her a quick kiss and then focused on where they touched, at the light she sensed in Nettle even when ensconced in her body. She focused until she felt that uncomfortable tightening, but this time, she searched for the way out and found it within moments, leaving her body with a happy cry.

She eyed the silvery cord attaching spirit to body and then willed herself into the plains, following the kidnappers' trail in the moonlight. The dark landscape seemed a little brighter, and the light of another campfire shone like a beacon. She hadn't yet seen any humans who glowed like the drushka did, but now she spotted a similar light around this other campfire; it had to be Horace.

They didn't seem so far ahead, but she could fly as a spirit far faster than she could walk or ride. Some of the tattooed people were asleep; others sat on watch. Their leader sat next to Horace, and he seemed asleep, his chest moving up and down. Mamet seemed the same, though she'd been trussed hand and foot.

Cordelia lingered around the tattooed woman, trying to spot any weaknesses, to see if she spoke with or favored any of her fellows above the others, but she stared into the fire as if she could see into it, and for a moment, her face creased in pain before it settled. Nothing there.

Cordelia didn't want to make Nettle nervous, but she found her disappointment growing as she flew back to her body. She liked the physical world, some of it more than others, but she wanted to explore this new power. It…freed her. As she saw Nettle carefully watching her body and stroking her hair, she hurried. Nettle definitely fell into the "better parts of the physical world" category.

As Cordelia settled into herself and opened her eyes, Nettle's expression went from worried to relieved, and she pressed her thin lips to Cordelia's forehead. "Welcome home, Sa."

"Horace and Mamet seem all right, if that makes you feel better."

"It does not. I prefer your body and spirit to be in the same place."

"I don't know if we'll be able to take them before they get to Celeste."

"Then we will have to sneak in after them. I will try to send this to the queen, but I do not know if she will be able to hear me over such a distance."

Cordelia grinned. "I've got an idea. You can use me like an antenna."

Nettle frowned. "A what?"

"Try to talk to her through me while I'm out of my body."

"How would this work, Sa?"

"Let's just try." Before Nettle could argue, Cordelia left her body again. She floated high into the air, the silver cord trailing out behind her. The plains spread out below, their campfire a tiny dot. Flutters of fear went through her at being so far off the ground, but that only added to the exhilaration.

She felt Nettle's call and tried to send it outward, reaching for the connection she felt to Pool. Funny how just a few days before this had scared the hell out of her, but now, with others counting on her, it seemed like a fantastic asset. Strange how the reverse was true for Nettle. Cordelia could feel her worry even as they both sensed a dim reply from Pool, who seemed to understand the message, and Cordelia got the hazy impression that Pool would try to follow if she could.

After riding all the next day, the walls of Celeste finally loomed before them. They'd bypassed several small settlements after Horace's kidnappers did the same. Cordelia told the geaver and handler to go back. They would sneak the rest of the way on foot.

The stone walls were a dull pink in the light of the high sun, and people wandered in and out of large wooden gates. Pairs wore vests or robes that hung past their knees, flaring open over baggy trousers that were wrapped at the ankles and partway up the calves. Everyone wore light colors, standing out against the dark clay of the road and the green grass. Cordelia eyed the ballistae on top of the walls and smiled as she remembered the one her uncle had given her.

Nettle gestured toward the river that snaked along the city's northern side. The delta beyond was a riot of flowering plants, and in the distance, the ocean flashed like a mirror. "Perhaps we could find a way to swim inside?"

Cordelia bit her lip and shook her head. It had never been one of her strong skills, and even now, it brought memories of almost drowning in the jaws of a prog. "Let's get a couple of those robes and sneak in at the gate."

"One look at my face would give us away."

"Not if we wait for dark."

"You think shawness Horace can afford to wait?"

"I don't think they'd drag him here to kill him. They must need him for something."

"Shawness Simon was right, then. He burned out both their powers because he thought these gods could not resist them."

She nodded. "So, they might hurt him, but they won't kill him, and he can heal anything they do."

"I pity him. Perhaps they simply desire whatever it was that gave them long life, and if he does it, he will remain safe." She mumbled something that sounded like, "This would never have happened in the swamp."

Cordelia didn't agree, but she knew enough not to argue. Nettle missed her home. All the drushka did, even those who were incredibly open to new experiences, like Shiv. But as Pool often said, "Our legs speak to our minds and teach them to keep moving forward." No one was going back to the swamp while the Shi, leader of all other drushka, wanted them dead.

"Let's get closer to the road," Cordelia said. "Then we grab a pair of people, wait for dark, and see what this city has to offer."

Sunset gave them a momentous gift, several pairs of Sun-Moon worshipers herding a pack of ossors inside the city. They'd seen plenty of creatures out in the country, but perhaps these were destined to be sold in the next day's market. As Cordelia and Nettle sneaked from the long grass into the road, the creatures shied away from Nettle, keening harshly as they went.

Nettle veered away, but Cordelia continued straight on, headed for where she'd seen one of the worshipers. She crept up behind him, spun him around, and punched him hard in the gut. When he doubled over, she bunched her hands into one large fist and slammed it down on the back of his neck. He collapsed, and she turned toward where a woman's voice was calling. As an ossor pulled out of the way, revealing the woman, Cordelia gave her a solid punch to the jaw before she could cry out.

She dragged both bodies out of the pack as the other drovers called for their fellows. She waved, careful to keep her face low, and hoped that signaled that everything was okay. Nettle stripped the worshipers of their outer clothing and handed one set to Cordelia. She didn't even glance at the symbol on the back as she put it on. Months ago, when she'd been firmly in the Storm Lord's camp, such an act would have disgusted her, but they were all just humans now.

"The animals will not let me get close," Nettle whispered.

"Stay to the back."

She helped herd the animals from one side while Nettle lingered near the side of the road, waiting for the herd to pass. Cordelia heard the keening begin as Nettle got too close, and the other drovers called to each other. They couldn't keep this ruse up all the way to the gate, not with the ossors panicking and the drovers wanting to know what was going on. They were going to notice the gap in their ranks.

Nettle must have realized the same thing. She called out, clapping her hands sharply, and the animals began to run. The guards on the gate shouted as the ossors charged.

Cordelia ran with the pack, slapping the big insects on the rumps, trying to rile them up. While the guards were distracted, she ran inside the gate, Nettle sprinting beside her. She didn't even register sights and sounds, too busy looking for somewhere to hide in the dying light. They ducked into the first alley and took several winding, narrow passages, staying out of the press of people that lingered near the open gate.

Unlike the hard packed dirt of Gale's streets, these were mostly mud with boards or bricks pushed in at random. She thought she'd seen paving stones on the main street, but it was clear the local residents took care of the alleys themselves, or no one did. Windows stood high above, none within the reach of any thieves that might prowl the alleys, but lines of washing waved above their heads, most of it being taken in for the night.

Finally, they turned into another narrow street and found a wooden gate crossing their path. Cordelia smelled some sort of livestock beyond, as if the people kept animals on individual properties instead of housing them all in one district. Hopefully, it was something smaller than a hoshpi or ossor.

She tested the gate. Locked or barred. Nettle looked back the way they'd come. "Voices."

Cordelia put her weight on one of the wooden slats, and it groaned, probably meant to do so by an owner tired of having his livestock stolen. She froze, but when no one came from the darkened yard, Cordelia listened to see if the voices were getting closer.

She thought they might have to fight again, but Nettle put her back to the fence and bent backward, slipping between slats too narrow for Cordelia. Once through, she put her hands on the ground and sank slowly forward, slipping her lower half through until she could draw her feet after her, all of it without a sound. She leapt to her feet in one smooth movement and unbarred the gate from the inside.

"Show off," Cordelia whispered as she passed. "Impressive, though."

Nettle wrinkled her nose and led the way through the small yard, careful not to approach any of the darker shapes that lined the brick walls around them. They unbarred another gate and slipped down the next street, moving farther into the city. Soon, though, they had to admit they didn't know where they were going. Cordelia had been hoping to break into another major street after dark, but once they had, she didn't know which way to turn. Gale was laid out as a grid, and it was easy to see all the options, but all the large streets here had a gentle curve, as if Celeste was laid out in circles, and they built high, much higher than Gale, so she couldn't see the largest buildings from street level. It didn't help that she and Nettle had to shy away from everyone, turning down another street or alley whenever they approached a noisier building. Even in dim light, Nettle's features were too much of a risk.

"I feel we have seen this street before," Nettle said.

Cordelia nodded. She was beginning to feel the same. "I need to search for Horace again." Nettle sucked her teeth, but Cordelia didn't let her get any argument out. "We need a direction."

They took shelter in another alley, in the dark behind a cart. Cordelia slipped loose of her body easily and drifted high, searching for Horace's light. As she'd guessed, Celeste was a succession of rings, and she spotted his light, along with two brighter ones, inside the city's largest building, dead in the center. If she were a god, that's where she'd live, too. It was practically a palace.

As she floated back to her body, she spied several people roaming the streets near her hiding place, casting their heads to and fro as if searching. She fell back into her body with a gasp and drew her weapon as she stood.

"We've got friends."

❖

As soon as she'd given the healer to the Lords and secured the Engali vermin in the basement of the palace, Fajir had gone swiftly to the walls. She'd known someone would come after the healer or the vermin or both. The healer was too valuable, and she supposed even a vermin could have allies.

She'd watched the crowds wander in and out the gates. A few times, she was tempted to succumb to boredom and let her attention wander, but each time she thought of Halaan and what he'd want her to do. So she kept watching, disappointed when night began to fall and no one showed themselves. She supposed any rescuers might be waiting for darkness, but with the gates closed, they would find it hard to sneak inside.

When the ossor stampede started, she'd clucked her tongue as the guards scattered. She'd have to speak to their seren about discipline, then she peered into the dying light as two of the drovers sprinted through the unattended gates.

Heart pounding, she followed them with her eyes until she got an idea of their route, then she ran down the stairs to where Nico and her squad waited. They spread out through the alleys, searching, picking up a glimpse of the intruders from time to time, but they seemed determined to become lost. She recognized the woman from their earlier fight, and the outsider stuck out despite the sun-embroidered robe upon its slender frame.

Now one of her people signaled that the two had gone to ground in an alley. Perhaps they were resting; perhaps they'd stopped to find their bearings. It didn't matter. She crossed the street at a sprint and poked her head around the corner, bone sword drawn. The alley was empty. She turned and signaled, but no one had seen them leave. A torch flared at the end of the alley, held by one of her soldiers; no one waited in the shadows.

Fajir snarled. Impossible that she should lose them completely! She waved the torchbearer away, sheathed her sword, and lit her own light, bending to study the muddy ground.

A slight creak sounded above her, and she rolled forward. The female intruder landed where she'd been, sword out to strike. Fajir threw down her torch and drew her sword. Before she could call for help, the woman lunged, leading with a blade made of wood, and Fajir grinned. It would be easy enough to slice through.

Their swords caught with a hard thwack, but the intruder's sword didn't crack as Fajir expected. She stepped back, reassessing, then pivoted so her back was to the wall. There were two intruders, after all.

The outsider let go of a washing line and landed, flanking Fajir, and she cried out as both intruders rushed her. She blocked the woman's sword, but the outsider had two daggers that punched forward. Fajir used the flat of her free hand to knock one strike aside and then twisted her sword down to the left, sending the outsider's arm toward the woman and forcing them to avoid each other's blades.

"Nice move," the woman said. "How long can you keep it up?"

Fajir pushed herself against the wall. "As long as you like." Bluster, and she knew it. Both of the intruders took wary stances; neither seemed a novice. At any other time, she might have even admired them.

Nico rounded the corner, and the woman spun to face him. Fajir launched a strike at her back, staying ahead of the outsider, but the woman was craftier than expected. She turned in mid dash, caught Fajir's arm and threw her at Nico. They crashed into one another, and Fajir carried him to the ground. As the woman leapt over them, Fajir tried to scramble to her feet, but the outsider kicked the support out from under the front of a cart at the alley mouth, and Fajir rolled away, calling for Nico to look out. Debris spilled all around them, and by the time they regained their feet, both intruders had fled.

Cordelia headed straight for the palace, and this time, she and Nettle didn't try for stealth. They ran hard, trying to create confusion by starting fights with people that had spilled into the streets from bars or houses, leaving a clear trail, but Cordelia had no doubt their pursuers could follow them anyway. It was about how difficult they could make the journey.

And by the sounds behind them, their tattooed pursuers were giving a good chase. In spite of everything that had happened, Cordelia couldn't help admiring them a bit. Maybe it had been too long since she'd fought someone who came close to her level of skill in combat.

By the time Cordelia and Nettle neared the palace, the sky showed a hint of gray. To Cordelia's surprise, the large structure had only a half wall, more of a suggestion of a wall than a real one, but maybe no one dared steal from the gods, especially not since they could turn brains into pudding. No one stirred inside the quiet first floor, the space large and open, dotted with columns and little gardens. They headed upward. When Cordelia's nose told her they were near the kitchen or larder, she opened a door and peered inside, seeking somewhere to hide before anyone stirred.

Seeing only barrels and boxes by the light of a lantern in the hall, she crept inside, gesturing Nettle with her. "A storeroom. We can hide."

Nettle lifted the lid from a barrel, and the smell of brine filled the room.

"Something that's been pickled." Cordelia reached past her, took a rubbery plant from the barrel and nibbled at it. "Sour but edible."

She heard Nettle sniff and then a delicate crunch. "Ahya. Just."

Cordelia felt for another barrel and shifted it in front of the door before they settled at the back of the room.

"How will we find shawness Horace in this great mess?" Nettle asked.

Cordelia leaned against her. "He'll be wherever the Sun-Moon is. Higher up."

"We wait for darkness again?"

"Might as well get some sleep if we can."

Nettle's fingers trailed up her thigh. "Sleep only?"

In the dark, Cordelia grinned. "You told me to keep my mind on the mission."

"Ahya, but tonight we risk death. Why regret at the same time?"

Cordelia couldn't argue with that.

CHAPTER FOURTEEN

Shaman Ap huddled in the dark basement with what remained of his sorry tribe. They'd lost many on the long journey from the Deliquois Islands to cramped, crowded Gale, most to illnesses, others to strange food or creatures. Two had been killed by the Storm Lord, just as the Contessa had been killed, and they'd be as honored as the rest, but first they had to finish their mission.

The youngsters among them worked for money, cleaning and carrying for the people of Gale. They were stronger, and they learned the language faster than their elders. Ap's faith had carried him many times over the long journey, and now he depended on it to get him over the shame of depending on others for food and shelter. He'd learned some of Gale's language but stayed in the basement most of the time. The unfamiliar sights and smells alarmed him; he'd often thought himself a coward. He should be out seeking to destroy the Storm Lord.

The Contessa had taught him about the human body's weak spots, sharing the knowledge she'd shared with all shamans so he could better rule their people, but with no idea how to get around the Storm Lord's lightning, it was best to remain hidden. He might be his people's only hope for revenge, but he needed stealth to do it. Some doubted that it even could be done. A few had fled in the night, and he hoped the spirit of the Contessa followed them to their graves.

Et knelt beside him. As one of the elders, he helped keep the spirits of the others up, but Ap saw in his face that he was beginning to waver. "We need more food."

Ap nodded, but the money had already run out. "We can weave more baskets to sell."

"We have no more reeds." He sighed. "This god is powerful."

Ap took the knife from his belt and laid it in front of them to remind Et that he couldn't question the Contessa. None of them could. Et eyed the knife and shut his mouth slowly.

"The Contessa must be avenged," Ap said.

Et stared, probably wondering if Ap was speaking to himself as much as Et. Ap sometimes wondered the same, but that didn't change the fact that the Contessa *did* have to be avenged, and it had to be the Deliquois that did it. Maybe he should go after this god himself, but he feared the resolve of the others would crumble if he died. His apprentice had already been killed, and he had yet to begin training another. They might all die before they finally killed the Storm Lord, but Ap couldn't let them give up. If they all died, perhaps the Contessa would still—

In a flare of light, the Contessa appeared before them, scowling. Ap froze for half a second before he threw himself to the dirt floor in prostration, hearing the others do the same.

"You haven't fucking killed him yet?" the Contessa said, her mouth still not moving with her words.

Fool, to think he could doubt! She always knew! "Please, your magnificence," Ap said, "please, have mercy."

"One simple job to do, and there's so many of you. I'd think one of you had a brain in his head."

"He is so well protected, Contessa."

She slashed a hand through the air, and a high-pitched shriek echoed through Ap's skull. He covered his head and groaned.

"Do I have to do everything myself?" she asked. "I can't be everywhere at once, and if I'm too distracted…"

Ap risked a peek and saw her staring at nothing, her form wavering as if she couldn't hold it together. He supposed it was harder, being dead. "Please, Goddess, do not tire yourself!"

She didn't look at him. "Maybe I've been doing too much. Maybe…" She shook her head. "I need to think about this. I need to think about what else I can do." Her spectral form walked above the ground, back and forth, and Ap and his people continued to press their heads against the floor as the goddess paced among them, muttering to herself.

"I know!" she shouted. "It's time to lure him out of the city, bring him into the fray."

Hope bloomed in Ap's chest. It was exactly what they needed. Away from the city, it would be easier to strike at the powerful god.

He'd have less people to defend him. Perhaps Ap or one of the others could blend with the Storm Lord's shamans, his mind readers and the like. "Yes, Goddess! Your wisdom knows no bounds! Outside of the city, we will strike and avenge you!"

She beamed. "Or maybe there's a use for him yet."

Ap's smile faltered. "Goddess?"

"Keep trying to kill him. It'll keep him on his toes. In the meantime…" She grinned. "I'm sure I'll think of something."

Ap did not doubt it.

❖

Patricia Dué stared up at the perfect blue sky, an endless bowl of turquoise with nothing to mark it but the giant cable that reached up through the atmosphere: the space elevator that ferried people and equipment from Earth up to the asteroid that served as Pross Co.'s space station. Just looking at it made her sigh contentedly.

Underneath her head, Jack's stomach shook as he chuckled. She reached up and poked him in the side. "Be a good pillow."

He raised his head and smiled. "What can I say? Seeing my baby content makes me happy."

A harsh launch siren echoed through the park, and Patricia sat up, eyes locked on the cable. "There they go!"

Everyone turned to watch as a massive capsule slid up the cable, starting the slow, day's journey to the asteroid above. Patricia shivered as she watched. Only a few more weeks of training, and that would be her going on her first long mission as a copilot, her first real taste of responsibility. She was so ready, had been ready for a long time; her life was finally kicking into high gear.

She couldn't look at Jack, didn't want her excitement dampened by what she'd be leaving behind. He could never truly hide his disappointment or his worry. She didn't want to have to repeat that she'd be back, they'd get married, and go on as planned, especially since it might not be true. They'd both considered the possibility that she'd get a taste for long missions and not want to come back.

She tried to lay down again, to pretend her thoughts didn't exist, but he moved, and her head knocked lightly against a hard floor.

"Jack! What the hell?"

Another siren sounded, and she looked for the elevator, but it had gone, replaced by the gunmetal gray of a ship's hallway. Her ship. Her mission.

"Jack?" But of course he wasn't there, not on the *Atlas*. There was no one but her.

Unless... She leapt to her feet and ran for the lift. Maybe she wasn't too late. Maybe they were still here, and she could stop whatever was about to happen. She could warn them about the crash. She wouldn't be under that damn bulkhead this time!

Patricia punched the code for the bridge, and the lift doors hissed shut. When it slowed to a stop, she stepped out, mouth open to call a warning, but the same hallway as before greeted her, not one she recognized. She ran, looking for doors, seeing nothing but a gentle curve that seemed to go on and on.

She ran for the lift again, but after another short move, it stopped at the same goddamned hallway. She tried the botanical habitat, Chrysalis, the mess. Nothing, nothing, nothing. She slammed her hands against the controls and screamed.

The lift doors slid shut before opening immediately, accompanied by the ding of an elevator from an old vid. Patricia paused before stepping out on a marble floor, her sneakers squeaking lightly. She heard the tinkle of piano music, but she didn't want this memory, didn't want to dine with Jack again. She had shit to do, places to go, people to see, as the old saying went. She had—

Blinding pain ripped through her right eye, cutting off her vision. She bent double, pressing the heel of her hand to the spot, but she knew that wouldn't stop the blackening of her vision, the pain rattling through her skull, a never ending view of the entire cosmos.

She screamed again as her fingertips sunk past where her eyelid should be, searching inside her skull for what was no longer there. Power reared inside her like a bright light, and she tried not to reach for it, tried not to lash out against this pain. She pushed the power away and staggered back to the lift, blinking tears from her one good eye.

The lift opened, but instead of the car, she saw a bright green planet spinning against the darkness of space. She knew this place. Desperate, she focused and flew toward it faster than any tech would allow, hurtling toward a dark tent on a grassy plain and then through that, into the body of a sleeping teenage girl.

Her eyes opened, two eyes. What the hell? Someone had left a candle burning. Who the fuck used candles anymore? There was another woman asleep beside her and a lot of leather around, like something out of a vid about ancient people. Another dream? She touched her hair, the blankets. So real. She hadn't felt anything this real in a long time.

Strong hands slid over her shoulders, and she froze. The woman was asleep; no one else in the tent. She smelled her own lotion, and out of the corner of her eye, she saw her own hand resting on her shoulder, wearing her engagement ring. The breath on her neck had a wintry chill, cold as a dead star.

"What do you think you're doing, sugarplum?" her voice said in her ear.

Patricia breathed deeply. "I'm alive."

❖

Natalya stirred as Kora muttered something. She was about to go back to sleep, used to random mutterings in the middle of the night, but when Kora screamed, "Get your hands off me!" she bolted upright.

"Kora?" They'd left a damn candle burning, and Natalya snatched it up before one of them could knock it over. When had she gotten so careless? "What's wrong?"

Kora stared without recognition. "Who are you?" She looked over her shoulder and tried to slide away from something that wasn't there.

Natalya hesitated. "Naos?" Storm Lord help them all if the goddess was having a nightmare in Kora's body. "Is that you?"

"You don't know?" She crouched like a hunted thing, casting her eyes back and forth, head cocked as if listening. "Is Jack here, too?"

Natalya sent out a gentle tendril of power, looking for signs of Naos, for any sign that something had gone wrong in Kora's brain. She sensed the telepathic link that tied Naos to Kora and gave it a nudge to see if that would cure the girl of this madness.

The link pulsed with power, and Kora collapsed. Natalya let out a breath, her head pounding. She'd never used her power with such a delicate hand. The world began to press in on her as it had when she was newly augmented. She gripped her blankets and breathed deeply, fighting to push it away. She felt for Naos, for the sanity that power could bring, but the goddess felt far away, and when she answered, it seemed as if she was more than one person, each scrabbling for power, unable to help.

Natalya used the tricks she'd learned and bottled her power so the rising tide couldn't become a flood. She clenched and unclenched her hands to ease the power inside her; it felt like massaging the world's largest cramp, and when it finally eased, Kora was stirring again.

"Maman," Kora said, "I had a bad dream."

"Go back to sleep." But she stayed awake and watched until Kora breathed deeply again.

The next morning, Kora seemed back to normal, though Natalya watched her closely. Every day before they marched, she heard the petty grievances of the plains dwellers who traveled with her. And the more people there were, the more grievances to sort out.

Kora frowned as she listened. Two youngsters from different clans had pledged themselves together, then the girl of the pair changed her mind and bonded with another fellow. Now the tribe she'd originally pledged her life to claimed she'd been seduced away from them. The chance for new blood was always a sticking point with the small clans.

Kora stared at nothing after everyone finished shouting. "Didn't I just do this? You were arguing about spears."

Natalya sighed. "That was different people."

"Are you sure?"

This time, Natalya couldn't help snorting a laugh. "They do sound the same after a while."

"Please, Child of the Goddess," the chafa of the slighted clan said, "this cur seduced the young woman with promises of her clan's wealth, but—"

"I did nothing," the other chafa said. "The young people fell in love. Nothing can stand in the path of that." She seemed smug where the other oozed righteous anger. Natalya wanted to smack them both. What did they expect Kora to do?

Kora put her hands on her hips. "I can't believe this is what a goddess is for."

Everyone looked at everyone else. Word of the headless chafa had gotten around.

Kora snapped her fingers. "I know what the goddess would do! She'd kill anyone that wasted her time."

They all took a step back.

"Or are you asking me to kill the two young people?" Kora asked the irritated chafa.

His mouth worked for a moment before he shook his head. "No, Child of the Goddess. I thought perhaps you would dissolve the bonding..." He trailed away as if also realizing this wasn't what a goddess was for.

Kora's voice whispered in Natalya's mind. "They're afraid of me, but don't worry. I remember my promise. I won't kill them."

"Good," Natalya mumbled.

Kora's power flared and towed Natalya through the assembled clans until she found the offending youngsters. She lingered with them long enough to find out that while chafas argued their fate, they were spending time in each other's arms.

Natalya tugged Kora away gently, and when she could focus again, she saw that everyone was still watching them.

Kora sighed. "Love is love."

The smug chafa beamed while the other smiled hesitantly, probably too afraid to frown.

"Anything else?" Kora asked.

Everyone was quick to say no.

"Then get ready, and let's go."

When they were as alone as they were going to be, Natalya asked, "Do you know what that means? Love is love?"

"I can love. I had a fiancé once."

Natalya fought down a tide of anger. "That wasn't you." She took a few deep breaths. "Did you really think about killing them? I know you wouldn't," she added. "I know you promised, but I thought..." She wasn't sure what she thought. She'd wanted to teach Kora that death wasn't the answer, and with Kora's realization that death was forever, she thought she'd done it.

"The goddess would," Kora said. "Sometimes, I can't tell us apart."

Yes, that was the problem, wasn't it? Even if Natalya could break Naos's hold over herself, she couldn't break it over Kora, too. They were too connected.

Kora shivered, mouth turned down. "I don't like it, though. I don't like thinking of them dead, not when I know them."

Natalya smiled softly. So, Kora could change for the better. Maybe that was what the night before had been about? "Do you remember anything about last night? Your bad dream?"

"There was a different voice in my head."

Natalya's chest tightened. "Do you know who?" A fourth person in their crazy little head party, just what they needed. "I thought it was Naos."

Kora shook her head. "Too different." She smiled slightly. "I liked touching the lovers' minds. They weren't thinking about death or power. It was nice."

"Don't spy on people," Natalya said automatically, the habits of Gale never leaving her.

"Did you ever have a fiancé?"

The thought made her laugh. "No."

"What did you have?"

"I had…" Friends? Lovers? There had been Horace for the one, and as for the other, she'd never been interested. "I had a life. Sometimes, it was happy."

Kora entwined her arm with Natalya's, content for the moment, at least until Naos took over her mind again.

CHAPTER FIFTEEN

Lazlo looked queasy, and the birth hadn't even started yet. As soon as Caroline had called for Dillon, he'd called for Lazlo. He didn't want anything to fuck this up. After he'd almost lost Caroline and his son to some nameless assassin, he'd been careful indeed.

And thoughtful. It was time to go on the offensive. No short forays into the plains. He needed a long campaign to start bumping his enemies off one at a time. Whoever these assassins were, he'd burn them out at the root, get whoever was in charge. And wherever he went, the assassins currently in Gale would probably follow him, and he'd take care of them, too.

Right now, he had the birth to worry about. As they walked toward the birthing room, Dillon rested one hand on Lazlo's shoulder. "Make this quick, okay? I don't want her to suffer."

Lazlo was frowning at nothing, his usual expression. "I've never delivered a baby. I've heard the time varies for everyone."

"Once you get the hang of it, you'll be able to make it go as fast as you want."

"Nice to know one of us is confident. Are you afraid of being bored?"

Dillon tried not to snap, but this attitude was getting on his fucking nerves. And none of his tricks worked on Laz anymore. Somewhere along the line, Lazlo had become immune to his charms.

They entered the birthing room together. Caroline was on a bed with an elevated back, allowing her to sit up. There was also a contraption in the corner that looked as if it would help a woman stand if she preferred.

Different yafanai stood around the room, but after a look at Dillon, they cleared out. Caroline's eyes widened as they left. Some were healers, and she probably feared being without them.

Dillon took her hand. "We don't need their help with Laz here." Lazlo didn't offer comment. Dillon kept his smile. "It'll be all right."

Lazlo's eyes slipped shut, and Caroline gasped. "Well," she said with a sigh, "it doesn't hurt anymore."

"You've been communicating with him," Lazlo said. "He's calm."

Caroline smiled, but Lazlo didn't look at her. His eyes opened slightly, and he hesitated before taking hold of the sheet that covered Caroline from the waist down. She glanced at Dillon before pulling her knees back and spreading her legs so Lazlo could see what was happening. Dillon was happy to be standing at the head of the bed. He'd never seen a birth in person, but something about staring at her...downstairs business with Lazlo beside him seemed wrong.

Dillon expected Lazlo to be the most embarrassed of the three, but he put on a professional air, and Dillon wondered if he'd helped birth animals in his biology studies. Maybe. Or maybe this detachment was part of the work Caroline and the other yafanai had done on him.

Or maybe he was just in the zone. He reached between Caroline's knees, and she looked to Dillon again, giving his hands a squeeze.

They both went silent, and Dillon looked from one to the other. "What's happening?"

She stared at nothing but still had an intent look. Lazlo's eyes had gone half-lidded, and Dillon noticed they breathed in time with each other. He shuddered and tried to tell himself not to be paranoid, but the silence was creeping him the fuck out. He cleared his throat. "I'm—"

"Shh," Lazlo said. "We're working."

Dillon's irritation inched up a notch, but he kept his mouth shut.

"Push," Lazlo said quietly.

Just like that? But Caroline grunted, and her eyelids fluttered as if she fought sleep. How much was Lazlo doing? Could she feel any of the birth pangs? Feel the baby as it left her? He barely had time to look from her face to Lazlo again before Lazlo was standing, a baby in his arms.

Dillon's mouth fell open. Just like that! Lazlo passed a hand over the baby's face, and he began to cry, a howl that filled the room. Caroline's eyes flew open, and she sobbed once, a happy sound as she came out from whatever stupor Lazlo had put her in.

Lazlo pinched the umbilical, sealing it with his powers. He laid the baby in Caroline's arms before turning his attention to the afterbirth. Dillon tuned that out and felt a smile overtake his face as his son squalled.

She kissed the baby's bloody forehead. "I never dreamt it would be so…easy."

He grinned harder. "I don't think it usually is."

She gave him a confused look, as if she'd been drugged. "Love's not usually easy?"

"I, uh, thought you meant the birth."

She looked back to his son. "I meant falling in love. I'm in love with this little guy. I was before, when we communed, but it never hit me until now." She kissed him again, and Dillon wondered if she'd let him go long enough to wash him.

"Well…" Dillon didn't know what to say, but another thought popped into his head, one he should have been thinking about, but it had totally slipped his mind. "What are we going to call him?"

"Evan," she said without missing a beat.

His old man's name, something he'd told her during one of their many pillow talks. Pride filled him, tainted with a bit of guilt that he hadn't given this as much thought as she clearly had.

"Thanks," he muttered. "That's…thank you."

She flashed a glorious smile.

Lazlo left without a word, and Caroline's friends hovered in the doorway. Dillon wavered, torn, before he said, "I'll be right back." Caroline's friends hurried to fill the space he left.

"Laz," Dillon said, hurrying to catch him. "Wait a second!"

Lazlo didn't look at him. "Congratulations. You should go back and be with them."

Dillon used to pride himself on how well he could read Lazlo, but now he wished for a little of that micro power. He couldn't tell if Lazlo was embarrassed or jealous or what. "Talk to me, buddy."

Lazlo's eyes bore into his, stricken, covered in tears, and his forehead was creased with such confused pain that Dillon nearly called the whole thing off and started working on a plan to let him go. "I'm missing…" Lazlo thumped his chest with an open palm. "Something is missing, and there's so much to feel, but I can't get at it!" He pointed down the hall. "I delivered a baby, and I can't feel anything."

Dillon rested a hand on his shoulder. "Take it easy, Laz. You'll be okay." God, he really wanted that to be true. He knew abducting Lazlo was a shitty thing to do, but he hadn't had a choice. He did want Laz to be happy, knew he could be happy if he'd just give this a chance.

Or maybe he wouldn't. Maybe he'd dissolve into a depression so deep, no one could get him out. Fuck, maybe Dillon would have to let him go.

For a moment, it seemed as if Lazlo might sag against Dillon and let himself be embraced, but he pushed away. "This isn't right. It isn't what I want." His eyes searched the hallway as if looking for something just out of sight.

Dillon supposed they could leave him in the plains or maybe walk him back to the rebels. His own memories would return in time. Of course, then he would hate Dillon even more, but wouldn't that be better than this?

Down the hall, Evan started to cry again, and Dillon thought of all the things that could have gone wrong, even with the healers. He thought of all the other women who'd soon be having his children. Beyond that, there was a future full of aches and pains, aging and death. Who would look after his children, his people?

His hand tightened on Lazlo's shoulder, and he thought loudly back at Caroline, at the other telepaths, hoping they'd pick up on the fact that he needed them. "It's all right, Laz. You and me, buddy, the way it's always been. I'll never leave you."

Lazlo's face relaxed, and Dillon knew the telepaths were working on him. He let himself be hugged from the side.

"I'm here whenever you need me," Dillon said.

Lazlo wiped his eyes on his sleeve and nodded before walking away, his panicky motions more stable. Dillon watched him turn the corner before letting out a long breath. Such a delicate balance, but he could have everything: Lazlo and his children and the people of Gale.

"And me," a voice said in his mind.

He sighed, hearing not only Naos but Carmichael, Paul Ross, Amy Lessan, and Marie Martin in that voice. "Whether I want you or not, apparently." When he turned, Naos lounged against the wall in her evening gown, arms behind her, head tilted to the side as she watched him with her good eye.

"How long have you been here?" he asked.

"Long enough to see your loin fruit. Well done."

He scowled. "What do you want?"

"Ooh, Daddy is ferocious." She snapped her teeth. "Mama likes."

"You want to see ferocious? Don't you have some worshipers on the plains? Want to see me wipe them out?" Yeah, that was the way. Kill them one at a time until he'd gotten them all.

"Come and get me, sugar. After I kill the Sun-Moon, you're next on my list."

He thought fast. "If you wanted us dead, why not kill us on the *Atlas*?"

"Why? Why? Why? I've got a why for you." She pushed off the wall. "Why does everyone keep asking questions? Kill my people before they kill you. That's the game! That's all you need to know! Who will be the last god standing?" She put her hands to her cheeks as if surprised, and her face lit with delight. "Oh golly! I hope it's me." With a laugh that echoed through his skull, she walked through a door as if it wasn't there.

Dillon hesitated a moment before he followed, checking to make sure she was gone. The room stood empty, but when he turned, Lessan waited behind him, face twisted with rot.

Dillon yelped and jumped back. Lessan popped like a balloon before she became Naos again, her laughter so loud it sent pain bouncing behind his eyeballs. He strode away, wanting to check on Caroline and Evan, just in case.

Even after he'd seen them, he couldn't get Naos's words out of his mind. Why in the hell was she attacking the Sun-Moon? And was she egging him on to get him to come or to get him to stay away? She could come after him next, and who knew why? Maybe there was no why. Hell, maybe she was just bored. Maybe having people with her on the station had kept her entertained, but once they'd all left, she realized how boring life could be without them.

And how deep was she in with the plains people? How far up their asses did her reach go? Was she talking to the rebels, too? Lining up all the pieces on the board? He'd heard there were people who were so good at certain games that the only real challenge they found was in playing themselves. Maybe Naos considered herself on that level.

And what the fuck did that have to do with him? He was already taking his troops out again. Now, especially as he had Lazlo on his side, he could wipe the rebels out, and maybe seeing them dead would help Lazlo find some calm.

He headed to his office. Time to start planning in earnest.

❖

Caroline lay in the dark with little Evan sleeping on her chest. She'd heard the Storm Lord's call, and even though she hadn't wanted to, she'd sent her mind out and soothed Simon Lazlo's troubled thoughts. She supposed they could break him given enough time, and he was powerful, but sometimes, Caroline didn't think he was worth the trouble.

A day ago, she would have censured herself for such a thought. Even a few hours ago, she might have done the same, but something had happened when Evan had moved through her, when he'd been brought into the world to breathe his first breath, when he'd lain on her chest, so warm and alive. She'd been nurturing him in her body for months, but now she knew he was a person, her little person, her little boy.

She kissed the top of his head as she'd done countless times already. When her friends had taken him to wash him, she'd missed him! Only three feet from her, and she'd missed him achingly, had nearly cried because of it. She knew what was happening inside her body; she knew about hormones and such. She'd smiled as her healer friends had told her again about the changes in her body, but that didn't change how it felt to be on the non-academic side of her emotions. They could theorize, but they couldn't know; feelings swept over her like the tide, and nothing in her wanted to fight them.

As much as she loved the Storm Lord, he'd been trumped by this tiny person in her arms, thoroughly beaten. She'd never expected that. She still loved the Storm Lord, but if she had to make a choice…

She clamped down on the thought. The telepaths in the temple still abided by the old rules of not listening to one another, but now they had the added edict, "unless the Storm Lord tells us to." As the most powerful telepath in the temple, she'd know if someone was prying into her thoughts, but she thought it best to keep her surface thoughts as quiet as she could. She made her shields tight enough to keep from reading others and to keep her own thoughts from wandering around. She'd never worried about it before, and she suddenly wondered who else might be having such thoughts. Perhaps the other women who were bearing the Storm Lord's children. Or maybe they wouldn't be like her until their children were born. Maybe not even then.

Now she did feel a stab of guilt. The Storm Lord had brought nothing but good things. He was a powerful, brilliant, handsome man, and she knew she should feel lucky he'd taken an interest in her, let alone doing her the honor of bearing his child. But when Evan made a gurgling noise in his sleep, she focused on him, and her heart didn't go back to normal until she'd checked to make sure he was all right.

Guilt again. She sighed and let her mind wander to Lazlo's. He was still awake. She'd been checking in with him, but he didn't seem to do more than stare at the walls and try to figure out why he felt so terrible. They should have been using healers on him as well as telepaths, but his own micro powers were too strong, and he'd catch them even more quickly than he did the telepaths. Still, her touch was gentle. After he'd healed her in the street and again during the birth, she'd felt a little bad about what they were doing, even if the Storm Lord wished it. She had a sudden thought about what it was like to be him, to have his memories altered. She wondered what it would be like if someone made her forget Evan when she knew she should have him.

Tears hovered in her eyes. Too painful. No, it was much easier to be angry with Lazlo for distracting the Storm Lord and tearing him away from his new child. She had no doubt he'd have been with her and Evan all afternoon if Lazlo didn't need so much handholding. It was clear he didn't want to be there, so why not let him go? Or if that was too dangerous, kill him. The Storm Lord wouldn't even have to do it himself. As Lazlo struggled against the telepathic blocks she'd hidden deep in his mind, Caroline soothed him again, wishing he'd accept his new mind and get on with it.

Evan stirred, and she kissed his soft head again. She'd have to hand over Lazlo duty soon. Evan's greedy tummy needed to be sated, and she wouldn't feed him while poisoning someone's mind. She sent a telepathic message to Marcus, asking him to watch over Lazlo while she nursed. A sleepy affirmation came back.

Caroline let her mind envelop Evan's, basking in his contentment. They were both drifting on a happy little cloud, when Caroline felt a ping from Marcus. Lazlo was asleep and dreaming. Soon he'd be having nightmares, but they'd dealt with those before. She told Marcus to keep her informed if there was an emergency, hoping he'd get that she wanted to be left alone.

Still, Marcus must have been searching for a way to keep himself awake; his updates became more regular. Lazlo's dreams were taking a bad turn. He was trying to remember the people he'd left behind, those the Storm Lord didn't want him to remember. Marcus was trying to shoo his mind away from those people, but there was a stubborn pair, Samira and Horace, former yafanai, and those memories were—

Shock hurtled through Caroline's body, a telepathic quake that made her cry out, jerking in her chair. Evan began to shriek, and Caroline gasped as pain careened through her skull. Lazlo had broken free of his telepathic blocks.

She sent a desperate call, and one of her friends stumbled through the door. She passed Evan over when every inch of her was crying out to hug him close and protect him. She didn't lay a telepathic blanket over his mind, didn't want to silence him that way. Her friend followed as she helped herself along the wall. She wasn't hurt; Lazlo had seen to that, but her body was still tired. She didn't know if she should be up and walking, but she had to hurry.

Other yafanai were in the halls, all of them wondering what the telepathic shriek had been. She gathered a few telepaths in her wake and sent them pouncing on Lazlo's mind. Working together, they weakened his mind and hammered him back to sleep. "Redo the blocks," she sent to the others. "And erase this evening."

They sent that they would, and she felt them go to work.

She opened the door to Marcus's room, but she already knew what she'd see. He hadn't responded to any of her calls. She sent for a healer and kept everyone outside as she stared at Marcus's still form, his bulging eyes, face creased in horror. Lazlo had sent out some kind of micropsychokinetic pulse, seeking whoever was feeding the blocks, probably thinking they were feeding his nightmares if he was thinking at all. More likely, he'd lashed out in his sleep, and his power had followed Marcus's like a fish after a lure.

The healer told her what she already knew. "I can't bring back the dead."

She choked back a sob. She and Marcus had trained together. They'd been close once, even lovers a few times. He didn't deserve this.

The healer shrugged. "Maybe Simon Lazlo—"

"Shut up," Caroline said. "Oh Marcus, I'm so sorry." Even as she wept for him, she checked on the other telepaths. Simon was asleep again, and the blocks were being rebuilt. He'd remember nothing about what happened, about what he'd done.

"What happened to Marcus?" the healer asked. "What did you feel?"

But not everyone knew about the Storm Lord's orders, and she couldn't explain. She wrapped her mind around the healer's before he had time to think. "He had a heart attack. It happens sometimes."

He nodded. "Shame."

Yes, it was. One that could have been avoided, and a small voice inside her said that this wasn't only Lazlo's fault. It was the Storm Lord's as well. As she thought of who else could have been caught in the pulse, those who could have been killed, like her and Evan, her guilt couldn't even rise to the surface.

CHAPTER SIXTEEN

Horace wasn't alone in his head. The dark, hollow place around him was one he only visited in his dreams, where a faceless figure sometimes chased him, but a new presence awaited him now, a dual presence, male and female combined. He tried to hide in the corners of his mind, but there was nowhere they couldn't find him.

"Good," the two voices said together. "If you've realized that, it'll save a lot of time."

With a burst of courage, he came out of hiding. It was his mind, after all, and these were intruders. He fought down every stray thought he'd ever had about not being good enough or powerful enough and transformed the darkness into a courtyard in the Yafanai Temple, a place he'd always felt at home.

At least until the Storm Lord arrived.

He shook away the dark thought and felt the sun on his shoulders, the gentle breeze that found its way through the open space. "Come out where I can see you."

They materialized in front of the table where he'd often communed with his fellow healers, Simon included. He'd seen them before, in the fields east of Gale. They were some of the gods Simon had been afraid of.

"The Sun-Moon," they said together. "We need your help."

He sighed. "Of course you do. Everyone else does, and instead of asking, you just take."

They tilted their heads. "We hoped Dr. Lazlo would be with you."

"If this is the way you treat your visitors, I'm glad he's not." He tried to wake up and leave his mind, but their power held him here. "You don't have to do this. I've never turned away anyone who needed healing."

"We couldn't risk it."

"I can't do anything for you if you keep me trapped in one corner of my mind, cut off from my power."

They released their hold enough so he could scan them. Telepaths, with one a macro-psychokinetic and one a pyrokinetic. Powerful enough to play with his mind however they wanted, but they couldn't alter him physically. Still, he didn't let himself think of escape, taking the problem one step at a time. He scanned them deeper and gasped.

"You have the disease! The same as the plains dwellers."

Their mental projections leaned on each other, blurring at the edges. "It spreads every day, and now that we're here, now that we're mortal..."

"You want children." He nodded slowly. "Look, you've been in my head. You have to know by now that I'll help you."

"We couldn't ask while you were near the Storm Lord. He can't know."

"Do you think he'd attack if he thought you were weak?"

He read their frustration. "He's...unpredictable."

That was true, but it didn't make it less infuriating to be kidnapped, especially not when Simon needed his help more than these two did. "I don't know if I can cure you on my own. With the plains dwellers, it took two of us."

"You must try." They stepped closer. "You know we can force you; we don't want to."

As if he wouldn't try, and being in his mind, they had to know that. But it seemed no matter how often he told them, they'd still rather threaten. Maybe that was the way it had been for them and their kind for too long, and they didn't know any other way to act.

The weight in his mind lifted, and he opened his eyes, sad that he wasn't in the courtyard but slumped on a divan in a large, open room. The Sun-Moon sat a few feet away, curled together on their own couch and staring at him.

He took a long look around, noting two doors and several open windows with the light of either early morning or late afternoon. He wondered how high up they were, thought of Simon's tales of escape. After he helped them, maybe he could do the same.

The Sun-Moon smiled. "We have a foothold in your mind," they said. "Nothing you can do will shake us loose."

He raised a finger. "Ah, but I only thought of escaping *after* I've tried to cure you. Or is that your not-so-subtle way of telling me you're never going to let me go?"

They didn't answer, and he saw no alternative but to cast his powers over them, looking for the disease and wondering what he could do when he found it without Simon to help.

❖

Once the light coming from under the door dimmed, Cordelia and Nettle sneaked out and along hallways that were open to air and light. When they reached an intersection, Cordelia waited while Nettle climbed outside the palace, along the frieze on the walls, scouting. She scuttled back after a few seconds and dropped to the floor at Cordelia's side.

"I saw our friend from earlier," Nettle said. "She walks the halls with her fellows, and her face is very angry."

"Shit. It's only a matter of time before they go room by room." She tapped her chin and tried to think fast. A quick jaunt outside her body had showed Horace on the highest floor of the building, and he wasn't alone. If someone raised the alarm before they got to him...

"How easy was it to climb out there?"

"For a drushka?" She spread her hands. "For a human, it could be difficult."

"But not impossible."

Nettle wrinkled her nose. "Nothing is impossible for you, Sa."

Pride and a bit of embarrassment washed through her. "We'll see."

Luckily, the people of Celeste tended toward heavy decoration on their buildings, especially the one dedicated to their most important denizens. Cordelia had no clue who had lived here before the Sun-Moon came to Calamity. Maybe they'd requested somewhere ornate to live should they ever want to visit. Maybe they'd been planning to do so for years.

Whatever the reason, Cordelia found plenty of handholds in leering gargoyles or ornate flowers. And the pale stone of the building stood out nicely even as the light of day faded, leaving them in moonlight. As she found another handhold and searched for the next, she wondered how many times the palace was broken into by the less faithful. But her next foothold felt more slippery than she'd thought. It took her weight, but her foot slid along it, and all the other holds within reach looked equally slick. She wondered if it was a coincidence or if she'd blundered into some kind of thief trap. Either way, she couldn't stay where she was, sliding into oblivion.

Nettle's hand clamped down on her wrist. The smooth surfaces didn't seem to bother her, and she'd clambered up the wall like a sticky-toed lizard. Her long fingers found cracks and crevices that Cordelia couldn't wedge her hands or feet into.

"You must jump when I say so, Sa."

"Where?"

"Straight up. I will guide your hand to a crack in the wall."

Cordelia glanced upward and saw nothing. "I don't see it!"

"Trust in me. Jump!"

Bending as much as she could, Cordelia jumped. Both her feet came free, and Nettle rammed her hand into a crack, sending spikes of pain through her fingers. She pushed downward, trying to hold on while her feet found two more sculptures. They were as slippery as the others, but the handhold made it easier to thrust her knees into the wall. She steadied herself as Nettle gripped her elbow.

"What the fuck are you holding on to?"

"There are many such cracks in the wall. Not as many as in a tree, ahwa, but enough."

Cordelia looked down and then up again quickly. The ground was too far away to believe, and she tried to hold on to that. "Fuck. This was a terrible idea. Why didn't you stop me?"

Nettle leaned far out, almost standing out from the wall. She made it look so easy. "It is not so high."

"How much farther?"

"I will see." She unhooked her feet and brought them to her chest, working her foot in under her current handhold. She bounced twice before letting go and lifting straight up on one leg. When she reached her full height, she passed her hands over the wall calmly, as if there wasn't a huge drop below, found a suitable handhold, and dug in before starting the process again, swinging up the wall as easily as Cordelia could stroll down a street. She disappeared from sight and returned a minute later.

"Not far."

Cordelia tried to hold in the disbelieving laughter. "You should go on without me."

Nettle started to help her upward again. "I would sooner leave my eyes behind."

"Sweet talker." She grunted as she pulled herself up.

"Have your mouth speak to your limbs and teach them to move. The wall is your enemy, Sa hunt leader, and I will help you defeat it."

When they finally reached a balcony, Cordelia didn't know if it had taken hours or days, perhaps years. She collapsed and breathed, her muscles reduced to burning liquid. She half expected their tattooed friend to be waiting and applauding, but they saw no one, and the room beyond was dark.

After a few moments of breathing, Cordelia eased upright, and she and Nettle slipped into the dark room, guided by a faint light coming from a room next door. They tiptoed around an empty bed and knelt next to the door, hearing voices before Cordelia opened it a crack and looked through.

She saw Horace first, sitting on a couch across the room, facing the door. His eyes were closed, but he was speaking to a pair who sat on a divan with their backs to the door. She'd seen them before, outside of Gale and when she'd scouted outside of her body: the Sun-Moon.

"We sensed you on the wall," they said without turning. "You could have taken the stairs, you know."

Cordelia looked at Nettle and put her hand on her sword. Nettle took hold of her daggers, and together they rushed into the room. After one step, Cordelia stumbled as buzzing filled her ears. Up became down, and the world turned on its ear. She fell forward, overwhelmed but still trying to curse as blackness closed around her.

Horace watched helplessly as Cordelia collapsed behind the Sun-Moon's divan like a toppled statue. Through the buzzing in his mind, he could only fumble for his power. He couldn't even call a warning.

Nettle sprang through the doors after Cordelia, and the Sun-Moon's power stabbed for her mind, too, but she wasn't alone in her head. No drushka was, as Horace had found out when he'd tried to use telepathy with them before. In her mind, they found the link to Pool, one that had gently denied Horace entry, but now it flared with the combined mental strength of the drushka. Nettle pushed back with evolutionary power, and the Sun-Moon slumped on the divan.

Their hold on Horace slipped. The Moon hurled Nettle across the room with her macro ability. Before Horace could try to cripple her, a sword point rammed through her chest from behind, through the divan. Cordelia was awake.

Blood dribbled from the Moon's mouth, and she stared at the sword point poking through her chest. The Sun screamed and leapt to his feet. Cordelia stood, leaving her sword where it was. The Sun's gaze locked on her, and his power coiled and burst outward, surrounding Cordelia in a shroud of flame.

"No!" Horace wrapped Cordelia with healing, keeping the flames at bay, though they swirled around her, trying to blister and maim and kill. Cordelia staggered, and through the haze of flame that consumed her clothing but left her whole, her eyes widened in wonder. After a moment, they rolled, and she collapsed again, but this time, Horace felt something odd about her, as if her mind slipped free.

Nettle leapt on the Sun's back and smacked the side of a dagger against his temple. He fell, and the flames winked out.

Horace scrambled to his feet and went to Cordelia, but he'd shielded her completely. She wasn't even warm. "Did she...did she leave her body?"

"Later. Are you well, shawness?"

"Yes, but the Moon won't be for long." He took hold of Cordelia's sword and before he could think too hard about it, yanked it free. The Moon gave a gurgling shriek. Horace dropped the blade and put his hands on her shoulders to slowly close her wound.

Nettle covered Cordelia with a small rug and then moved to face the Moon. "Is it wise to heal her, shawness? I know it is your nature, but she is powerful."

Horace clamped down on her macro power once he was sure the sudden shock wouldn't kill her. "I'm keeping her power subdued. I can't break her telepathy; her connection with the Sun is too strong. Since telepathy doesn't work on you, we should be all right. And if we let her die, I doubt we'll make it out of here alive."

Nettle looked at the Sun as if entertaining the idea of killing him, too, making sure they'd have a better chance of escape, but Horace shook his head. He wouldn't let her kill someone who was unconscious, and he knew Cordelia wouldn't like that, either. Luckily, Nettle didn't press, watching Horace work instead.

He moved around the divan, healing as he went. The Moon's eyelids fluttered, and she wiped the blood from her chin. He filled a glass of water from the pitcher on the table and handed it to her.

She took it and looked from him to Nettle. "Well?"

"You and your mate have stolen our shawness," Nettle said. "We will take him back now."

"We need him." She glanced at where the Sun laid on the carpet. "I'm guessing he'll be all right?" Her voice was even, but Horace sensed her fear.

"You have the same disease as the Svenal," Nettle said. "Do not bother to lie. You have the same smell. To cure this sickness, you need two shawnessi, Horace and Simon, and Simon has been taken by the Storm Lord."

"We know. We never should have let Lazlo go, but we were hoping to catch both of you at once. We can't lose the one healer we have."

"We're in your city," Horace said. "I know it would be a big fight to leave. Lots of people would get hurt. You'd get hurt."

She stared.

"I don't want that," he said. "I don't like hurting people, but Nettle is right. Help us get Simon back, and we can all work together." He nodded toward the back of the divan. "Or would you rather try to argue with my stabby friend?"

The Moon seemed to consider, but the other door burst inward, and the same tattooed woman that had captured him stepped through, followed by a host of guards.

❖

Just as when Cordelia first left her body, the pull of being killed and healed at the same time threw her spirit out. She catapulted into orbit again, and before she had a chance to look for any smidgen of her lifeline that might have followed her here, the same immense presence as before moved toward her, the copilot.

"It's the little bee! Have you reconsidered my offer? Come to stay?"

"Just an accident, sorry," Cordelia said.

"I'm surprised no one's squashed you yet."

Cordelia had to chuckle, even if the copilot made her so nervous it was hard to think. "The Sun-Moon just gave it a good try."

The presence moved closer, though Cordelia still saw no body to speak of. She did see something glittering in the distance, the sun striking metal in orbit.

"The *Atlas*," the copilot's voice said in her ear. "Impressive, no? You little groundlings are always so hungry for metal."

"A ship?"

"Once, now a satellite, though I suppose it could be a ship again if it were properly motivated." She sighed, and her voice seemed to change a little, sounding lost but infinitely more human. "The skip drives are broken. We can't go home."

"Right. Speaking of home…" She tried to drift away, but the presence held her like an anchor.

"Did you say Sun-Moon?" it asked in its normal, confident voice. "Are you a pain in their ass?"

"Um, when I'm not on fire, but I just came for my healer."

"Are you in the market for a new god? I've got lovely rates and a free gift!"

Cordelia didn't know how sarcastic she could be given the fact that the copilot could keep her here.

"Naos," the voice said distractedly. "I liked being the copilot once, but now it's all Naos. Ooh, tell the Sun-Moon I'm coming for them, but use a dramatic voice, something impressive. Think seer, like a vid about ancient Greece."

"Sure," Cordelia said, still lost but unwilling to argue with someone who could pluck things out of her head. "You're coming for them personally?"

"No, silly, with my army. Didn't I mention?" She sighed. "I have an army, and it's really big, and I'm coming for the Sun-Moon and maybe the Storm Lord is, too, and I'm going to be the last god standing unless someone is as entertaining as you." She said it all in a rush. "Have I forgotten anything?"

"How big of an army?"

"See how focused she is! You should be mine, you know. Just a little more drifting, and I'll add you to my collection!"

The shining *Atlas* was coming closer, or maybe she was getting drawn in by it, though she didn't know how that was possible in her spirit form. A suffocating feeling overcame her, drowning or being buried alive, she couldn't tell. "No."

The voice kept chattering on, and Cordelia started to struggle, but if the copilot, if Naos, was paying attention, Cordelia couldn't feel it. She gasped for air with no lungs and fought to get away, to help Nettle, help Horace, warn everyone about this disembodied madwoman who claimed to have an army on Calamity's surface.

The babble faded, and she sensed someone else, that lonely presence who'd spoken of skip drives. "Go," it said.

The space around Cordelia lightened, and she struggled free before she was hurtling toward the planet again, streaking into her body like a falling star.

When she opened her eyes, the first thing she noticed was the foot in the middle of her back. The second was that the floor was ice cold beneath her, and the third was that she was naked and partway under a rug.

"She's awake," someone said.

Cordelia tensed. One good push...

"Leave her be, Fajir," someone else said. "Everyone, be calm."

"That's a good idea." She knew that voice, Horace.

When the foot lifted, she shifted away, standing and taking her rug with her. She saw her blade and scooped it up before moving to the corner of the room where Nettle stood with Horace. She wrapped the rug around her like a towel, but it was barely big enough to go around her hips. Liam would have made some crack about sexy fighting.

The Moon still sat on the divan, healed; must have been Horace's doing. The Sun was slumped beside her, and she and Horace were staring at one another, probably having some kind of mental standoff. Behind the divan stood the tattooed woman, Fajir, Cordelia guessed, and a host of other guards, all with weapons drawn.

"What did I miss?" Cordelia asked.

Nettle kept her eyes locked on the guards, her daggers drawn. "We have explained that we need shawness Simon if we are to...aid these gods with their problems."

The Moon inclined her head. So, there was some secret at play.

"She's going to help us get him back?" Cordelia asked.

"We do not relish an assault on Gale," the Moon said.

Naos's conversation played through Cordelia's mind. "You might not have to." Quickly, she told them what Naos had told her, her references to the *Atlas* and skip drives making the Moon's eyes widen and hopefully backing up her story.

Still, when she told them that an army of indeterminate size and maybe the Storm Lord were coming to attack Celeste, Fajir said, "Lies."

Cordelia sighed, but she would have thought the same thing. Skeptical always looked good on a guard, especially a leader.

"Will you permit me into your mind?" the Moon asked.

Cordelia looked to Horace, who nodded slightly.

Nettle tensed again. "If anything harmful happens to Sa…"

Fajir took a step forward. "You'll do nothing."

"Enough," the Moon said. "I think we all understand one another."

A tingle passed over Cordelia's scalp, but nothing as great as before. If she hadn't known what was happening, she might have thought it a stray breeze.

"She's telling the truth," the Moon said, her voice disbelieving. "What is Naos playing at? Why attack us? Why now?"

"Could you ever get a straight answer out of her?" Cordelia asked.

The Moon ignored that and stared at nothing.

"The Storm Lord may bring shawness Simon to us," Nettle said.

"I know he'd agree to help you in order to keep the peace," Horace said. "So would I, but you have to put an end to these threats, thinking you can take what you want. We don't work like that!"

"Shut your mouth!" Fajir barked.

"Here's your chance to prove you're better than the Storm Lord," Cordelia said. "We could be allies."

The Moon tilted her head and nodded. "Heal the Sun, and we'll talk about it." She gestured over her shoulder, and Fajir and the guards sheathed their weapons.

CHAPTER SEVENTEEN

As the soldiers and yafanai made preparations to leave Gale, Dillon felt freer than he had in months. He knew people bothered him as little as possible with the day-to-day running of the city, but the chance to leave it all behind was nearly as freeing as when he'd first left the *Atlas*.

There were some drawbacks. Little Evan would have to be left with a nurse. A stricken look had taken over Caroline's face when he told her he needed her to come. He'd had to massage and cajole; hormones were probably screaming at her to stay with her baby. He'd promised they'd be gone as short a time as possible, and she'd agreed. Still, he wasn't looking forward to the crying ahead. He'd make sure she had her own tent so they could have a little space.

All that was left was to wonder whose side he'd be on when he reached Celeste: Christian and Marlowe against Naos or the other way around? If they killed all of Naos's troops, they still couldn't get at *her*. She'd make more eventually, but with Lazlo in Dillon's camp, he could kill them forever, too. Might be nice to have a recurring enemy to knock around. On the other hand, if Christian and Marlowe were dead, Dillon would be free to pillage their city, maybe convince their followers to turn to a stronger god. He'd have to think of a better name than Celeste; that was for damn sure. Unless the former Sun-Moon worshipers decided Naos was the better god. Or she decided it for them.

No, better to hide and watch at first, let them tear each other's throats out, and he'd mop up whomever was left. As strong as they all were, he had yafanai, railguns, and powered armor. He'd mow down the remainder and pick through what was left.

In his mind, he counted the yafanai. The pregnant ones would have to stay behind, as well as the youngest acolytes. The others could either ride on carts or be bolstered by Lazlo and the healers. His armors could pull the carts. He'd bring a few servants along, people to cook and clean and fetch. Maybe after the plains dwellers saw the full might of Gale, they'd join the ranks of his faithful.

After a few sessions with Caroline, of course.

❖

Lazlo read every emotion in the Yafanai Temple as news spread that they were going to Celeste. It didn't matter who'd spoken to whom, or who was supposed to be keeping quiet about what. There was no stopping a rumor once it got started, especially one as tantalizing as a big fight. Some were calling it a war, even.

He'd have thought they'd had enough of combat. Some still spoke about the night of the boggin attack in hushed or angry tones. Some were too traumatized to speak of it at all, but others were excited for war, and he wondered if they were the lucky few who hadn't had to fight, who'd managed to hide and not lose anyone they cared about. He couldn't believe such a person existed. They had to be as rare as unicorns. He laughed harder when he realized the Galeans wouldn't have any idea what that was. He'd been laughing a lot at random things lately. When someone caught him, he blamed the brain damage, and they nodded sympathetically, which made him laugh harder.

Well, some of them nodded sympathetically. Caroline was a ball of anger. With her deft touch, he hadn't caught her poking around in his mind again, but she could probably do it so he wouldn't feel her. Still, once he knew how angry she was with him, he couldn't help seeking her out with his senses, as if her anger brought him clarity. It felt worlds better than Dillon's hope or anyone else's sympathy. Her emotions seemed pure, and as he sat in the courtyard of the temple one day, he remembered something similar Dué had once said.

He'd been sitting in the mess, nursing a cup of coffee and reading one of the many novels stored in the *Atlas's* computers. Sports fiction, he'd read it before, probably a hundred years before that moment, but because of the way his brain regenerated, he remembered it exactly. He'd been trying to forget that fact, trying to lose himself in the story, when she'd come in.

Her steps were always jerky, as if she couldn't find a rhythm. She took a seat near the wall, facing the door, her left eye darting around the room, but at least she wasn't focused on him. She didn't get any food, nothing to drink, and he was starting to think he should leave when she spoke up.

"It's nice, isn't it?"

Lazlo didn't know if she was talking to him or not. She didn't look at him, and he didn't know how to respond, so he slid off the stool and headed for the door.

"Linear emotions," she said. "A nice good fight."

Yeah, she probably didn't need his help with whatever she was doing, but a half second later, the door slid open again, and a couple of breachies walked through, having an argument. They didn't seem to notice him, and he had a brief thought that he was either invisible, or it was time to swing his power around a little.

But of course, he never did that. Funny thing was, they didn't seem to notice Dué either, and everyone noticed her. She wore a broad smile as the breachies argued about one of them saying something the other thought was insensitive, and he was suddenly so glad he didn't have a love interest on board, lonely as that was.

Unless he counted Dillon, which he was not doing that day.

"One following the other," Dué's voice said in his mind. "Cause and effect."

He looked back to her, but she'd vanished, and he realized she'd never been there at all. She'd been projecting herself in his mind. Her chuckle echoed in his head, and he brought his shields around as tightly as he could, hoping that if they didn't keep her out, she'd at least take the hint. The arguing couple looked at him at last as if sensing his power.

"Sorry," he mumbled, even though they were the ones who'd ignored him, but now he'd gotten their attention. Cause and effect. "Sorry."

At the time, he hadn't worked out what she meant, but now he had an inkling. Caroline was angry with him, and she had to have a reason, a real reason. The sympathy givers and Dillon, they felt sorry for him, and their reason was that he was injured, but that rang false.

Caroline felt right. He'd done something, and now she loathed him. Cause and effect. He went inside, searching for the bright light of her anger. When he found her holding her baby and talking to some people near the kitchen, he thought he'd open with an inquiry about the child's health then lead into what had been happening between them, but he knew the child was fine.

He blurted, "What did I do?"

Their conversation went silent, and he felt shock from Caroline as well as the loathing. "What?"

"Don't play games with me, not you, too."

People were staring, and she grabbed Lazlo's arm and led him away from her friends. Stunned, he went along. Only Dillon grabbed him. Other people didn't touch him at all, and he preferred it that way. No one had gone out of their way to make him feel welcome since...

Who?

He snarled and jerked his arm back. "What the fuck is going on?"

"Watch your mouth," she said, glowering. "You want to know what's going on? Do you? We're in mourning."

"For...the boggins?"

She sneered and opened her mouth then shut it again. "For Marcus."

He searched his memory and came up with a face glimpsed only a few times. They'd never spoken. "One of the telepaths."

"One of us. He's dead."

"I'm sorry. Was there something I could have done? No one called for me, did they?" He tried to think, but his brain felt so muddy.

Her expression went from angry to unreadable, and he sensed anger mixed with sympathy, but it felt truer than the sympathy of others.

"I don't think there's anything you could have done," she said quietly. "And you're right where the Storm Lord wants you to be, so..."

A strange phrase. "He wants me to be near the kitchen?"

She sighed and rubbed her forehead. "Thank you for helping with Evan. I appreciate it, but unless we have to speak, I'd rather we stay away from each other." She held up a hand before he could ask why. "That's just the way I want it, all right?" She stalked away, and he couldn't follow, couldn't disregard her wishes so casually. Funny, no one had ever loathed him before.

Well, he had the effect. Now he just had to find the cause.

❖

Samira listened to the rumors about what was happening in Gale and tried to think of what it might mean for Simon. To the drushka, Gale had seemed busier. They were gathering wagons just outside the palisade on the eastern side as if preparing for some kind of market day outside the city, but they'd never done that in the past. It worried everyone, and she heard more than one person saying the Storm Lord was finally coming for them.

Liam, an ex-paladin, tried to comfort everyone, and Samira watched his efforts with interest. He had a nice, smooth way of talking to people, a sense of humor that made people relax, but the way he spoke to those who were eager to do battle with the Storm Lord made her think he wanted that, too, that he was hoping the Storm Lord wanted another fight.

If so, he was a fool. He'd seen the weapons and armor. How did he think the drushka could compete with that? Samira sat cross-legged in the grass, and Reach sat next to her after a moment to check her bandage. With her ministrations, the wound was healing nearly as fast as it would if tended by a yafanai.

"Why would the Storm Lord retreat from his attack once he had Lazlo," Reach said, "only to come back again? Is there something else he wants?"

"The rest of us? Simon said he was greedy."

"Ahya, it could be."

"Do you want to fight him, Reach? For killing Paul Ross?"

Reach went silent and stared into the fields. "When Paul first died, I would have given anything to tear his murderer to pieces, but I saw how grief infected Sa and some of the others, and I knew it was like a wound. It would never stop bleeding unless staunched. And I saw the value of living in little Paul, in Sa, in others." She wrinkled her narrow nose. "If the opportunity came, I would kill the Storm Lord, but I will not rush in foolishly to do so. I will not risk all."

Samira nodded. She felt the same about killing, but she'd risk all to save her friends, the little family she'd put together. "If he is coming, maybe there'll be a way to grab Simon."

"You think the Storm Lord will leave him behind, and we can sneak him out of Gale?"

"Or if he brings him, maybe we can take him back, whatever will get the least of us killed."

Reach chuckled. "Or none. Prefer none, Usta."

"If he comes this way, do we run? You know what he can do, and I know you don't want to risk the tree."

Reach tilted her head. "And what do you know of the tree?"

"I know it moves. It's the drushkan home, right?"

Reach wrinkled her nose again. "An apt word. You know we drushka communicate over distances."

"Like telepaths." She frowned. "Are you telling me the tree has something to do with that?"

"Ahya. Now the queen has felt a disturbance from Nettle. She fears they may be in danger."

Samira nearly held her breath, thinking of Horace and Mamet. "Anything specific?"

"Not over such a distance. But if the Storm Lord comes this way, perhaps it would be better to move toward Nettle and Sa and see what has become of them."

"What about Simon?"

"We will not abandon him, Usta, fear not. The drushka can be in many places at once."

Comforting words, but as the day wore on, she found herself looking more and more to the west, toward where Gale lay over the rolling hills. She tried to hold on to the hope that the drushka wouldn't abandon her, that Cordelia would succeed in freeing Horace and Mamet, that Simon would be all right until they could get to him. She tried not to think about all the bad things that could happen, tried not to wonder about the various outcomes, if the Storm Lord would kill them all.

When she saw Lydia again, Samira knew she'd been secretly looking for the ex-prophet, even though she knew what Lydia would say if asked to see the future. When Samira struck up a conversation, she tried to talk of anything else, but Lydia sighed.

"I've seen that expression before. The answer is still no."

"I was trying really hard not to ask."

"Were you hoping I'd offer?"

"There are too many possibilities!" Samira sat down heavily. "I want a little assurance that everything will be all right."

"Okay. Everything will be all right."

Samira gave her a flat look. "You didn't..." But she didn't know what Lydia using her power looked like. She'd heard the gift of prophecy worked quickly. Or was it the curse of prophecy? "Did you..."

Lydia's smile turned sad. "I was more in love with Freddie than I ever thought I'd be with anyone. After she died, I couldn't help thinking I should have seen her future sooner. And I *know* it doesn't help. And then I had to reassure myself that I did the right thing. I would've seen her die, only I would've had to wait for it to come, devastated before anything ever happened. That's all that seeing the future can change: how you deal with what's going to happen before it happens."

Samira lined up a row of arguments in her head. If she'd seen Freddie die, surely she could have avoided it, maybe even left Gale before the boggins came, but if she'd seen Freddie die in Gale, something would have happened to drag them back.

Lydia was staring, and Samira nodded. "I understand," Samira said. "If there'd been something you could've done, you would've done it."

Lydia shrugged. "As long as I'm not looking, it's as if events are uncertain, but after I see them, there's no turning back." She rested a hand on Samira's shoulder. "So, everything will be all right."

"Thank you," Samira said. "You're a good person, Lydia. I'm sorry I didn't get to know you and Freddie better."

"We were in our own little bubble most of the time." Her lips quirked up. "And how do you know I'm a good person?"

"A bad one would've done what I asked and let me suffer."

She chuckled softly. "Freddie always said you seemed sweet." She walked away, and Samira let her be, thinking on the possible futures again and promising she would try her best to make sure everyone she cared about made it out alive.

CHAPTER EIGHTEEN

Of all the fights Cordelia ever imagined being pulled into, one between the Sun-Moon—Horace's kidnappers—and the enormous presence of the copilot—through plains dweller proxies—had never occurred to her.

She supposed they could try to run. The Sun-Moon had given her, Nettle, and Horace a room in the palace, one close enough for easy mental eavesdropping. But now that the Sun-Moon had seen into all their minds but Nettle's, Cordelia got the idea that the telepathic duo could "follow" them everywhere.

Late in the night, she asked about Mamet, and the Sun-Moon turned her over to Fajir, saying that they'd promised Mamet to her, and Cordelia would have to bargain to free her. She dressed quickly in some borrowed clothing before returning to the guard captain, or seren, as they called her.

Even though Fajir had kidnapped Horace, Cordelia couldn't help but admire her, seeing in her some of the qualities Cordelia valued most in herself. She supposed that if the Storm Lord hadn't proven himself to be a murderer, she'd be even more like Fajir, still serving as a lieutenant in the paladins, one day to be captain.

Fajir eyed her new clothing and smirked. "What happened to your rug?"

"I'm saving it in case we dine somewhere fancy. Give me Mamet."

Fajir sneered and said nothing.

"Now, now," Cordelia said. "We've got a deal going on with your gods. Don't make me knock on their door."

Fajir turned away and muttered something about vermin as she walked down the hall. Even that didn't faze Cordelia. After all, she'd once had some very uncharitable thoughts about Sun-Moon worshipers. Hell, "vermin" might have been one of them.

Of course, that didn't mean Cordelia wouldn't give Fajir shit about it. Paul had once told her that the way to see a person's true nature was to ruffle their feathers and see what dropped out. "Don't like Mamet's people?" Cordelia asked as they walked. "Or is it all plains dwellers that you're forever crying about?" She gestured to Fajir's cheeks.

Fajir took a deep breath, but Cordelia saw redness creeping up from her collar. "They killed Halaan, my true mate."

"Mamet did? When?"

"One of her kind, just before the Lords arrived."

Cordelia licked her lips and thought about what she'd do if someone killed Nettle, if she was now being led to a corpse. "Is she alive?"

"Yes." But there was the barest hint of a pause.

Great. If Mamet had been harmed, Simon wouldn't cooperate easily. Of course, given how he'd spoken of the Sun-Moon, he wasn't going to cooperate easily anyway. At least Horace could fix whatever had been done, but Mamet wasn't likely to forget. And the Sun-Moon wanted them all to stay in Celeste until Naos's army had been dealt with. That might be a hard sell to someone they'd tortured.

And torture didn't sit well with her, no matter the cause. If someone killed Nettle, she wanted to believe she'd rip them apart and be done with it, no need for torture. She didn't even like kicking an opponent once he was down. She looked at Fajir again out of the corner of her eye. If it had been a person rather than the swamp that killed her parents, and that person had gone on living, would she have turned into Fajir? The Storm Lord knew she'd beaten up enough people in impotent rage, even though no one caused her parents' death.

But the Storm Lord still lived, and she wasn't out to torture all the faithful she could get her hands on. But then, she'd seen the universe, learned that the living were more important than the dead. Maybe no one had ever bothered to tell Fajir.

"Did you get the one that killed Halaan?" Cordelia asked.

By the tightening of Fajir's face, Cordelia guessed no.

"The Storm Lord killed my uncle, and I never got revenge either," Cordelia said as they turned down a long hallway and started down a staircase.

"Why not?"

"I would've been killed if I'd tried, and my people needed me. The living are more important than the dead. Since you're here leading your people rather than out hunting plains dwellers, you must understand that."

Her nostrils flared, and she gave Cordelia a look that said she'd rather be out there than here serving her Lords, but she didn't seem as if she wanted to say so aloud. "I will have my revenge one day, and until then—"

"Until then, you should do your duty and leave the rest of the plains dwellers alone." It came out angrier than expected, and she knew she was speaking to her slightly younger self, the one that had broken more than a few bones. There could have been greater injuries, too. She'd never stuck around to find out.

Fajir turned on her. "I cannot reach the one that killed Halaan while I serve the Lords! I must do something so his spirit can rest!" Her hands curled into fists, and Cordelia saw her own anger reflected back at her. Fajir threw one hand into the air. "I don't expect a heathen like you to understand. You can have all the lovers you want, but you'll never have a partner."

"That is so…" Cordelia took a deep breath. Now was not the time for a religious debate. She tried to think of what she would have wanted to hear. "So go after the one that killed Halaan. Take off, and get it done."

"I can't abandon the Lords! And I couldn't ask my fellows to do the same."

"Go alone."

She leaned back as if slapped, and Cordelia realized she'd never been alone in her life. A moment passed, and Fajir shook her head. "Do you want your vermin or not?" She strode away again.

They went down to a basement underneath the cool ground. The only light came from infrequent torches, and they did little to drive off the darkness. The Paladin Keep had a few holding cells, but nothing like this dank dungeon with its many wooden doors, damp walls, and sense of terrible purpose.

Fajir paused. "You said the Lords wanted you to have the vermin, but they said nothing to me."

Cordelia cursed inwardly. She'd been hoping that wouldn't come up.

Fajir stared at her for a few seconds and then smiled. "They told you to bargain for the vermin, didn't they? They left it up to me."

Cordelia shrugged, but she knew that if she didn't do something quick, Mamet would be lost. "I'll help you get Halaan's killer," she said quickly, surprising herself. "Just him. I know Nettle will come with me, and no one tracks like a drushka."

Fajir paused again, and Cordelia knew she'd have to find a way to get out of this later, find a way to convince Fajir that vengeance wasn't everything. "Agreed."

Fajir went to one of the last doors and unlocked it. Inside, Mamet hung by her arms from a ring in the low ceiling. Her head rested against her chest, and ropes cut into her wrists. Her clothing had been torn here and there by what looked like whip marks, and blood left red trails through the dirt streaking her body.

Cordelia had known it would be bad. She'd expected that any sympathy she'd been nurturing toward Fajir would be blown away as if by a strong wind, but she couldn't help thinking that she could have gone this way, too. If her life had taken a few different turns, she could have turned into this torturing madwoman.

"Cut her down."

Fajir stared for a moment, her tattoos like gaping holes in the dim light. She slit the rope, and Mamet began to fall. Cordelia lunged forward and caught her.

Mamet stiffened in Cordelia's arms, and Cordelia had to smile when Mamet tried to kick her. She blocked with one knee and rocked Mamet back so their faces were in the light.

One of Mamet's eyes widened; the other was swollen shut. Her face was covered in purple bruises, and her lip had been split open. Her dark hair stuck to her forehead with sweat and blood. "You?" she croaked.

"You shouldn't have gone tense. It gave you away." Cordelia tried to work the rest of the rope loose, but the blood-soaked hemp didn't want to unwind. "Wow, kid, think you could have bled some more and made this harder?"

Mamet blinked before wheezing a laugh. Tears began to ooze down her cheeks, and once her hands were free, she wiped them away. "My arms hurt."

"That's the blood coming back."

"Where is Samira?"

"Safe with the drushka."

Mamet sagged, and Cordelia hauled her upright. "Can't rest yet," she whispered in Mamet's ear. "We're not with friends. You have to walk up the stairs, or I can carry you."

Her jaw tightened, and it looked painful, but she didn't wince. "I will walk." They started out, and she added, "Please, help me."

Cordelia hooked a hand under Mamet's elbow. "Easy now, one step at a time."

Mamet used her as a crutch, and she hoped it looked as if Mamet could let go at any time. Their trip up was a long one. It must have felt like centuries to Mamet. When they made it to Cordelia's room, and the door closed behind them, Mamet collapsed on the rug.

Cordelia lifted her onto a divan, and Nettle fetched two buckets of warm water and an armload of towels. They knelt before Mamet and began cleaning her face. She slept through it, tired beyond reason, it seemed.

"Where's Horace?" Cordelia asked.

"Still attempting to heal the Sun-Moon." Nettle dabbed at Mamet's face. "I thought young Mamet might awaken when we started to wash her, but she is snoring like a hoshpi."

"Her body must know it's in safe hands." Cordelia lifted Mamet's shirt, trying to see the extent of her injuries. "It's hard to tell where the dirt ends and the bruises begin. Look at her ribs!"

Nettle clucked her tongue. "She is purple. Not her natural color."

"It means bleeding under the skin."

Nettle gestured to Mamet's torn trousers. "How far do we wash?"

"Probably as much as we can. I don't think she minds."

When they started to tug her trousers loose, Mamet's eyes fluttered open. "Samira?"

"You should be so lucky," Cordelia said.

"It is only we two, young one," Nettle said. "Be at ease. We seek to clean your injuries."

Mamet went red under her bruises but didn't seem to have the will to fight.

"We won't look unless we have to," Cordelia said. "And we won't tell Samira. She'll have to wait and be surprised."

Mamet nodded and fell asleep again when they were washing her knees.

Long after dawn the next day, Mamet sat up and listened as Cordelia told her what had happened. She asked again about Samira and about the rest of her kinfolk that had been left in Celeste when she'd first escaped, but Cordelia had to admit she didn't have any more information.

Horace still hadn't returned, but as long as Mamet didn't move, she didn't seem to be in too much pain. When she listened to their plans to pretend to be allies of the Sun-Moon, her expression darkened. "I don't want to fight my own people."

"I don't think the Engali—"

Mamet scowled harder. "Any plains dweller will be more my people than these." She glared around as if the very walls offended her. Any small sound made her jump, and once or twice, she stared at a shadow as if it might attack. Cordelia wondered if anyone she'd attacked in Gale ever had a morning this bad.

Nettle rested a hand on Mamet's, and she nearly leapt out of her seat. "Be easy, young one," Nettle said, her voice soft, almost a croon though she was no shawness. "Do you wish to speak of your time here?"

Mamet trembled, and Cordelia thought she might cry, but she breathed deeply. "I heard some names, Fajir and Nico. Halaan. But I only know who they are because you told me. It was so dark. They... there were...whips. Kicks." Her free hand tightened to a fist. "They only laughed when I asked them why. They said the rest of my kinfolk who were captured with me are dead. They said if they'd gotten hold of me when I was first captured, I'd be dead, too. I tried so hard not to cry."

Cordelia hurt for her. "You're free now. You don't have to think about it."

"I'm sorry I tried to kick you. I'd been thinking about escape for so long."

"It was a good effort. I'm proud of you, kid."

Mamet smiled and then grimaced as if it hurt her. "I don't know if I can pretend to be their ally. And if Fajir makes you keep your promise, you'll have to hunt one of my people."

"It won't come to that," Cordelia said. "I'll...think of a way out. And we'll get out of this fight, too."

"We can see about your fellows who are still imprisoned here," Nettle said. "They might be alive."

"Do you think Fajir will give them to us without another bargain?" Mamet asked.

Cordelia shrugged. "With Horace distracting the Sun-Moon by trying to figure out how to heal them, we might be free to poke around, see what we can find."

Nettle leaned close and kept her voice down as if the Sun-Moon could hear through walls. "They cannot read my mind. Perhaps I can arrange an escape that we will appear innocent of." She grimaced slightly. "Though I do not like deception. Sa tells me it is all right to deceive your enemies, but…" She frowned harder.

Mamet smiled a little. "I'm in your debt, honor bound to help you, but I'd like to see my people free."

"We won't forget them," Cordelia said. "I've been spending too much time with the drushka, and now I'm trying to make everyone part of my tribe."

Mamet smiled a little wider. "My parents would like you."

Cordelia sat up straighter. "Doesn't everyone?"

Nettle touched her knee. "You would not care if they did or did not."

"Just you."

Mamet sighed as she looked between them, clearly a kid in love with love. "Do you think we will have to fight for the Sun-Moon at all?"

"Well, I doubt Naos's army will ask if we're Sun-Moons before they kill us, so maybe."

"We could hide," Mamet said softly. She flinched as if the thought was new and unsettling.

"I'm not so good at that," Cordelia said.

"*We* are not," Nettle added.

"But to fight by the side of…" Mamet shivered.

"We can't leave without Horace," Cordelia said. "And they've got a hold on him."

Mamet nodded, and Cordelia could almost see her mind working. When the moment came, could she lift her sword in defense of those who'd killed her people? Could any of them promise they would?

But, Cordelia told herself, she'd already done that. No matter that she'd said she could get out of hunting an Engali, part of her hoped she could pull Fajir out of this vengeance spiral, and maybe one dead plains dweller was all it took. She felt as if she had to do it just to prove it could be done.

No, she thought. She should focus on escaping and not having to think about any of this shit anymore.

Horace came in later that day. When Cordelia asked if he'd know if the Sun-Moon were listening in on their conversation, he shrugged, clearly exasperated after spending the morning and afternoon with them. "They're too powerful. They contacted their people from space. They can speak through them. Do you know why Fajir speaks our language? The Sun-Moon put it in her head. *Put it in her head!* They can use their telepathy *through* their worshipers. They can project not just thoughts but images. If they wanted, they could probably make us think we were seeing them right now or hide themselves from our sight if they were here."

Cordelia grinned. "So that's a no?"

He gave her a dark look. "No."

In the end, they decided to keep their voices low and hope for the best.

They spent the rest of the day resting, but just before nightfall, Fajir knocked on the door and told them she had news. Mamet seemed torn between the desire to run and the need to rip out Fajir's throat. Nettle sat beside her, one long arm slung around her shoulders.

Fajir didn't even look Mamet's way, and Cordelia resisted the urge to snap at her.

"Our scouts have found this army," Fajir said. "They are three days from here, perhaps four if they move slowly."

The scouts had to have been moving fast indeed. But they wouldn't have to come back before they reported, not with the Sun-Moon listening in.

"A big force will have to move slowly," Cordelia said, thinking of her time in the swamp. This wasn't difficult terrain, but more people equaled more problems that could slow an army down. "All warriors or others, too?"

Fajir shrugged. "Everyone, it seemed. They come from the southeast."

Cordelia nodded. Even if she managed to escape with the others, they'd have to turn north to avoid any confrontations with scouting parties. "Did your scouts run into theirs?"

"This Naos doesn't use scouts." Fajir frowned as if the idea perplexed her.

"If she's powerful enough," Cordelia said, "she won't need people to see in front of her. And she might be sucking up everyone in her path. She might do the same to your outlying villages."

"Our people would never leave the Lords!"

"Your Lords aren't the only ones with telepathy," Horace said. "If Naos is powerful enough, she won't need words to convince them."

"Most are fleeing into Celeste," Fajir said. "This army is too great to meet in the plains, but you don't have to fear. The walls will protect us."

"We are not afraid," Mamet said in a strangled whisper.

Fajir finally looked at her, a glance of pure disdain, before turning to Cordelia again. "That's all the Lords wish you to know. If you want me to hold your hand some more, you know where to find me."

Cordelia would rather have broken her hand at that moment. They'd barely had a fight before, but Cordelia wouldn't mind another. Still, for the sake of the peace, she let Fajir walk out the door. Like so many things, she'd have to wait.

CHAPTER NINETEEN

Liam rested on Shiv's abdomen as her small tree sheltered them from the sun. Pool had asked him and Reach to be go-betweens for her and the plains dwellers, sort of like ambassadors, Liam supposed, though he'd never thought of himself as such.

Both Onin and Wuran had kept their clans close since the Storm Lord had attacked. Liam told them Pool planned to move if the Storm Lord came this way. She wanted to be closer to Sun-Moon territory in order to find Nettle, Cordelia, and Horace. The two chafas had glared at each other as if declaring they might fight in Pool's absence.

Liam said there'd been enough killing, and Reach cautioned them about risking the people they had left. After two long, arduous days, Onin had offered reparations for those his clan had killed, and the two chafas seemed to reach an uneasy peace. Many people had died, but the clans could both either move on or finish the job and annihilate each other. Even then, Wuran seemed as if he might not fully accept peace until Onin offered to die for the crimes his clan had committed. Wuran accepted that offer at last, and that brought an end to things.

Liam had caught Wuran's arm before he could leave. "I wanted you to know how much I admire you for even coming to this meeting. I don't know if I could've done the same."

Wuran smiled, though the pinched look around his eyes said he still carried an undercurrent of anger. "When you travel east, we may follow."

"You will always be welcome," Reach said.

He nodded with a faraway look. "Some of our people were visiting family in the far south when we were attacked. Now they have returned and bring rumors of a gathering of clans moving east, too. I think something larger than all of us might be happening."

When Pool heard this, she said they'd move sooner rather than later, not wanting to get caught between the Storm Lord and this new group. She wanted to stray farther to the north and stay away from any humans. Liam hoped Cordelia wasn't caught up in any strange fights. Best to rescue them quickly, Pool said, and get out of the way, with scouts trailing behind looking for a way to spirit Simon Lazlo out of the Storm Lord's hands.

From his place under the little tree's branches, Liam sighed. Simon Lazlo could rot with the Storm Lord for all he cared. If Simon hadn't healed the bastard after Liam shot him, they'd still be in Gale, out of this mess. He'd be a lieutenant, Cordelia would be captain, and things would have just continued as they were.

But would that have been enough? Negotiating between the two chafas had been difficult, but he'd done it, leaving him with unexpected pride. He'd had plenty of practice keeping calm in the face of irrational anger, let alone anger that had a cause. And no matter how enraged they were, the chafas couldn't hold a candle to his mother.

Shiv passed a hand through his hair, followed a moment later by the leafy tendrils of her tree. They tickled his nose and made him sneeze.

"You are not sleeping," she said.

"I was wondering if I talked the chafas into something, or if all they needed was a little room to think for themselves and decide not to kill each other."

"Reach told me you led them to that but let them *think* they led themselves."

"I've never led anyone to anything before."

"Who else is there to lead the humans now?"

"Cordelia," he said.

"Sa is not here. Besides, your people have need of two leaders, or so Reach tells us, one of the body and one of the mind. Sa enjoys battle more than you."

He barked a laugh. "The mayor's niece leads the paladins, and the captain's son leads the people?"

"Two circles, each locked with the other."

He looked into her lean face. "Does that bother you?"

Shiv threw her head back and laughed. "I like Sa, and I like you. We are all excellent good friends."

He ran a finger over her lips, and she nipped him gently. "If I see a chance to attack the Storm Lord, I don't know if I'll be able to stop myself. I don't know if I can be like Wuran."

"Reach could teach you."

"She has, a little."

Reach had told him he must find the answer in himself; no one could teach him the ways of inner peace. She'd reminded him that the price of the Storm Lord's life might be his own death, and he must consider all those he'd leave behind. It'd been a good speech, but he still didn't know if it would be enough.

He thought of all his friends, closer than family; of Shiv, whom he was still getting to know, but every layer he uncovered he liked better than the last; and he loved Cordelia without question. And if he was going to truly be a leader, if there was no one else who could fill that role, he couldn't leave them.

Liam sat up and pulled Shiv close, kissing her deeply and forgetting the rest of the world for a while.

The next day, the scouts told them that the Storm Lord's army was leaving Gale. Pool's tree moved north, leaving a trail of drushka behind her. The Storm Lord moved fast, and when it seemed he might be able to see the tree, Pool laid it down, not taking any chances. Liam kept near Pool with Samira, but Reach was one of the scouts. Shiv sat beside her mother, her little tree next to her, and her eyes as unfocused as Pool's as they watched and listened.

"Reach can see the Storm Lord," Shiv said softly.

Liam's heart thudded. He wished he could have been one of the scouts even as he was glad he wasn't. He wondered if Reach had volunteered because of what they'd talked about. Had he stirred the flame of vengeance inside her? Surely she wouldn't risk leaving her son an orphan again.

Samira shifted. "Can she see Simon?"

Pool didn't respond, though Shiv's eyes shifted across the ground as if searching. "Yes, he rides upon a cart at the Storm Lord's side."

Samira grunted and looked pained. "Is he…"

"He is unbound."

Liam could see the questions gathering, but he caught her eye. "Let them watch."

"And smell," Shiv said, her vision clearing briefly before going distant again. "Reach says the humans smell differently than when she lived there; not a wholly unfamiliar smell, but one she has not associated with humans before. She cannot name it."

Odd, but Liam didn't know what they could do with that.

"None of our concern now," Pool said.

They watched until the Storm Lord was well into the plains.

"Are you looking for a way to get Simon back?" Samira asked.

"Yes," Pool said impatiently.

Samira stood to pace.

"Easy," Liam said.

She shook her head and seemed as if she didn't know whether to laugh or cry. "I'm usually a lot calmer than this."

"It's a bad time for everyone."

"Someone follows the Storm Lord," Shiv said. "A group of... families? They have children among them and follow far behind the army."

"Who could that be?" Liam asked.

Pool focused on him. "Go to Wuran. He must see these newcomers and tell us if he knows them."

Liam ran, not stopping until he was among the tents of the Uri. Onin had died the night before, executed by his own people, but there'd been no celebration. The mood in the tents was as somber as before. They still mourned their dead.

Samira trailed Liam, and he slowed to let her catch up. She was a risk, just as he was, but since they weren't going near the Storm Lord, her power might be useful.

Wuran agreed to go with them to see these new people, and they gathered up Reach on their way. They spied on the little group of families that followed the Storm Lord's track, but Wuran shook his head as he studied them.

"I don't know them." He frowned hard as the children struggled to keep up with the adults. "They might need help. We can find out what they want at least. Perhaps you should stay behind, Reach. No offense."

Reach's eyes took on an unfocused look, but without a chain of drushka, she was probably having a hard time communicating. "I think Pool would agree. I will be watching."

"I'm coming with you," Samira said. "If they turn nasty, I can help."

Liam nodded. "The three of us, then."

Ap froze when he saw the strangers, but they made no move to hide. They stood in the open with bare hands, no weapons in sight. Of the three, one was dressed like the people of Gale, though they'd come from the wrong direction to be part of the Storm Lord's pack.

"What should we do?" Et asked.

One of the newcomers dressed as the plains people did, and Ap supposed they might be curious. As he watched, one of them waved, a friendly smile in place. He said something to the other two, and all of them tried a gesture that seemed friendly.

There were probably more of them hiding. Ap took Et and one of the young girls who was better at the language of Gale and went to meet them, leaving the others to keep going slowly.

The man who'd waved said hello in the language of the plains, which Ap had learned some time ago. "I understand you," he said, though the words felt rusty and unused in his mouth.

"I'm Liam, this is Samira and Wuran, chafa of the Uri. We're from a clan to the north."

"I am Ap, shaman of the Deliquois people. Greetings."

"The Deliquois?" Wuran said. "The islands to the south?"

Liam looked blank, but Samira brightened. "I've heard of you! What are you doing all the way up here?" She seemed to notice her outburst could be rude and closed her mouth, cheeks going pink.

Ap suppressed the urge to chuckle. After all the hiding in Gale, some forthrightness was refreshing. "We're traveling."

Liam nodded slowly, but Wuran frowned as if he didn't believe.

"Are you travelers as well?" Ap asked.

Liam glanced at the others and said, "We're following the Storm Lord. He has one of ours, and we're going to rescue him."

Samira looked at him in surprise, but Wuran kept watching Ap. Ap copied Liam's slow nod. "So, you're sure I'm not his ally?"

"I can't help but notice you're *traveling* in his tracks," Liam said, "rather than with him. Is there something he took from you, too?"

Ap felt anger creeping along his neck as he relived the Contessa's death, but he kept his face expressionless. "He killed our goddess."

Now they all exchanged looks. "If it's revenge you're after, killing him won't be easy," Liam said. "I did it once, but he didn't stay dead."

"We've noticed."

They all smiled even though they were discussing grisly business.

"We were a peaceful people," Ap said. "Not so long ago." He told them of the Contessa's death. They seemed confused, understandably so. The goddess had never revealed her magnificence to them.

Samira shook her head. "The children, too?"

"They can stay with the Uri," Wuran said. "I know you've no reason to trust us, but surely—"

"No," Ap said, "we'll stay together." He didn't add that their task would fall to the children if the adults should fall. "Please, don't try to stop us."

"Wouldn't dream of it," Liam said. "I hope you get the bastard."

The others glanced at him, but Samira licked her lips. "If you see our friend…" She gave a quick description, and Ap said they weren't out to kill anyone but the Storm Lord. He didn't add that he hoped this Simon Lazlo didn't get in the way. They parted peacefully, though Ap noticed they watched his people until they were lost from sight.

Wuran scratched his head as the Deliquois moved on, but he didn't speak until they were out of earshot. "How did his goddess speak with him beyond the grave?"

Liam shook his head, remembering what Cordelia had told him about the Storm Lord attacking the Sun-Moon and some others in a field after Pool had first left Gale. There had been at least one dead body; it could have been their goddess. "I'm guessing someone else was using telepathy on them, but I don't know who."

"Maybe the Sun-Moon," Samira said. "All these so-called gods were at each other's throats at one time or another."

"Or this man and his people are insane," Wuran said.

Liam shrugged. "I hate to say it, but they could be a good distraction."

"For getting Simon back!" Samira beamed, but he was thinking of a chance to strike at the Storm Lord. He didn't think Ap and his people would care who killed the Storm Lord as long as it stayed done. Samira sighed, and her smile faded. "I feel bad for the kids."

"What can we do?" Wuran asked.

She didn't bring up taking the kids by force, a smart move. As someone who'd recently had his children kidnapped, Wuran wouldn't be up for any plan that involved abduction.

"I'll take my clan and ride ahead to the Engali," Wuran said. "I can warn them you might be coming close to their territory and tell them of all these strangers and weird goings-on."

"Or they might find themselves pulled into this gathering of clans near Celeste," Liam said. "It's a good idea." And it would get the Uri far from the Svenal, which would benefit everyone, even with Onin dead.

Once they returned to Pool's tree, Wuran left. Pool packed up everyone, and once she heard about these new humans, she stayed closer to the Storm Lord's trail, their scouts watching him closely to see what he might do. She had no doubt he would realize he was being followed, and if he turned his soldiers to deal with the Deliquois, she intended to be ready.

"But we must still be cautious," Pool warned.

"But this is our chance!" Samira said. "There was no way to attack him in Gale, but if we can get his people to split up, the tree can handle him."

"Usta," Reach said, "everyone knows your thirst for blood, but the tree cannot be used so hastily."

"I'm so sick of waiting!"

"The Storm Lord's weapons shredded my sister queens in the swamp," Pool said, staring at Samira with cool green eyes. "I will not have the same done to me or my tribe."

Samira shut her mouth with a snap.

"If the Storm Lord turns," Liam said, "the Deliquois will be slaughtered."

Reach spread her hands. "Wuran asked them to travel with us, and they refused."

"They are not of our tribe," Pool said.

He nodded, though it sounded cold. Samira didn't say anything, but she looked torn, as if she was thinking of the Deliquois on one hand and Simon on the other.

Reach touched her arm. "Do not be ashamed, Usta. It is natural to care for one's own above all others."

Samira shook her head. "If we can, I'd like to keep everyone alive *and* get Simon back." She stared at the ground, redness growing in her cheeks. "I thought you were foolish to want to attack the Storm Lord before, but now…I'd like to give him a bloody nose."

"Me, too," Liam said. "Pool's plan is solid. We get as close to the Storm Lord's army as we can, using drushka so his telepaths can't read their minds, and we wait for his troops to make a move toward the Deliquois. If they do, we strike."

CHAPTER TWENTY

Gale's army moved faster than Dillon expected. The paladins pulled wagons loaded with supplies and yafanai, their armor giving them nearly inexhaustible reserves. With luck, it would only take them three days to get to Celeste.

Dillon enjoyed the feel of the powered suit on his body. He enjoyed the sight of the rolling hills and the fresh air. It sucked that he hadn't caught up to any renegades or plains dwellers yet, but maybe they were all hiding. Wise, if boring.

He had Caroline and the other telepaths minding Lazlo, so Brown was in charge of the scouts and rear guard, and when she told him someone was following them, she seemed almost as eager as he was.

"Any idea who?" Dillon asked. On some of his earlier missions, long before he'd come to Calamity, his soldiers had to worry about colonists sneaking after them, usually kids who wanted to join up, but he doubted that was the case now.

"No, Storm Lord. I could take some telepaths and get a read."

"No need. Take a few troops and go have an old-fashioned look-see."

She nodded. "I'll get some of the leathers out of the carts to watch our back and flanks. They could use the exercise."

"Everyone needs practice." He wondered who the fuck could be back there, though. The renegades, most likely. He smiled. This day was getting better and better.

As soon as she was gone, he asked Caroline to keep half an "ear" on them, just to be safe. She agreed, but he spotted a current of unhappiness in her stiff shoulders. She cast an angry glance Lazlo's way, and he couldn't blame her. Laz had been whiny lately. Dillon had considered leaving him behind, but he was too useful, and he'd straighten up given enough time. Shape up or ship out, as the old man had said, and from the look on Caroline's face, she'd thought of plenty of places to ship him to, as long as they were hell and gone from her.

Dillon called a break, not wanting to get ahead of the rest of the troops. Besides, with Brown taking the armors, there was no one to pull the wagons, and he damn sure wasn't going to pull them himself. It was okay. Even though they were riding, the yafanai seemed to appreciate the stop. They walked around, stretching their backs and chitchatting. The servants handed out cups of water and snacks. Dillon leaned against Caroline's cart and wondered if he should ask how she thought their son was doing or if that would only make her grumpier.

"Hmm." Caroline squinted to the west with the slightly constipated look of a telepath in action.

"What is it?" Dillon asked.

"Some of the paladins are coming back."

"Already?"

"Brown found some people she didn't recognize. They ran. Some of the paladins are chasing them, but there's something else." She shook her head. "I can't get a clear read with…" She cast another glance at Lazlo.

He nodded. "Ask Brown—"

"Look out!" Lazlo cried.

Dillon whirled around, freeing his sidearm. The rolling hills of grass hissed softly in the breeze. "What? Laz?"

"I saw…" His hand dropped.

Dillon waited. "What?"

Lazlo didn't answer, only mumbled something.

Dillon leaned close to Caroline. "What happened there?"

"Maybe he's snapped." She shrugged as if she had no pity. Or maybe she expected Laz to snap under the strain, but she didn't know him. She looked where Lazlo had pointed and frowned. "I'm not getting anything, at least anything I've—"

A small stone whizzed from the grass and smacked against her skull with a dull thwack. She toppled into the cart.

Dillon crouched. "Everybody down!"

Some obeyed. Others froze. Stones flew from the grass like swarming wasps, pelting yafanai and the remaining leathers with remarkable precision. Some bounced off invisible shields as the macro-psychokinetics sprang into action. Dillon lowered his visor and stood. The stones ricocheted off him with hard plinks, but they couldn't hurt him.

He reached for Caroline's pulse, made sure she was alive, and then headed into the grass. "Laz, heal Caroline!"

At the merest hint of movement, he fired off a shot and winged something that yelped. He jogged forward, but whoever it was vanished, leaving nothing but a spray of golden fluid to tell where it might have fallen. Not human, then. Probably drushka.

Another rock bounced off his helmet, and he headed in that direction, using his targeting sensors and hurling a bolt of lightning. Another yelp, and another body gone when he arrived. He followed their retreating forms far into the grass, and it wasn't until the wagons were out of sight that he realized he'd been drawn away. A stupid move, maybe, but as he'd proven, there wasn't any way the drushka could hurt him.

Of course, the wagons were another matter.

"Fuck!" He didn't know how many the yafanai could handle, but he didn't want to lose any finding out. He turned back, but a snake hurtled from the grass and wrapped around his ankle.

"Gah!" He tried to pull away, but the snake stretched, its long body hidden under the soil like a tree root. More of them shot upward and curled around him. He thought of carnivorous plants then remembered the walking tree. Drushkan trickery. With a quick flex of his power, he pumped lightning into the roots, and they shuddered but held tight. He shot at one and went for his blade with his free hand. They wouldn't hold him for long.

He yelped as they yanked him backward, overcoming his stabilizers with a harsh whine. Even with the armor, there were too many. As they jerked him underground, burying him in darkness, he cried out, the sound echoing inside his helmet.

"Calm the fuck down," he growled to himself. It was all right. His visor was down. He had enough air to get free as long as he stayed calm. With slow movements, he tried to wriggle for the surface, but a root caught his feet and dragged him back into place, releasing him before he could shock it again.

Clever fucking bastards were waiting for him to run out of air. With the armor, it could take a while, but it would happen. He shifted upward. No movement. He shifted again, waiting for the next root to tug him down. He gave it a jolt but couldn't tell if he did any damage, and he couldn't keep it up forever.

The drushka were probably packing the dirt above him, entombing him. Sweat trickled down his spine, and he shut his eyes so he wouldn't see the darkness. He tried not to think of what it would feel like to suffocate, if he'd go to sleep or gasp for his last breath. The armor began to seem uncomfortably tight. He told himself he was imagining that. He couldn't be crushed, but it was cold comfort.

In his mind, he called for Caroline, for any of the telepaths. He kept his teeth clamped shut, not wanting to suffer the indignity of another scream.

❖

Lazlo didn't bother to get down and hide; none of the stones came near him. He knew he'd seen something! He was afraid for a moment that he'd gone insane enough to hallucinate, but now everyone could see. It gave him a happy little charge.

He heard Dillon's order to help Caroline, but as he looked at her, he knew that was the wrong thing to do. All his questions about Marcus had turned up nothing but a random death. No one else thought he was connected, but Caroline blamed him still. Maybe it wasn't something he'd done but something he'd distracted her from doing? Well, Lazlo was determined not to be a distraction any longer. He'd let her sleep. A hazy memory of healing Dillon when he shouldn't have swam through his memory, gone in an instant, but he knew he'd made the right choice.

"Get down," someone whispered.

One of the yafanai was gesturing wildly, but Lazlo stared around him. The breeze felt cooler, the air more clear, and from high on the wagon, he saw someone sneaking through the grass: long-limbed, brown and gray people, their skin covered in tattoos. No, not tattoos. It was natural, like bark. He knew them. One reached the side of the wagon and grinned at him with sharp teeth.

"I know you," Lazlo whispered.

The creature held out a hand; its fingers had an extra joint. Lazlo glanced around, but no one else seemed to notice. Maybe he *was* hallucinating, but when other Galeans tried to poke their heads up, another hail of stones made them duck again. Lazlo resisted the urge to laugh.

"Come, shawness," the creature said softly. "Your tribe awaits."

Bells and alarms were going off in his mind, but were they warning him to stay or go? Well, he knew what life among Dillon's people was like, and Caroline wouldn't stay unconscious forever. He slid down from the cart. Several human voices called out, but he ignored them and stared into the face of the maybe hallucination that seemed realer than Dillon. Oh well, if he was going to sink into psychosis, he might as well enjoy himself. The creature pulled him along, keeping both of them low as they retreated into the grass in the opposite direction Dillon had taken.

The creature paused often, and Lazlo cast his senses back, sensing it as one of the micros healed Caroline. As soon as she was awake, he felt her telepathic call. She acted concerned for his safety, but he sensed her anger and frustration, as if she hoped something bad would happen to him even as she seemed guilty for thinking that.

"Piss off," he thought back.

She pushed harder, trying to make her suggestions into commands.

He winced and resisted the urge to rush back to her side. "What about Marcus?" he thought, hoping to distract her.

Her anger slipped into rage and, she sent a telepathic spike designed to knock him out, but his shields were up and ready, his own power strengthening his mind so she couldn't overload it. The micro added his power to hers, trying to bludgeon a way past Lazlo's shields. He grunted under their assault and slowed the creature down. He couldn't run *and* fight. The creature grabbed his arm, and Lazlo sent his power over it by accident, feeling its connection to sun and soil, all the rhythms of flora that were so familiar, botanist that he was at heart. He'd felt something like this before. He knew these creatures. Drushka.

It drew its arm back, making a sucking sound. "Shawness?"

Caroline stabbed his brain again, and he snarled. "I have to get away. I can't walk. They're…"

The drushka lifted him, snaking one arm over his legs and the other under his back. It leapt up and ran, ignoring any cries from behind. A wave of force sent them stumbling, but the drushka didn't fall. Caroline's attacks grew panicked, hammering, using the micro to add to her mental battering ram. She still aimed to wound, but it seemed she'd stopped caring if she accidentally killed.

Oh, if she wanted a real fight…

Lazlo tried to shut down her power center but found that fortified by the micro. He switched and aimed for her body instead, attacking her heart, her brain, her spine. Her pain rocketed through him as her scream echoed through the plains. The force attacks vanished as he used her distraction to thump the powers of those around her, but nothing matched the pain in her voice. He had enough time to hope he hadn't killed her before they were over a hill and out of sight.

Samira couldn't believe their luck. Not only had the armored paladins chased the Deliquois people, as Pool hoped they would, but they'd left the Storm Lord alone, making him far easier to ambush. Pool had been afraid she'd have to bury all his troops at once.

Even better, the drushka had managed to whisk Simon away. Now she just had to keep the armors busy so Simon could get clear, and Pool could kill the Storm Lord. The leathers were still chasing the Deliquois, but the armors had turned back. She hid in the long grass with some of the drushka and waited until the drushka fired slings, making the paladins turn with guns drawn. Samira hit them with a force wall, sending them tumbling over. Liam told them the armor wouldn't function without the batteries, so groups of drushka swarmed over the soldiers, seeking to unplug their power cells and leave them to flop on the ground.

Some soldiers flung the drushka away like rag dolls. An armored swing could shatter them, and none of them could dodge a bullet, so they hit and then leapt for cover again. As one paladin freed himself and took aim, Samira gave him a psychokinetic shove. When another drushka went flying, Samira caught him in midair and set him on the ground.

"Usta!" One of the drushka heaved a battery her way. She caught it with her power and dropped it near her feet. Another drushka grabbed it and ran, heading for Pool. Three more came her way, and she sent them all hurrying behind her. If they couldn't take captives, they could at least rob the soldiers of their greatest weapons. That way they could never hurt Simon or anyone else again.

Caroline's world became pain and fear. She could feel the yafanai working on her, trying to heal her, but nothing could take away the cramps that flooded her body, curling her limbs into themselves and sending spikes of agony through her torso and back.

"Organ failure!" she heard one of them say.

"What the fuck did he do to her?"

Simon Lazlo had done this, set off some kind of cascade of agony, her body rebelling against itself, killing her.

Fear tried to overrule the pain. Evan. What would happen to him? She couldn't leave him alone! But he would have the Storm Lord, wouldn't he? The thought should have been a comfort, but there was just so much pain.

They were trying different things now, equally useless, and one of the other telepaths was trying to access her thoughts, but she denied them entry, not wanting anyone to feel this agony, not wanting even the chance that her son would someday know what she experienced at her death. She tried to say his name and failed.

"What is she saying?" someone asked.

She put out a brief, telepathic call, trying to tell them this was all Simon Lazlo's fault, that he needed to be stopped, or he would drag all of them down, including the Storm Lord, but they all cried out, and she knew she had to be sending her pain and little else.

Still, one of them said, "Something about the Storm Lord?"

"And Simon Lazlo."

"Why? We already know this is his fault."

But they didn't know the whole story. Few did. She wanted them to ask questions, to debate with the Storm Lord if they could, if it was safe, but she couldn't form coherent signals, could barely think them. She cried out again for her son, and they kept working on her until she pleaded for them to stop, for everything to stop, so this agony could leech away.

"Enough!" someone said. "Enough, can't you hear her!"

"We can't just let her die."

She sent out a last, desperate telepathic burst, making them all cry out again and stagger back, their power leaving her, and she could take one final shuddering breath before merciful darkness surrounded her.

CHAPTER TWENTY-ONE

Celeste stretched near a delta with the ocean beyond. Its rose colored walls glowed in the sun, and what Natalya could see of the buildings seemed to shine. The ocean looked like polished metal, with a yellow cast like flames. When she'd first heard of the ocean, Natalya had pictured something like the swamp, with water that just sat there, but even from a distance, the ocean seemed to move and rock as if swirled by a giant hand.

Kora said, "It reminds me of San Francisco Bay."

Natalya glanced at her, expecting to see Naos's smirk, but this was Kora's open, honest face. Natalya was about to point out that the memories weren't hers, but Kora frowned.

"No, it doesn't," Kora said. "Those aren't my memories. It's not the same." She stared at Natalya as if having a revelation.

Before Natalya could respond, Kora's head snapped back as if someone had grabbed her by the hair, and when she looked to Natalya again, her right eye shone fiercely blue. "What have you done to her?"

"Nothing!" The air left Natalya's lungs in a rush as Naos's power closed around her, cutting off thought. Her head burned as Naos tore into her mind, ripping through memories that played in Natalya's mind like a vid. She went through every conversation with Kora, every treasonous thought Natalya had ever entertained.

"And you were so happy to have a replacement," Naos said with Kora's mouth, the words coming with a harsh growl. "And now you're trying to take her away from me?"

"She's just a girl!"

"She's mine. You're mine. Every single creature in this world or the next is mine!"

Natalya fell to her knees. She'd thought nothing could be worse than the overwhelming feeling of too much power, but now Naos took everything away, robbing Natalya of every sense except sight, and even that narrowed to a long tunnel. She'd known this would happen. She'd tried to pretend it wouldn't, but part of her had always known it would come to this.

"No!" Kora staggered, and Natalya sagged as the power released her, and all the feeling came rushing back to her limbs, her lungs. Kora pointed at empty air as if someone was standing there. "We need her!"

The tone sounded different, though the voice was the same, and Natalya knew this was the confused person she'd once met in the tent late at night. Natalya staggered to her feet, coughing, as Kora, Naos, and this new entity argued with each other, though Kora probably didn't get many words in. Was there even room for her?

The plains dweller army crept forward, staring at their mad godchild. Natalya waved them back. She sent a cautious tendril of micro power and sensed two connections to Kora. She wished again for telepathy so she could see what was going on in that mind, but did she really want to know?

As quickly as she'd started fighting with herself, Kora took a deep breath. The second connection faded slowly, and Kora turned back to Natalya, still with that one blue eye.

"Goddess?" Natalya asked, hoping she sounded scared. She felt it. She only hoped Naos had forgotten what prompted this particular explosion in the first place.

"It doesn't matter," Naos said with a wave. "I'm here now. I'm staying."

Natalya stayed silent, keeping even her thoughts from having expectations.

Naos smoothed down Kora's simple shirt. "Shall we begin?"

"Begin what?" Natalya looked back at the army and at Celeste's stone walls. To get that much stone, they probably used ships or barges to quarry the mountains to the north. Natalya wondered how many mines they had. "You want to attack the wall?"

Naos sneered. "You *attack* the people *inside*. The wall is just an obstacle."

"Right." Not only was it tall, but large weapons stood atop it, and she could see archers waiting. Obstacle indeed. Naos was staring at her. Fantastic. "Um."

Naos's lips wobbled, and she brayed a laugh. "Your face! You should see it." She laughed for a solid minute before wiping her eyes. "Oh man. Now." She turned to the wall, and Natalya sensed power filling her, growing until Natalya fancied she could see it as well as sense it. Her own macro powers were drawn in without her say-so, and she felt the immense strength flooding Kora's limbs. How could one person contain it? Kora would be torn to bits, and Natalya opened her mouth to say so when Naos flung the power outward, compressing it into an invisible ram that slammed into the walls of Celeste and blew a hole clean through in a boom of exploding stone.

Cordelia approved of the plan to defend Celeste. Fajir had told her about the archers and the ballistae on the walls that would hammer the enemy before they even came close to the gates. And if by some miracle the plains dwellers managed to get in, infantry would be waiting, with more archers stationed on the highest buildings and inner walls. And if those should fail, the Sun-Moon would wait along the main thoroughfare with their two friends from the *Atlas*, Lisa and Aaron, just in case.

All non-combatants had already moved to the city center, near the palace and out of the way. Cordelia hadn't liked the idea of crowding the civilians so close together. If a fire or close-quarters fighting started, they'd be trapped. Fajir agreed and argued with her fellow serens that even with all the precautions, barricades should be built through the city to slow down any troops. She seemed to be the only commander who wasn't completely cocky, but as people who knew Naos personally, the Sun-Moon agreed with her, and the barricades were built.

To Cordelia's dismay, the Sun-Moon planned to keep Horace close when the battle started. She'd been hoping they could sneak away in the commotion, but when the opportunity didn't arise, she thought it best to keep everyone as safe as possible. So Horace and Mamet stayed with the Sun-Moon near one of the barricades, and Cordelia decided to look over the defenses with Nettle and Fajir. She'd been peering over Fajir's shoulder at a map, standing near the wall, when the whole world shrunk to the size of a roar that lifted her off her feet and covered her in shards of stone.

Her breath wheezed in and out of her lungs as she lay in a pile of rubble. With a frown, she tried to remember what had happened. She'd been looking at a map. And now…all this rock and dust. How did that make sense? A twisted man lay next to her, blood streaming down his face. His mouth was open, but he didn't make a sound. Was he mute, or was she deaf?

She felt her own face and found it sticky and dusty. Everything was dusty. The Sun-Moon should have cleaned if they were expecting company. The thought made her laugh, and she couldn't hear herself either.

Bits of rubble quietly rolled away as she stood. That wasn't right. The street shouldn't have been covered in stone. People moved through the hazy air like ghosts, and she watched them pull Fajir out of the pile. Her face was slack, her head bloody. Someone grabbed Cordelia's arm, and her hazy memory said, "Nettle." She had streaks of gold along her face, and her mouth moved as if shouting.

"What happened?" Cordelia tried to ask.

Nettle dragged her into a jog, but she'd never felt like staying still so much in all her life. Her stomach lurched, and she threw up in the street, but Nettle didn't let her stop.

"The wall," Nettle called, her voice so faint. "They will be coming!"

Cordelia tried to turn, fumbling for the wooden sword on her hip, but Nettle kept pushing her to run.

"Horace will heal you!"

Dimly, she thought she should at least know what Nettle was talking about, but it wasn't until they reached a barricade and a wide-eyed Horace ran toward her that she realized something had gone wrong. Her mind cleared like mist before the breeze.

"What the fuck happened?" She gripped Nettle's arm. "Are you all right?"

"Scratched. Something hit the wall, some force. The enemy will be pouring through."

"I felt something," Horace said, "some great macro force like…" He blanched. "I think I've felt it before, but it couldn't be her."

"Who?"

"My friend Natalya, you remember her? Before we left Gale, she was augmented like me. I…thought I sensed her a minute ago."

Cordelia looked back the way they had come; dust had blown up the street, and shouts came from around the corner. "How strong is she? If this Naos is still in orbit, maybe she needs someone here to guide her hand."

"It does not matter," Nettle said. "How can we stand against such a force?"

"We can't." Horace looked back to the barricade; the Sun-Moon stood staring into the city. Who knew what the fuck they were even doing?

Horace went to the other wounded, healing Fajir along with some others. Cordelia thought about trying to stop him, but no matter how Horace felt about someone, he was a born healer, and as the drushka said, you couldn't stop a shawness from fixing people.

But the Sun-Moon were distracted. The battle had begun. Now would be the time to slip away. She crept close to Horace, Nettle with her, but realized they were missing someone. "Where's Mamet?"

"She's not with you?" Horace asked.

Cordelia swore. All the warnings, and she'd still managed to get herself lost. "We left her here."

"She went to find you."

"Shit! How long ago?"

"I have no idea."

Cordelia looked to the Sun-Moon again; they were talking with Fajir. "Come with us, Horace, and—"

"No," the Sun-Moon said loudly. "He will remain here, under Fajir's watch."

Cordelia fought back the urge to curse again. "Fine. We'll find Mamet on our own."

She and Nettle ran toward the sounds of combat that were echoing through the street. Plains dwellers had taken advantage of the hole in the wall, and knots of people fought amongst the debris. Some plains dwellers might even have made it farther into the city before the Sun-Moons caught them.

In all the chaos, Mamet could have easily taken a wrong turn or been forced down another street by the combat. They were soon in the thick of the fighting, and Cordelia's heart sank. She didn't want to fight her fellow humans, not like this. They might be under some mind control garbage. She thumped heads where she could and saw Nettle using her claws, the paralyzing poison rarely strong enough to kill unless someone had a bad reaction, but their chances of survival were better than with a slit throat.

"There!" Nettle cried, pointing ahead.

Cordelia saw Mamet among the fighters, but she stood shoulder to shoulder with other plains dwellers, hacking at Sun-Moon soldiers. "What the fuck?"

"Perhaps it is telepathy," Nettle yelled.

"If that were true, we'd all be affected, wouldn't we?"

Nettle sucked her teeth. "I will get her."

Cordelia wanted to argue, but Nettle squeezed between the Sun-Moons and leapt up, elbowing a plains dweller in the face. She tackled Mamet and dragged her through the crowd before anyone had a chance to realize what had happened or where the drushka had sprung from and then disappeared to in half a heartbeat.

"What the fuck are you doing?" Cordelia yelled when they were out of the fighting.

Mamet was panting, her face red, and Cordelia noted tear tracks down her cheeks. "I was looking for you."

"And so you joined the other side?" Nettle asked. "Or do my eyes fail me?"

"They're my people." She gestured wildly with her sword. "I got lost! I saw some plains dwellers, and I hid. They were caught by Sun-Moon archers. Some were killed. I told the rest to surrender. I said if they threw down their weapons, they wouldn't be harmed." Her mouth wobbled, and one small sob escaped. "I yelled it so all could hear, and I know the Sun-Moons understood me. And when the plains dwellers surrendered, the Sun-Moons shot them!"

She slashed her sword through the air, and Cordelia was tempted to wrestle it away from her. "They looked like me," Mamet said, "dressed like me. I've seen their faces in the faces of my neighbors, my clan. They don't go about in pairs or have tattoos or torture people!"

"These are not your kin," Nettle said softly.

"They're closer than the Sun-Moons! And if the Sun-Moon get their hands on my family, they'll treat them just as they treated me. At least all these people would do is kill me!"

Cordelia sighed. "I don't trust the Sun-Moon to give us clean towels, let alone let us go, but we can't fight them, not yet. We have four of us to think about, and they're keeping Horace close."

"I would say now is the time to look for your kinsmen," Nettle said. "But with the fighting, we must look for a chance to flee."

The fighting was getting closer. "We have to go, Mamet," Cordelia said. "And if I knew how the Sun-Moon would react, I would tell you to get as far away from here as possible, but while they still have Horace, I don't know if we can risk making them angry. They almost killed us once, and we had surprise on our side."

Mamet swallowed hard, and Cordelia watched her weighing her options. She didn't know any of them. She could run, no matter what she'd pledged, what sort of bonds she said they'd formed. She was young, probably hadn't figured out what kind of person she would be.

In the end, she nodded. "But I won't help them kill anyone else."

Cordelia nodded, and Nettle seemed pleased by that answer.

❖

Natalya couldn't get over the sounds. She'd killed people with the goddess before, but they'd always been at least fifty feet away. Now, as the screams of the wounded and dying surrounded her, she didn't know if that had truly been distance or something inside herself. She supposed it didn't matter. The crunch of breaking bone and the dull, wet sounds of weapons hitting flesh assaulted her senses as much as the terror-filled cries of the living, whether they ran toward death or away from it, and she couldn't get away from them.

She stayed by Kora's side, and now they stood within Celeste itself; there had been no more great displays of power after the wall. Naos swayed slightly, eyes half-lidded. Blood landed on her in a fine mist as someone got their brains bludgeoned out, and she turned her face toward it as if it was a cool breeze.

Natalya flung away a Sun-Moon worshiper who got too close. "Goddess, end this!"

Naos ignored her. The Sun-Moon worshipers had scattered at first, caught off guard, but they were quickly organizing into rows of deadly infantry supported by archers on the high wall or scattered along the tops of buildings. The surprise of the attack wouldn't last much longer, but Naos didn't need it to. She could end this anytime she wanted.

"Naos!"

Her eyes snapped open, and Natalya thought she was going to answer, but she smiled, her right eye even more brilliant blue. "There they are." She grunted and grabbed her chest as if someone had punched her.

Natalya sensed another presence attacking the link between Kora and Naos, not the other person who'd shared it with them before. It had to be the Sun-Moon, but they were attacking with telepathy, trying to subdue both Kora and Naos and succeeding against neither. They should have been trying to distract her instead. Or they should have attacked with all the powers at their disposal, but like all telepaths, they thought it the superior power.

Naos gathered her own considerable telepathy and began to hunt for them, but Natalya sensed glee in her rather than the desperation of the Sun-Moon. If they wanted to fight with mind powers, it seemed she'd take them up on it rather than just flatten their city.

Natalya looked to the growing press around them. They could soon find themselves alone, and Naos seemed too distracted to fight, but what did she care? It wasn't her body in danger.

"Fall back!" Natalya called. "Organized retreat."

Around her, the dwindling army obeyed, and they inched toward the wall. Natalya kept her hands on Kora's shoulders and guided her slowly.

"No!" Naos called.

Natalya let her go. "Goddess, we must—"

"Lead the army out of the city!"

"Uh…yes, I will. We were—"

Naos grunted and pushed her arms out as if shoving an invisible foe. Natalya felt a strike of huge telepathic and micro-psychokinetic power but couldn't tell where it went. "There. That should take care of them for a while." Naos turned toward the wall, and when Natalya didn't move, Naos slapped her, but there was no power behind it. "Move!"

Natalya cried to the army to fall back and felt it as Naos sent out a telepathic call to withdraw. They filtered out slowly, Natalya still guiding Naos along as she muttered to herself, her eyes tracking invisible enemies. She kept calling someone else stupid and finally yelled, "He's going to die anyway!" She slashed a hand through the air. "This is the last time we do what you want. Enough of this!"

Facing the gates, Naos spread her hands apart, and the plains dwellers that stood between her and the wall scooted gently to the sides of the street. Naos stalked toward the gates, and Natalya followed. She ducked as Naos flung her arms upward as if slamming a window open. A wall of force flew from her in a cone, and buildings blew apart like split kindling. Natalya ducked at the deafening crunch as buildings collapsed, and stones were torn from the street. The gates blew outward, followed by tons of debris that scattered outside the city as if someone had dragged a hand through a pile of dirt.

All sound ceased, the voices of plains dwellers and Sun-Moon worshipers alike falling silent. All stared at Naos, and Natalya knew she had to have the same amazed look. As Naos strode from the city, Natalya waited a few moments before catching up. The plains dwellers followed, but no one else. Natalya didn't blame them. Even considering standing up to such immense power had to seem the height of foolishness.

Patricia Dué walked the Atlas's halls, peeking into conduits and checking the wiring. The engineers had already done their inspection, and the ship wouldn't depart for hours, but it was her first long mission. She wanted to get to know the ship she'd be helping to pilot. She'd done this last minute check for every tub she'd ever flown, and the *Atlas* put them all to shame.

She spotted a missing bolt on a hatch cover and clucked her tongue. One missing bolt wasn't likely to cause a crash, but she didn't like the laziness it spoke of. What mistakes might be behind the hatch if the outside was so sloppy?

She put her toolkit down and strained to catch the remaining bolts with her wrench, but they were just out of reach. She put one foot on the toolkit and tried again, but the kit slipped, and she lurched backward with a yelp.

Someone caught her elbows, stopping her fall. "Climbing the walls before we even get to the boondocks?" a man's voice asked.

Patricia turned, and the rescuer flashed a brilliant smile. Late forties, maybe early fifties, he radiated masculinity from his square jaw to the calluses on his hands. His thumb glanced along her forearm, making her teeth clench. Something about him made the small touch seem as intimate as if he'd caressed her bare breast.

He let go as she turned, and she eyed the crisp gray uniform, the black piping, a combo that complemented eyes that seemed more gray then blue. The stripes of a Pross Co. colonel graced his shoulders, and she looked for the stitching that gave his last name as Tracey.

He raised an eyebrow, and she knew she was staring. She'd never been a blusher, so she swallowed instead. "Thanks." Her mind raced, trying to find out what it was about him that was so fascinating. She'd never been interested in someone at least ten years her senior. Jack was a handsome man, but when Colonel Tracey chuckled, secret places in Patricia's core tightened as if pulled by a drawstring.

She sensed power in his muscled frame; maybe that was it. This wasn't someone who worked with numbers all day, who sat at a desk. No doubt he used his hands for all sorts of things, and he was a soldier. If he was a colonel, he'd seen combat, had fought for his life and the lives of others.

She'd walked away then, but now, when she had this moment to live again, she wanted to stay, wanted them to peel each other out of their uniforms and fuck right there in the hallway. She opened her mouth to tell him, but he'd gone still, frozen in time, stuck in the unchanging past.

"I thought you loved Jack," her own voice said. Naos leaned against the wall in a black evening gown, fidgeting with a string of diamonds around her neck. She pulled it taut with one finger, the stones dimpling her skin.

"I did love Jack," Patricia said. "Do love. Something."

Naos tapped her chin. "During pre-flight check on the bridge, you were thinking about our dear colonel, weren't you, wanted to sit on his console and wrap your legs around his head."

Patricia edged away, looking for another memory, but Naos stayed with her, floating through the air as if there was no gravity.

"Don't you think you should have been paying attention, hmm? Did you cause the crash? Is that why you were so willing to let me in?"

"Nichols caused the crash! He was the pilot. I was just running the numbers."

"Yes, double-checking his work. Maybe everyone would have been alive and happy and sane if you'd done your job instead of fantasy fucking Dillon Tracey!"

Patricia turned, fist raised, but Naos caught her in an invisible grip. She laughed, her with all the power, and Patricia with all the pain.

"You want me to abandon my war?" Naos said. "For him?"

With a flash that made her gasp, Patricia remembered what she'd been doing before she'd gotten lost in the past again. She'd heard a telepathic cry for help. Naos's shields had been wide open on that battlefield, and Patricia had been able to peek through, but it wasn't the battle that interested her. It was the people she'd once known, and one of them was in desperate trouble and calling for help with all his might, but he wasn't a telepath. No one else could have heard him.

"We have to help him!"

"No!"

Patricia flexed what little power she'd managed to find within herself, trying to manipulate the real body she had to share.

Naos shut her down with a snarl. "He's going to die anyway." She muttered something about being foolish and stupid.

"But you want to be the one to kill him, don't you? You want to kill him with your hands, her hands."

Naos frowned harder, but Patricia knew the argument was working. "This is the last time we do what you want." Naos flickered and disappeared.

Patricia sagged against the hallway. A ghostly ribbon hung in the air where Naos had been, and Patricia knew what that was, too. She was seeing it more and more recently: the attachment to the world, the one Patricia could occasionally follow. Sometimes it led to the girl, sometimes other places, other people. Patricia clutched it and watched as Naos sent out a psychic tendril, seeking Dillon. His mind was tight, panicky, and Patricia could see through his eyes. He was entombed in blackness, and she sensed the thunder of his heartbeat. In his mind, Naos began to sing.

He didn't bother to reply out loud, but Patricia heard him think, "Come to watch while I die, nutbag?"

A confident thought, but in his mind his terror was more transparent than if he'd spoken aloud. It should have made him less in her mind. In any other man, it might have, but now she wanted to save him more than ever.

"Don't read too much into this, sugar," Naos thought at him. "It's just because you've got a part to play."

But that wasn't all, and Patricia knew it. She'd been able to upset Naos's plans, to jangle around in her mind like a loose screw until Naos took her seriously. She was gaining power.

Naos moved Dillon upward through the dirt; a macro pulse shielded him from the roots he feared. As he rose, he laughed and thanked her, his gratitude real, and though Naos ignored it, Patricia delighted in every sensation.

CHAPTER TWENTY-TWO

Samira sent her third battery away from the fight, crippling another paladin. Many of them now had to open their visors and shout to one another. She braced to grab another battery when the air glowed white around her, blinding her as the sky cracked with thunder. She staggered and rubbed purple spots from her eyes only to see that a nearby drushka had been reduced to a smoldering pile of flesh. When the smell washed over her, she gagged and grabbed her mouth. The hair on her arms stood on end, and she whipped around, looking for him. He stalked toward the battle to her right, his visor open and murder etched on every feature.

"Oh no."

Another drushka ran to her. "The queen is in pain! The Storm Lord is free!"

"Keep fighting!"

He yelled something else about Pool, but Samira gathered her power around her as the Storm Lord's eye fell on her. She didn't know if she could stop him, but she wasn't going to wait to try. She hurled a wall of force and knocked him over. At least *she* had a chance of withstanding him. She had to give the drushka more time to get Simon!

When he stood, he looked past her, and Samira heard a slithering sound accompanied by heavy thumps that made the ground tremble. She risked a look and saw Pool's tree thundering toward the battle. Its long roots whipped out and knocked the Storm Lord flat again.

Another battery was freed, and Samira sent it Pool's way. Thunder boomed across the sky now, and the clouds opened like an overturned bucket, sheeting everyone with rain. Another bolt lashed out, and the drushka screamed as it left a black scorch mark across Pool's trunk. The tree bent and swung a branch, hurtling the Storm Lord into the air. He landed hard on his back, but Samira had no doubt the armor could protect him. He slipped in the wet grass, and the rest of the paladins ran toward him. Several shot at Pool where she rode in the tree, but the limbs folded over her, and more drushka leapt from the branches to join the fight.

Samira gave the paladins another shove and ran for the tree. Her strength was flagging and her head pounding without Simon to cure her fatigue. She didn't know how much longer she could keep this up. After another macro shove, she caught sight of a drushka running toward them out of the haze of rain. She thought he might have gotten thrown clear of the fight when she noticed he was carrying someone, a human.

"Simon!" She ran toward them, whooping for joy.

One of the paladins turned and lifted her weapon. She called something about not letting them have the healer, and others went for their guns.

"No!" Samira pulled another wave of force from her core, sending pain bouncing between her ears, but the shot rang out just as the wave threw the paladin prone.

A fine red spray doused the drushka's face as Simon's head jerked to the side. He went limp, and the drushka stumbled.

"Simon!" Samira cried. She skidded to a halt.

The paladin who'd shot Simon was getting to her feet. Samira's vision went cloudy as her teeth came together hard. She reached deep within, grabbing every ounce of power and ignoring the pain twisting her head off. With a cry of inarticulate rage, she set a wall of force across the paladin's body, seeking to rip her in two. The armor shrieked as loudly as the woman inside, but Samira snarled and pushed harder, feeling the armor give along with muscles and ligaments, organs and bone.

Another paladin fired at her, but she knocked the bullets away, pulling reserves from places she didn't know she had. She tasted copper. Her nose was bleeding. Pool's tree reached Simon and his rescuer and lifted both into her branches. The Storm Lord turned, and she thought he'd aim at Pool again, but he pumped a bolt of lightning into the paladin who'd shot Simon, and Samira thought she heard him cry out.

A limb snaked around her torso and lifted her into the air. "I'm not done yet!" But she had to let the paladin go as the drushka returned to their branches. Samira screamed, desperation turning into a final prayer that the Storm Lord had ended Simon's killer.

The limb placed her on a branch, and she fell to her knees. The drushka and humans scattered through the branches had a hazy, dreamlike quality made dimmer by the rain. She wiped her face, leaving red smudges across her hands, but the rain cleaned them at once. It might already have washed away Simon's blood.

The drushka had his body. She had to find it. She grabbed the first drushka that passed, wadding her fists in his shirt. "What did you do with him?"

He replied in drushkan, lifting his hands. She pushed him away and staggered along, calling Simon's name. The unknowing drushka stayed with her, muttering.

Shiv dropped in front of them. "Usta, you must calm yourself."

"Where did you put Simon's…body?" Her voice broke, and she sobbed, loud and hard until Shiv had to support her. One minute alive and the next dead, after everything they'd done? Life couldn't be so cruel. She tried to ask where he was again but could only manage a keening moan. Shiv was talking to her, and there were people all around, trying to console her, but what was she supposed to do now? Where was she supposed to go?

"Usta, come with me," Shiv said as she cupped Samira's cheeks. "Come."

One of the watching drushka said, "Queen's daughter, you cannot—"

Shiv gave him a harsh look. "I have decided."

She led Samira away, and Samira spotted Lydia in the crowd. She wanted to fly at the ex-prophet, to tear her apart for not warning this would happen, but before Samira could gather whatever power remained to her, the tree lifted her and Shiv higher into its limbs.

Shiv led her to a group of branches as dense as a basket, and she eyed them curiously, even through her grief. At a wave from Shiv, the branches parted enough to crawl through, and Shiv led the way inside.

Samira blinked as they entered a world of soft, golden light. Pods hung from the branches all around them, and as Samira stepped close to one, she saw a tiny drushka inside, a baby. From those the size of a fist to some so big she couldn't get her arms around them, the pods all held infants in various stages of development. Near the largest, Reach stood with several other drushka, one of whom held a mewling baby. Samira looked past them to the pod itself.

Its occupant filled it completely, making great bulges along the sides and interrupting its oval line. Samira walked toward it woodenly, hypnotized by the naked man inside; his legs were pushed up to his chest, and his arms locked around them. His head rested on his knees, face turned toward her, eyes closed. His hair swayed inside the golden liquid.

"Simon." She put a hand to her mouth. "Is he…"

She touched the pod's slick, smooth surface. She could see the bullet wound in his head, a precise little hole. Occasionally, a small jolt of red blood leaked into the golden fluid, turning it a darker amber.

"He is alive," Reach said. She had red and golden smears of blood on her clothes, in her hair. "I cannot repair the wound as I cannot sing away the metal." She looked to Shiv. "One human here was bad enough, but two?"

"Shawness Simon will not remember," Shiv said, "and Usta had become useless with grief."

"How is he alive?" Samira asked.

"Shawness Simon has a connection to plants. We sensed it when he touched the connection of the drushka, but we can only keep him alive like this and not forever." She took a cloth from her bag and wiped Samira's nose, but Samira barely felt it. "We need a human healer. We need shawness Horace."

Samira swallowed hard. She didn't understand about the connections to plants and the drushka, but she understood the pod was keeping him alive. She took a deep breath. They hadn't failed to save him. It was just going to be more complicated than they thought.

She looked from the pod to the rest, to the babies, the newborn. One of the drushka bounced the baby softly, saying, *"Chee, chee, chee,"* before speaking to Shiv.

"She worries because the baby is thin," Reach whispered. "We had to remove him early to make room for shawness Simon."

"Will he be all right?"

"Ahya, I think so. The queen feeds the children differently at every stage. The last is mostly her blood, to bind the children to her so that they will be tied to their tribe."

Shiv unwound a bandage from her hand. Samira hadn't noticed it until then. She had a wound below her knuckles which she held above the baby's head. When she flexed, golden blood dribbled into the baby's mouth. It ceased mewling and lapped at the liquid, its tooth-filled mouth working and swallowing.

Samira turned away, so many emotions warring within her that she didn't even know how to process that.

"We are lucky the young queen is here with us," Reach said. "She gives the blood while Pool is occupied."

Samira stared at Simon and felt the heavy hand of fatigue across her shoulders. She wanted to be happy he was alive, but if they couldn't get to Horace, there was no guarantee he'd stay that way. "Can I stay with him?"

"Ahya. We ask you, Usta, please do not tell other humans of this place. Not even Sa knows of it. We wish it to remain a secret."

Something about keeping secrets from their closest allies should have sounded off to her, but as she sank to the ground and stretched her neck, she found she was too tired to consider that, either. "Fine, whatever, as long as I get to stay."

❖

Liam took charge of the captured batteries. During the fight, he'd told Pool all he knew about where the armor might be vulnerable. Now, as they fled, he scrambled through the tree, trying to think of another way to help.

They'd captured one prisoner, a paladin who'd gotten caught up as Pool rescued a group of her people. The drushka had taken his armor's battery, but he still gave them a hard time. Liam jerked him around by his armored shoulder and punched him in his open helm, three hard hits, and the man went limp. He recognized Clemensky, who'd been a private when Liam left Gale. He wondered if they'd all been promoted since then.

"Strip his armor," Liam said, "and plug the battery back in." He took the paladin's sidearm, but someone touched his shoulder.

"The queen asks for you."

He kept the gun as the drushka led him to Pool where she steered the tree. "They follow us," Pool said, her gaze unfocused. "Their bullets, the Storm Lord's lightning…" She shuddered, and Liam knew she was feeling the hits.

"Put me where I can see them."

She lifted him to the back of the tree, and he saw the armored figures running in Pool's wake. With their armor still powered, they were keeping up easily, but Liam knew there were more than a few back at the battlefield with no power to speak of. He took aim and fired, hitting one paladin in the knee, though the bullet couldn't penetrate the armor. The paladin still stumbled enough to be left slightly behind.

Liam took another shot and missed. "Fuck." He took a deep breath and exhaled slowly before shooting again. He hit another paladin in the hip, but she shrugged it off, drew her own sidearm and fired into the tree. The branches closed over Liam, and he heard the dull thud as the bullets buried themselves in the bark.

"Shit," Liam mumbled. "Sorry, Pool."

Well, if he couldn't fight them from the tree, time for Plan B.

"I need that armor," he said.

"You go to fight them?" one drushka asked.

"I can keep them busy long enough for you to get away." For Shiv to get away. He only wished she was here so he could say...

What? That he loved her? He did, he knew that, but he fell in love so often and so easily, he wondered if it meant anything anymore. She made him feel worth more than just his body, which was something great. He had every intention of coming back, but he wished she were there so he could say that out loud and know that she'd miss him if he didn't.

He dressed quickly, smiling as the armor came to life. He'd never been as excited about it as Cordelia, but it was exhilarating all the same. "Ask Pool to throw me at the Storm Lord. He's the one in the lead, with the fucking stripes on his armor."

The drushka looked uncertain but touched the bark with the unfocused look drushka got when speaking mind to mind. "The queen says we will find you."

He didn't have time to respond before a branch curled around his waist and flung him straight for the Storm Lord. He held his arms out, and they crashed together in a screech of metal that sent them spinning across the grass. Liam grunted and tried to keep hold, his visor down, the speaker crackling as it came too close to the transmitter inside God's own helmet.

"I've tackled God," he thought. It made him laugh as they skidded to a halt with Liam on top, but the Storm Lord tried to buck him off, and calls were coming through his helmet as people started shouting.

"Get off me, you bastard!" the Storm Lord said, his voice growling in Liam's ear.

Liam grinned, seeing only a shadow of his face through both their visors. "Make me."

The Storm Lord gripped Liam's shoulder. Liam freed his sidearm and fired all around them, driving the other paladins back.

"No lightning?" he asked as he drove his knee downward, powered armor against powered armor, trying to drive the Storm Lord into the mud. "Are you tapped?" He felt a jolt, but it was so weak, his visor display flickered but steadied. The rain was still falling, but even it had become a trickle. "God having a little trouble getting it up?"

"Get him off me!" the Storm Lord shouted.

Liam holstered his sidearm, tucked his limbs around the Storm Lord and rolled, using his armor to move them both. The Storm Lord struggled, but when they hit the crest of a hill, gravity did Liam's work for him, and they went over the rise, Liam on top again. He rode the Storm Lord down the hill, sledding on God.

"I'm going to kill you, motherfucker!" The Storm Lord's fist caught him in the side of the helmet.

Liam jerked, his ears ringing in spite of the armor. He brought his gun out again and fired right into the Storm Lord's visor, hearing the reverb in his own ears and knowing it must have been deafening in the Storm Lord's. "That's for my mom!"

And he really wanted to stay, to claw the Storm Lord out of his armor and kill him seven different ways, but the other paladins were running down the hill, and if they killed Liam, they would be after Pool like a shot. He thought of Shiv and remembered everything Cordelia had tried to teach him about the living being more important than the dead.

"Come and catch me, assholes!" he cried as he ran, heading north. The crack of their guns was dulled by his helmet, but he felt the strikes against his back. The shockwaves had him gasping and stumbling. They didn't penetrate, but dull pain spread through his lower back as if someone had hit him two sharp whacks with a big stick. He tried to run in a random pattern and fired behind him until his clip emptied. Someone shot him again, then a fourth time, and ache spread through him, arcing with every step.

He kept running, using the power of the armor and the vision of Shiv to keep going. It'd been afternoon when the fight had begun, and now night was falling. He hadn't known they'd been fighting and running that long.

There were several more shots; one caught him on the shin and one on the hip. They were trying to stop him, not kill him. He risked a look over his shoulder and saw that the Storm Lord wasn't among them. Only a handful pursued him now, and he wondered if the others had stayed behind because he'd deafened the bastard.

When the sun finally set, he didn't activate his armor's glow but kept running through the dark. He changed direction again and again, hoping he wouldn't hit anything unexpected, but the ground vanished beneath him.

He fell hard into a gulley and tried to tuck into a roll, but he hit a rock and jolted to the side, making all his aches and pains scream as one. He kept his lips shut on a cry. When he came to rest, he wrestled his helmet off and gasped for breath, listening. He heard a sound like someone running, but it headed in a different direction and faded quickly, leaving him alone with the sound of the wind sighing through the grass.

He breathed deep and took a moment to be happy he was alive, even with pain winding through his back, and his lungs burning in his chest. His battery seemed to be losing charge. Maybe the others' were, too, or they might have caught him. Overhead, the stars brightened to life as the light faded, and a meteorite streaked across the sky. The air was crisp with the promise of a cold season ahead. And he was alone on the plains with no idea how to find Pool.

She was headed east, so he supposed he'd start trekking that way, hoping to meet up with her in Sun-Moon territory. He put his helmet back on and started walking, going carefully in the dark. When the armor became heavier, he wondered if he should dump it, but he heard a noise in the grass, something moving.

He paused, thinking of every predator Wuran had told him about, but the chafa liked to spin tall tales. Whatever it was, it didn't sound too big. He tried to activate his armor's glow, and managed a weak light barely bright enough to pick out the grass around him.

"You ruin your night vision!" a drushkan voice said.

Liam breathed a sigh that turned into a laugh and then a cough. "Cordelia always said no one tracks like a drushka."

"With the scent of your metal skin, it was easy." The speaker stepped into the dull light: Smile, one of Nettle's friends. "Come."

"Gladly." Liam stripped the battery out of his armor, and one of the drushka carried it, not wanting to leave it on the plains. Walking in un-powered armor brought back happy memories of patrols with Cordelia, and he tried to focus on them instead of the arduous walk through the dark. After who knew how many hours, they arrived at Pool's tree, and after he'd stripped out of the armor and told her what had happened, Shiv was waiting.

"Fool!" she said as she knocked him to the ground and crawled into his lap. "Fool a thousand times to risk yourself so!"

Liam settled her in his arms, trying to ignore his aches and pains. "I couldn't let them catch you."

She kissed him hard and laid her cheek against his. "You are a good mate, even if you make me worry. We rescued shawness Simon, but he is still in danger. We go now to seek shawness Horace."

Liam nodded. That had been the plan anyway, though with Simon Lazlo out of commission, they were still down a healer. He noticed the bandage wrapped around her hand and peered at it in the dim light. "I don't want to sound like your mother, but you weren't fighting, were you?"

She wrinkled her nose. "A scratch, and not from the fight. As you say, Shi'a'na would have my hide."

"Then how—"

"Let us leave off questions. I am chilled." She snuggled deeper into his arms, and they left off speaking for a time, though Liam called for a shawness soon after.

Dillon trudged back to camp surrounded by a few of his paladins. Most of them had chased the maniac who'd tackled him, and the rest stood around like worried parents. One plucked a blade of grass from the shoulder plate of his armor, and Dillon resisted the urge to yell at her to leave him be.

Lazlo was dead. That was the only thing that mattered.

"Orders, Storm Lord?" someone asked.

"I'll give you an order when I'm damn well ready!"

They recoiled as they should, and he wondered who was supposed to be giving them orders. Brown, probably. But she'd shot Lazlo, and then Dillon had pumped a bolt into her, killing her. He hadn't been thinking, had only seen her take the shot, and his power had just reacted.

He lowered his visor. The bullet hadn't dented it, but the noise had deafened him for a full ten minutes. Even now, it seemed as if the world's volume had been turned down while someone was ringing an imaginary bell.

And Lazlo was dead.

He looked to the horizon, where the man who'd tackled him had disappeared. He didn't want to run anymore, didn't want to make this day any shittier than it already was. Why the fuck had he listened to Naos? He could be safe in Gale right then, Lazlo and Brown alive. But no, he'd gone off, thinking to catch her or the Sun-Moon while they were vulnerable, and now everything was one big fuckup.

Back in camp, the yafanai were in an uproar, bustling about. They had to know Lazlo was gone, but they couldn't know he was dead unless…

Dillon spotted some of the other paladins, the leathers and those who'd had their power cells stolen. They were clustered among the wagons, and one ran to Dillon, his mouth open.

"I know about Lazlo and Captain Brown," he said, not wanting to hear it again in case someone thought he should be informed. He wondered if they'd brought Brown's body back.

The man shut his mouth and then opened it again. "And Caroline, Storm Lord?"

"What about her?"

He quivered. "She's…she's dead."

Dillon shook his head and pulled his helmet off. "Sorry, my ears are still ringing. You said what?"

The man blanched, and Dillon tried as hard as he could to look like a man who wouldn't be fucked with in that moment.

One of the paladins stepped up, Brown's second in command, Lea. "Caroline is as dead as Captain Brown, sir."

Oh, this one was going to take it hard, but he couldn't even think of that yet. "How the fuck? Was it the drushka?"

"No, sir. The yafanai tell me that Lazlo did something to her, sir."

"Some kind of cascade attack," one of the yafanai said hurriedly. "She was suffering multiple organ failure, dying as quickly as we could heal her until…" He shook his head. "We did all we could, I swear."

Dillon waited for that to come crashing down on him, too, but it couldn't get through his already spinning head. He tried to put it in order. Lazlo killed Caroline, then Brown killed Lazlo, then he killed Brown. All that was left was for someone to kill him.

He waited for Lessan then, but she didn't appear, nor did Naos or any of her circus. She'd pulled him out of the ground, but he still didn't know why. Maybe she knew this was coming, knew how much it would fuck him up, and she wanted to watch him suffer.

Lazlo was dead, and that hurt more than Brown or Caroline, more than the accusation in Lea's face or the grief on others. He tried to get mad for Caroline's sake, tried to remember all that had happened between them in order to summon grief. His son would grow up without a mother, without a biological one, anyway.

Nope. Nothing would get past Lazlo. Even when he'd left, there'd been hope that he'd come back, the best friend Dillon had ever had. But there was no coming back from a bullet to the head.

The volume of the world went back to normal, and the ring faded. He looked down to see one of the micro-psychokinetics withdrawing her arm. "Is that better, Storm Lord?"

He nodded. "Where are the bodies?"

"Caroline is on the wagon, Storm Lord," Lea said. "With Brown."

He'd have to nip that in the bud soon, but not right then. He'd let his soldiers grieve as they would. "Make camp."

They bustled around, and Dillon sat on the end of the wagon beside two bodies that had been wrapped together in a tent. Covered up, he couldn't tell which was which. He wondered what the soldiers thought they were going to do with two fucking bodies. They couldn't take them all the way to Celeste and then back to Gale. They'd be pretty ripe by then. The smart thing to do would be to bury them on the plains.

"Everyone underestimated him," he said to the bundles. "Even the three of us." Grief welled up inside him, and he couldn't even tell who it was for. Probably Lazlo, but the others would catch up to him. "I'm sorry I let this happen. I'll tell Evan…" He trailed away, unable to think of anything. "Should we just go home?"

He knew what his old man would say: if he went home now, all the suffering and the dead would be for nothing. There was such a thing as counting losses, but this was too damn many for nothing to show for it. No, best to learn from this what he could and keep going, only now he had his sights set on the fucking drushka, too, and he wouldn't be fooled again, wouldn't be lured.

He nodded. He'd bury Caroline and Brown at Celeste, with the Sun-Moon and Naos and the drushka and whoever the hell else got in his way.

❖

When Ap had first seen the soldiers coming after them, he'd ordered the others to take the children and run while he stayed behind. Some had protested, thinking he'd be killed; others argued that they wanted to slow the soldiers' pursuit as well, but he had no intention of getting in their way. He told them he would hide and then join the Storm Lord's followers while the rest of the Deliquois distracted the soldiers. They had run then, saying they would all see each other again in the Contessa's embrace.

He hid, cramming into a hollow under a nearby boulder. It stank of whatever animal had sheltered there, but Ap shut his eyes and found his center. He'd schooled his thoughts to nothingness, letting the feel of wind and grass, rock and earth fill him. He'd let the soldiers pass and then pressed on to the bulk of them, where several were in disarray, milling about, mourning one of their own. He'd waited until one man wandered out to relieve himself, and then Ap had rammed his knuckles into the man's head, just where spine met skull. After he'd lowered him to the grass, he'd pressed his hands around the man's windpipe and held his thumb against the artery that led to the brain.

It'd been easy enough to strip him. He looked like a servant rather than one of the mind benders, so if Ap stayed away from the other servants, he might be okay. He saw how those who were served didn't always look at those who served them. And if Ap acted as if he'd always been there, they would think he had. When the Storm Lord had come back from the plains, Ap didn't let himself feel glee. Knowing the abilities of those around him, he kept his thoughts blank or on the services he was to perform. He lit fires when instructed and helped someone set up a tent. Even when he heard in passing that his fellow islanders had gotten away, he didn't let himself feel relief.

Instead he watched the Storm Lord and waited. When the god went to sit alone on a cart, Ap thought he might get his chance for revenge, but a soldier watched the Storm Lord closely with an unreadable expression, and Ap settled in to wait.

CHAPTER TWENTY-THREE

From a room high in the palace, Cordelia leaned out the window. Even at night, the swath of destruction was like a scar across Celeste. The Sun-Moon worshipers had piled what they could in front of both massive holes, but they had to admit the only reason Naos's army hadn't charged back through was because it must not want to.

"We can't fight that," she said.

Sitting on their divan, the Sun-Moon ignored her. Horace had healed them from Naos's telepathic attack, but they still clung to one another, both pale. Naos's assault had almost burned out their minds as much as staring at the sun would burn the eyes.

"What do you suggest?" Fajir asked from where she leaned against the wall.

"She doesn't want surrender," the Sun-Moon said.

"Then evacuate," Cordelia said. "Everyone over the wall closest to the sea. Put those who can't walk in boats, and then everyone up the coast. Let her have the city."

Fajir sneered. "I never thought you a coward."

It might have gotten a rise out of Cordelia in the past, but now she shrugged. "So you want to stay and be turned into kindling?"

"Why did she not destroy the city at once if she can do so?" Nettle asked. "Why this one show of power? Why wait?"

"Perhaps there are limitations," the Sun-Moon said. "She's still on the satellite, but we sensed her telepathic connection to someone in the army. Perhaps the connection has a fault. Or perhaps whomever she's connected to convinced her to leave. It might be someone with their own power."

Cordelia looked to Horace, and she knew they were thinking the same thing. "Someone with their own power" could be Natalya. She used to be Horace's friend. Perhaps she'd discovered he was in the city and made Naos leave before he was hurt. "Did you find out anything about this connection?" Cordelia asked.

"A young mind," they said. "Probably female. We couldn't read it, not while being attacked." They clutched each other a little harder.

And Cordelia didn't want to talk anymore in front of them. "We should get some rest while we can."

"We need to plan," Fajir said.

"Sure, you think of a plan that will get rid of the closest thing we've ever seen to a real god, then come find me."

If that hurt the Sun-Moon, they didn't show it, but Fajir's lips pressed into a thin line. "Lords, if you will it, I'll consult with the other serens."

The Sun-Moon waved her away. As Cordelia started out of the room with Nettle and Horace, the Sun-Moon added, "Don't even think about leaving."

Cordelia fought the urge to scream. "I know."

"We don't want you to forget."

Once they were safely in their own room with Mamet, Cordelia said, "I don't suppose you've learned how to block them?"

He sighed. "I think I can tell if they're actively listening, and right now they're not. They might sense it if we leave the city."

Cordelia ran her hands through her hair. "Why can't I be involved in the regular fights? Guns and blades? Why is someone always throwing lightning bolts or force waves or telepathic attacks?"

"Says the woman who can leave her body."

She shook her head. "We have to get out of here. What are the chances that Natalya is out with that army?"

"She's not what I'd call a young mind, but I know I sensed her."

"Who's Natalya?" Mamet asked.

"An old friend of Horace's. We think she might be... I don't know. Caught up in this? Anyway, she might help us escape."

Horace looked out the window. "I can't see Nat doing all this, no matter what happened to her. At least, she wouldn't have before being augmented. She went a little...overzealous at the end."

"One way to find out," Cordelia said. "Can you reach her from here?"

"Over so many minds and at such a distance?" He shrugged. "Maybe, but *finding* her is the problem." He rolled his lips under. "If you go out of your body, I can follow you telepathically, and you can search with me. That might be better than fumbling around with the world's greatest telepaths nearby."

"What if we run into...her? Naos?" Cordelia shivered.

"We shouldn't seem any different than any other mind," Horace said. "If either of us senses her, float like hell back to your body."

"Great." The last few times, that hadn't been an option, but maybe the Sun-Moon were right, and Naos was distracted.

"If you reach your friend," Mamet said, "what are you going to ask her to do?"

"Leave, if she can manage it," Cordelia said. "And take Naos with her."

Mamet shook her head. "Shouldn't you ask her to attack? If we know when it's coming, we can escape."

Now they all looked to one another, and Cordelia glanced at Horace. "They're not listening," he whispered.

Cordelia almost laughed, but now seemed like a fine time for whispering.

"Mamet," Horace said, "think of all the people in the city—"

"Some of them deserve to die," Mamet said, her fists clenched.

"That might be true," Cordelia said softly, "but this isn't our fight on either side. The best thing we could do is figure out how to leave with the least amount of bloodshed, not switch sides."

"No matter who wins this fight, it could be bad for us," Nettle said. "Where might the victors turn their eyes next?" Before Mamet could speak again, Nettle laid a hand on her shoulder. "But when the warriors of this city are next distracted, no matter the cause, you should search for your captive kin."

Mamet took a deep breath then nodded, and Cordelia knew the captives had been on her mind since she hadn't gone looking during the first attack. But then, there'd been a lot of fuckups during the first attack.

"Ready?" Horace asked.

Cordelia laid on one of the divans, her head in Nettle's lap. "Be careful, Sa," Nettle said, her thin lips gliding across Cordelia's forehead. "Return to me unharmed."

She would have loved to promise, but she could only kiss Nettle's long fingers, let her eyes fall shut, and slip free of her body.

Shapes seemed sharper to her astral eyes; the world a little easier to see even at night. Cordelia looked down on the heads of her friends, except for Horace, who stared up.

"I'm with you," he said in her mind, his lips unmoving.

"Right." She drifted out the window and over the city, not stopping until she was among the campfires of Naos's army. Even at night, many people wandered to and fro, their camp far enough from the walls that they were in no danger from ballistae or arrows. Small lights burned within tents, and she wondered how many plains dwellers were having sleepless nights, how many wondered what in the hell they were doing here, and how many had seen the destruction and felt fear instead of pride.

"How are you doing?" Horace asked. "I'm getting hazy pictures from your mind, but I don't want to dig."

"The army's pretty spread out. Do you sense anything?"

"Many minds below you. You'll have to get closer."

She headed for the middle of the encampment where a tent stood alone, the others giving it plenty of space.

"Wait!" Horace called. "There are three minds and two bodies in that tent."

Cordelia began to drift back the way she'd come.

"One of them is Natalya."

Cordelia paused, torn. She spotted a glint coming from the tent, a sliver of blue light like the silver one that anchored her to her body, only this one came from the sky.

"Go!" Horace said. "Go, get out—"

A flood of white noise drowned him out, and Cordelia felt Naos's immense presence surround her. "Well, well, well! Fancy meeting you down here!"

Part of the blue light peeled away and reached out to Cordelia. She hung frozen, just as before, and the light shifted into the ghostly form of a woman, tall and wild-looking and missing her right eye.

"So you can come see me when I'm aground. Fascinating."

"I'm in the city," Cordelia said, hoping that would gain her something; maybe some fondness on Naos's part would turn her away.

"Shame." Naos drifted around her and gripped the silver cord that led back to Cordelia's body, twining it around one finger.

Cordelia groaned as cramps spiked through her. It wasn't fair to have pain with no body. "Stop," she gasped.

"I wonder what would happen if we cut this? Would you float around forever? Do you think that after a hundred years of not being able to touch anyone, you'd beg me to collect you?"

"Is...is Natalya here?"

"How do you know her? Are you a people collector, too?"

"I just want..." She trailed away as another bit of blue light broke off from the strand and curled like a serpent around Naos's shoulders. It hovered near her ear as if speaking, and she tilted her head, listening.

With a start, Cordelia realized she could move again. She'd have to go around Naos to get back to her body, so she edged that way, hoping to remain unobtrusive. Naos gestured as if speaking out loud, not paying Cordelia any mind. When she began to fade, Cordelia got ready to flee, but Horace popped back into her mind.

"Can you hear me?"

"Yep, and I'm getting the fuck out of here!"

"Wait! I can't sense the three minds anymore. Now there are just two."

She looked back to the tent; the blue light had dissipated, but it wasn't gone. "Horace..."

"When will we get another opportunity? I sensed something like four minds there at the end, but now just two. It...should be safe."

Cordelia could hear Fajir in her head calling her a coward. And here she thought that hadn't bothered her. "All right. I'll get closer."

Natalya rubbed Kora's back in gentle circles. The goddess had departed her violently, leaving her shuddering on the ground. When she possessed the girl, she often forgot to feed herself, and she definitely forgot to rest. Natalya supposed Naos didn't have to do either of those things often, but it was Kora who felt their lack.

Kora's eyes moved back and forth under her bruised lids. She shuddered in her dreams. Natalya used as much of her micro powers as she dared and tried to ease Kora's pain, but as she'd thought to herself many times during their journey, she wasn't a healer.

"Natalya?" a new voice asked: Horace's voice, a telepathic message.

It was a trick, had to be, but Naos wouldn't know Horace's voice, wouldn't have perfected his tone of concern. But of course she *could* do it. She'd dig it out of Natalya's own mind. "What is this?"

"Nat, it's me. Horace."

It did sound like him, and she tried to think of what that might mean, if Naos had gobbled him up and ransacked his brain. "How?"

"I'm in Celeste. It's a long story. How are you part of Naos's army?"

"Another long story." If this was a test, it was the most bizarre one yet. "What do you want?"

"Did you make her leave today? Can you get her to go away for good?"

Natalya laughed and heard the edge to it, but she wouldn't give in to hysterics. Not yet. "Might as well convince a firestorm to die down. I'm in over my head, Horace. She doesn't listen to anyone. I don't know why she does anything."

"Nat…I'm so sorry I couldn't help you more. I should have made sure you were all right before I left Gale."

That old Horace guilt. She had to admit she'd used it against him a few times, but now it made her chuckle. "It's not your fault. Simon Lazlo made me like this, and Naos was the only one who could help me." She sighed. "I want out, Horace, for me and for this girl."

"Don't blame Simon. It was all the Storm Lord's idea. We all have to get away from anyone who calls him or herself a god."

She couldn't argue with that, at least.

"Tell me about the girl," he said. "She's linked to Naos?"

"Not completely. There might be a way to separate them, but I don't have the power."

He went silent, and she wondered if he knew how much it bothered her to be powerless. The whole reason she'd taken the augmentation in the first place was to surpass everyone, to always be the person everyone called on, depended on. She'd thought Naos could help her get there, but the price was too damn high.

"My friends and I might be able to think of something," he said at last.

"Are your friends the Sun-Moon? Because she's going to go after them hard, Horace."

"We'll see what we can do, Nat. I'll contact you again. It was good to hear your voice."

She sensed his genuine feeling and smiled, even though she still found him too sappy for his own good. As the contact faded, she clenched her fists and hoped he wasn't a trick. Before, she would've prayed to the Storm Lord, but now she didn't know who to turn to. And she had no doubt Horace would be back. At least, he'd try. He'd also promised to help her in Gale and hadn't been able to see it through.

Now, though, he had the lives of his friends to consider, and he was always better at keeping his promises when someone besides himself was on the line. As Kora groaned in her sleep, Natalya stroked her hair, more hopeful than she'd been. Now all she had to do was hide her hope from Naos.

❖

On the balcony, Cordelia lay in Nettle's arms. They'd begun the evening in bed after Cordelia had returned to her body, but they both missed the feel of the wind and the open sky. She didn't think Nettle was a fan of wide open spaces, but it seemed any nature was preferable to being trapped in the house of the Sun-Moon.

Cordelia teetered on the edge of sleep, still freaked out by her brief touch with Naos. Part of her feared having her spirit collected while she wasn't paying attention. When she heard a creak in the courtyard below, her eyes opened. She paused, waiting, and when the creak came again, she sat up. Nettle woke and slid to her knees without effort to look into the darkened courtyard below.

"Someone gathers," she said softly. "Many people, by the sound."

Cordelia saw only shadows on top of shadows, but they were on the move, and she thought she spotted the glint of something shiny in the moonlight. A candle flared but was quickly snuffed, and she thought she saw someone in leather armor. Not townsfolk, then.

"Where are they off to?"

"Running from the battle?" Nettle asked.

If that were true, and a bunch of minds were leaving Celeste at once… "Wake the others. Time to go."

They woke Horace and Mamet, who blinked at them groggily, but Horace's quick telepathic scan revealed that it wasn't deserters below them. In fact, the Sun-Moon seemed to be down there with them.

"Can you tell what they're up to?" Cordelia asked.

He gave her the same look he always did when she asked if he was a match for their power. "I'm not going to try reading their minds or anyone around them, thanks. I don't want my brains leaking out my ears any more than you do."

"We have to find out what they're doing."

"If they've left the palace, this is my chance to free my kinsmen," Mamet said. She looked to Horace. "I'll come when you call."

They agreed and split up. Cordelia, Nettle, and Horace hurried down through the palace, stepping over clumps of sleeping civilians. Once on the ground, they trailed a column of soldiers through the city until they got to the head, trying to stay in the shadows. The Sun-Moon walked toward a gathering of ballistae that sat near a lone torch, just inside the breached gates. Fajir marched at the Sun-Moon's side, and after a small sigh, she veered toward where Cordelia tried to stay in the dark.

"You may be able to hide from me," Fajir called softly, "but not from the Lords."

With a shrug, Cordelia marched into the open, Nettle and Horace with her.

"Before you ask," the Sun-Moon said, "we're attacking Naos's army when she least expects it."

"Are—"

"We're not insane," they said.

"What—"

"We need to strike while they're still in disarray."

Cordelia clenched her fists. "It'd be nice if you stopped answering the fucking questions before I ask them."

Fajir drew her sword, but after a glance at the Sun-Moon, she sheathed it. They had little smiles, and Cordelia reined her temper in, not wanting to give them a moment's amusement.

"When you communicated with their camp earlier, we sensed Naos's distraction." They nodded at Lisa and Aaron, the companions they'd brought with them from space. "If she stays distracted, the four of us might have a chance to defeat her forces, maybe even kill her host."

Horace started to speak, but Cordelia laid a hand on his arm. "So you were listening," she said.

"Of course." Barely a tingle passed over her scalp as they spoke in her mind. "We can be stealthy when we want to." With a chuckle, they added, "You seem to attract her attention somehow. Do it again, and we've got her. The faster we drive her away, the faster you can leave."

She didn't believe they'd just let her leave, but if they were fully embroiled in the conflict...

Nettle leaned close to her ear. "I will guard your body."

Cordelia nodded. "I'll distract her and retreat. You hit her with everything you have."

"She won't know which way to turn," the Sun-Moon said.

Horace leaned up toward Cordelia's ear. "I promised Nat we'd try to help!"

"You don't think hitting Naos hard enough to make her leave everyone alone will help?"

He sighed. "After the attack starts. I'll tell Nat to run."

❖

Natalya sat outside the tent, gazing up at the star-filled sky. She hadn't been able to sleep after Horace contacted her, so she'd decided to sit outside rather than risk waking Kora. She wasn't a telepath, so she couldn't listen for Horace's mind, but she kept a micro-psychokinetic link on Kora, hoping she'd get a heads-up if Naos returned.

A tingle ran along that connection, and she looked into the tent to see Kora sitting up. She'd lit a candle, and before Natalya could speak, she laid a finger against her lips. Her eyes were their normal brown. Kora pulled Natalya in with a telepathic connection, and Natalya heard Kora's voice speaking in Kora's own mind. "Goddess, is that you?"

"I'm not a god and neither is she."

It was the other voice, the one Natalya had heard before, but it had never spoken to Kora like this, not with such sureness of itself.

"I'm learning," the voice said as if hearing Natalya's thoughts, too, and maybe she could, being as powerful as the goddess.

"Yes and no," the new voice said. "I want to *be* again. I want to be free, to not need her permission."

"The goddess must have her way in all things," Kora said loyally.

Natalya frowned, but the new voice laughed. "Poor thing. You really are broken, aren't you?"

Voices lifted through the camp, and Natalya turned back toward the night. Cries of alarm and surprise turned to screams. Natalya got to her feet, trying to see what was happening, trying to feel it; a lot of people were hurt.

Kora climbed out beside her. "The people think the goddess has turned on them!"

"You have to stop—"

Kora put her hands over her ears. "So many people hurt! So many thoughts and voices! They want me to help them. Some want me to kill them, but you said killing is bad!"

"Get yourself together!"

"What do I do?" Her power fluttered, as if she wanted to direct it but didn't know where. "They're dying forever!"

Natalya pulled on Kora's arm. Maybe now they could run, but where? Naos would find them. Where the hell was Horace when she needed him?

"Goddess, help me!"

"No!" Natalya cried, but Naos's arrival scorched the air, and she flailed backward, tripping into the tent and collapsing it. By the time she fought free of it, Kora had gone. "Kora?" People were still screaming, torches bobbing here and there. Kora had taken the candle. "Kora!" She turned toward the tent perimeter. A torch flew high into the air, a bright arc that landed in the long grass and spread its glow as the grass caught fire.

Natalya picked up her downed tent in a psychokinetic grip and smothered the fire. With a sound of snapping sinew, another tent exploded. She staggered back, thinking someone was using macro powers, but she spotted an enormous spear protruding from the tent's remains. Something inside it glistened, blood. Someone had been in there.

She remembered the war machines on top of the walls, but they were too far away to do this. Maybe someone had brought them closer. A new group of torches stood together at the edge of the field, beyond the tents. A group of plains dwellers charged them and were tossed away or immolated by fire. The Sun-Moon had come.

She looked for them, spotting two people standing close together and staring at the field. As she watched, they grasped their heads and bent double. Her senses told her Naos was attacking them, so she looked again for Kora. Maybe the goddess would be distracted, and Natalya could finally take Kora and flee, but the question of where still remained.

"Horace," she thought as loudly as she could. If he could attack Kora's connection while Naos was busy, maybe he could sever it and find a way to shield her and Natalya both. But she had to find Kora first.

"I'm here," he said in her mind. "Get ready to run."

CHAPTER TWENTY-FOUR

Cordelia floated above a battle she couldn't hear and searched the ground below. The Sun's fires turned it into a series of flickers, bringing combatants into sharp relief before throwing them into shadow again. Ballista bolts caught fire as they smashed into tents, and people were thrown into the air by the Moon's invisible hand.

Cordelia searched for that telltale blue glow and finally spotted it near the edge of combat. She willed herself toward it but had only a vague idea of what to do when she got there. The plan was to get Naos to notice her, but she really didn't want that to happen again.

Still, no time to run from a fight. Distract and retreat. Right.

"Fuck it." She hurtled toward the blue glow and through it, trying to pass out the other side and hurry back to her body, but she stuttered to a halt as images and memories raced through her mind, one after another, the whole of the universe trying to fill her head as it had before. She willed herself to fucking move, to go faster, and the feeling eased as she passed out of the glow. She hurried toward the city as fast as she could, but before she reached the edge of the field, that titanic force seized her again.

"What the fuck do you think you're doing?" Naos's voice roared in her head.

Cordelia grunted and struggled. She felt Naos's power waver, probably the Sun-Moon attacking her. "Horace!"

"Here," he said. "Naos is attacking the Sun-Moon now."

Which meant the plan was working, but it wouldn't keep working if Naos killed the Sun-Moon. Cordelia turned, bracing herself, and hurtled through the blue light again.

It splintered, and she crowed, thinking they'd broken the link, but it only stabbed toward many bodies, the lights becoming thin threads. As she focused on one, it seemed to disappear. She turned for her body—best to retreat if the whole plan was fucked—but one of the threads coalesced into the ghostly woman she'd seen earlier.

"Horace!" Cordelia cried.

Naos lifted a hand, and Horace's voice melted into nothing.

"Nice try. Let me give you a kiss as a reward." She blew along her palm, and Cordelia cried out as her spirit tumbled backward. She tried to lift her hands and shield herself, but she had no hands, and she'd never felt so powerless as her spirit lifted high into the air. She hurtled across the landscape, away from Celeste, and darkness grew around her, the lights fading into the distance. Her silver life cord unwound like a rope going over a cliff.

Cordelia screamed, but no one could hear, even if there'd been someone around. She struggled and reached for Horace, but nothing could stop her, and her lifeline grew thinner and thinner before it dissolved into nothing. When she finally whirled to a stop, darkness surrounded her, with nothing to show the way home.

Cordelia's pain rattled through Horace's brain, and then her mind was gone as if she'd never existed. He turned from healing the Sun-Moon, but Naos was no longer attacking them either. "I have to get to Cordelia!"

They waved him away. "Stay close."

He ran to the side of the road where Nettle watched over Cordelia's body. Blood trickled from her ears, and she shuddered and jerked. Horace healed her body, but her mind was just…gone. "What happened?"

Nettle bent over her, and Horace caught, "Sa, come back to me," but Cordelia didn't respond. The screams from the battlefield were coming closer. Horace had sensed it as Naos splintered her own link so she could control multiple people at once. He didn't know if they could all wield her awesome power, or if she was just maneuvering them like puppets, but it sounded as if the battle had turned.

"Shawness," Nettle said, "what has happened to her?"

"I don't know." He sent his mind out again, but there was so much telepathic chaos, not to mention the random attacks from the Sun-Moon, and he couldn't find Natalya without Cordelia acting like an antenna. He laid a hand on Nettle's shoulder. "She's not in there anymore, but we'll find her."

"How?"

Again, he had no idea.

Nettle stood, her lean face without expression. "I will find this girl, this host of Naos, and kill her. Perhaps then Sa will come back to her body."

"Wait, you can't just—"

"Guard Sa, shawness."

"Come back! You might hurt Natalya!"

Nettle took off into the battlefield, and Horace watched through the haze as she stabbed one young girl through the neck before she was lost to smoke and darkness.

"Damn it!" He took a deep breath and sent out a telepathic call for Mamet.

"Almost there," Mamet said. She jogged around the corner, and Horace waved her over.

"Help me move Cordelia somewhere safer."

"What happened?"

Horace explained as they shifted Cordelia into a nearby house, and Mamet went pale as she listened. "Do you think Nettle's plan will work?"

"I don't know! We have to get after her. If she kills Natalya, there's no telling what Naos will do."

Horace hoped the Sun-Moon were too busy to notice as he slipped past the wall and onto the battlefield. "There!" Mamet whispered.

Nettle leapt from the shadows and killed another woman before fading into darkness. Horace ran after her, both he and Mamet trying to keep away from pockets of fighting. Horace sent out small telepathic bursts, searching for Natalya. Maybe she would know what to do with Cordelia, and they could get her back and leave this place behind. He had a brief thought that they should have brought Cordelia's body with them, but that would have slowed them down. When Mamet dragged him out of the way of two brawling fights, he knew it was too late for second thoughts.

Natalya felt Naos all around her, but not like when she was speaking in Natalya's head or inhabiting Kora. She filled the plains dwellers and made them throw themselves at the Sun-Moon soldiers. Natalya didn't know whether she was targeting the people guarding the Sun-Moon or the Sun-Moon themselves, but the reckless attacks threw lives away.

One thing was certain, Naos wasn't currently with Natalya, which meant now was the time to act. Horace had told her to run, but she had a better idea. She had to attack the link. A jot of loss surprised her. So much for being the chosen one. She'd never wanted to be Kora, but the thought that she was no longer worthy of even a fraction of the goddess's attention irked her. But now wasn't the time for lamentations. If Naos was busy spreading herself around, Kora might be free, too.

She found Kora standing in the middle of the field, head thrown back and eyes wide. One of the Sun-Moon's long spears hovered in front of her, suspended in midair. Natalya grabbed it with a macro-psychokinetic shove and hurled it into the dark. She put her hands on Kora's shoulders and reached for the link with her micro powers. She tried to adjust Kora's brain, but it resisted her. She cried out for Horace, hoping he was still listening. When he'd disappeared, she'd feared he might have been killed.

"Natalya?" he asked in her head.

She whooped. "Help me! I'm with Kora. We have to break the link now."

"I'm on the battlefield. Where are you?"

She looked around, but the chaos was impossible to follow, and the darkness made distances hard to gauge. She caught a flaming tent with her powers and tossed it into the air. "Here!"

"If we break her link, will that free the rest of the plains dwellers and stop this?"

She didn't know and hoped he wasn't listening too hard when she said, "Yes! Hurry!"

He linked with her mind, not shoving in as Naos did, but offering his telepathic powers and letting her use her micro powers to focus them both. They'd communed sometimes in Gale, and the memories came flooding back. The link twitched under their combined assault, and Natalya felt Naos's attention turn toward them.

"More!" Natalya cried.

He reached for someone else, and she felt another power join theirs, the telepathic might of the Sun-Moon; she wasn't about to argue. They attacked the link as one, and Kora screamed, a cry that echoed all around them. Across the field, plains dwellers screeched in gut-wrenching dissonance, and Natalya had to resist clapping her hands over her ears.

The link shuddered, collapsing like foam in a storm, but before it could wink out, Naos's connections to the other plains dwellers snapped shut, and her mind overtook Kora's, her power butting against Natalya and the others and swamping them. The force of it launched Natalya off her feet and sent her flying.

She landed hard, grunting, and the air rushed from her lungs. She tried to use her micro powers to heal herself, but Naos stalked closer, a blue glow shimmering around her, around Kora's body.

"You miserable fucking shitbag!" Naos's hair whipped in an invisible wind, and her eyes blazed with fury, the blue light dancing like smoke as it made spectral faces near her shoulders. "I'll teach you!"

Natalya tried to move but an invisible hand gripped her so hard she couldn't breathe. She lifted from the ground, hovering. One of the spectral faces stared over Kora's shoulder, showing Naos's true face—leaner and older than Kora's—but both faces wore an evil grin as Naos lifted one hand, index finger pointed at Natalya's right eye.

"Lessons to learn, prices to pay," Naos said. The finger didn't shake, didn't move a fraction off course as it slid forward. Natalya couldn't even gasp as it filled her vision. With her left eye, she stared at Kora and willed the girl to stop the goddess.

The fingertip grazed her eye, burning, but she couldn't cry out. Naos paused, and Natalya had a fraction of a second to hope for mercy.

"Mercy is earned." Naos drove forward in one smooth, violent motion.

Pain blocked out everything but the feeling of hot fluid rushing down her cheek. Naos released her voice, and she shrieked until her throat felt shredded. As her screams turned to sobs, Naos finally released her, and she fell to the ground.

"I'm going to need a little time to recover. You *hurt* me." Naos forced Natalya's head up and smiled. "I'm almost impressed." She flicked the raw flesh inside the empty socket, and Natalya summoned up another scream. "Hopefully, this little reminder will keep you out of trouble."

As Naos departed, Natalya slumped to the ground, Kora beside her.

"No!" Kora crawled closer. "I hoped it was a dream." She lifted Natalya's head, probably trying to help, but the pain doubled, tripled.

Natalya turned her head to the side and retched. She couldn't even manage another scream, could only grunt and sob. Kora wiped her cheeks and chin, murmuring, "I'm sorry. I'm so sorry." She petted Natalya's hair and called, "Someone help!"

"Natalya?" Horace's voice. What the fuck had taken him so long?

"Can you help?" Kora asked.

Someone took Natalya's hand, and healing energy flowed into her. She sighed as the pain ebbed away, and Horace's power carried her away from madness and into a comforting black abyss.

❖

As Natalya fell asleep, Horace turned his attention to the girl. She was filthy with soot, and tears had carved clean tracks down her cheeks. He felt her link to Naos and knew this was the one Nettle had gone looking for.

"I don't know what I am," she said.

So, she had some of Naos's power even when the goddess wasn't around. Horace had expected Naos's vessel to be horrific, a mad warrior covered in blood, not this young girl who gripped the hem of her shirt like a lost child.

Mamet had her sword out and was looking between all of them as well as watching a battlefield that had ceased battling. All it had now was the pop and crackle of random fires and the cries of wounded people.

"Grab Natalya's legs," Horace said. "We're taking her back to the city."

The girl's eyes widened, and Horace thought she might protest, but she said, "Yes, good! Take her so the goddess doesn't punish her again!" She scrambled to her feet.

Mamet helped Horace lift Natalya. Horace hesitated, not knowing if he should invite this girl to come with them, not knowing if Naos could take her over with impunity. He decided not to ask. If he couldn't break the link, there was every chance the Sun-Moon would kill her, and he didn't know if he could stand by and watch such a thing.

"What about Nettle?" Mamet asked when they were halfway across the field.

As if to answer them, someone hissed nearby, and Nettle peeled away from the shadows. Mamet suppressed a cry but let go of Natalya's legs and fumbled for her sword before she recognized who it was.

"I followed you," Nettle said. "Who is this?"

"My friend Natalya."

"And the girl you left behind?" Nettle stooped to support Natalya's midsection, lessening the burden so they could go faster.

Horace swallowed and didn't answer.

"Shawness?" Nettle asked again.

Horace sighed. "She's the one we were looking for."

"And you did not kill her?"

"I couldn't!"

"First you leave Sa, then you let the person who injured her go?"

"That was Naos, not the girl!"

"You said they were linked, shawness. Are they not the same?"

When Horace said nothing, Mamet added, "She didn't look like a goddess."

"If we killed her, would Sa's spirit return?" Nettle asked.

Horace shook his head, thinking fast. "I...don't think so. I healed Cordelia, and I don't think her body would be alive if her spirit wasn't still around somewhere, so we have a little time."

"That does not answer my question."

Horace took a deep breath, sick and tired of all the killing. "Please don't do anything until I've had a chance to talk to Nat."

"We will take her into the city with Sa. But after this is done, I will return here, shawness, taking Mamet with me, and once you know the truth of this girl, you will contact Mamet with your mind. If killing the girl will help, it will be done."

Horace wanted to argue, but Nettle's tone said that wouldn't go over well. He had to nod and hope there was a way to keep as many people alive as possible.

CHAPTER TWENTY-FIVE

Don't fucking panic." Cordelia would have taken a few deep breaths, but she still didn't have a body. She tried not to think of herself as the only person she would ever speak to again, but no one else could hear her.

"Shit, shit, shit." If she'd had fists, she would have been looking for something to pound, but that was as off the table as anything else.

"No, calm. Fucking calm." Telepaths could hear her. She had to find her way back to Horace. Good, a plan. That was good. Now, which way?

She willed herself upward, but the night below was an endless sea of moving grass. The occasional rock flashed white or gray, but how the fuck was she supposed to find her way back to Celeste, and what would happen when she got there? Would Naos send her right back into the middle of nothing?

The moon was on its way down, so she could find east easily enough, but she had no idea how far north or south she'd gone. Why hadn't she paid attention to Wuran when he'd tried to teach her about the stars? Why did the plains dwellers have such good alcohol?

She drifted higher still and saw a light in the distance, but it wasn't the light of fires or the blue glow of Naos. It had a pure, non-flickering quality that filled her with hope.

"Pool!" She headed for it like a shot. She'd been able to touch their connection before when she'd left her body. Why not now? She willed herself faster and faster, and as the tree came within sight, she saw dark streaks marring its light like wounds in the bark. She paused by the enormous trunk and saw the burns. If Pool had caught fire, the marks wouldn't be so precise, and she realized with a start that they were lightning strikes. The Storm Lord had attacked the drushka.

Anger burned in Cordelia's heart. No one could leave them the fuck alone, it seemed. She sensed drushkan power at work, the shawnèssi trying to sing away the tree's wounds, but they would be a long time in healing. Cordelia drifted downward and threaded past the limbs rather than trying to move through them, not wanting to do anything to interrupt the drushkan connection as she'd interrupted Naos.

She found Pool dozing in the high branches, her green hair spread around her, and the white glow suffusing her dark skin. Cordelia hesitated, but her problems wouldn't wait. "Pool, I need your help."

Pool's eyes flew open. "Sa?" She looked near where Cordelia hovered and reached out. "I hear you." Cordelia told her story so quickly, Pool held up a hand. "Your memories flow like water, Sa. You must slow yourself."

"I'm sorry. I'm new at this mind to mind stuff. I need my body back!"

Pool held her arms out, and the white glow extended from her, engulfing Cordelia, but unlike Naos's overwhelming force, this wrapped around her rather than immobilizing her. She heard the whispers of many voices like wind sighing through leaves, but it didn't intrude on her consciousness. She smelled greenery and earth, and for the first time since she'd started for Celeste she felt real calm.

"We will journey to reclaim your body together," Pool said. "All that is done can be undone. Remember this."

"What happened to your tree? The Storm Lord?"

"I sensed the attack on Nettle's mind, and so we were speaking of coming to your aid when the Storm Lord ventured from his city. We attacked and retrieved shawness Simon, though he is terribly injured and needs shawness Horace. Some of us are dead." She fell silent, and Cordelia felt her sorrow, the sorrow of all drushka to find one of their kind missing where before they had been whole.

"This is such a mess," Cordelia said. "I'm sorry, Pool."

Pool smiled. "I feel your grief, Sa, and it is welcome. Do not worry. We will see you whole again."

"What if I can't be?" If she'd had a body, she wouldn't have been able to choke the words out, but there was no hiding like this. At one time, the idea would have scared her to death. "Naos asked me how long I could be alone before I turned to her from loneliness."

"Hear me, Sa." Certainty flooded Pools words even though she wasn't speaking aloud. "The drushka will never abandon you. Do not abandon hope."

Cordelia felt grateful, but she didn't know how long her body would last without her inside it. And if her body died, the rest of her would fade away.

Unless she didn't, and she *was* doomed to float around forever, watching the people she cared about yet unable to touch them, to speak with them except through Pool or Horace. Before she gave in to despair, Pool's light flowed around her again, and she sank into it, letting it comfort her.

❖

The fighting seemed to be done for the moment, but Horace didn't know which deity to thank. After they'd come back inside the city, they'd collected Cordelia's body and moved both her and Natalya a little deeper inside the city to a small, unattended house. Horace hadn't seen the Sun-Moon, but even Nettle seemed to think better of escape at the moment, not with a mad goddess right outside the walls and two unconscious bodies to haul around. Horace pointed out that if they moved Cordelia too far, she might not be able to find her way back to herself, but he didn't add that he also wanted to help the young girl in the field if he could. He couldn't get her small, dirty, hopeful face out of his mind.

Nettle and Mamet went back outside the wall despite Horace's protests, and now he watched Natalya sleep on a narrow bed inside a small, abandoned bedroom. He wondered briefly who'd lived here. The room held another bed, probably for a partner, and it called to him, but he resisted the urge to close his eyes, focusing on Natalya instead.

Ever since he'd been augmented, he'd wondered if he could regrow a missing limb or eye, then when Simon had taken his power, it hadn't seemed worth the time to ponder. Now he tried but found he couldn't do anything except seal the cavity and nudge away infection. Either it was beyond his power, or Naos had done something to prevent this sort of tampering, but how was that possible? Maybe it was just a case of having nothing left to work with.

"Nat," he said gently, using his power to wake her.

Her remaining eye flew open, and she tried to sit up. "Kora?"

Horace pushed her back down. "It's all right, Nat. You're safe."

She had to turn her head to focus on him. "Horace?" Her hand went halfway to her empty socket before it fell.

"I'm sorry. I couldn't fix it."

"It's not your fault." She stared at nothing, and he didn't want to use telepathy on her, but he needed answers.

"Tell me about Kora, Nat."

She barked a humorless laugh, and her left eye filled with tears. "Is she all right?"

"Fine when I left. Do you know what Naos did to Cordelia?"

"Who?"

"One of the paladins. You met her in the swamp. She can…leave her body. Anyway, Naos separated her from her body, and I have to figure out how to undo it. Would Kora know how? Does she know how to get rid of Naos?"

Natalya stared at him a long time, and he recalled that he was never good at hiding things from her. "You're going to kill her. You think that'll undo all your troubles." When he didn't respond, she grabbed his arm, fist knotting in his shirt. "She's only four years old, and Naos stole her. She grew her overnight, implanted false memories. Kora has no idea what's happening, Horace!"

It took him a minute to figure out what she was talking about, and then he felt sick to his stomach even thinking about it. "That's disgusting! How is it even—"

"None of what happened is her fault. You can fix her, Horace. It's what you do!"

And you couldn't blame a shawness for being a shawness. "She has some power on her own, right? Or is that just Naos, too?"

"I don't know, but if you sever the link, the power might go. You can fix your friend without Naos's power, Horace. Make Simon Lazlo help you. I'll help you!"

He read her desperation, certain she at least was willing to *make* Simon do things. The idea sickened him further. "I need to contact my friends. You should get some rest."

"Please don't hurt her. Tell your friends not to hurt her."

"I will. Rest, Nat. It's almost over." He wished he could believe that. He left the room and closed his eyes, trying to block out everything as he searched out the only alien mind near Celeste. He still couldn't contact Nettle that way, so he reached for Mamet instead, finding her nearby. "It's Horace."

Mamet's mind jerked in surprise. "I will never get used to this."

Horace relayed what Natalya had told him and waited while Mamet did the same for Nettle.

"Nettle asks if we're supposed to kill the girl or not."

"She's a four-year-old!" Horace said. "We can't! She can't!"

"I think she's joking. Maybe. She wonders why you didn't tell us not to kill the girl instead of taking so much time to explain."

As if that would have worked. "Are you coming back?"

"Nettle says we'll stay out here and watch. She says consult the Sun-Moon and tell them what you've learned, see if they have thoughts about this link. Perhaps it's weakened now."

"Might be worth a check." He shut off the connection and went to see if Natalya needed help going to sleep. He didn't know why it still felt so natural to urge a wounded person to sleep. He could cure their fatigue as well as heal their wounds, but Natalya had been through something traumatic and needed real time to heal.

So, of course, she had gone out the window. He cast his senses out and found her in the street. He sent a telepathic call, but she shut him out with her micro abilities. He ran from the house and tried to track her with power, but she did something to herself, used her abilities in a way he'd never seen, shifting the signatures of her body to blend in with those around her. When she reached a crowd of people carrying a host of wounded, she vanished from his senses. He cursed and tried to follow as best he could.

Even as she hurried through Celeste, Natalya's power felt ahead of her, searching for Kora while hiding from Horace. She skipped over the multitude of plains dwellers and looked for that special signature of someone whose body felt newer than it should. As soon as her power touched Kora, Kora's mind drew her in as it often did. Natalya stumbled but kept going, seeing the streets of Celeste one moment and the plains of Kora's mind the next.

Kora was in a dream of Naos's again, sitting on green grass and watching a long metal string that led high into the sky.

"Kora, what are you doing?"

Kora turned as if Natalya was there with her and not just in her mind. "Mom made me a new party dress." White and pink, it had ribbons on the sleeves. "It's my birthday."

Before Natalya could argue that it probably wasn't, Naos appeared next to her. Natalya stumbled again, but when this Naos spoke, she had the other voice, the one that sometimes tempered the mad goddess.

"I loved that dress," the other Naos said. "She didn't often make me things, but that dress was special."

Kora grinned. "Maman loved me." She reached toward her throat. The bone necklace appeared there, and she was dressed once again in leather. "I didn't want to hurt you, Natalya."

"It's all right, Kora. You can wake up now."

The pleasant landscape stayed the same, blinking in and out of Natalya's vision.

"I've tried to be helpful," the other Naos said. "When I could."

"Then wake her up!" Natalya shouted, but the other Naos didn't seem to hear her.

There were other people in the grassy park, but as Natalya watched, they transformed into plains dwellers. She thought Kora might be waking, but these plains dwellers lurched in haunting steps, blood pouring from wounds across their bodies.

Kora stood. "Change it back."

"I'm not doing it," other Naos said. "I'm sorry, Kora."

"Wake up!" Natalya shouted. "You can do it, Kora!"

Kora put her hands over her ears again. "I don't want to go back! I don't like the hurting. I don't want to break my promise!"

The dead plains dwellers stabbed one another with weapons made of smoke. They bled and screamed but didn't fall down, hurting each other over and over.

"Do you think you'd be better off where we found you?" It was the same voice as before, and the same woman sat there, but Natalya knew she'd changed into the real Naos. She managed a wink in Natalya's direction before her right eye faded to a black void.

A headless corpse staggered toward Kora, and she screamed. "Make it stop!"

Naos looked to Natalya. "This is on you. You put ideas in her head, and then she saw you turn against me, so I'm having to scare her into accepting me again."

"Stop it. Stop this." Natalya reached for Kora, but she wasn't there.

"I want to go home!" Kora cried.

"You are home, dearest." Naos forced Kora's hands down so she had to see the dead killing one another over and over. "And this will be home forever if you try to keep me out ever again." She looked back to Natalya. "After you were gone, you see, she tried to deny me. She's never done that before."

"Leave her alone! If you want to punish me, punish me."

Kora screamed. "Take it away! I'll do anything, please!"

"That's what I like to hear," Naos said.

Natalya sobbed and called for the other Naos, but no one answered. Kora faded slowly until she seemed like an afterimage next to Naos, who turned and gave Natalya a final wave. "See you soon."

The vision faded, and in Celeste, Natalya picked up speed. They tried to stop her at the hasty barricade at the edge of the city, but she flung them away with power and pushed her way through, ignoring the shouts behind her. The world turned gray in dawn. The ground was a ruin of scorch marks and overturned earth, and corpses dotted the field as if spilled from a giant sack. The fires had gone out, and the air turned chilly. A low fog rolled in, lingering with the smoke.

People moved through the haze like ghosts, and she didn't know if they were helping the wounded or looting them, maybe consuming them in this mad world. She headed for Kora, dreading what she'd find. Even across the field, she sensed the link, pulsing like an evil heart in Kora's mind. When she saw the smirk, she knew girl and goddess were joined, maybe for good.

Natalya shook her head, not knowing what to do. Her empty socket itched, but she didn't bother to use power to ease it. She'd let this go on too long. She should have done more, should have tried harder to break the link when she had the chance. Maybe death was the answer, but every inch of her argued against that. There had to be a way. But as Naos stalked closer, Natalya sensed the difference in the link. It infused Kora in a way it hadn't before, and Natalya bet that were she a telepath, she wouldn't get any sense of Kora at all.

"What have you done?" Natalya asked.

"What I had to."

"You killed her."

She held out Kora's arms. "Does she look dead to you?"

"She feels dead."

Naos put on a pout. "Well, now you don't have to feel so sorry for her. She's resting comfortably in an endless sleep. How's the eye?"

Natalya resisted the urge to touch the empty socket. "You can't just do this." Inside, she called herself a moron for even saying such a thing. Who did she think she was dealing with?

"Who indeed?" Naos said. "I must admit, I'm impressed. I thought for sure all the fight had gone out of you."

And it had, in a way. Maybe what she'd meant was that she was too tired to deal with any of this anymore. Maybe it would be better to be dead.

Naos backhanded her with such force it lifted her from her feet. She landed in a heap again, the air rushing from her lungs. She shouldn't have come back. She'd been free, and she'd come back for Kora. She tried to heal what had to be a broken cheek, but her power snapped off.

"Take her eye, and she still doesn't learn," Naos said. "You're mine. Your life, your death, your everything. Nothing will ever happen to you again without my permission."

Natalya tried to respond, but her jaw wouldn't work, and pain roared through her, making her cough and choke.

"Here, let me help you." The pain slowly leeched from Natalya's face. "Now, how do I teach you so that the lesson sticks, hmm? If I take your other eye, how will you see? An arm? A leg? No, I can't have you hopping after me."

Natalya drew a ragged breath. A crowd of plains dwellers had wandered toward them through the fog, all healed by the looks of things, but she couldn't know for sure without her power.

"Ah ha!" Naos said. "There's a thought."

Pain stabbed through Natalya's head, blocking out her vision from somewhere inside. It faded quickly, and she was left wondering what happened, but Naos turned and moved away. She still looked like Kora, like a normal girl, but Natalya couldn't feel her anymore, couldn't sense the link. Was Naos still keeping her from her powers? But she didn't feel the same block as before. She raised a hand to her neck and felt for her pulse, could only feel it with her fingers, not with her mind. She reached out to a nearby stone, but it wouldn't obey her command to rise into the air.

Her powers. Gone. Stolen. One of the few things she'd ever cared about gone as quickly as dirt swallowing a raindrop.

Tears clouded her vision, her one-sided vision, and rolled down her cheek. Loss upon loss. Her eye, then Kora, now this. Why not just kill her? She'd thought what Simon Lazlo had done had been the worst thing, to offer supreme power that her mind couldn't handle, but to have it all taken away?

She wept for Kora and her power, smart enough to know which meant more to her. In the field, Naos laughed, and Natalya sobbed in a way she hadn't done since childhood, when power had been far in her future, and she'd had no idea what really mattered.

CHAPTER TWENTY-SIX

In the light of dawn, Horace marveled at how empty Celeste had become. Doors hung open, and debris dotted the street: spilled baskets, torn blankets, a few trinkets. But the closer he got to the barricades in front of the gates, the fewer people he saw. He didn't even bother to search for Natalya anymore. He knew where she'd gone; he sensed great power in the field beyond. Natalya must have found either the girl or the goddess that possessed her.

"Nat," he whispered in frustration. Why couldn't she have waited for him?

There were some guards lingering near the wall, and he hesitated, not knowing if he should follow her out there. He thought to send a message to Mamet, but he didn't want either her or Nettle to get involved if Naos was throwing power around again. He heard one of the guards saying that people were fleeing the city to the north, as Cordelia had suggested, but it was too late for her, maybe even for them if Naos chased them up the coast.

Even with his senses pulled back, Horace spotted another power nearby, undoubtedly the Sun-Moon in one of the structures near the breach. Before he could pull his power wholly back, he felt their telepathic call, a summons they could easily turn into a command. He groaned and stepped into a dim building. He sensed their pain from the night before and healed them in moments. If they were going to end the war, they needed their strength.

"Well, that didn't go as expected," they said. "It was a good plan, but all it did was cripple your friend and kill ours."

Horace looked to the numerous wounded and dead lying in the room and spotted Aaron, one of their friends from space. His eyes had rolled back to the capillaries, and his face was slack, mouth open. Horace didn't sense any wounds in the body. Naos had probably destroyed his mind as she was going to destroy Nat's.

"Two friends crippled?" the Sun-Moon asked. "How unfortunate."

He sighed. "Please stop spying on my thoughts. And yes, I want to attack the link to Naos again. It seems the only way to stop this without killing more people. Unless killing lots of people is what you want?"

"Trying to read our thoughts now? We don't want you forgetting who's the stronger power here."

His temper began to boil. Usually anger and resentment and all the other bad shit other people nurtured in their hearts rolled off him. He knew the Sun-Moon were speaking from a place of pain, one where they feared Naos could overpower them, but they didn't want to admit it. They were scared, and he didn't even need power to confirm it.

But he was sick and tired of being pushed around. "What do you want?"

"Don't go far again. If you want to brood, do it inside the city. Fajir will look after you."

She waited near the door, and as he left, happy to not be in the Sun-Moon's presence whether they wanted it or not, he felt another jolt of anger. He took a few deep breaths and sensed the Sun-Moon turning their attention elsewhere, probably commanding their troops. They weren't even bothering to keep a close eye on him. Either they thought they had him cowed, or they thought he was scared. Maybe they knew he'd have a hard time leaving Cordelia behind. So they left him with a babysitter who had no actual power.

An idea began to bloom, but he kept it muted, his shields tight. "I need to find my friends."

"Where are they?"

"Out there."

She shook her head. "Call them here with your mind."

He opened his mouth to tell her off but shut it quickly and crossed the street to a narrow alley. He glanced at her smirking face and knew she was pleased he would simply obey. He threw a telepathic shield around her, and she didn't seem to sense it, probably not sensitive to power at all. When he felt nothing from the Sun-Moon and heard no warnings in his head, he used his micro powers for a little punch to her brain, knocking her out. As her face went slack and she fell, he felt a jot of guilt but also one of satisfaction. Too late for regrets. He only hoped Cordelia would be all right on her own for a few hours.

He kept his shields tight as he ran for the other hole in the wall, and it was easy enough to send the guards telepathic signals to look the other way and allow him to slip through into the field.

He sent a quick signal to Mamet, and they met up with each other. He told them what he'd done, but now he was out here, he wasn't quite sure what to do. "It just…feels good to do something I'm not supposed to."

Nettle wrinkled her nose. "Ahya, Pool has taught us this, but I will not leave Sa. Perhaps if the Sun-Moon are still distracted, we may sneak Sa outside and be done with this place."

Horace bit his lip. "Well…"

Mamet sighed. "I know you want to help your friend Natalya and this possessed girl, Horace, but can't you see now how hopeless it is?"

Nettle held up a hand, stopping them from arguing. "I hear the queen!" She froze. "She is coming. I hear her faintly, but the thoughts she sends me…" She frowned hard before smiling widely. "The queen has Sa's spirit!"

"Is this more…" Mamet tapped the side of her head.

"Shh," Horace said. "What else?"

Nettle beamed again. "The queen has shawness Simon!"

Horace's heart lifted, and he saw an end to all their troubles, though he dreaded bringing Simon into the middle of this. At least he was used to dealing with these people. "That's so—"

"He is gravely wounded," Nettle said softly. "He needs your aid."

And now his chest did a different sort of lurch. "Shit! Wounded where? How?"

"I only feel her concern. She wants you to come, shawness. Go and heal him."

"Right, but Cordelia—"

"I will fetch her and take her somewhere secret. Take young Mamet to guard you."

"If the Sun-Moon realize I'm gone, they'll come after you."

Nettle grinned. "They cannot attack my mind, and with Sa's spirit gone, they will not sense her, either."

"They can still light you on fire or tear you apart!"

"Then I will keep in motion, and they will not find me. I will work to get outside the city and come meet you. Now go! I will tell the queen you are coming."

He and Mamet ran in the direction Nettle pointed them in. She warned them not to stray and Pool would find them. Horace could only hope they wouldn't be too late.

❖

Fajir climbed to her feet, her head throbbing. "Lords?" she asked. "Was it as you suspected?"

"He was waiting for his chance to flee," the Lords said in her mind.

Fajir nodded, wondering why they'd let the rogue healer knock her out if they'd known what he would do, but she knew they had their reasons. "Shall I go and fetch him?"

"No. The aliens were communicating with one another, and we couldn't read their thoughts, but Horace's came through loud and clear. He left to heal the other healer, and then they're all coming this way."

Fajir felt their relief. This battle had taken a toll on them, but like their people, they'd persevered, and now it seemed they'd get everything they wanted. Fajir moved back toward where Nico and her troops waited. After this battle was done, and the Lords had the healers, her life could return to normal, but the idea only made her anxious. She loved the Lords, accepted their will in all things, but Cordelia's words hadn't given her a moment's peace since all this had started. Strange. Cordelia had said nothing that Fajir didn't already know. She knew she could run from her duties and find Halaan's killer. She knew Nico would offer to come with her, but something about having those words spoken by an outsider clung to her like smoke.

She heard Cordelia's promise in her mind again: she would aid Fajir in hunting down Halaan's killer. Nico would be spared the shame of abandoning his duty, and Halaan's spirit would finally rest, and Fajir could die as she should have died so long ago.

In the street, Fajir spotted Nettle sneaking into one of the houses and taking out Cordelia's body. She knew she should stop the alien, should hold Cordelia's body hostage, but the Lords might command Cordelia's death. Then the promise would go unfulfilled forever.

Fajir turned and continued up the street.

❖

Samira hovered between awake and asleep. She leaned forward, head resting against the pod that held Simon's body, but she didn't care enough to either sit up or lie down. She could hear Reach shuffling around, tending to the other pods. Samira's brain kept trying to make words into a dream, some exhausting cacophony of images that robbed her of where she was and why, then something slight would wake her again.

She rubbed her forehead and found it slick with the fluid that coated the pod. If that fact would have disgusted her before, she could only blink at it now.

Reach touched the back of her head. "You have been leaning on the pod too long. Your hair is a fright."

Samira sighed something like a laugh. "Where are we?"

"Drawing closer to this city of the Sun-Moon. Shawness Horace comes, or so the queen has told me."

Samira sighed again, but some of her tension left her. Simon was still floating in his pod, still alive, and now Horace would save him. She leaned back and began to slip into sleep when the sound of a dull crack seeped into her consciousness just before Reach cried out.

She sat up, blinking. "What's happening?"

"The tree has been shot again. The Storm Lord or his paladins must have found us."

The tree lurched. Pool was no doubt moving in an erratic pattern, trying to make herself harder to hit. Reach cried out again, and Samira struggled to her feet.

"You must go, Usta," Reach said. "The queen has need of your power."

Samira nodded, trying to clear the fog from her brain. She slicked her hair back and left the basket of branches. They were so close to healing Simon now, to making sure everyone was back together. She damn sure wasn't going to let the fucking Storm Lord spoil everything again.

Drushka were pouring from the branches onto the plains. Pool's roots lashed several armored paladins, tossing them around the field. Samira spotted Liam donning armor and one of the stolen batteries.

Several drushka gathered around Samira, and one said, "As before, Usta? We rob them of power?"

She nodded, and the root lowered them to the ground. Her power flowed sluggishly, but she directed it toward as many paladins as she could. Pool's roots wrapped around one paladin and slammed him into the ground. Her branches struck others and flung them away, but they never seemed to tire. Samira knocked one over and shoved him over a hill, and pain began to build in her forehead. She hadn't gotten enough rest!

One of the drushka tossed a battery in her direction, and she knocked it up to Pool, not waiting to see if it was caught. The pain spread through her temples, blinding her, and she staggered.

The drushka rushed to cover her, but she could barely see them, couldn't hear them. She reached for her power again, but it refused. A drushka carried her to the ground as a shot rang out, and she couldn't do anything to catch herself. As her head bounced against the ground, sleep caught her at last, and there was no denying it.

Across the plains, the tree was easy to spot, the tallest thing for miles outside of Celeste. Horace grinned when he saw it, before the shots broke the stillness of the early morning.

"Run!" he said to Mamet, charging for the tree. It had to be the Storm Lord. Who else on Calamity had guns? Mamet kept up, but her eyes said it all. What were they supposed to do against a bunch of paladins?

But all he had to do was get close enough to heal Simon. Even amongst so many minds, he'd always be able to pick Simon out of a crowd. They kept running, though it was still a long way, the tiny figures fighting in the distance.

"We should sneak," Mamet said.

"No time!" And he didn't want to sneak. He wanted to run in and finish something for once, something he hadn't been able to do on this whole adventure. Mamet kept up with him, her expression calling him crazy, but she wouldn't abandon him. She seemed to take great stock in her word.

"I'll try to reach him from here," Horace said. "You'll have to guide me." He slowed a little, searching for Simon. He wouldn't be on the ground but in the tree, and there were more alien minds than human ones.

To Horace's power, Simon shone like a bright light among the branches, and when Horace sensed the bullet in his skull, he stumbled.

He hadn't realized things were so dire! Mamet supported him, steering his steps, and Horace reached out again with his power, latching on to Simon.

Mamet yelled something, and Horace staggered under a surge of vertigo as he fell. He was rolling down a hill, feeling the grass sliding under him, rocks bruising his skin, but he kept the contact. He concentrated on that bullet fragment, but they were still too far.

Push, he told himself. Gently. He grabbed the bullet again. Millimeter by agonizing millimeter, he eased it out. Mamet was pulling him to his feet, but his body had become a dream. The bullet slipped, nearly out, a little more. So close!

Hot pain seared his chest, and he felt another bullet sliding under his own skin. Now they both had bullets! How romantic. He pushed the bizarre thought away along with the pain. His body didn't matter. The pain faded to a cold wave that passed through him, leaving his focus intact beyond Mamet's shouts.

Horace let his legs crumple. He didn't need them anymore. The tiny bullet was the only thing that mattered, and it had such a little way to go. He gave it a final tug, and it slipped free, and he could let go of everything, joyous.

CHAPTER TWENTY-SEVEN

Simon opened his eyes to a world of glowing gold. So warm, so comforting. He wanted to sink back into bliss, but he had a nagging feeling, punctuated by a sharp pain in his head, that people needed him to get up. With a flick of power, he healed a small hole in his skull, and with it gone, clarity followed, and he remembered.

Dillon, Gale, Horace. Everything. But he couldn't be angry, not in this plant womb. It felt as if his love of botany had physically manifested in order to cradle him. He sent his power out and found the wounds in the tree. Pool and her drushka were fighting for their lives, but that wasn't all. He used Pool's senses to search farther and found Samira and Horace, both needing his help.

Rage began to seep through the bliss like the little red ribbons his blood left in the pod's fluid. Someone was outside, watching him. Reach. He stretched the skin of the pod and let her feel his anger, his desire to come out. Her eyes widened, and he felt her surprise that they should be so connected. Pool was surprised, too, but he couldn't let either of them distract him.

Reach sent him calming feelings; he couldn't hear her song, but he could feel it, and it urged the pod to open. As the lips above him folded back, he stood, desperate to stretch. The pod ripped along the top, and he grabbed the branch above him. Reach steadied him, helping him down as he tried to remember how to stand.

And breathe? He bent double, coughing and sputtering, heaving fluid. Reach patted his back, but he used his power to help himself, and she gasped again.

"Shawness, I can feel you like a drushka!"

He sent her a jot of healing power, strengthening her, washing away her fatigue and using her as a conduit to do the same to the rest of the drushka. Something nagged at his senses, not drushkan but connected as he was. He felt it coming closer and had a momentary thought about ghosts as a hazy form glided among the branches, but even without a body, he recognized her.

"Cordelia Ross?"

Reach turned, but if she could feel Cordelia it seemed she couldn't see her. "Where?"

"I hear you!" Cordelia said, a thought that passed through the drushka.

"I have to go." He couldn't stand still. The air felt supercharged, crackling with the energy of the tree, with the drushkan connection. He started through the branches, but Reach grabbed his arm.

"Perhaps some clothes, shawness?"

For a moment, he almost didn't bother, but even with the rage, with the rebirth, he was still himself. "Fine." She went to find something, and Cordelia hovered beside him.

"You're glowing like fire," Cordelia said. "Nearly drushkan, but more... I don't know."

"Looks as if the drushka have changed us both. I'm sensing you with my power, but neither of us is a telepath, so we shouldn't be able to talk."

"Through the drushka? They need your help, Simon. There's a fight—"

"I know."

Reach hurried back with some clothing, and he dressed quickly as she muttered about two humans communicating as drushka. Simon felt another bullet punch into the tree, and he sent another wave of healing energy through his feet, into the branches.

Reach shivered and laughed. "Perhaps not such a bad thing."

Once dressed, he strode away from her. Someone was using micro powers; it had to be Horace. He'd been shot, but he was healing himself slowly. Good. That would save some time. Simon searched for Samira and found she'd been lifted into the branches. He didn't even need to be near her to heal her with a thought.

"Take me to the field."

Pool's branches lowered him to the ground. Cordelia hovered in the air beside him, and Reach rode with him as well. He wanted her close.

He might need contact with a drushka or the tree to access his connection to Pool. The thought surprised him. With all the anger he felt, he knew he should have been half a step away from gibbering. He should have been lashing out and swearing and damning Dillon to hell and back, but he felt an eerie calm. He sensed humans and drushka on the battlefield, their bodily rhythms similar but different. Reach called something, but he didn't listen, paying attention to blood and sap and soil. They were all cogs in a great machine, and he was the monkey wrench. All he needed to do was throw his power over them like a net.

The firing and the yelling stopped; even the drushka fell silent, though he didn't catch them up as he had the humans. The armored ones stood frozen as if they'd been paused in time, but that was just their armor holding them up. The others had fallen to the ground. The drushka milled around, wondering at each other, seeking information from Pool.

"What have you done?" Reach whispered.

"I've interrupted them." He'd once seen Dué do the same, but he didn't mention that. "Even their neurons can't fire without my permission."

"Will they die?" Cordelia asked.

"Not unless I let them."

"Wow," she said, and he supposed that summed it up perfectly.

"I can't hold them forever," he said, speaking to Pool through Reach. "If you're going to disarm them, it has to be in the next few minutes."

"Where are you going, shawness?" Pool asked in his mind.

"I'm going to kill Dillon." He nodded, never so certain of something in all his life.

"I'm coming with you," Cordelia said. "I'm not missing that."

"I also," Reach said, "so that we can all speak with one another."

"Okay, but just you two." He didn't want to give Dillon the opportunity to use anyone else against him. He was pretty certain Dillon couldn't hurt a ghost, or whatever Cordelia was, and he trusted a drushka to stay hidden. With one more cast of his power, he sensed that Horace had healed himself and was coming closer. Simon wanted to hold him with terrible fierceness, but Horace would want to come with him, and Simon couldn't have that.

Instead, he cast his senses wider, borrowing from Pool again. Dillon wasn't on this battlefield. He was somewhere else, closing in on Celeste. Simon pinpointed him and started moving. But Dillon wasn't the only interesting thing in Sun-Moon territory. Simon sensed many wounded and dead. "What's been happening?"

Cordelia told him about a great battle with Dué, or Naos, as she was calling herself. When she told him about a connection between a plains girl and the space station, he stopped her. "Can you describe this connection? This blue light?"

"Um, it was images, lots of them. Pain, probably because she sees everything. It would drive anyone crazy. Can you do something about it?"

"I don't know yet." It almost made him giddy, almost shook his calm, but he made himself keep to center. Killing Dillon was the most important thing here. He'd deal with Naos when and if he had to.

"I'm sorry I didn't tell you about your uncle when it happened," he said, wanting to get anything off his chest that still lingered.

"I'm sorry I hit you."

He nodded. He'd deserved it. It had been the first pain he'd felt in a long time. "I feel as if I've spent years in limbo, and I'm not talking about the tree. You know, I thought one time that I'd always heal Dillon, that I could never let him die, but now I've never been surer that I have to kill him. I've never killed anyone, not a human being."

"This one deserves it."

"Ahya," Reach said. "We will kill him on behalf of those we loved and lost."

Horace's arms were up over his head, and the ground slithered underneath him. Someone was dragging him? He opened an eye and watched the sky go by for a few seconds before he noticed that someone had hold of his feet. Mamet. Oh yes, there'd been a fight. He'd fallen? He'd been healing Simon, and then he'd fallen, but that wasn't what was hurting so much.

Right, there was pain, a lot of it, but he could always fix that. And once the pain was driven away, the wound could be healed. "Mamet. Stop." His legs dropped.

Mamet leaned into view. "You healed yourself!"

Horace sat up, blinking. "Simon! The bullet! Did it work?"

"I don't know. I dragged you away after you got hurt." She rubbed her forehead. "I don't know anything anymore."

Horace smoothed away the strain in her. "Thank you, but we need to go back."

There were still shouts and gunfire, and Horace thought for a moment that Mamet would try to stop him, but she eventually agreed, both of them picking up speed when the noise ceased. By the time they reached the tree, a strange tableau lay before them. Drushka stood around a handful of half-naked humans who'd been bound so tightly with vines, it was a wonder they could breathe.

"The drushka won!" Mamet said.

Horace sent his power over the captives, detecting something strange, though he couldn't quite put a finger on it. Liam stood in armor near the captives, and when he saw Horace and Mamet, he waved them over.

"Your boyfriend learned some new tricks," Liam said.

Horace couldn't help beaming. "He's all right?"

"Better than that, I'd say."

"Where is he?"

Liam spread his hands, a drushkan gesture. "He said he was going to kill Dillon and walked off. That's the Storm Lord, right?"

"Yes." And if Simon was angry enough to kill, the Storm Lord had to have done something truly awful to him in Gale. "Which way did he go?"

"I don't think he wanted anyone to follow him."

"That's not going to stop us," Samira said as she joined them. She smiled, and Horace felt like throwing his arms around her, but before he could get the chance, Mamet beamed and took her hands.

"You're all right!" She seemed as if she might hug Samira and then kissed both her hands instead.

Samira grinned and wrapped her arms around Mamet's neck, drawing them together for a long kiss. Mamet's eyes widened before she returned the favor.

Horace studied Samira with his power. She'd been healed, too. He cleared his throat, but that didn't stop them, and he finally said, "Well, time to get going!"

"We're all headed in the same direction," Liam said. "Let's go together."

"As long as we go now."

❖

With the arrival of dawn, Dillon had decided to march without the paladins who'd been chasing after the lunatic who'd tackled him. They'd catch up, he was certain, and they might have some dead drushka or renegades to show for it; it'd be especially nice if they bagged the asshole who'd given him so much trouble.

He smelled smoke before he caught sight of Celeste. The area directly in front of the walls was all churned mud and burnt grass, quite the shithole, and groups of people seemed to be mixing it up near a big hole in Celeste's wall. He stood with his hands on his hips, trying to watch and see who had the upper hand. If the dead bodies in the field and the holes in the wall were any indication, both sides had gotten some hits in.

"There are people using yafanai power down there," a telepath said.

He nodded but didn't bother to explain. That would be the Sun-Moon and maybe Naos if she'd decided to join in.

"Leave the wagons," he said. "Break out the railguns." What little ammo they had left for the big guns might as well be used here. "Form into your squads. Let's poke our noses in a bit, see who bites." If both sides were tired, he could take them all in one swoop.

He knew some of his people could be killed. He could be killed. Even knowing that, he wanted this. Everything in Gale had gone ass up, but this fight fell pure somehow, even with the death it had caused. The enemies were clear, and all he needed to do was kill them.

Lieutenant Lea brought him a railgun, the man's face as impassive as a corpse's, and Dillon didn't know if that was just him or if he was still pissed about Brown. Some of the yafanai seemed nervous, milling and shuffling. He scattered them among the soldiers, knowing they'd do what they had to once the killing started.

Patricia Dué waited just behind Naos, sensing an ending coming but not knowing when it might happen or where. She looked through Kora's eyes and felt as if she was watching a vid, but unlike when she relived her old memories, she'd never seen this before.

Naos let their senses drift through Celeste. Lives fluttered against her thoughts like butterfly kisses. The fragility of them was amazing, as if she was standing in a room full of candles, and any sudden movement would snuff them.

"How very poetic," Naos said. "I should let you out more often."

But she wasn't letting, not exactly. She was slipping, but Patricia didn't tell her that. Naos searched through the candle flames until she found a mind from the *Atlas*. Lisa, one of the breachies. Her thoughts danced around them: loves, fears, a childhood theft that still sometimes filled her with shame. Naos took Lisa's mind with her power and squeezed. A long scream from just inside Celeste rewarded them.

"What did you do?" Natalya asked.

Even as Naos turned, Patricia sighed, wishing this one would learn to keep quiet. "I liked you better when all you cared about was power," Naos said.

"You took that away, remember?" Natalya asked.

She was alive with rage, and Naos lapped it up like honey. She loved strong emotions, especially when she knew exactly where they were coming from and why. Patricia thought it was one reason Naos enjoyed tormenting her. She snuffed more lives, heard the screams, the cries of rage, the desire for revenge. She cackled, and Patricia cringed to hear it.

"You're insane," Natalya said.

Naos gestured, and one of her followers punched Natalya in the gut. Natalya doubled over, retching. Naos waved the follower away. She held them so tightly now. She thought they couldn't be trusted. Some had already run away.

"Insane," Natalya wheezed, desperate, it seemed, to poke the bear.

"Why do you have to ruin all my fun?" Naos asked. "Do you need more lessons? There's little of you left that I can take away." She raised a hand, and Natalya drew back. "Ha! Two for flinching!"

One of the followers kicked her hard, sending her to the ground with a grunt before he kicked her again.

"Ooh, I think that was a rib!" Naos said.

When Natalya didn't answer, Naos turned her attention back to the city. She sorted through the flickering lives until she spotted two that seemed brighter than the rest. "Ah ha! The Sun-Moon again."

Patricia tensed, trying to keep her thoughts quiet as Naos attacked Lieutenants Christian and Marlowe with her mind. Patricia braced herself. If Christian and Marlowe rallied and forced Naos to leave Kora, Patricia was determined to stay behind. But Naos caught the lieutenants with her micro powers, and they barely struggled. They were weak, tired; even their awesome power had been dulled by fatigue. All it would take was a little push.

Patricia felt panic creep up on her. The lieutenants were her greatest hope, but she didn't know what she could do to help them, trapped as she was. She felt around with the residue of power left to her and sensed *him* nearby. He could help her, even if he was only a distraction.

One of Naos's followers died, then another, and another. "Dillon is here," Patricia said quietly.

Natalya was screaming about guns, and Naos released the lieutenants and turned her senses west. She commanded the followers to fall and make themselves into smaller targets. Then she grinned as she sensed Dillon and his toys.

"You can't save him now," Naos said. "Not now that he's attacked us."

Patricia stayed silent, watching, waiting.

CHAPTER TWENTY-EIGHT

Simon kept his senses fixed on Dillon, but now Naos's followers had gotten in the way as the two groups tangled with one another. "Damn, damn, damn." Aggravation disrupted his rage-calm, but he took a deep breath.

"Shawness?" Reach asked.

"Naos's army is in the way."

"Well," Cordelia said. "You're going to have to go around her or through her."

He sighed. Stopping her might mean saving some of the plains dwellers who'd gotten mixed up with her. Besides, if he had to fight Dillon first, he didn't want to take on Calamity's most powerful deity while winded.

He switched his senses to Naos, the woman he'd always thought of as Dué, but he supposed he should change that thinking now. She'd gone from the bizarre, powerful creature that barely got involved in life to a war mongering, power-hungry monster. He sensed her vessel easily, moving from Celeste to where Dillon was attacking her western flank. He also sensed her power extending from the vessel like spokes on a wheel, piercing every plains dweller around her.

"We're going to need help," he said. "Not just me, but Horace and the Sun-Moon and all the yafanai."

"Think they'll agree to that?" Cordelia said.

He grinned. "I don't give a rat's ass. I don't need them to agree. And we're not going to attack the link where it meets the girl. There's only one way to kill a diseased plant."

"At the root, shawness," Reach said.

"Just so, shawness. We're going to break this link and make it so she can never have another."

There were some plains dwellers on the fringe of the army, running from Dillon or maybe trying to take cover. Simon put them out with a thought. "This should be close enough. I'll gather the power, and Cordelia, you'll deliver it."

"Me?"

"Unless you know someone else that can fly. And once Naos is finished, we'll put you back where you belong."

He felt her fear, then excitement overtook her. "I've been waiting to get back in this fight!"

With a chuckle, he used his power to find the Sun-Moon. They'd been injured, but that helped him at the moment. They'd be less likely to struggle. Across the distance, he borrowed their telepathic power and added it to his own, sort of like a communion, but they didn't have any choice. He felt their protests but disregarded them and collected any micro or telepathic yafanai, using his power to merge them into a weapon.

Casting his senses behind him, he sent an invitation to Horace. Horace lent his power eagerly, almost gladly, and Simon had to smile. To this giant cord of power, Pool added the weight of drushkan telepathy, though they'd never used it as a weapon against one that wasn't their own. Simon didn't even know if it would work, but it coiled around the human power as a vine might, adding weight.

When Simon searched for Naos's vessel again, he found she'd only taken a few steps, seemingly oblivious to his presence. Well, maybe she was too focused on Dillon.

"Ready?" he asked Cordelia.

"Fuck yeah."

Simon coiled the waiting power through her, using her as a conduit as she'd told him Horace had earlier.

"Shit! I feel so…heavy."

"All in your mind. Now, up you go. I'll stay linked with you, like a transmitter, and you'll take the fight to her."

"Oh yes," she said. "Fuck yes."

"Steady. Follow her blue light all the way to the space station, quick as you can."

She streaked away, and his senses went with her, all of the hopes of those in Celeste going, too.

❖

Cordelia gritted teeth she didn't have and forced down the desire to whoop with joy. She was fucking invincible. Through their connection to the drushka, Cordelia felt Simon in her mind as if he was an extension of Pool's tree. She raced up the blue cord that connected Naos to the ground, not touching it, just tracing it to the hunk of metal that she'd always thought of as the unwinking star, the *Atlas*, a satellite in orbit. As the atmosphere thinned and blue gave way to black, she paused at the multitude of stars, remembering infinity.

"Focus," Simon said in her mind.

She moved toward the *Atlas*, enough metal to satisfy even the greediest Galean, and stayed with the blue light, passing through the hull and floating down corridors until she finally found Naos in the flesh.

She'd expected more, a body as titanic as the power that emanated from her, but she was a normal looking woman. She floated in the middle of a room as if someone had turned the gravity off. She wore a blue jumpsuit, and her hair spread out around her like seed fluff. Her mouth was open, her eye half-lidded, and her empty socket a dent in her face. She was alone, would be alone forever if they succeeded.

"You can't afford pity," Simon said. "Just touch her. I'll do the rest."

Cordelia would have taken a deep breath, but because of this woman, that wasn't an option. She flew, taking all the power with her as she punched up through Naos's torso. "Remember me?"

The eye flew open, and Naos thrashed in mid-air, staring at Cordelia. Her power hammered against the forces Simon had gathered, but his attacked from a multitude of directions, outflanking her left and right.

With a snarl, Naos rammed a hand into the space where Cordelia's chest would have been. "Ghosts can be killed if one knows the right spots."

Cordelia screamed as agony wormed through her. She hadn't known she could hurt like this, like someone was tearing her apart.

"Hang on, hang on," Simon said in her mind.

The pain leveled off, and Cordelia fought the urge to run. Fucking swamp couldn't kill her. Fucking God couldn't kill her. She'd be damned if she'd let some space-bound megalomaniac kill her.

"I channeled her attack away," Simon said, "and two yafanai are dead. You have to give me more time!"

"Oh *yes*." Blood oozed from Naos's nose and floated away as little red beads. "Stay here, little bee, far from the good doctor. Stay and let me rip you to shreds!"

The pain spiked, and Cordelia cried out. Thoughts fled as if her mind was unraveling, little parts of her slipping away piece by piece. "Fuck. You." The pain lessened; someone else had died, but she felt Simon chipping away at the link. She howled into Naos's face and stayed where she was, trying not to think of what she was losing, memories she might never get back, her very awareness. She could die up here, and only Simon would know what happened. He'd have to tell Nettle and Liam as well as all her friends and makeshift family.

"Yes, think of your friends," Naos said as the pain roared again. "If you leave now…" She trailed away, and her face screwed up as she stared at nothing. "Patricia Dué, what the fuck do you think you're doing?"

When the attack had first started, Naos had pulled both herself and Patricia back from Kora, leaving her nearly alone. Well, she couldn't be alone anymore. There wasn't enough left of Kora to occupy her body, but Naos was good at splitting her attention.

With all the different powers hammering at her, the link was dissolving, taking any chance for Patricia's freedom with it, but what could she do? Help Naos fight? As the link grew weaker, Naos had to pull more of herself out of Kora, out of all her followers. Power against power, she'd win or at least live, but her ability to link to the ground might be gone.

Patricia tapped into a bit of that power, redirecting it her way while Naos was distracted. She used micro-psychokinesis and telepathy like a scalpel, sawing her and Naos apart as if they were conjoined twins. Her thoughts locked on how amazing it would feel to be alone for the first time in over two hundred years, to walk, to speak, to just exist. She worked as quickly as she dared, feeling herself sliding out of her own body, but it hadn't been hers since she'd been forced to share with this stranger. No, share wasn't the right word. She'd been taken over, and as much as she would have loved to have her own body back, she knew that ship had sailed.

"Patricia Dué, what the fuck do you think you're doing?"

"Saying good-bye."

She was so close now. Naos couldn't stop her, and if Simon Lazlo or this new attacker sensed her, they didn't try to stop her either. She cut the last ties to her old body and flew down the link as it buckled behind her, Simon Lazlo's power shutting it down forever.

❖

Natalya watched Naos stagger around the field, putting her hands over her head and screaming, cursing, spouting nonsense. Around them, plains dwellers shook their heads as if trying to clear them. The gunfire had stopped, and everyone seemed to be going crazy at once.

Whatever it was, Natalya saw a chance. She leapt on Naos, knocking her to the ground. "Kora, if you're still in there, I'm sorry." Without Kora, Naos would no longer have a vessel. She might possess Natalya again; she might kill her, but at least this particular madness would be over.

And Kora deserved some peace at last.

Natalya locked the bend of her elbow around Kora's neck and flexed, using her other arm for leverage. Her injured ribs ground together, making her swear and spit, but she kept up the pressure. Kora's hand beat against her weakly, as if the body barely held the strength or the wherewithal to fight back. Tears crept down Natalya's cheeks, and she tried to remember the last time she'd cried twice in one day. Now seemed the right time, when she didn't know if it was goddess or girl trying to fight her off.

"I'm sorry," Natalya said. "Let go. You'll be free."

The plains dwellers crowded around them, but none attacked. Maybe they didn't know whether or not they should, or maybe they wanted to be free, too. "Stay back," Natalya said, just in case.

Kora's thrashing grew weaker, and Natalya thought she ought to say something, to explain how Kora had changed her or try to say what Kora meant to her, but when she thought it might be Naos listening, she couldn't do it. Kora's last attempt to fight her was a light graze, almost a caress, then she went limp. Natalya began to let her go when a bubble of force exploded from her, pitching Natalya away.

She landed on her neck, nearly doing a backward somersault. The air rushed out of her, but the pain went with it. As she fell over, she marveled that she felt nothing at all. The plains dwellers stared at Kora in shock before they took off at a run. Natalya tried to turn and watch them, but her body wouldn't obey. Her limbs were like stone.

She heard footsteps, and then Kora stood over her, gazing down with one blue eye and one brown, but she didn't glow or smirk. As she knelt at Natalya's side, her expression seemed apologetic. "I didn't mean to hurt you, sorry. It's all a little fuzzy."

Natalya tried to respond, but her voice wouldn't work. Everything was going gray around the edges. What had happened to Kora?

"She's gone," this new person said, the other Naos. "You'll be dead soon. I could heal you, but I think that would complicate things, and something tells me you're ready to go, so I won't make you stay."

Natalya's world faded to a narrow pinprick before going black. Kora was dead. Maybe that was all right. And Natalya wouldn't have to live with the knowledge that she'd helped kill the one person who'd really loved her, despite the fact that Naos had forced them together. Her own breath stuttered in her ears, faltering, and then stopped.

Naos went still, gaping at nothing, her face a mask of disbelief.

"It's done," Simon said in Cordelia's mind.

Cordelia floated away. She'd never felt so tired. Moving was a chore; existence itself had become painful. "I'm…tattered."

"We'll fix you," Simon said. "Come home."

Cordelia began a slow drift out of the room.

"Where do you think you're going?" Naos stared, still with her sense of menace even if she'd lost the fight. "Your friends cut the link, but you're still here, and I seem to have a vacancy."

"Simon," Cordelia said. "Can I get a little help?"

"Paging Dr. Lazlo, Dr. Simon Lazlo." Naos cupped a hand to her ear. "He must not be in the building." A pang of effort crossed her face, and her empty socket seemed to flare.

Cordelia tried to drift faster. "Simon, are you fucking shitting me? Please, say something!"

Naos held out a hand, and Cordelia's progress halted. Slowly, as if moved by the smallest of air currents, she drifted toward the center of the room. She struggled, but it felt like wearing armor in a bog.

"I'm a little hurt," Naos said, "so this is going to be slow and painful. I know I gave you a choice before, but now, well, beggars and choosers."

Cordelia readied herself, not knowing how she would fight but wanting to go down swinging. "If you trap me in your head, you're going to have one angry passenger."

Naos smirked.

"Cordelia?" Simon's voice said.

"It's about fucking time!"

"Sorry, but since the delicate work is over, I had to gather some brute force."

Cordelia gasped as power filled her anew. This wasn't the work of telepaths and healers. It was the crushers, the hurlers, the macro-psychokinetics like Samira and the Moon, and on top of that, Cordelia felt the electric punch of the Storm Lord and the burning power of the Sun.

It made her giddy, dizzy. "I'm kind of hurt," she said, "so this is going to be short and painful." Simon showed her how to guide the power, and with a roar, she threw it at Naos, the waves of force, the charged lightning, fire, everything. It left her so quickly, it dragged her spirit forward as it blew Naos against the wall.

Naos howled, her mouth open, skin rippling and blackening. She bounced off the wall and began to drift into the room, limp and lifeless.

"No!" Simon cried. "She's not dead. Get out of there before she recovers."

Naos grasped at her blackened, dented flesh, but even as Cordelia watched, the dents healed, and pink skin began to show through the blackened spots. Cordelia fled as quickly as she could, moving from the station into space. As she drew near the atmosphere, she felt Simon's power helping her along, giving her a boost.

"I can't wait for you," he said. "There's still Dillon to deal with."

She'd wanted to be there, to see that, but now… "Believe it or not, I've had my fill of fighting today. Just make sure he knows part of his death is for my uncle Paul."

CHAPTER TWENTY-NINE

Simon told Reach about the fight with Naos as it was happening, and she relayed what she knew to the other drushka so he wouldn't have to speak through her. It was almost as good as having comms.

Now though, with Cordelia safely on her way back, Simon straightened his borrowed drushkan clothing and marched toward Dillon again. The plains dwellers fled around him, but he let them go, keeping his thoughts on his true target.

"Are you well, shawness?" Reach asked.

"Very." He thought he'd be tired, but he'd let others do the bulk of the work for once. "You might want to hide. If he thinks he can get at me through you…"

"Ahya." When they finally saw Dillon, she ducked into a nearby ditch. "I will be watching."

He nodded, barely hearing her. Dillon was bent double, breathing hard. He'd taken his helmet off and wiped his mouth as if he'd recently thrown up. All the yafanai lay in the field, either unconscious or dead, and the paladins milled around, many of them clustered about Dillon or barking orders at the servants to help the yafanai. Simon kept walking, not bothering to hide, but he kept his power close to the surface, ready to do whatever he needed.

"Storm Lord," one paladin said, "the enemy ran off, sir. Who do we fight?"

Dillon shook his head, probably too tired after Simon borrowed his power, but Simon didn't help him, not one little bit. "It's like…someone pulled me out of my body." Dillon looked up, and when their gazes met, the bastard *smiled*.

The other paladins turned to look, and Simon put them to sleep. Those without powered armor fell. The servants either ran or ducked. Dillon opened his mouth, and Simon shut it for him, interrupting him as he had the paladins at Pool's tree. Should he just do it? Just like that?

No, he wanted Dillon awake.

Simon let Dillon's mind and face go free. Dillon blinked stupidly before that smile crept over him again. "You're alive! Ah, Laz, I'm so glad! What happened?"

And that was almost enough to make Simon tear him limb from limb. "Well, for a start, I'm not anyone's slave at the moment."

"Laz—"

"You know, even dogs get to pick who they care for."

"I needed you."

"I don't care. I don't know why I'm even letting you talk. There is no possible excuse I'd accept. Not one!"

Dillon sighed. "So? You going to kill me?"

"All I have to do is decide on a method."

He felt Dillon's skepticism, and he knew it was well deserved. Even now, with rage like a bright spark inside him, doubt climbed up from the depths. He couldn't do this, couldn't kill Dillon.

Yes, he fucking could! He damned himself to hell and back and told himself to get on with it, to kill the man quickly and be done. He'd be safe; Horace would be safe. He tried to summon the memory of all the people who would be safer with Dillon dead, every goddamned human and alien on Calamity.

And Dillon's children would grow up without a father.

One of the servants stood. Simon turned in his direction, poised to knock him out, but the man's face was an intense mask, his eyes fixed on Dillon's back. He slipped a little knife out of his sleeve, and his lips climbed into a snarl. A disgruntled Galean come to steal the kill?

It was the coward's way out, but Simon breathed easier. After all, Dillon had fucked up his own people as much as everyone else, and a knife was as good an instrument as any other. And, a cowardly voice inside Simon's head whispered, if he was just holding Dillon still, the murder wouldn't be on his hands.

Dillon wouldn't even see it coming.

"It's not murder," he said softly. "It's an execution." He looked into Dillon's eyes, those that had so often haunted his dreams. "Cordelia Ross wanted you to know that this is partly for her uncle Paul."

Dillon's eyes widened. "You're actually going to do it?"

"You've hurt everyone for the last time."

His mouth opened and closed. "Will you...take care of my son?"

Simon didn't know if this was a ploy to be saved, didn't know if he could care for a child, but the man with the knife was drawing closer. "I will." And now there were tears in his eyes, but it wasn't for the man in front of him. He mourned the friendship they could have had. "Good-bye, Dillon."

"Laz, I want you to know—"

Simon watched on every level as the knife entered Dillon's neck, as his face went from surprise to a sort of wonder. Simon shut his eyes as the sliver of bone slipped between the vertebrae, as Dillon's armor held him up as his eyes rolled back. As his heart beat its last, Simon drew back into himself, happy Dillon hadn't been allowed to try whatever trick he'd thought of there at the end. He wiped away the few tears that had managed to escape.

The assassin stared at Simon before turning, grabbing some water skins from a fallen yafanai and fleeing into the plains. Simon didn't know his story and didn't care. He stepped to Dillon's still standing form and yanked the battery free so Dillon could fall in a heap. It seemed more appropriate that way.

As he walked away, he sought out a new rhythm, Horace's heart, and headed for it like an arrow.

❖

Patricia held her breath and waited until Simon Lazlo and his drushka had departed. Whether from her own efforts to remain unseen or from his preoccupation, he hadn't noticed her, and she wanted to keep it that way.

She ran to Dillon. His heart had stopped, and his brain was almost dead, but there was something she could do about that. She wrapped her hand around the knife and pulled it free. Blood gushed after it, but Patricia capped that off, using the power she'd brought with her down the broken link. It was easy enough to heal the spine, too.

She rolled him over using macro power and surveyed his handsome face. With a caress, she closed his eyes. Maybe she should leave well enough alone and let the dead stay dead? No, she couldn't spend eternity by herself. Alone in her head, yes, but she'd never been good at being alone in body. She restarted his heart, keeping his brain alive, but kept him asleep as she went to work.

"No more tyrant colonel, I'm afraid," she whispered. "Can't have you running off on a tear all the time."

She skimmed through his mind, used to dealing with inner psyches after hundreds of years as one. She siphoned all of Dillon's memories and implanted them in her own head for safekeeping. In their place, she inserted his near worship of Patricia Dué, chafa's daughter, from a plains dwelling tribe who were all dead but her and her loyal servant, Jonah. She smiled, liking the name; it suited him.

She studied his brain, saw how his power worked, and copied it in her own brain, too; that might come in handy. She didn't want electrokinesis to perish from Calamity. With a few flicks of power, she unbuckled the armor and cast it away. Little by little, she worked on his appearance, turning his hair silver but leaving the eyes gray. She cut a jagged scar into his cheek and healed it, leaving an attractive, pale line.

She shook him awake with her power. "Wake up, Jonah. Time to leave."

He blinked sleepily. "Mistress? What happened?"

She helped him to his feet, supporting him with power and leading him to the north. "It's not safe here."

With a last jolt of power, she implanted memories into the soldiers and yafanai that still slept in the grass. There had been a mighty boom of thunder, she told them, and the Storm Lord rode away on a bolt of lightning to battle Naos in heaven. They wouldn't look for him, not after that. The thought made her laugh.

The tree was hard to miss, but Simon didn't spare it a glance. He reserved his gaze for Horace, whose determination shone like a beacon. Simon grinned and watched the mirror of his expression flash across Horace's face. All of their senses were wide open, and Simon felt every emotion Horace had for him, not Dillon's want but genuine caring.

"I want every part of you," Horace said in his mind. "More than just your power, though that is nice." He winked.

Simon picked up the pace. "I love you, too. Know that."

"I do." They reached one another at last, and Simon opened his arms, drawing Horace in, and their lips came together as their power embraced, reuniting them in every way. Healing energy spiraled outward, mending injured drushka, Naos's army, the Sun-Moon worshipers, and the Galeans alike. Everyone it touched it rejuvenated, even the Sun-Moon as it cured their disease.

It healed everyone but the dead.

Simon thought of Dillon and allowed a small part of himself to mourn, but Horace wrapped himself around that pain and healed it, too. Simon leaned in, letting himself be cured at last.

They parted, both breathless, but before Simon could get another kiss, Horace said, "The Sun-Moon are behind you."

"I know."

Pool's tree moved close as Simon faced the dual gods. A branch lowered Pool to his side. "We are with you, shawness."

He didn't know if he'd need her help, but he appreciated it. "We already healed you," he said loudly. "Something else you need?"

"Thank you, but—"

He shut off their power, making them stagger. "No buts. And you're welcome. Now, to borrow a phrase from someone I used to now, 'Fuck with me or my friends again, and I'll kill you.'"

Their mouths dropped open.

He waved them away and turned his back.

Horace had a surprised smile. "I don't know whether to be appalled, elated, or completely turned on."

Simon grinned and hugged him close even as he used his power to track the Sun-Moon as they walked back into their city.

Behind Horace, Samira held out her arms, tears swimming in her eyes. "Is it my turn?"

Simon gave Horace a final squeeze and then hugged her as she sobbed. She'd had her fatigue cured, but she needed sleep; they all did. He held her and thanked her, and after a moment she stepped back and wiped furiously at her face.

"You're so strong, Samira," he said. "You'll be all right. We're all okay."

She laughed through her tears. "I don't feel strong. I might need some help getting out of here."

Reach touched her arm. "Ahya, Usta. We will all go together."

"Please, shawness?" Nettle approached with Cordelia's body, and Simon cast his senses out again, looking for her spirit.

"Here she comes."

"I feel as if I'm coming home from a three week bender with two broken legs and a spike through my head," Cordelia said through their link with the drushka.

Simon chuckled. "You're almost there."

She floated back down to her body, and Simon felt the power of the drushka reach for her. He used it, braiding it like a stalk and pulling pieces of Cordelia's spirit into it. She balked a little, and he knew she had to be thinking of Naos, but she needed a new way to attach herself to herself, and the drushka were all he had on hand. As the light from her spirit and Pool's energy blended, it secured her to her body again.

"I can make this permanent," he said, "so you can never leave your body or be forced out again."

She paused and then said, "Just make the cord a little stronger, okay? I think I'd miss being able to fly."

He chuckled but did as she asked, and her eyes fluttered open as her spirit sank back inside.

Nettle bent over and kissed her forehead. "Welcome home, Sa."

Pool gathered all her people into her branches, leaving the plains dwellers to scatter to the wind. Liam said he'd find Wuran when they got back home and tell him to spread the word that Naos was dead, that everyone should return to their lives.

"Tell him that if the Sun-Moon start killing people again," Cordelia added, "they should send for the badass healer to take care of it."

Simon ignored that, tired of being badass for the time being. Where home would be was a different story. Cordelia didn't want to leave the paladins or the yafanai unconscious and near Celeste, so the drushka took them all prisoner, leaving only the dead behind. Simon left them to it, preferring to stay close to Horace and Samira. But with the soldiers subdued and Dillon dead, there seemed to be nothing standing between the former renegades and Gale, though Simon suspected it wouldn't exactly be easy to go home again.

When they were out of sight of Celeste, Mamet asked to be lowered to the ground. "I've freed the Sun-Moon's captives," she said. "I should go home."

Samira's shoulders sagged, but she smiled softly, always happy to sacrifice her own happiness for whatever someone else needed. "Mamet, I just want you to know—"

"Come with me?" Mamet asked.

Samira's mouth fell open. "I…give me a minute." She grabbed Simon's arm and pulled him aside.

"You should go," he said before she could ask.

"You've stopped needing me already?" She laughed, but he knew the question was serious.

"I'll always need you, and I'll always love you, but you shouldn't let that stop you. I want you to be happy. You're the truest friend I've ever had."

She nodded, but he felt her doubt. She'd been seeing to other people's needs for so long, maybe she didn't know how to see to her own. Well, she'd have to figure it out. "Go," he said. "Have a rest, see what happens. We can always have more adventures later."

She chuckled again and nodded, but he still felt her waver.

"Don't live with regret," he said. "You can always come home again, no matter what."

She hugged him close. "I love you, too."

"You better say something to her. She's trying to be stoic, but she's a mess."

She stepped back. "While I'm gone, no getting kidnapped, no getting shot." Her voice broke, and she had to take another breath.

"Samira, I'm so sorry you had to be alone, that you had to…" When she seemed almost in tears, he stopped. "Go, go! Mamet's mom and dad won't wait forever."

She gave him a playful slap on the arm then went to Mamet. "Yes."

Mamet whooped. One of the humans from Pool's tribe approached them, and Simon recalled the ex-prophet of Gale, Lydia. "Can I come?" she asked. "I can't go back to Gale. They'll want me to be a prophet again, and I just…won't." She took a deep breath but seemed on the verge of tears. "I won't be any trouble. I can do things—"

Samira took her hand. "Of course you can come."

Simon relaxed a fraction. As long as she had someone to look after, Samira would be fine.

The tree lifted the rest of them, and they were off again. They'd have to make a quick stop with the Svenal to finish curing them and pick up their pseudo yafanai, then it would be on to Gale. The Galeans would be in need of a good leader, and when he looked at people like Cordelia and Pool, he knew they'd get it. All that stood in their way was the long walk home.

EPILOGUE

Fajir paced up and down her room inside the palace. Sitting on her narrow bed, Nico's gaze never left her, but what answers could he hold that she hadn't already thought of?

All the vermin were gone. Those she'd kept in the cells had been freed, no doubt by Cordelia's pet vermin. She cursed herself. She should have been paying better attention.

"And her word is worthless," Fajir muttered. "She told me she would help me hunt Halaan's killer, traded her vermin's life for that, but she's gone!" And to think Fajir had let her slip away!

"She could come back," Nico said.

Fajir snarled. It was possible, and hope bloomed again, but she tried to quash it. She'd let hope guide her once before, let the stranger's open face fool her into thinking Halaan's killer could be closer than she thought. "The Lords will have too much need of us to clean up the mess the city has become."

Nico shifted on the bed. "We could go, Seren, you and I."

A nice offer, one she trusted, but she couldn't put him into contention with the Lords. She'd planned to risk just her own life. She thought again of going alone, but the idea still filled her with fear. She'd never been alone, not in the whole of her life. How could she do so now? How could she get revenge with no one to witness it?

"We could ask the Lords," Nico said. "I'll ask them."

Loyal Nico. There had to be a way to keep him safe and not be alone. "We'll volunteer to ride after the tree, to make sure they've gone, and so we can check on the villages. We'll catch them. I'll remind her of her oath." She smiled. Cordelia prided herself on honor and loyalty. Fajir had sensed it, and the Lords had confirmed it. Cordelia had always been planning to escape, but she hadn't abandoned her friends, and she'd been drawn into conflicts with those that needed helping. If Fajir demanded she keep her promise or be dogged by Fajir forever, she would agree; anything to keep her friends safe.

Nico kept with her as she gathered what remained of her troop and got permission from the Lords to ride out. With ossors underneath them, they rode hard, and Fajir could almost feel the distance to Halaan's killer growing ever shorter.

Enka, envoy of the Shi, sat on a rooftop in Gale. With the Storm Lord and his soldiers gone, she had been able to sneak in and out of the city at will, spreading the second part of the Shi's poison.

The wind shifted, and she relished the new smell of Gale's denizens. The first part of the poison had spread to nearly everyone, and with the introduction of the second, weakness was spreading faster than even the Shi had anticipated. Soon, Gale would be hard-pressed to find anyone strong enough to stand against the drushka.

The Shi would soon send her queens closer. Enka wondered if they would take the buildings apart or leave them. Which might warn the other humans to stay far from this place? Which would anger or frighten the Anushi enough to make her run for the swamp again? Without his city, how long would the Storm Lord and his soldiers live? So many questions, but Enka was certain the Shi would have the answers. All she had to do was wait.

About the Author

Barbara Ann Wright writes fantasy and science fiction novels and short stories when not ranting on her blog. *The Pyramid Waltz* was one of Tor.com's Reviewer's Choice books of 2012, was a ***Foreword Review*** Book of the Year Award Finalist, a Goldie finalist, and made *Book Riot*'s 100 Must-Read Sci-Fi Fantasy Novels By Female Authors. It also won the 2013 Rainbow Award for Best Lesbian Fantasy. *A Kingdom Lost* was a Goldie finalist and won the 2014 Rainbow Award for Best Lesbian Fantasy Romance.

Books Available from Bold Strokes Books

A Quiet Death by Cari Hunter. When the body of a young Pakistani girl is found out on the moors, the investigation leaves Detective Sanne Jensen facing an ordeal she may not survive. (978-1-62639-815-3)

Buried Heart by Laydin Michaels. When Drew Chambliss meets Cicely Jones, her buried past finds its way to the surface—will they survive its discovery or will their chance at love turn to dust? (978-1-62639-801-6)

Escape: Exodus Book Three by Gun Brooke. Aboard the Exodus ship *Pathfinder*, President Thea Tylio still holds Caya Lindemay, a clairvoyant changer, in protective custody, which has devastating consequences endangering their relationship and the entire Exodus mission. (978-1-62639-635-7)

Genuine Gold by Ann Aptaker. New York, 1952. Outlaw Cantor Gold is thrown back into her honky-tonk Coney Island past, where crime and passion simmer in a neon glare. (978-1-62639-730-9)

Into Thin Air by Jeannie Levig. When her girlfriend disappears, Hannah Lewis discovers her world isn't as orderly as she thought it was. (978-1-62639-722-4)

Night Voice by CF Frizzell. When talk show host Sable finally acknowledges her risqué radio relationship with a mysterious caller, she welcomes a *real* relationship with local tradeswoman Riley Burke. (978-1-62639-813-9)

Raging at the Stars by Lesley Davis. When the unbelievable theories start revealing themselves as truths, can you trust in the ones who have conspired against you from the start? (978-1-62639-720-0)

She Wolf by Sheri Lewis Wohl. When the hunter becomes the hunted, more than love might be lost. (978-1-62639-741-5)

Smothered and Covered by Missouri Vaun. The last person Nash Wiley expects to bump into over a two a.m. breakfast at Waffle House is her college crush, decked out in a curve-hugging law enforcement uniform. (978-1-62639-704-0)

The Butterfly Whisperer by Lisa Moreau. Reunited after ten years, can Jordan and Sophie heal the past and rediscover love or will differing desires keep them apart? (978-1-62639-791-0)

The Devil's Due by Ali Vali. Cain and Emma Casey are awaiting the birth of their third child, but as always in Cain's world, there are new and old enemies to face in post Katrina-ravaged New Orleans. (978-1-62639-591-6)

Widows of the Sun-Moon by Barbara Ann Wright. With immortality now out of their grasp, the gods of Calamity fight amongst themselves, egged on by the mad goddess they thought they'd left behind. (978-1-62639-777-4)

18 Months by Samantha Boyette. Alissa Reeves has only had two girlfriends and they've both gone missing. Now it's up to her to find out why. (978-1-62639-804-7)

Arrested Hearts by Holly Stratimore. A reckless cop with a secret death wish and a health nut who is afraid to die might be a perfect combination for love. (978-1-62639-809-2)

Capturing Jessica by Jane Hardee. Hyperrealist sculptor Michael tries desperately to conceal the love she holds for best friend, Jess, unaware Jess's feelings for her are changing. (978-1-62639-836-8)

Counting to Zero by AJ Quinn. NSA agent Emma Thorpe and computer hacker Paxton James must learn to trust each other as they work to stop a threat clock that's rapidly counting down to zero. (978-1-62639-783-5)

Courageous Love by KC Richardson. Two women fight a devastating disease, and their own demons, while trying to fall in love. (978-1-62639-797-2)

One More Reason to Leave Orlando by Missouri Vaun. Nash Wiley thought a threesome sounded exotic and exciting, but as it turns out the reality of sleeping with two women at the same time is just really complicated. (978-1-62639-703-3E)

Pathogen by Jessica L. Webb. Can Dr. Kate Morrison navigate a deadly virus and the threat of bioterrorism, as well as her new relationship with Sergeant Andy Wyles and her own troubled past? (978-1-62639-833-7)

Rainbow Gap by Lee Lynch. Jaudon Vickers and Berry Garland, polar opposites, dream and love in this tale of lesbian lives set in Central Florida against the tapestry of societal change and the Vietnam War. (978-1-62639-799-6)

Steel and Promise by Alexa Black. Lady Nivrai's cruel desires and modified body make most of the galaxy fear her, but courtesan Cailyn Derys soon discovers the real monsters are the ones without the claws. (978-1-62639-805-4)

Swelter by D. Jackson Leigh. Teal Giovanni's mistake shines an unwanted spotlight on a small Texas ranch where August Reese is secluded until she can testify against a powerful drug kingpin. (978-1-62639-795-8)

Without Justice by Carsen Taite. Cade Kelly and Emily Sinclair must battle each other in the pursuit of justice, but can they fight their undeniable attraction outside the walls of the courtroom? (978-1-62639-560-2)

21 Questions by Mason Dixon. To find love, start by asking the right questions. (978-1-62639-724-8)

A Palette for Love by Charlotte Greene. When newly minted Ph.D. Chloé Devereaux returns to New Orleans, she doesn't expect her new job, and her powerful employer—Amelia Winters—to be so appealing. (978-1-62639-758-3)

By the Dark of Her Eyes by Cameron MacElvee. When Brenna Taylor inherits a decrepit property haunted by tormented ghosts, Alejandra Santana must not only restore Brenna's house and property but also save her soul. (978-1-62639-834-4)

Cash Braddock by Ashley Bartlett. Cash Braddock just wants to hang with her cat, fall in love, and deal drugs. What's the problem with that? (978-1-62639-706-4)

Death by Cocktail Straw by Missouri Vaun. She just wanted to meet girls, but an outing at the local lesbian bar goes comically off the rails, landing Nash Wiley and her best pal in the ER. (978-1-62639-702-6)

Gravity by Juliann Rich. How can Ellie Engebretsen, Olympic ski jumping hopeful with her eye on the gold, soar through the air when all she feels like doing is falling hard for Kate Moreau, her greatest competitor and the girl of her dreams? (978-1-62639-483-4)

Lone Ranger by VK Powell. Reporter Emma Ferguson stirs up a thirty-year-old mystery that threatens Park Ranger Carter West's family and jeopardizes any hope for a relationship between the two women. (978-1-62639-767-5)

Love on Call by Radclyffe. Ex-Army medic Glenn Archer and recent LA transplant Mariana Mateo fight their mutual desire in the face of past losses as they work together in the Rivers Community Hospital ER. (978-1-62639-843-6)

Never Enough by Robyn Nyx. Can two women put aside their pasts to find love before it's too late? (978-1-62639-629-6)

Two Souls by Kathleen Knowles. Can love blossom in the wake of tragedy? (978-1-62639-641-8)